H

BLOODROOT

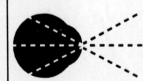

BLOODROOT

AMY GREENE

LARGE PRINT PRESS
A part of Gale, Cengage Learning

GALE
CENGAGE Learning

Detroit • New York • San Francisco • New Haven, Conn • Waterville, Maine • London

GALE
CENGAGE Learning·

LIBRARY OF CONGRESS CATALOGING-IN-PUBLICATION DATA

Greene, Amy, 1975–
    Bloodroot / by Amy Greene.
        p. cm. — (Thorndike Press large print basic)
    ISBN-13: 978-1-4104-2501-0 (alk. paper)
    ISBN-10: 1-4104-2501-0 (alk. paper)
    1. Families—Fiction. 2. Appalachian Region—Fiction. 3. Large type books. I. Title.
    PS3607.R45254B57 2010b
    813'.6—dc22   2009050754

ISBN 13: 978-1-59413-457-9 (pbk. : alk. paper)
ISBN 10: 1-59413-457-X (pbk. : alk. paper)

Published in 2011 by arrangement with Alfred A. Knopf, Inc.

Printed in the United States of America
    1 2 3 4 5   15 14 13 12 11
ED060

For Adam, Emma, and Taylor

■ ■ ■ ■

ONE:
BYRDIE LAMB AND
DOUGLAS COTTER

■ ■ ■ ■

Byrdie

Myra looks like her mama, but prettier because of her daddy mixed in. She got just the right amount of both. The best thing about Myra's daddy was his eyes, blue as the sky. They'd pierce right through you. Myra ended up with the same blue-blue eyes. I always figured she was too pretty and then John Odom came along. Now I'll die alone. It's not that I'm scared of being alone with this mountain. I love it like another person. I just miss my grandbaby. Me and Myra's mama wasn't close. Clio had little regard for me or Macon either one. Myra's the daughter I always wished I had.

I didn't see nothing wrong with John Odom at first, but even if I'd seen that snake coiled up inside his heart I wouldn't have tried to stop her. I could tell by her eyes Myra had to have him whatever the outcome. Now I know the outcome is no good.

9

This morning I went to see her and it broke my heart in two. I can't stand to think about what he might be doing to her beside of them tracks. Through the years I got tougher than a pine knot, but something about getting this old has softened me up. I reckon I have too much time to think about my troubles these days, without Myra here to talk to.

I should have seen what was coming after that time she got in late from the library. She was supposed to have been studying with one of her school friends. But I caught a funny shine in her eyes. "What have you been up to?" I asked.

She went to the sink and got a glass of water, gulped it down like she'd been in a race. She turned around and her cheeks looked hot. She smiled with water shining on her lips. "I'll tell you later, Granny, I promise. Right now I want to keep it just for me."

"You're silly," I said, but the way her eyes shined made me nervous. Then I got busy tidying up the kitchen before bed and forgot all about it.

When I finally laid down, I fell asleep as quick as my head hit the pillow. Thinking back, it was an unnatural sleep, like I had drunk a sleeping potion. I had a dream that

I was standing on a rickety bridge over muddy water. The roar of it was so loud I couldn't hear nothing else. Then I seen there was things getting carried off in the rapids. It was pieces of our house on Bloodroot Mountain. The leg off of my favorite chair. The quilt I made for Myra when she was a baby. A drawer out of the kitchen buffet. A baby doll Myra used to play with. Some floorboards and a few shingles and even the front door came rolling by. Then there was a crack and my foot went through the boards of that old bridge. It started coming apart, jagged pieces dropping and rushing away, until I was hanging on by a scrap of rotten wood, my feet dangling over the water. If I fell it would carry me off, too. Finally I couldn't hold on no longer. Just as I was dropping, I jerked awake, wringing wet with sweat. I set up on the side of the bed, heart thudding so hard I was afraid it might give out on me. I should have knowed right then. Grandmaw Ruth always said it's bad luck to dream of muddy waters.

Doug
Last night I closed the door to the smokehouse where the bloodroot is kept in cardboard boxes, away from the mice and bugs.

I stood there with my back against it, looking across the yard. The house was dark with my parents sleeping and all my brothers gone. Behind barbwire the pasture made a chain of starlit humps. I took the feedbag, heavy with corn, to the barn on quivering legs. The cows are sold and the field was still, but from the barn came fitful knocking sounds. Wild Rose never rests. Daddy had to put her up because she's been getting loose more often. I think I know why. Myra Lamb is gone from her house down the mountain and Rose has been looking for her.

I went to the black opening of the barn and turned on my flashlight. The knocking sounds stopped at once. I could sense Wild Rose waiting for me in the shadows of her stall. The smells of manure and damp hay turned my stomach. Walking deeper into the barn, I saw the reflective shine of her glassy blue eyes and wanted to turn back.

"Rose," I said. "I brought you something good to eat."

The horse didn't stir as I came down the aisle, like she knew what I was up to. She's never liked being touched, but she usually lets me strap on the feedbag. I was hoping the taste of sweet corn would hide the bitterness of what I'd laced it with.

"You hungry?" It was hard to hear myself over the thudding of my heart. Part of me couldn't believe what I was doing. Maybe I was still in bed asleep.

Wild Rose took a few steps toward the front of the stall. I could hear her breath snuffling through the wet channels of her nostrils. Somehow, even before she charged, I knew that she had figured me out. She exploded out of the stall door as she had out of the trailer the first time I saw her, a storm of splintering wood and pounding hooves, with a scream that threatened to split my head in two. I dropped the feedbag and the flashlight and clapped my hands over my ears. I felt the hot passage of her body like a freight train in the dark, the force of it knocking me down. Then she was gone, out the barn opening and across the hills, leaving me to lie in a mess of spilled corn and bloodroot.

Byrdie

When I was a girl I lived across another mountain in a place called Chickweed Holler. Until I was ten years old, me and Mammy lived with Grandmaw Ruth, and two of Grandmaw's sisters, Della and Myrtle. I used to crawl up in Grandmaw's lap to study her face and follow its lines

13

with my finger. She stayed slim and feisty up until the day she died of a stroke, walking home in the heat after birthing somebody's baby. Myrtle had hair soft and white as dandelion fluff that she liked for me to comb out and roll for her. They was all good-looking women, but Della was the prettiest. Her hair stayed black right up to the end of her life, and she didn't have as many wrinkles as Grandmaw. I reckon it's because she didn't have to work as much in the sun. She was the youngest and Myrtle and Grandmaw still babied her, old as all three of them was.

It was just me and Mammy after my daddy passed away, so Grandmaw took us in. We lived in a little cabin with a porch up on stilts. I liked to play under there, where they kept mason jars and rusty baling wire and all manner of junk for me to mess in. Chickweed Holler was a wild place with the mountains rising steep on both sides. From Grandmaw's doorstep you could see a long ways, wildflower fields waving when the summer winds blowed. That land was in our family for generations and Grandmaw and my great-aunts loved it as good as they did any of their kin.

All the neighbors thought the world of Grandmaw and her sisters. They was what you call granny women, and the people of Chickweed Holler relied on them for any kind of help you can think of. Each one of them had different gifts. Myrtle was what I've heard called a water witch. She could find a well on anybody's land with her dowsing rod. People sent for her from a long ways off. Sometimes they'd come to get her and she'd fetch the forked branch she kept under her bed and hop in their wagon. She'd be gone for days at a time, depending on how hard of a trip it was. Della was the best one at mixing up cures. She could name any root and herb and flower you pointed at. Another thing she was good for was healing animals. She could set the broke leg of the orneriest hunting dog and it wouldn't even bite her. One day I seen her in the yard bent over the washtub scrubbing and a bird lit on her shoulder. It stayed for a long time. If she noticed, she didn't let on. I stood still, trying not to scare it away. When I told Grandmaw about it later, she said animals are attracted to our kind of people, and so are other people of our kind. She winked and said, "Don't be surprised if the feller you marry has the touch. People with the touch draws one another." I've always remembered that, but I don't reckon Macon had none of the gifts Grandmaw and her sisters had. I didn't either. It's odd how the touch moves in a family. You never can tell who'll turn up with it.

Grandmaw had the best gift of all. She claimed she could send her spirit up out of her body. She said, "You could lock me up in the jailhouse or bury me alive down under the ground. It don't matter where this old shell is at. My soul will fly off wherever I want it to be." She told me about a time she fell down in a sinkhole when she was little and couldn't climb back out. She had wandered far from the house and knowed her mammy and pappy couldn't hear her. She looked up at the sun between the roots hanging down like dirty hair and wished so hard to fly up out of there that her spirit took off, rose, and soared on back to her little house in the holler. That's when she figured out what her gift was. She had no memory of being stuck in a hole that day. What she remembered was watching her mammy roll out biscuit dough and romping with her puppy dog and picking daisies to braid a crown. Grandmaw wasn't even hollering when a man out hunting came along and his dog sniffed her out. That's the gift I wish I had. I'd go back to Chickweed Holler right now and see if everything still looks the same.

Doug

It doesn't take as much to poison a horse as people think. You just have to know what to feed one. A few oleander leaves, a little sorghum grass, a bit of yellow star thistle and a horse can choke faster than the vet can get there. Tie your horse to a black locust or a chokecherry tree and it could be dead within minutes. Bloodroot is dangerous to horses, too. We have a carpet of it growing down the side of our mountain when springtime comes, thriving under the shady tree canopy high above our house. We have to walk quite a piece each year to find it. Daddy says such a lush stand is rare these days. My brother Mark, Daddy, and I used to go up there with hand spades and a sack, noses red in the leftover cold of winter. Bloodroot can be harvested in fall but the leaves have died back, so it's harder to know where the plants are. That's why we always made the trip in early spring, when the flowers are spread across the slope like the train of a wedding gown. We had to be careful not to damage the roots. When Mark and I were small, Daddy would yell at us if we were too rough, "That's money y'uns is throwing away!" He taught us to shake the roots free of clinging black soil and brush off the bugs and pluck away any weeds that

17

might have got tangled in. Then we had to move fast because bloodroot is easy to mold. We'd head back down the mountain with our sacks to spray the roots with the water hose attached to the wellhouse spigot, washing away the dirt. Once the roots were clean we put them in the smokehouse to dry for about a week. Daddy or one of us would check them for mold once in a while, and when they broke without bending they were dry enough to store. Sometimes we got up to ten dollars a pound. I've heard bloodroot's good for curing croup, and it's even been used for treating certain kinds of cancer. Some of it we kept for ourselves, to use on poison ivy and warts. I've known bloodroot to last in a cool, dark place for up to two years. It will also kill a horse. Daddy told me so last spring, the last time we went up the mountain to dig.

It was March and still cold enough to see our breath. Daddy lumbered along beside me and Mark walked on ahead because, even though we're both grown, he always had to be the fastest. We heard the crack of Wild Rose's hooves before we saw her.

"Dang horse," Mark said. He hoisted himself up by a sapling onto a shelf of rock. "She's loose again."

Daddy shook his head but I saw a grin

ripple under his beard. His beloved Rose could do no wrong. Not far up the mountain we saw the bloodroot, a lacy white patch littered with dead leaves. Wild Rose stepped out of the trees near the scattering of flowers and stood looking down at us, tail switching. Her beauty took my breath away.

"I don't believe I've ever seen her stray this far from home," Mark said. "She must be looking for something to eat up here that she's not getting in the pasture. Do you think she needs a dose of vitamins, Daddy?"

Wild Rose blinked at us indifferently for another second or two, then lowered her head to crop at the mossy grass beside the patch of bloodroot. All of a sudden Daddy sprang forward and threw up his arms. "Hyar, Rose!" he shouted. "Git!" Wild Rose turned and thundered off between the trees, tail high.

"Shoot, Daddy," Mark said. "You scared me half to death."

"Wouldn't take much of that bloodroot to kill a horse," Daddy said. He straightened his stocking hat and picked up the sack he had dropped. He moved on with Mark but I stood looking after Rose for a long time.

"This here's a three-man operation, Douglas," Daddy finally called. I went and joined them on my knees among the flowers.

19

Byrdie

There was others in the family that had the touch, but some didn't use it for good purposes. Grandmaw always said it can draw ugly things to you if you're not right with the Lord. Whenever she talked like that, I figured she was thinking about her cousin Lou Ann. Most people thought Lou Ann wasn't all there, but that was no excuse for her to be so hateful. She was a granny woman, too, but the neighbors didn't go to her unless they was ashamed to go to Grandmaw and Della and Myrtle. Sometimes a girl would go up to Lou Ann's to get rid of an unwanted child she was carrying. Lou Ann knowed what kind of root to use. She wasn't above putting a curse on somebody, either. When my great-grandpaw died, he left the best plot of land to Grandmaw and her sisters. It liked to drove Lou Ann off the deep end. She told Grandmaw that she was putting a curse on them that wouldn't be lifted until there was a baby born in our line with haint blue eyes. Haint blue is a special color that wards off evil spirits and curses. Grandmaw said, "That old devil knows ain't nobody been born with blue eyes in our family for generations." It was true, all of us had brown and green eyes. Lou Ann went down to Grandmaw's house and pronounced her curse, then she climbed back up the hill and shut the door on her little shack perched on a ledge and never spoke to Grandmaw or the great-aunts ever again. I seen her sometimes setting on her porch and even though I couldn't make out her face from such a distance, it seemed like her mean eyes was piercing right through me. After she laid that curse Grandmaw said awful things started happening to her and her sisters. Grandmaw, Myrtle, and Della all lost their husbands right close together, and two of Della's grandbabies was stillborn. Myrtle's house burnt down across the holler, and that's how come she moved in with Grandmaw. Even though I lost all five of my children, I don't believe in curses. But I was still glad all the same, the first time I seen Myra and she opened up them big haint blue eyes to look at me.

After Lou Ann died, Grandmaw and the great-aunts painted the doors and window-sills of the house haint blue to keep her mean old spirit out. Anytime that blue started to fade in the weather, they'd get out the paint can and freshen it up. Mammy said they kept it up until the last one of them, Myrtle, died at the age of ninety-two, after I had done married Macon a long time ago and moved off to Bloodroot Mountain.

Doug

Daddy believes he knows that horse better than anybody, just because he loves her better. But nobody knows Wild Rose better than me, and sometimes I think I hate her. I've studied her for years now. Many times I've tried to enter her body, wishing to know how to enter Myra Lamb's. I've stood at the fence and watched Wild Rose grazing on the mountain, a dark outline against the pale sky right before the sun is gone, and sent my soul across the rolling green searching for entry, maybe through the tear ducts of the blue glass eyes, maybe through the snuffling channels of the downy nose, or through the grass she rips from the earth and grinds between her big square teeth. Most of the time Wild Rose stands a few yards off with her head lowered, staring back at me. Her tail keeps moving, flicking off flies, but it's me she's concentrating on. She's known for a while that I'm up to something, way before that stunt I tried to pull with the bloodroot last night, when I heard for sure that Myra got married. I guess I've wanted to poison Wild Rose for a long time, ever since the day I saw her standing beside the bloodroot patch.

She probably knows everything about me just by looking at my face. I bet she's noticed how I don't smile or talk much because of this front tooth, broken off and brown with rot. Daddy didn't have the money to take us to the dentist when we were kids, and since I've been old enough, I haven't gone. The truth is, this tooth embarrasses me, but I'd be more ashamed to have it fixed. My brothers would say I'm trying to make myself pretty so I can get a girlfriend. A big part of me was glad when all six of them moved off one by one, four of them heading north to work in the factories, two of them fighting in Vietnam. For a long time there was just Mark and me, until he joined the service, too. The house is lonesome now, but at least I'm not the butt of all the jokes anymore.

My tooth got broken when I was seven. It happened one Saturday when Daddy and I went to Millertown after shoelaces. We headed out every week, whether we needed anything or not. Daddy talked more on those Saturday trips than the other six days of the week put together, whistling and tapping the truck's steering wheel all the way down the mountain. Looking back, he needed that time away from the farm and all the worries that come with it. He'll never leave Bloodroot Mountain because the Cotters have lived here for generations, but I wonder if he ever wants to dust his hands of this place and move on.

Millertown was the big city to me back then, before I went to Knoxville with Daddy once to buy a washing machine. Now I see it for what it really is, a country town with old houses and glass-sprinkled lots and the smokestacks of dirty-looking factories looming over everything. The buildings on Main Street are falling into disrepair but they still have character, with tall windows and painted brick and arched doorways. Even in 1963, when I was seven, not many people shopped there anymore. Once the Millertown Plaza was built, with a supermarket and a department store, the downtown seemed outdated. There was only Odom's Hardware, the dime store, the drugstore, a shoe store, a television repair shop, and a shabby restaurant where roaches skittered along the backs of the torn vinyl booths. Some people still feel like Main Street is the heart of the town. There's a society of blue-haired ladies dedicated to preserving what they call the historic district. Daddy still shopped there when I was small, because it was what he was used to. He's always been set in his ways and it took a while for the Plaza to win him over.

The Saturday that my tooth got broken, we climbed into the truck and headed out as usual. Ordinarily Mark would have come along, but he was in trouble for misbehaving at church. Daddy and I had been to the dime store for shoelaces and were passing Odom's Hardware on our way to lunch when I saw a sign in the window advertising a junked car for sale. Daddy stopped to examine the sign and decided he wanted to take a look at the car. He claimed he might want it for parts. That's the way he is. He goes all over the countryside dickering with other men just like himself, silent and gruff with greasy caps on their heads and plugs of tobacco tucked in their jaws. No matter how Mama fusses, he'll drive from one end of Tennessee to the other collecting junk, or even out of state if he hears about a bargain. Half the time he brings back things we don't need and can't use. Once it was a box of hammers, and another time he hoisted an old unicycle out of the truck bed when he got home. Mama really threw a fit over that one.

We waited until after lunch to see about the car. Daddy took his time and had two cups of coffee. I drank a chocolate milkshake. Coming out of the restaurant, Main

Street was deserted because everything closed early on Saturdays. It gave me an empty feeling. We got into the truck and went to a house with dark upper windows and old furniture setting on the porch. It might have been fancy if it hadn't looked so rundown. When Daddy rang the bell, a man came out and said the car was in the backyard. He called Daddy by name as if they already knew each other, but I couldn't place the man myself.

We went around the house and saw the car up on blocks in a thatch of weeds with its hood propped open. Daddy crossed the yard behind the man to have a closer look. I stood around with my hands in my pockets, wishing they'd get down to business. There were toys in the backyard, but no sign of the kids they belonged to. It was a sad place and I wanted to go home. I drifted to the edge of the yard and looked at the weedy lot next door. It was littered with junk and trash, almost like a dump. I lingered there for a while, daydreaming about nothing in particular. Then the back screen door of the house screeched open and slapped shut. I turned and saw a boy coming down the concrete steps with a basketball under his arm. He was bigger than me, tall with black hair and white skin. He dribbled the ball a couple of times on a bald spot of ground before noticing me. When he saw me standing at the edge of the yard, he stopped and looked me over with suspicious eyes. I didn't know how to talk to other kids besides my brothers, so I hoped he would go back to his dribbling. My heart sank when he walked over and spoke to me.

"Hey," he said, and bounced the ball between us a couple of times.

"Hey."

He stared at me for a minute, so hard I felt my ears turning red.

"You want to see something?" the boy asked finally.

"What?"

"A skeleton."

I didn't answer. I thought he was picking on me.

"Not a human skeleton, dummy. A dog one."

"Oh."

"You want to see it?"

"Where's it at?"

"Over there." He tilted his head toward the weedy lot.

"I guess."

He tossed his basketball back into the yard and I watched it bounce a few times before it came to rest by a rusty swing set. To this

27

day, I don't know why I followed him. I had a bad feeling from the minute he sized me up with his mean black eyes. We walked into the weeds and as we got farther from the house I grew more and more nervous. I looked back over my shoulder at Daddy and the other man, bent under the car's hood.

"I want to go back," I told the boy.

"Come on. It's right over here," he said.

He took me by the arm and dragged me down a glass-littered path, past a heap of charred garbage and an old mattress spilling stuffing. Finally we came to the edge of the lot, where dark trees crowded close to a rickety board fence. I wanted to cry, but didn't let myself. I could see the bones ahead, glimmering white in a mess of green vines. The boy steered me roughly by the shoulders until the skeleton was at my toes.

He wanted me to be afraid, but the dog bones weren't so bad once I saw them close up. They were wound in a shroud of morning glories and the flowers made them almost beautiful. But it turned out a dead dog wasn't the most interesting thing to be found in the weedy lot. When I knelt down to have a better look at the skeleton, something shiny caught my eye. Glittering in the weeds near the dog's skull, I saw the tip of a rock poking out of the earth like a headstone. Right away, I lost interest in the bones and reached out to touch the rock. Back then, Mark and I collected quartz. We called the shining chunks we found field diamonds, and this was the biggest one I'd ever seen.

The field diamond was half buried and wouldn't budge at first. The boy knelt to see what I was doing and soon he was helping me dig out the rock with his fingers. I grew afraid that he would try to claim the treasure since he had done some of the work, so I was determined to be the one who pulled it free. I gave one last yank and suddenly I was holding the quartz in my hand. I brushed off the reddish dirt and we looked at it together, the boy leaning over my shoulder. I always wanted just one precious thing for myself. Ever since I could remember, Mark got everything with his clamoring mouth — more milk, more candy, more toys. He was two years older than me but he acted like a baby, always bellowing until he got his way. Most of the time, I would rather have done without than to be like him. But this once, I wanted the prize all to myself.

"Let me see it," the boy said.

As soon as he spoke, I knew. He'd steal it and run off as Mark would have done, and

I'd never see it again. As much as the boy intimidated me, I clamped my hand down on that dirty chunk of something special and said, "It's mine."

"Give it," the boy said. His voice was calm enough but I can still see the awful look on his face. My guts turned to jelly. I should have given it to him, but I couldn't bring myself to. He tried to pry open my fingers but I tore my fist away and ran. I heard him chasing and before I knew what was happening, the boy had knocked me down. My head bounced off the ground like his basketball had done and all the wind wheezed out of my lungs. I barely noticed how bad it hurt. All I felt was the rock flying out of my hands. I rolled over and tried to find it in the weeds, but the boy had already snatched it up.

He could have taken it then and left me alone. I was too scared to fight. I would have given it to him. But the boy wasn't satisfied to steal my rock. He straddled me and I saw something crazy in his eyes, something more than meanness. He drew back with the chunk of quartz and brought it down on my mouth. There was a bright flash of pain and I must have screamed because our daddies came running. It took them forever to reach us.

The boy told them I fell and hit my mouth on a rock. I didn't contradict his story, mostly because my smashed mouth hurt too much to talk. I don't know if Daddy and the other man believed him or not. They seemed more concerned with the blood wetting my shirt. I didn't realize until we were in the car on the way to the doctor's that my new front tooth was broken. Maybe that's when I knew, somewhere inside, that I wasn't meant to have a wild, precious thing like that field diamond all for myself. And even if I could buy it, as Daddy bought Wild Rose years later, it would never really be mine.

Byrdie

I wish I could remember Chickweed Holler better, but some things happened there I'll never forget. I liked going dowsing with Myrtle. Sometimes if she traveled on foot to a place not too far, I could leave the holler for a while and see somewhere new. The soles of my feet used to itch at night and Myrtle claimed it meant my feet would walk one day on foreign ground. That's how come she took me. She thought I ort to travel. One time Mammy let me go to the next county with Myrtle and we had to camp overnight. Mammy was worried but

Myrtle said, "Why, we'll have a big time."

When the sun went down we stopped to rest under a lonely tree in a wide open field. All day long we had walked and talked. Myrtle was good to ask questions to, because she talked to everybody just the same, didn't matter what their age was. The whole day it was just like Myrtle told Mammy. We was having a big time. But when we settled down for the night in that long, lonesome field, not a house in sight for miles, I started missing Grandmaw and Mammy. Myrtle must have seen I was fixing to cry. She said, "Come on now, little birdie. Let's build us a fire. I brung some chestnuts for us to roast." The idea of roasted chestnuts worked to cheer me up some, and gathering branches took my mind off being homesick. Pretty soon we had a good fire going. We set looking into the flames as the dark came creeping over the field grass. It was hard to look away from the light of it, even though it hurt my eyes. After while Myrtle went to fishing around in her dress pocket. I thought she had the chestnuts in there, but she pulled out a little sprig of something leafy instead. She held it up for me to see in the firelight.

"What's that?" I asked.

"This is my favorite herb," she said. "Do

you know why?" When she grinned her mouth stretched tight across her toothless gums. Her eyes reflected the flames back at me and I felt a little bit scared of her. I wanted my mammy more than ever.

"It's called myrtle, like my name."

"Oh," I said. "Where's the chestnuts?"

"Just a minute, little birdie. I want to show you something. If you throw this myrtle in the fire, the face of the one you're bound to marry will rise out of the smoke."

I just blinked at her at first. I didn't want to see a face in the smoke, but I didn't want to disappoint my great-aunt Myrtle, either. She was always bragging about how big and smart I was. She held out the sprig and after a minute I took it. I looked at the flames and they put me in mind of orange snakes dancing. My heart went to flying. I throwed that myrtle in the fire before I could chicken out of it and the fire dwindled down to just about nothing. Me and Myrtle both watched like we was under a spell, waiting for something to happen. Directly the smoke came rising up, slow and thick and black. At first I couldn't make nothing out, but then I started seeing it. There was a pair of black eyes looking out at me. I wanted to back away from the fire but my legs wasn't no use anymore. Then a straight nose and a fine mouth and some waving locks of coal black hair formed out of the smoke. I got so scared I couldn't breathe. When I finally found my legs I scrambled away from that fire and ran. I yanked down my bloomers and squatted to make water in the grass before I wet all over myself. Myrtle came to check on me and I tried not to cry as we walked back to the fire. She didn't say nothing but I knowed she felt bad for scaring me that way. She pulled me close and held me against her before we bedded down for the night. I forgot about that face until years later, after I seen John Odom for the first time. It wasn't my own future husband's face that came swimming up out of the fire to look at me. It was my granddaughter, Myra's.

Doug

I was twelve when Wild Rose came home in a trailer. Daddy opened the door and she burst out like a thunderstorm. I stood back in awe of such a powerful creature of God. It was easy to see that He had made her with love, carving out her velvet nostrils with His most delicate tool, sculpting every muscle under that shining hide. The way Daddy was always dragging something home, I wasn't surprised when he told us he'd found a horse. He said he'd wanted a paint horse with blue eyes ever since he was a boy. One day he went to see about a tractor a man had cheap in Dalton, Georgia, and found Wild Rose instead. What surprised me was how crazy Daddy was over that horse right from the start. He would stand at the fence for hours just watching her graze. It must have been love at first sight. One morning I looked out the kitchen window and saw them together in the pasture. I was up early and the ground was still stiff with frost. I took my coffee and sat on the back steps watching as Daddy tried to ride Wild Rose. For a minute, she even let him put the saddle on. He crept up to her side, one foot in the stirrup, and hauled himself onto her back. The instant the horse felt Daddy's weight, she threw him. He landed so hard, it seemed I heard the thud of his body hitting the ground from several yards off. I wanted to go see if he was all right, but I knew his pride would be hurting.

Thinking about Wild Rose coming home in a trailer reminds me of the first time I saw Myra, dropping out of a tree behind the church house at the homecoming dinner. Her dress flew up like a parachute, tiny legs waving and black hair floating out behind her. Myra had been around my whole life, because the Lambs lived down the mountain and went to our church, but that was the first time I took notice of her. Myra didn't cry when she landed, but Mr. Lamb rushed to her side, dropping his paper plate and splattering food everywhere. He spanked her in front of the whole congregation and I didn't blame him. He was scared. It was only natural to be protective of something so precious. I knew the feeling myself, even as a small boy. You took extra care of your special things. That's how I thought of Myra, as something extra special and wild. The wild part was scary to Mr. Lamb and me both, because it meant we were always in danger of losing her.

From the day she dropped out of that tree behind the church, I thought about Myra all the time. I followed her around school once first grade started, even though I was too backward to make friends with any of the other kids. Naturally, once Mark realized how I felt about Myra, he decided he wanted her, too. He set about stealing her attention every chance he got, making her laugh by pulling faces and burping in the library.

When Mark and I were old enough to go off by ourselves, we walked down the mountain to play with Myra as often as we could. She liked to wear dresses in warm weather, even though she was a tomboy, because she couldn't stand for her legs to be confined. I guess it was easier for her to run away from us with a floppy dress on. Sometimes she disappeared into the woods at the end of the day without a word and we learned not to look for her. She always came back out to play again. The three of us spent nearly every weekend shooting tin cans with my BB gun and catching grasshoppers and wrestling in the mud if we got mad at each other. Myra jumped on my back and bit me once because I beat her at a game of marbles. She was a spoiled brat, but I didn't mind. I was her fool from the minute she jumped out of that churchyard tree.

It was best when we ran off alone together. I followed her places where Mark wouldn't go, into dripping caves littered with bones and hollow logs squirming with sow bugs. I wasn't afraid when I was with her. We played all over the woods, not concerned about trespassing. My family and the Lambs and the Barnetts were the only ones living near the top of Bloodroot Mountain. The women shared their gardens and wherever the hunting was good a neighbor was welcome to shoot what he could. Fences were meant for keeping livestock in and strangers out, not for each other.

Bloodroot Mountain is small as far as mountains go. Daddy says it's not even a thousand feet at the summit, but as a child it was the whole world to me. I knew that at the bottom of the mountain, a little over twelve miles down winding roads, through farming communities like Piney Grove and Slop Creek and Valley Home, there was Millertown, and about sixty miles beyond that was Chickweed Holler, where Myra's granny came from. I had traveled that far with Daddy and seen the lay of the land, long stretches of corn and high grass, bridges over foaming waters, and white farmhouses scattered on hills. But the minute I got back home, with none of those places visible through the trees, I forgot about them. There was only Bloodroot Mountain and I didn't mind because Myra was up here with me. The whole mountain belonged to us and we knew its terrain like our own bodies, every scar and cleft and fold.

But one fall morning, when I was ten, the three of us found something we hadn't seen before. It was an abandoned cistern high on the slope behind the Barnetts' house, half covered in dead vines. Myra pulled back the growth to reveal a stone opening edged with moss. Bright leaves floated on the surface of the murky water collected inside. I held my breath as Myra knelt to look closer. I'd heard tales of children drowning in wells and cisterns. Suddenly the trees I had lived under all my life seemed like giants peering over our shoulders, some so tall a grown man couldn't have reached the lowest branches. I looked back toward Mr. Barnett's house, a swatch of dingy white peeking up through the skinny trunks. It seemed so far below us, like there were no grownups around for miles.

"Oh," Myra said. "Poor little thing."

Mark crouched beside Myra and I took a step forward, not wanting her to think Mark was braver than me. I leaned over and saw a baby chimney swift floating among the leaves. I swallowed hard and inched a little closer.

"Must have fell out of a nest," Mark said, glancing into the trees overhead.

"Chimney swifts don't live in trees," Myra said. "Look, there's a nest in here."

When she pointed I saw an empty cradle of straw in the shadows below the cistern's opening. It made the bird's death even sadder somehow, that its corpse had been left behind. I lowered myself beside Myra, the earth cold under my knees. I couldn't look away from the dark clump of feathers, the tiny, sealed-shut eyes. We peered into the cistern for a long time, like mourners at a graveside. I didn't notice until it was almost too late how far over Myra was leaning, her top half nearly lost in the dank gloom. Then we heard the crack of twigs and the thrash of fallen leaves. Before I had time to wonder who was coming, a big hand hauled Myra away from the cistern's stone mouth by the back of her dress. Mark and I scrambled to our feet, eyes wide. It was Haskell Barnett standing there with a crease between his bushy eyebrows, leaning on the handle of his axe.

"Myra Jean Lamb," he said. "Your grand-daddy would skin you alive if he caught you up here messing around. And you boys ought to get a switching, too."

The three of us stood in a line gaping up at him. I was half afraid he would take matters into his own hands and do the switching himself. He frowned down at us, maybe waiting for one of us to speak up, but my tongue was stuck to the roof of my mouth. Then Myra burst out crying, which was a surprise to me. She wasn't prone to tears.

"Here, now," Mr. Barnett said, softening right away. "I didn't mean to make you squall. But I told Byrdie and Macon I'd always watch over you. What would they think if I let you fall down a dadburn hole?" He put his big hand on top of Myra's head and she dried her eyes hard on her sleeve. I knew she was embarrassed to have cried.

"Please," she said. "Don't tell Granddaddy, okay?"

"I won't this time," he said. "But don't you younguns be messing around that old cistern anymore. Now come on to the house. Margaret's made banana bread."

I looked back to where the chimney swift floated, the loneliness of its corpse still tearing at me. I was sorry to leave it behind but I wanted to follow Mr. Barnett. If it was true that he swore to watch over Myra, we were in on something together now.

Byrdie

One morning I woke up with the thresh. My mouth was broke out so thick with sores I couldn't hardly swallow. Della said, "Ain't but one thing'll take care of this."

Mammy was standing over my bed looking worried. "What?" she asked.

"A man that's never laid eyes on his father."

"Who'll we take her to?" Myrtle asked, standing in the doorway with her hand on

41

her hip. She looked blurry to me. My mouth hurt so bad I couldn't see straight.

"Clifford Pinkston's the closest," Grandmaw said, leaning over to rub my hair.

"You can't tell me Clifford Pinkston never seen his daddy," Mammy said. "I went to school with him and I seen his daddy my own self a hundred times."

"Howard Pinkston ain't Clifford's daddy," Grandmaw said. She was done getting her headscarf on. "He was an orphan and the Pinkstons took him to raise." She turned back to me and when she smiled I felt a little better. "Come on," she said. "We'll get you fixed up right quick. Clifford just lives down the holler a piece."

I had seen Clifford's house before, on the way to other places. It was about two miles from ours, perched on the edge of a bluff near the bottom of the holler, a weathered three-story with a boarded-up window on the top floor and a wraparound porch that sagged down in the back, overlooking a patch of rocky farmland. There was always goats and geese and peacocks strutting around in the yard. In winter I could see his chimney smoke puffing up through the trees. Grandmaw told me on the walk that he lived by hisself because he was too backward to get him a woman. Mammy said she didn't believe he ever said two or three words when they was in school together.

"What makes you think he'll help us?" Mammy asked.

"Why, Clifford's always been a good neighbor," Grandmaw said.

He was out on the yard splitting wood when me and Mammy and Grandmaw came up. He took off his hat when he seen us. My mouth hurt too bad to think about much but I took note of the fine figure Clifford cut when he stood up straight. He was long and tall with strong brown arms. I could see his muscles with the sleeves of his shirt rolled up. When we got close my nerves went away because of how kind his face was.

"Hello there, Clifford," Grandmaw said.

"Hidee, Miss Ruth," he said.

Then he nodded to Mammy. His face and ears turned red.

"How are you making it, Clifford?" Mammy said. "It's been a long time since we was in school together." She smiled and I pictured her as a girl. It crossed my mind that Clifford might think she was pretty. It made me feel funny to think of my mammy as a woman and not just the one who bore me. I wasn't used to seeing her around men her own age. My daddy died when I was a baby, so I didn't remember them being together.

"This'n here's got the thresh," Grandmaw said, and set me out in front of him by the shoulders. "I was hoping we could trouble you to help us out."

The way Clifford looked at Mammy, I knowed he wouldn't refuse her anything. Then he looked down and studied me real good. I felt a warmness spreading in my heart like I never knowed before. He had the kindest eyes I ever seen. He seemed familiar someway. I had the queerest thought that he was my daddy, even though I knowed my daddy was dead. He knelt down before me so our faces was close. I could smell his sweat where he'd been working in the heat. I stood still as I could, waiting to see what would happen. He took hold of my face so gentle, and it was like I always needed to be touched that way by a man's fingers, after all them years being raised by women.

"Open your mouth, Byrdie," Mammy said. Her voice was thick and fuzzy, like it sounded when she woke up in the mornings. It seemed to me like the world had quit turning and Mammy must have felt it, too. I did as she said and Clifford leaned in to cover my lips with his own. He blowed warm wind in my mouth and down my swelled-up throat. I could feel my lungs filling up with it. It was such a relief someway that I wanted to squall. He pulled back from me, still holding my face, and we looked for a while in each other's eyes. It seemed like even the birds in the trees had quit making noise. Then Grandmaw said, "Well, that ort to do it." I looked up at her and Mammy standing over us. Mammy's face was white as a sheet. She was staring at Clifford with something like worship in her eyes. She'd felt the power of what he done the same as I did.

"Why don't you come up and eat supper with us tonight?" Mammy asked. Her voice still sounded far off. "It's the least we can do to thank ye."

"Maybe tomorrow night," Clifford said, and I could tell Mammy was disappointed. She probably figured he never would come.

Sure enough, the next day when I got out of the bed my thresh had cleared up. I was feeling better, setting out on the porch playing with a doll, when I looked up and seen Clifford coming. He waved his hat and I ran to tell Grandmaw and Mammy.

"Well, I'll be," Grandmaw said. "I never dreamt he'd turn up."

It was true Clifford was backward, but he was so struck on Mammy he couldn't resist her. Pretty soon he was coming to supper just about every night, and bringing me and Mammy presents. He took us to town and the fair and all kinds of places. I got to where I loved that man just about better than anything, and so did Mammy. When he asked Mammy to be his wife a few months later, I reckon I was more tickled than she was. I got to wear baby's breath in my hair to the wedding. After the knot was tied, I figured I had a new daddy. I started calling Clifford "Pap," and all of us was happy.

Doug

Besides Myra, Haskell Barnett was my only friend. After he pulled Myra away from that cistern, we were allies in my mind. The Barnetts' grown children had moved up north and they were lonesome for the sound of small voices, so they treated Myra and me like their own flesh and blood. We loved playing at their house. Mrs. Barnett was always baking and Mr. Barnett showed us how to build forts and shoot with slingshots. Mark stopped visiting once he got older, but Myra and I still went there even after we were grown. Sometimes Myra and Mrs. Barnett embroidered or cooked together while I helped Mr. Barnett with the outside chores. He paid me but he didn't have to. It was nice being alone with him. He was quiet when I needed him to be, but he also told good stories.

When I was eleven, we took our first walk together. All afternoon I had handed him tools as he worked under his truck, until he slid out into the springtime sun and said, "I need to stretch my legs. You want to come with me?" We went far up the mountain, but not to the top because the way was too rugged and steep. Not even Daddy ventured to the summit anymore, after breaking his leg as a boy. Daddy said there was a grassy bald on top of Bloodroot Mountain where his grandfather used to drive his cattle to. It was a dangerous trip but the high mountain grass was better for the cows and it was cooler up there in summer. Walking with Mr. Barnett, I wondered if my great-grandfather's motivations had less to do with his cows and more to do with spending time alone where it was quiet, away from his duties on the farm. I thought about Daddy's story, how one day he decided to see the top, even after he'd been forbidden. He fell trying to scale the steep cliffs and lay for a day and a night before he was found. He claimed to have seen some frightening things while he was lying up there but wouldn't say what, only that if I ever went farther than the big rock over the bluff, he'd skin me alive. I never would have risked it, but sometimes I dreamed of my great-grandfather driving his cows up those rocky slopes to reach a meadow that must have been like paradise to him.

The woods looked different walking with Mr. Barnett than when I was alone. At the time the change was hard to understand, but looking back I see why. It was because he still observed the mountain with wonder, even though he knew it better than I did. As we passed through dark patches of shade into clearings like rooms of light, he paused to touch ridges of fungus growing on bark, stopped to catch a moth and study its wings, bent to pick up an arrowhead. When I was with him I saw it too, how magical everything was.

We came to a place where the cotton-woods were thick, shedding their seeds in drifting white tufts. Small clouds floated all around us like something from a dream, lighting on Mr. Barnett's shoulders and the top of his head, where the graying hair was still matted down from his cap. We stood watching for a while, faces lifted to the sun. "Look, Douglas," he said. "How pretty it is. Makes me think about the Lord."

His words made my arms prickle with goosebumps. I understood what he meant so well that, after a few seconds of holding my breath, I couldn't resist telling him my secret. "That's how I feel about Myra," I said, closing my eyes so I didn't have to see his face. "She makes me think about Jesus." I expected him to laugh, but he didn't. He put his hand on my shoulder. He must have already known. From then on, we took walks together at least once a week. The only thing I couldn't tell Myra was how much I loved her, so I told Mr. Barnett all about it instead. He never said I was too young to be in love, even though I was only eleven. When I told him how I felt about Myra, he believed me.

I didn't expect before I started talking how much there was to tell, but Mr. Barnett didn't mind. He knew I needed our walks and he made time for them. I poured my heart out to him a thousand times over the years, not bothering in those cool autumn evenings or snow-dusted mornings or shade-speckled summer afternoons to cover my broken tooth. He didn't look at me anyway. That's what made it so easy to talk to him when I could barely say two words to anyone else but Myra. It was how he reached out to touch a leaf with a worm inching across it, how he bent to examine a hoof mark or paw print, how he plucked a persimmon and popped it into his mouth, as if he wasn't listening. But he always was. "She'll come around, Douglas," he'd say. "One of these days."

I didn't do all the talking on our walks. He told me stories, mostly about the times he had with Myra's grandparents growing up. When Mr. Barnett lost his older brother in the war, Macon Lamb was the closest thing he had to one. Since he was the only boy left in a house full of sisters, he was always at Macon's heels. "He's the one taught me how to smoke and chew both," Mr. Barnett said. "Some people didn't like him because he was quiet, and they took that for hateful. But I knowed the kind of man he really was. He'd do things you didn't expect, like whittle something and give it to you for a present. One time I caught him off by hisself hid in the corn patch, reading a book of poems. His face got red as a beet and he flew so mad I thought he was going to fight me, just because I knowed he liked to read poems. But Macon never stayed mad for long."

Mr. Barnett talked about Myra's granny, too. He said he could see why Macon was drawn to Byrdie, even though she wasn't

50

much to look at. She was brash and sassy and tough. "I seen her bury every one of her children and take to her bed for months at a time," Mr. Barnett said. "But someway she always got back on her feet. It was Macon that never got over it. Since their youngest, Clio, got killed, he's been scared to death something might happen to the baby she left behind. Myra's the only thing he's got left of Clio. That's why he watches over that youngun like a hawk."

I loved hearing stories about Myra as a baby, how Macon and Byrdie doted on her. Mr. Barnett said they worked hard to make a good home for her to grow up in, and I can't think of a better one than what they had. It's pretty all over Bloodroot Mountain, but the Lambs have the best spot. When the trees are bare you can see far into the woods from their back steps, and from the front window you can look down on the winding dirt road and the creek rushing alongside it. Mr. Barnett still liked to walk up the mountain on summer evenings and sit in Byrdie and Macon's yard, drinking sweet tea or lemonade and talking about the Bible way into the night. "I can remember watching Myra toddle around when she was a baby, catching lightning bugs," he told me once. "She'd come running to show us how they

51

lit up her hands." He stopped walking then to look at me. "I can see why you love her, Douglas," he said. "That little girl is special." It seemed like he was trying to tell me something, but I was afraid to ask what it was.

Byrdie

It was sad to leave our cabin with the haint blue door and go live with Pap on his farm, even as much as I loved him. We still seen Grandmaw and the great-aunts but it wasn't the same. Me and Mammy lived there on Pap's farm until I was fifteen years old, when Grandmaw died. It was an awful time and after we buried her we got to where we couldn't hardly stand Chickweed Holler and all the memories there. Pap said one day maybe we ort to move down to the valley. He'd struggled so long with the rocky soil on his farm, he believed he could do better somewhere else. Me and Mammy agreed to it because we needed to run away from our grief. Much as we cared for Della and Myrtle, it was hard to be around them without missing Grandmaw so bad it liked to killed us. Pap got word of land for sale about sixty miles east, in a little farming community called Piney Grove. He bought ten acres off a man named Bucky Cochran that owned a big dairy farm and everything else along the five-mile stretch of road between our place and his house, a two-story yellow brick with white trim and fancy columns on the porch. Pap built us a log cabin with a loft where I slept in a feather bed Mammy made for me. Every day I'd slip off from my chores to set by the spring-house where we kept a jug of fresh milk tied up in the ice-cold spring. I'd pull it up out of the water and close my eyes and take a long drink and it seemed like nothing in life could taste sweeter. I thought it was the prettiest plot of land I ever seen, too, until I came up here to Bloodroot Mountain.

I took a job cooking and cleaning for Bucky's wife, Barbara Cochran, and we found us a church not far from the house. That's where I seen Macon for the first time. I never was good-looking like Myra, even before I got real old. My ears stuck out and I had a good head of hair but it had an ugly color to it, like dirty dishwater. It's a wonder Macon took to me, but he wasn't no looker hisself. Had a puckered face and scraggly whiskers and a brown birthmark over his eye shaped like an island off of the globe I seen at the Cochrans' house. Every chance I got I'd sneak and spin that globe and run my fingers over the shapes. Macon's birthmark put me in mind of all them shapes that stood for places I'd like to go. Sometimes the soles of my feet still itched in the night. Up until he died I had that island to run my fingers over whenever I wanted to.

Piney Grove Church was about two miles down the road from us, and about the same from the foot of Bloodroot Mountain. I guess you could say me and Macon met in the middle. He caught my eye right off, setting over in the amen corner with suspenders on. I've thought about what drawed me to Macon, besides that island birthmark, and I believe it was being able to tell right off that he was a man. He wasn't but eight years older than me but there was something about the way he carried hisself. He'd give his sisters stern looks when they went to giggling on the back pew, and every time he led prayer his voice rung up in the rafters. I could tell just by setting in the church house with Macon that he'd know how to treat a woman and run a farm and be a good daddy like Pap. Even though I was only fifteen, I knowed I wanted to marry a man like him.

That's how come I stood close to him every chance I got and tried to get myself noticed. Seemed like it took forever for him to figure out I was around. Then finally at the Easter egg hunt me and him and some of the other older ones was picked to hide the eggs. It was springtime and chilly out. The churchyard grass was bright green and slick with dew. My feet was wet in them thin shoes I had on, but I couldn't hardly feel it. All I knowed was Macon Lamb being close by. Every once in a while I'd ease up on him, like I was hiding another egg, and catch a whiff of his soapy-smelling skin.

I seen him pass through the gate to the graveyard and finally he was off by hisself. The others headed around back of the church where the trees and outhouses was, so it was just me and Macon. I went with my egg basket amongst the tombstones, some of them old enough to where the names was rubbed off. Such a quiet came over me, with the sky blue and the birds singing. There's always something peaceful about a graveyard.

Macon was bent over hiding an egg at the base of a stone carved like a lamb. It was a child's grave and I've wondered more than once if that wasn't the Lord warning me and Macon of things to come. I crept up behind him and said, "I didn't know we could hide these out here." I liked to scared him to death. He jumped sky high and both of us laughed. Then he stood there looking at me funny, eyes twinkling like they did when he was up to mischief. "I reckon we can," he said. "Nobody told me any different."

"Well," I said. "Where do you reckon would be a good place to hide this'n?" My mouth was dry as a bone. I was holding up this nice pink egg, I still remember it. That's when Macon finally noticed me. We hid the rest of them eggs together.

Doug

In the winter right before I turned twelve, Myra got chicken pox and stayed home from school for a week. At recess I sat by the chain-link fence at the back of the playground poking sticks and brown weeds through the diamonds into the churchyard grass on the other side, my fingers stiff with cold. I looked at the graves and thought of climbing over to lie on top of one where it was quiet and still, away from the thud of basketballs and the screams of my bundled up classmates lunging under the net, white bursts of breath pluming out of their hoods. Without Myra, they intimidated me a little, even though we were all the same. Before the new high school was built, in 1970, kids of all ages from across the county were

56

bused in to Slop Creek where the red brick school building stood beside a Methodist church at the end of a dusty dirt road. We were mostly the children of farmers and I guess I should have related to them. But it wasn't just my classmates I couldn't get used to. Myra and I hated everything about school. In first grade, we were always in trouble for hiding. We'd slip into the janitor's closet, eyes stinging from the bleachy mop water. Once we ran into the field behind the school with the teacher calling after us. We went deep into the high weeds, laughter making us breathless. When the teacher found us she paddled us both, two licks. I was miserable without Myra, half mad at her for being sick. I drew up my knees and tried to be invisible but it didn't work. A girl from my class named Tina Cutshaw saw me and walked over.

"What are you doing?" she asked.

I didn't look up at her face. I already knew it, pale with slit eyes and a fuzzy ring of dun-colored hair. She sat in the desk next to mine staring at me all day. I looked at her shoes instead, mud-crusted brogans with the laces untied. They were probably hand-me-downs from her brother, a bone-thin boy who was always throwing up. There was a rumor that he needed surgery on his stomach but their parents couldn't afford it. Tina's father drew a disability check and her mother had run off with another man. I didn't answer her. I waited for her to go away, but she sat down in the grass close to me. I scooted over. When she breathed through her mouth I could smell her rotten teeth.

"Where's your girlfriend?" she asked.

My heart leapt to hear Myra called my girlfriend. I thought at first she was making fun of me, but I glanced at her eyes and they were serious. Maybe Tina Cutshaw wasn't so bad. I poked a twig through the fence. "She's got the chicken pox," I said.

Tina was silent for a minute but I could still feel her watching me. It made my skin crawl. "You oughtn't to mess with that girl," she said finally. She plucked a thistle and twirled its stalk between her thumb and forefinger. Part of me wanted to ask what she was talking about, but I didn't. I glanced at her dirty face. She grinned and tickled herself under the chin with the thistle's prickly head. "Don't you know about her people? My mamaw said they're witches. You better watch out. She'll put a hex on you."

I turned away from Tina Cutshaw and stared through the chain link at the silent graves, wishing for her to disappear. I could feel my ears reddening.

"It's true," she said. "Mamaw told me. If you keep hanging around with that girl, you'll be cursed the rest of your life. All kinds of bad things will happen to you."

I should have got up and walked off but somehow I couldn't move. Then I felt a touch under my chin, a sly tickling. I jerked away and she dropped the thistle in my lap. I pressed my face into the chain link so hard that my cheeks and forehead hurt. "What's wrong, Doug?" Tina Cutshaw asked. "I can be your girlfriend if you want."

After school I walked down the mountain to see Mr. Barnett, chest tightening as I passed the house where I knew Myra was sick in bed. I found Mr. Barnett hammering on his roof, where a storm had blown off some shingles. I waited on the porch until he came down, trying not to think about Tina Cutshaw and the prickle of her thistle's head.

"What do you say, Douglas?" Mr. Barnett said, coming around the house with his hammer. He stopped grinning when he saw my face. "Lord have mercy, boy. You look like you done lost your best friend." I stared down at my shoes, not ready yet to talk.

He left the hammer on the steps and I followed him across the yard, hands stuffed deep in my coat pockets against the cold. Halfway up the slope, when I still hadn't spoken, Mr. Barnett asked what was on my mind. "Something happened at school," I said. I told him about Tina Cutshaw all in a rush, barely stopping to pause for breath. When I was finished, light-headed and dizzy, I waited for him to say it was nonsense. He moved silently under the winter trees, eyes tracking a red bird, until I began to think he wouldn't respond at all. Then he startled me by saying, "I figured you'd hear it sooner or later. That talk's been going around ever since Byrdie came here from Chickweed Holler." I stopped and stared but he walked on without me. I hurried to catch up.

"Back when Byrdie and her mama first came to Piney Grove to worship, there was an old busybody in the congregation by the name of Ethel Cox. She had something ill to say about everybody. My mama was in charge of organizing the bake sale that year and she held a meeting at our house. Well, there wasn't much talk about a bake sale that night. It was stuffy so Mama had opened the windows. I stood outside smoking and heard the whole thing. Big old Ethel got up and said, 'Before we get started, there's something important that ort to be addressed.' She was always trying to sound proper. I peeped in and seen her standing in front of one of the chairs Mama had arranged in a circle, big as a Sherman tank in that flowered dress she wore all the time. She said, 'I'm talking about that Pinkston woman and her girl that's been coming to Sunday morning services. I thought I knew that woman the minute I seen her. I got to talking with my second cousin that lives in Chickweed Holler where the Pinkstons come from, and I figured it out.' Then she took a big pause. The other ladies was getting restless. It was hot and they was fanning theirselves with paper fans Mama got from the funeral home. I could tell they wished Ethel would get on with it. Ethel said, 'That woman's mother is Ruth Bell, one of the Chickweed Holler witches.' I knowed she expected everybody to gasp and carry on, but they just looked at her like she was crazy. She said, 'Ain't you all ever heard of the Chickweed Holler witches?' Her fat cheeks was turning red. Mama asked her what in the world she was talking about. She never could stand Ethel Cox. Ethel said, 'The women of that family has been practicing witchcraft up in them hills since time out of mind. I been hearing stories about them all of my life.' Mama said, 'Now, Ethel, you know there ain't no such thing as witchcraft.' Ethel looked mad enough to spit. She pushed her glasses up on her nose and said, 'Well, them Bell women thinks there is. They're up yonder making love potions and casting spells, and who knows what all. We can't have people like that joining our church.' Then Mama got Ethel's goat real good. She said, 'If what you say is the truth, it sounds like they need to be in church just about as bad as you do.' I believe Ethel would've choked Mama dead on the spot if she could have got away with it. She stood there for another minute red in the face, mouth working like a fish on dry land, trying to think of something else to say, before she finally set back down. If it hadn't been for Mama, Ethel Cox might have got her way and run Byrdie off."

He fell silent and we walked on for a while, our shadows long on the frozen ground. I listened to the wind stirring through the trees. It sounded like an incantation. "Mr. Barnett," I said at last. He glanced at me and kept on walking. "Do you believe it?"

He seemed to think it over, maybe deciding if he should go on. "I never did buy that talk about witches," he said. "But sometimes

I thought about it. Like one time I walked up the hill to take Byrdie and Macon a cake Margaret made and seen Myra sleeping under a tree. She was just a little bitty thing then, must have got tuckered out playing and laid down right yonder in the shade to take a nap. I walked up to make sure she was all right before I went in the house. That's when I seen the butterflies. They was lit all over her arms and legs and in her hair. There was even two or three on her face, all sizes and colors with their wings opening and closing. I shut my eyes, thinking I might be seeing things. But when I opened them up, all of the butterflies was still there and Myra still sleeping away. She looked like a child out of a fairy story. For some reason, I was scared to death. Directly Myra opened her eyes and blinked at me. I kept still and held my breath to see what she would do. It took her a second to notice anything was unusual. Then she raised up her arms and said, 'Look, Mr. Barnett. Look at the birds.' I never told anybody this story except for you, Douglas. Sometimes I wonder if I dreamed it."

There was nothing else to say after that. We walked out of the woods and parted without a goodbye. Dark was already falling across the mountain as I headed home. I was late for supper but I stopped in the road for a while anyway to look up at Myra's house. The front windows glowed and there was smoke rising out of the chimney. I tried to send her a message in case mind reading was one of her powers. I love you, I shouted without words across the rushing creek and the rocky ground and through the walls that kept me out. Then I moved on, feeling empty and lonesome and like someone cursed.

Byrdie

I never will forget the first time Macon took me up Bloodroot Mountain. It was the spring of 1913, not long after that day we hid Easter eggs. He lived up here and took care of his pap that had a stroke and his two sisters after their mammy died. We had to take a mule and cart, because there wasn't no roads back then. There was just a dirt track that you could ride a horse or mule on. It was getting to be afternoon and the sun glared in our eyes all the way up the mountain. Shadows fell across the road and I was nervous. Mammy hadn't wanted to let me go but I had begged Pap. Now I was having second thoughts. It seemed like Macon was taking me off to some hainted place. I pictured all kinds of creatures hiding in them woods, but they was pretty even though they was thick. The creek was pretty, too, rushing down off the mountain alongside the track. I tried to sit back and enjoy the ride but every time I looked down my belly sunk. It was a long ways to the valley below. By the time we got up here I was about half sick. Then we rounded a curve and glimpsed the house up on a hill with a little barn off to the side, the sky bright blue over top of its red tin roof. The sun was shining down on it through the trees, the edges of the leaves tinged with gold. It looked so nice my heart fluttered.

Right when I thought we'd never make it, we started up the path to the house. Macon said, "Yonder it is." From the minute I seen this place, I knowed I was home. Macon and his sisters had kept it up good. The paint on the house looked fresh and the tin roof had a pretty sheen to it. The barn looked new and there was hogs in the lot. There was flowers of every color and birdhouses in the trees. I didn't know it yet, but Macon had built them hisself. When we got out of the cart, Macon's sisters came to meet us, both of them quite a bit younger than him. They looked alike, skinny little things named Becky and Jane. I couldn't wait to get ahold of them younguns and fatten them up.

Walking across the yard, Becky said, "I got some beans, but they ain't soft yet."

Macon asked me, "Why don't we take a walk before supper?"

"I don't know," I said. "These ain't walking shoes."

"Surely a country gal like you's had a few blisters. I believe you'll be all right."

Macon took ahold of my hand and led me behind the house, dragging me up through the trees until I was just about give out. He was laughing at me by the time we got there. It took forever and I was starved. I figured dinner was already on the table.

"You crazy thing," I said to Macon. He pulled me close and kissed me hard.

"Looky here," he said, pointing at the ground. He was panting, just about out of wind his own self. "This here's why they call it Bloodroot Mountain."

"What is?"

Macon knelt and pulled me down with him. "These here flowers." He rubbed a white petal with his finger and that tenderness made my heart ache. Then he started to dig around the flower with his hands. I didn't know what he was doing, but I didn't want to ask. It was so quiet, except for the sounds of mountain woods. It felt like a ceremony, like we was in church down there on our knees. Macon pulled the flower out of the ground and held it in his hands where I could see the root. It was fleshy and about as thick as a finger, looked like part of a human being. I got cold chills all over. Something came whispering through the trees, sounded like voices or a long breath. Just like that day in the churchyard, I smelled Macon, the musk of his whiskers, the clean of his clothes. Then he fished out his knife and cut the root in two pieces. When I seen that blood seeping out it was like everything slowed down. Home rushed through my mind, thoughts of Mammy and Pap and my childhood days in Chickweed Holler. It seemed like my whole life was leading up to this very minute. I had a bad urge to turn around and run fast as I could back down the mountain, but then Macon looked at me and his birthmark darkened like it did when he got excited about anything. I thought of Myrtle saying I'd walk one day on foreign ground and decided this was as foreign a ground as my feet would touch. From then on the soles of them quit itching. I made my choice and that was it. Macon was my home and far as I was concerned any wedding we had was just for show. I'd done cleaved myself to him right yonder under the trees, kneeling over that bloodroot flower. Looking at its red root sap, I was overcome with something that felt like the Holy Ghost. I seen all the generations that would come out of me and Macon. I seen our blood mixed up together, shining there in the gloomy light.

Doug

The Sunday after Daddy brought Wild Rose home, Mark whispered to Myra during preaching, "We got a horse." Mama whipped around and shot him a look, so he hushed. Myra didn't seem that interested, but after the service she was bored enough to come with us up the mountain to see Wild Rose. Walking to the fence, I had an uneasy feeling. I could sense Myra moving away from me. I wanted to grab hold of the floating skein of her hair as if we were in a cave and might get lost from each other. But I hung back as Mark led her on, calling for the horse with a handful of sweet corn.

We had to cross the first hill to find Wild Rose, and Mark and Myra took off chasing each other. She was giggling and out of breath, the belt of her green dress dragging the ground like a dead garter snake. When Mark was around I usually found myself tagging along behind them. I ran to keep

Myra in my sight. She skidded to a stop when she saw Wild Rose grazing on the next hill. Mark tripped and went sprawling, the corn flying out of his hand. "Shoot," he said, still laughing. He tried to look up Myra's dress as she stood there awestruck. Wild Rose lifted her head and looked at us. I thought she would take off as she always did when people came close to her. But it was different this time. She lengthened her neck toward us and sniffed the air, then walked slowly to where we stood, muscles working under her velvet hide. Even Mark got quiet. The horse kept coming until she stood in front of Myra, close but still out of reach. I wanted to shout or clap my hands, anything to drive Wild Rose away, but I couldn't move.

"She's got blue eyes," Myra said.

"She's a paint horse," Mark said, trying to recover a few kernels of corn. "They got eyes like that sometimes."

"They look like yours," I said. I don't know if Myra heard me. Her fingers were trembling at her sides, eager to touch the horse's white-streaked nose. Wild Rose stared at Myra, hide twitching. When Myra finally reached out her hand, the horse got spooked and galloped away. Myra stared after her for a long time. Like Daddy, she was smitten. But I knew she loved Wild Rose for a different reason than Daddy did. Daddy loved her because she was something different than he was. Myra loved Wild Rose because they were the same. I guess it doesn't matter why, but both of them loved her better than they loved me. I moved closer to Myra as we stood in the pasture, trying to claim her back somehow.

"That horse is crazy," Mark said, getting to his feet and knocking clods of dirt from the knees of his good pants. "Ain't no use fooling with her."

Byrdie

If I think too much about John Odom wearing that ring I get mad enough to bite nails in two. The first time I seen it was at the Cochrans' house the day me and Macon snuck off to get married. I used to walk all the way over yonder to work with my big ears hid under a headscarf. I had to start out when it was still dark if I meant to get there in time to fix the breakfast. Most times I'd show up on the doorstep already wore out.

That dairy farm they lived on stunk to high heaven, but you'd never know it by the way Barbara Cochran put on airs. Bucky was the biggest farmer in three counties and they was the richest people I knowed. Bucky came from money to start with, before he ever decided to farm. His pap was a doctor and I always heard Bucky was a disappointment because he didn't get none of the family brains. Used to be the church'd hold baptisms over at Slop Creek, which runs down off the mountain and through Piney Grove, but they had to quit after Bucky came in with his spotted heifers and dirtied up the water. Now them boys of his has built chicken houses that'd knock you down in the summertime. I swear I can smell them all the way up here. That's how them Cochrans are. It don't matter to them about their neighbors, as long as they're raking in the money.

Every morning I'd unlock the back door and let myself in the house. Usually I'd get to work while Barbara Cochran was still asleep, but that day she came down the stairs wrapped in her pink chenille bathrobe and said, "Byrdie, honey, would you mind to clean the oven this time? I've got people coming in from North Carolina for the weekend." She always talked to me real sweet, the same way she spoke to her little house dog.

She bustled around all morning and didn't even eat the breakfast I fixed. Around ten o'clock she lit out for the beauty shop. I was straightening up her room and seen she'd left her jewelry box open, all in a fizz getting ready for her company. That silver box was always setting on her dressing table and I'd run the feather duster over it without thinking twice about what was inside. I was a God-fearing girl and Barbara Cochran never had any reason to mistrust me before. But I'd slipped in the back door that morning with Macon Lamb on my mind. We was running off to get married. Pap didn't want to let me go being just fifteen, but I couldn't wait no longer to be Macon's wife. It was all I could do to concentrate on my chores. The only reason I went to work at all that day was to collect my pay. She left it every Friday on the kitchen table under a candlestick.

I was fixing to close the jewelry box back when that ring caught my eye. It was a man's ring and what it was doing in a woman's box I'll never know. It sure didn't look like anything Bucky would wear. I don't know the history of that ring either, or what it meant to Barbara Cochran, but it must not have been much because I don't believe she ever even noticed it was missing. She never asked me one thing about it. Granted I never did go back to work for

Barbara Cochran because Macon was the old-fashioned kind that thinks a woman should keep her place at home, but I did run into her in town a few times over the years. She was just the same as ever, talking to me like she might scratch me behind the ears any minute.

I seen the ring in that tangle of riches and it seemed too dark of a red to be ruby. Might have been garnet, I still don't know for sure. It was like them blood-colored drops of root sap Macon showed me up on the mountain, a cluster of precious stones the shade of the love that was running all through me dark and deep. I snatched it up before I even thought, like my hand had a mind of its own. I stuffed it in the sole of my shoe and walked on it the whole time I was cleaning Barbara Cochran's house. End of the day I took my pay out from under the candlestick and left a note in its place, saying I wouldn't be back to work no more, as I was getting married to Macon Lamb.

I left the Cochran place and limped on that bloodred ring all the way to the corn-field where me and Macon agreed to meet, holding back tears of pain. I reckon I felt too guilty to carry it in my hand. I went fast down the third row of corn like we planned, stopping just long enough to kick off my shoes and take out the ring. I must have sounded like a storm rustling through the corn because Macon was grinning when he stepped out, head and shoulders spangled by the sun falling down through the stalks. When we kissed all of them long, skinny green bodies was like an audience for us. Then I pulled back, heart working overtime, and asked him to hold out his hand. He did and I dropped the ring into it. He opened his eyes and whistled at the beauty in his palm. He studied it closer and said, "Where in the world did you get a thing like this?" and I blurted out, "That old Barbry Cochran gave it to me for a wedding present." My face was so hot I know it had to been red as fire but he never questioned me, even though it didn't make a lick of sense given the kind of person we both knowed Barbara Cochran was. I hope he always figured I took that ring and just didn't say nothing because he wanted to keep it as much as me. I could tell he felt like I did about them red stones. I'd like to believe we was in it together and I had no secrets from him. The guilt of stealing that ring devils me to this day, but back yonder in the cornfield, when Macon tried it on his finger, I didn't feel as bad. It fit so good, seemed like it had finally been give back to its rightful owner.

Doug

When school let out the summer of my fourteenth year, it was like being turned loose from prison. All three of us were in high spirits when we got off the bus at the foot of the mountain, laughing and running most of the way up the dusty road. Mark and I waited outside as Myra stopped to ask her granny if she could visit Wild Rose before supper. She came out smiling, cheeks flushed and hair blowing back as she ran to us.

We were panting by the time we made it to our house but Mark wouldn't let us go in for a drink of water. He said, "I got something better in the chicken coop." I followed Mark and Myra out to the tree line where the old coop leaned next to the wire fence. Mark had to wrestle the door open and the stink hit us right away. Daddy used to store junk in there but the smell of chicken droppings was still musty and strong. We climbed over the rusted tools and tractor parts and broken dishes and made a place to sit in one corner. Mark reached between some boxes and pulled out a jar of sloshing liquid.

"White Lightning," he said.

Myra covered her mouth, eyes wide. "Where'd you get that?"

"This old boy at school, Buddy Roach.

His daddy makes it."

"You better hope Mama never finds it," I said.

Mark grinned and held the dirt-smeared jar up to the light falling through the chicken wire. "I believe I can outrun her," he said, and took a long swig. He squeezed his eyes shut and coughed and wiped his mouth with the back of his arm. Myra laughed and clapped her hands. I twisted my head away, burning with jealousy.

Mark was laughing, too, trying to catch his breath, eyes streaming water. Then he held out the jar to Myra. "I dare you," he said. "Just one sup."

My back stiffened. I wanted to reach out and grab her wrist as she took the jar, halting it on the way to her lips, but my dread of being mocked won out. I knew Mark would tell me not to be a chicken and Myra would probably think less of me, too. I saw how she was looking at him. Even if she liked me best, it was my brother she admired.

At first she thrust the jar back at Mark, spluttering and choking, but he handed it back to her. "First drink always burns going down," he said. "You'll get used to it."

He was right. We passed the jar around a few times and the more we drank, the easier the fiery liquid went down and settled in my stomach, radiating heat. I kept watching Myra and before long her face looked different to me, cheeks and eyes bright in a way I didn't like. After a few drinks the world tilted each time I moved, but I didn't refuse the jar when it came to me. Myra and Mark seemed to find everything funny. Pretty soon they were laughing at nothing, looking at each other and busting out in foolish giggles. Moonshine didn't have the same effect on me. I just felt dizzy and green around the gills. I was about to pretend I heard somebody coming, anything to get out of the stinking heat of the chicken coop, when Myra said, "I want to go somewhere."

Mark took another long swig from the jar. "There ain't nowhere to go," he said. "That's the trouble with being stuck up here on top of a mountain."

"This isn't the top of it," Myra said. "Granddaddy went to the top and he said you could see all the way to town." Her words sounded slurry. I took the jar from Mark and forced myself to drink, even though I was heading fast toward being sick.

"It's not that high," I said. Myra wobbled getting to her feet. She stood there swaying in the slick-bottomed shoes she'd worn to school, not made at all for climbing.

"My daddy's been, too," Mark said. "He claims there's a field up yonder."

Myra's eyes lit up. "There's a field? Maybe that's where Wild Rose goes when she gets loose." I could picture Rose grazing, long neck bent, in my great-grandfather's mountaintop paradise. I knew Myra would never rest until she saw it.

"Let's go up there," she said.

Mark tried to get up and they both laughed when he tripped over the rusty tines of a rake and nearly fell back down again. "I will if you will," he said.

I couldn't keep quiet anymore. "Don't you remember what happened to Daddy?" I asked Mark, trying to sound calmer than I felt. "It's too steep of a climb."

Then Myra said something that cut me to the bone. "Why do you have to be such a baby all the time?" I could feel the blood draining out of my face.

Mark slapped me hard on the back and I almost tipped over. My head was swimming. "Buck up, private," he said. "Have some gumption about you."

Myra narrowed her eyes at me, as if they were having trouble focusing. "If he's too yellow," she said, "we'll just do it without him."

I stood there for a minute unable to speak,

hating both of them, until Mark said, "If we're going we better head out, so we can make it back before supper." I could have told him there was no way we'd be back before supper. We were guaranteeing ourselves a whipping, but I kept quiet. I moved to let them pass and then followed them out of the chicken coop into the sun. We looked over our shoulders as we ducked under the fence, Mark holding the barbed strands apart for Myra, and disappeared into the thick pine trees that marked the beginning of our woods. Mark and Myra stumbled ahead, half leaning on each other, and I wanted to knock their heads together. I thought of turning back and telling Daddy what they were up to, but in the end I stayed my course.

The climb was easy at first. There was a footpath worn up through the trees, but I didn't feel any better about the fix I was in. It didn't help how the moonshine sloshed back and forth in my stomach. Several times I had to stop with my hands on my knees until a dizzy spell passed. At first Mark and Myra pretended they were still having fun. I tensed up each time she slid on loose rocks but Mark would get behind her and push, tickling her ribs under her blouse. It wasn't long, though, before their giddiness wore off.

The terrain wasn't very rugged but it labored straight up through trees so tall we couldn't see their tops even when we craned our necks. After we had walked for what seemed like hours, sweating and pale and thirsty, the footpath began to disappear under a scrawl of twisted roots and ferns. I was so sick-feeling, it took every ounce of my will not to give up and sit down. At some point Mark must have realized it was still a long way to the top. I could see our predicament dawning on his face. Now he would be the baby if he suggested turning back. I was heartened a little to see my brother getting his comeuppance, and relieved that the climb wasn't as dangerous as we had been told.

But just when I began to think Daddy had exaggerated, we came to a place where it seemed the mountain's rock core had erupted through the pebbled dirt surface of the slope and heaved it almost in two, each side studded with scrubby bushes and tall, thin trees jutting at angles across the divide. It was still daylight and not much cooler in spite of the elevation but there was fog up ahead, curling close to the ground and clinging to the tree trunks. We all stopped and Mark and I exchanged nervous glances. I knew he wanted me to be the yellow baby she had called me, to let on like he was only turning back to appease his cowardly little brother, but he wasn't going to get away with it. Then Myra started climbing again, maybe imagining Wild Rose grazing in a mountaintop meadow, or maybe just being stubborn. We had no choice but to go on behind her.

I mustered what little strength I had left and pushed myself upward, arms heavy and tongue dry and the rancid taste of moonshine still thick in the back of my throat. The incline was almost vertical and it was a struggle to keep my balance on the rocks. I bit my lip, shaking with exhaustion, trying to see through the sweat in my eyes. When I glanced up, I realized that Myra was out of sight. She had disappeared into the fog and Mark wasn't far behind. There was nothing between the leaning trees but blank sky and the mist that had risen up to claim her. I went cold with dread and scrambled to catch up with them. That's when I began to lose my hold, fingernails clawing for purchase in the crumbling dirt. In those slow seconds before dropping, heavy and helpless like in a dream of falling, I turned my head to the side and saw another outcropping. Some of the pines there were broken off with their tops bowing down. Between the rise I clung to and the mountain's other jagged face a buzzard was circling. Then my arms and legs gave out and I was flailing backward, hands searching in vain for something to grab. The tumble down was fast, a blur of ground and sky, before my head cracked on a stone.

Mark said later I wasn't out for long because my eyes were open when they got to me. The first thing I remember is Myra bending close and I was glad to see that she was sorry. She never said so but she didn't have to, the guilt was all over her face. Mark helped me up and my head hurt so bad that I almost passed out again. It felt like a bowling ball on the end of my neck. They dusted me off and examined my scrapes and cuts before we started down. I'll never forget how Myra looked back over her shoulder into the fog. That night I was so dizzy and sick that I stumbled out of bed and threw up twice. Afterward I lay in my room, head pounding and backside raw from Daddy's belt, thinking about what Tina Cutshaw had said in fifth grade, that bad things would happen to me if I kept on loving Myra. I guess I knew even back then how things would turn out.

Byrdie

The summer after we got married, Macon took me home to Bloodroot Mountain and I been here ever since. Them was good years when I first came here to live. I'd set on the back steps looking off through the trees, breaking beans or shucking corn, or weaving me a rug for the floors. Sometimes a wind would come along smelling so sweet, like creek bank mud and pine needles and rainy weather. It'd lift my hair off of my shoulders and kiss my forehead the same way Macon did at night, and I'd know for sure I belonged here. But I did get homesick sometimes. I missed Mammy and Pap and our cabin in Piney Grove. They was less than five miles from the foot of the mountain and we still seen each other at church, but it was hard to be away from them during the week. Sunday afternoons Mammy would cook dinner for me and Macon and as much as I loved our house on the mountain, I'd wish sometimes to crawl in my feather bed up in the loft and sleep the day away. I was jealous of my time with Mammy and Pap and it was irksome when our Sunday dinners got interrupted. Word had got around about Pap's gift for healing and many Sundays there'd be a knock on the kitchen door. He'd get up from dinner and somebody would be standing at the back steps with a baby on their hip. Pap would take the baby around the cabin, I guess for some privacy, and cure its thresh like he done mine. Then he'd come back in and set down at the table like nothing ever happened. Just being around Pap for a little while would set everything right with me and I'd head back up the mountain with Macon, happy as a lark again.

I helped Macon take care of his own pap, Paul Lamb, until he had another stroke and died. Then I took Becky and Jane to raise, until they growed up and married some boys that worked for the railroad. I learnt them how to sew, not just mend socks and put buttons back on, but how to make curtains and dresses. Where they'd been so long without a mammy, there was a lot them girls didn't know. I learnt them how to make pie crust and how to season their beans and how to make their biscuits fluffy. I wasn't much older than Becky and Jane and we had a big time together. In the summer worshing clothes we'd bust out in a water fight, or making bread we'd throw flour on one another until we was white-headed and the kitchen was a mess. It was worth cleaning it up for all the fun we had. If the chores was done sometimes we'd run off in the woods and play hide-and-go-seek. Macon would get mad enough to spit when he'd come in from the barn and see me acting like a youngun, but he got over anything pretty quick.

Before the road came through Macon farmed for a living. When the Depression hit, a lot of the men around here went off to work in the mills and coal mines, but Macon stayed with me. The banks started closing in 1929 and nobody on the mountain had two dimes to rub together. It was hard to buy sugar and salt and coffee, but we had a milk cow and laying hens and hogs to render fat for lard. We worked long hours in the hot sun until our fingers was blistered and our backs was sore. Once Roosevelt got in things started looking up for us, but it took years to climb out of the hole we was in.

Macon worked on the road when it came through. Him and the other men got out here and dug it with picks and shovels. I hated to see Macon give up farming, but I reckon he was happier working with his hands on cars for a living, after people in these parts started driving. Before he went to fixing motors down at the filling station in Piney Grove, he liked to whittle and build things out of scrap wood. He'd make birdhouses and whirligigs to put in the yard, and he could whittle any kind of animal you asked for. Me and him'd set out in the yard as the sun was going down and I'd love to watch him work a block of wood, his fingers moving that knife so swift. I was glad to be his wife.

I didn't even mind taking care of poor old Paul before he died. Every morning I'd make Paul some mush and spoon it between his lips. Macon'd be down to the barn and Becky and Jane off to school. It was peaceful with just me and Paul in the house. I'd lead him to the front room window and feed him there so both of us could see the mountain and the sky. Then I'd get me a pan of soapy water and worsh him one piece at a time. Some days he'd look at me like he knowed what was going on, but others seemed like he was in a dream. I always believed he was dreaming about his life up here on the mountain, working the land and playing with his younguns. I figured he had it all stored up in his heart, didn't matter where his body was at or what kind of shape he was in.

I got to where I loved old Paul, but he didn't live long after me and Macon got married. Wasn't long after we buried him down at Piney Grove Church that Becky and Jane was gone, too. I cried and cried when they ran off with them railroad boys. They was the only sisters I ever had. They used to come and visit sometimes before their husbands decided to move up north. They still write me letters but they never did come back. I don't see how they stand it up there where it's cold and the people's so different.

Besides Becky and Jane, I had younguns of my own. Not long after me and Macon got married I was expecting, and none of us got too excited about it. It was just how things was. You got married and went to having younguns. The first one was Patricia. She was awful tiny and didn't want to nurse them first few days, but I never doubted she'd take off. It never entered my head that Patricia might die, or that any of my younguns might not outlive me. Once Patricia took to nursing, she got fat as mud. Becky and Jane helped me with her, and then Jack and Sue when they came along, one right after the other. For a time I was nursing both of them at once, like twins. I used to set in a rocking chair in front of the kitchen door catching the breeze with one in each arm. I felt a contentment when I was nursing my babies that I reckon I'll never know again.

Then all three of them, Patricia, Jack, and Sue, died of the diphtheria one winter. It was the year that Sue, my littlest, was turning two. I liked to lost my mind. I didn't take them to the doctor right at first. It was before the road came through and we was snowed in that winter. Sometimes it's like I dreamt them up, it's been so long ago. I still can't figure out how come me and Macon not to catch it. Them first days after the last one, Patricia, passed on, I waited for the fever to come. I wanted so bad to get sick and die. It was like a bridegroom had left me at the altar. I went out of my head and Macon didn't know how to tend to me. Mammy and Pap came up the mountain to stay a few days but Mammy couldn't do much with me, either. She tried putting on a cheery face and talking like I hadn't lost my babies but I laid on the bed I'd birthed them in and wouldn't get up. I didn't want to eat and they had to pry my jaws open to force broth down my throat. I'd look past them as they fought me to Pap, standing there watching with bright light shining all around him. I don't believe I imagined it, even in the state I was in. He never fussed or paced the floor or begged me to eat like Macon and Mammy did. He just stayed there in the room. Day or night I could open my eyes and he'd be setting at the foot of the bed, watching over me. I guess, looking back, I decided to come back to my life because Pap was still in it. I got better, but for a long time I went through my days living over and over that time when my youngguns was getting sicker and nothing could be done. I got to where I thought it might not have really happened. I made up my mind they was still alive, just off somewhere playing. I don't know when I figured out the bridegroom wasn't coming for me and started putting one foot in front of the other again.

I guess some part of me must have died anyhow because it was easier when my boy Willis got killed. It's awful to say but it's the truth. I had Willis in 1924, three years after Patricia, Jack, and Sue was gone. I didn't want to have no more babies for a long time because I was scared of losing them, but Macon begged me to. I never seen that man beg to nobody before, but he got down on his knees as I was trying to hang the worsh and clung to my legs. "This house is too lonesome, Byrdie," he said. "I can't stand it." People might have thought Macon didn't have no feelings, but his heart was softer than just about anybody else's you could find, including mine. He loved younguns and animals better than anything, and couldn't be happy unless there was a child or dog underfoot. I gave in because I couldn't stand to see Macon that way, and we had Willis.

Willis wasn't no good, from the time he was little. He'd bite my nipple hard as he could soon as his teeth came in, and would fight me with his fists anytime he didn't get his way. Willis broke my heart every day he was alive. I don't know what went wrong with that boy. I reckon it had to been something me and Macon done. Someway or another, we wasn't cut out to raise younguns. That might be how come the Lord took them from us. All I can figure out is we spoiled them too much. I believe we ruint Willis and Clio both by smothering them, and I reckon we did the same thing to Myra when she came along. I treated Willis like a little king, made him sugar cookies every day until nearly every tooth in his head rotted out, and he still hated me and Macon both.

Whatever made Willis that way, he was meaner than a striped snake. He got stabbed in a bar fight when he wasn't but twenty years old and bled to death. The ones that done it throwed him off of a bluff and he laid there a week until somebody found him. I never did feel like Willis loved me. Maybe that's how come it was easier to take. Besides that, me and Macon still had Clio. She came to us late in life and you'd think we would have learnt our lesson, but we couldn't help petting Clio rotten, too, until she growed up and turned against us. I believe she blamed us for being born on a mountain. Why, we didn't ask for her no more than she asked for us. That was the Lord's doing.

Doug

For a while after my fall on the mountain Myra wouldn't look at my face, even when we were laughing. I wanted to tell her she was forgiven but that would have been like accusing her. I knew she didn't want to talk about what happened so I kept it to myself, until the day we sat in the barn loft eating peaches. Her eye caught mine and darted away and I couldn't stand the awkwardness anymore. "We can climb to the top again if you want," I said. "I bet we could make it this time." She turned to me, sucking shreds of peach from a wrinkled pit. She took the pit from her mouth and closed her hand tight around it. I held my breath, waiting for her to speak. After a while she opened her palm, looked down at the peach pit, and said, "Let's bury this and see if anything grows." I didn't bring the subject up again. It would only have made things worse between us.

It's true that Myra and Wild Rose are two of a kind. That's why they took to each other so quickly. If I believed that talk I heard about witches, I'd figure Wild Rose was Myra's familiar. But there's one difference I can think of between them. Wild Rose never let me within arm's reach of her, but I got away with touching Myra once. It was because of the poems. All through elementary school Myra and I had the same teachers, and in high school we always had at least one class together. Junior year it was English. Myra loved the poems we studied, especially Wordsworth. "It's like he's talking about here," she said. "He wrote this one a few miles above a place in England called Tintern Abbey, but I can tell he feels the same way as I do about Bloodroot Mountain. Does that make any sense to you?" I said yes, but it didn't matter to me. I just liked hearing her talk.

Whenever she knew that Mark was away from home, she would come walking up the mountain to find me, carrying one of her books, wearing a floppy old dress with the sun in her eyes. Just to make sure, she always asked, "Where's Mark?" I'd smile with my lips closed over my broken tooth, knowing she needed to share the poems she loved with somebody quiet. I'd say, "Mark's gone hunting," or fishing, or down to the pool hall with some of his friends. Then she'd ask if I wanted to take a walk. She didn't really have to ask. She knew I'd follow her anywhere, branches slapping my face in her wake.

Most of the time we went to a big rock high on the mountain behind her house and I'd sit there with her for hours, listening to her read. But that day we decided to walk down to the creek branch instead, where it runs downhill beside the road. She was quiet and I thought maybe she had spied an animal or bug she wanted to touch. She could track for hours, shushing Mark and me, telling us to go away, even though we never did. But there was no lizard, no squirrel or frog this time. She was only thinking.

When we came to the creek branch we crawled under the pink rhododendron together, where its low branches made a cave of shadows sprinkled with coins of light. She read for a while, but I could tell there was something on her mind. Finally, she put down her book and sat on a rock with her feet in the water. I stared at them through the silt-swirling ripples. They were long and slim, smooth on top and leathery on the bottom. "I got a chickadee to eat out of my hand," she said, dipping her cupped palm in the water.

"How'd you do that?"

"You know that stump behind the house where Granny scatters seed? They come in droves this time of year, all different kinds of birds. I've been sitting there every day with my hand out. They're used to me now."

"Reckon they think you're part of the stump?"

"I am," she said.

She lowered herself off the rock and into the branch, her dress darkening and spreading in the water. She lay back on the rocks with light shifting on her face, fingers of creek water closing across her middle.

"Can I tell you something?" She closed her eyes and propped up on her elbows. The water trickled over her thighs and played with her dress tail. I couldn't stop looking at her pale body, stretched out long and hard in the creek branch.

"Yeah."

"I'm afraid you'll think I'm crazy."

"I won't."

"I thought . . . it was like . . . that chickadee was my mother."

Myra had never mentioned her dead mama to me before. "Like reincarnation?" I asked. "Better not let the church folks hear you talking that way."

Myra smiled. "Not exactly."

"Like a ghost or something?"

"More like a spirit. Like she's still here."

"The Bible says there's two places people go when they die."

I looked at her stomach, the black dress gathering in neat wrinkles where her navel was hidden. I imagined a dark slit filling with water.

"I wonder about her. You know she moved off to town with my father when she was seventeen. I can't figure out how she could leave this place. She must not have been like me."

I lowered myself into the water beside Myra. The cold took my breath. "Does it make you sad?"

"Hmm?"

"That she wasn't like you?"

"I don't know." Myra sounded sleepy, drunk on the feel of the creek lapping at her fingers, running like a cool scarf over her elbow bends, gliding under her heels and between her toes, and all the smells of blossoms and muck and mottled toadstools risen like yeast in the shade. Looking at her,

95

a feeling came over me that she might do the same thing her mama had done. I wouldn't have believed that Myra could leave the mountain, but I hadn't seen until then how she longed for her mama and wanted to know about her.

"You'll go, too," I said, leaning over her.

Myra took in a deep breath, black hair coiling out in all directions, a nest of water snakes. "Never," she exhaled, and I felt the cool rush of her breath on my face. I put my hand on her wet stomach and it tightened under the slippery fabric of her dress, but she didn't open her eyes. I leaned in and pressed my mouth, ever concealing the broken tooth, against hers. But I'm no fool. It was Bloodroot Mountain she tasted when I kissed her lips. I might as well not even have been there. I knew it then and I know it now. I never tried to kiss her again, but I'm glad I took my chance when I saw it.

Myra drove Mark out of his head, the same as she did me. He tried to kiss her a million times when we were teenagers. She always laughed and wriggled away as if he was playing with her, but I knew it was for real. I saw how his smile dissolved and his eyes flamed up. In high school when we went to the movies he would try to touch her in the dark, his hand sliding onto her ribs and moving up toward her breast. She would bend back his fingers until he cried out and the people behind us fussed at him to be quiet. He'd try to pretend that he wasn't mad, walking through the lighted lobby to the parking lot where Daddy's old truck was waiting for us, but I knew what his anger looked like.

Mark hated me when he discovered how Myra sought me out. He caught us one day coming back from a walk. He was home early from a fishing trip because nothing was biting. He watched us as he took his pole and tackle out of the truck bed to put in the smokehouse. Myra waved but he didn't raise his hand in return. I walked her down to the road and when I came back he was sitting on the porch steps blocking my way.

"She won't ever have you," he said, his eyes reminding me of that crazy boy who broke my mouth with a rock when I was seven. "Ugly old snaggletooth thing."

I climbed up the porch steps and he let me pass. I knew he was right. I couldn't put into words why I'd never have Myra. It had nothing to do with how I looked. It was something else I couldn't explain. I wanted to tell Mark that I love Myra's wildness and hate it at the same time. I'm jealous because

I can't be it, and want it because I can't have it. The only way to love Myra is from a distance, the same way Daddy loves Wild Rose.

Byrdie

Pap lived to be a good age, but it still liked to killed me when he died. He never did get sick or feeble. He worked right up until the end, when that tractor he'd had ever since we moved to Piney Grove turned over on him. The doctor said there wasn't nothing to do but wait for him to die. Thank goodness me and Macon got to the cabin before he passed on. The front room was packed full of people from the community he'd helped down through the years and it touched my heart to see how many had loved him. They parted to let me through and the first thing I seen was Mammy kneeling at his side. When she looked up at me her eyes was like holes and I had to turn my face. I stood at the end of the bed and took hold of Pap's foot sticking out from under the quilt. I rubbed it through his old sock, feeling the hard corns and thick toenails he'd always pared with a knife. His face was so white it nearly blended in with the pillow. All of us waited, not speaking, for him to go. When he finally breathed his

98

last, the breath went straight up. I seen it with my own eyes, a glow that rose and evaporated against the ceiling like steam. I held on tight to Pap's sock foot, tears running down my face. Then I closed my eyes and prayed to the Lord that he wasn't the only one of his kind.

I didn't get to be there when Mammy died. After Pap was gone I begged her to come and live with us on Bloodroot Mountain but she wouldn't hear of it. Her and Pap had put a lot into that farm and she meant to keep it going. She took to wearing overalls and every time me and Macon visited she was out in the field or the garden sweating under the hot sun. She was like Pap and Grandmaw Ruth, worked right on up until the day she died. She passed away in 1939, just a few months after Clio was born. A woman from the church found her in the bed and the county coroner said she went peacefully in her sleep. That's exactly how I want to go, fall asleep one night and wake up in Glory.

With Mammy and Pap gone and the Great Depression on, it was sad times. The only thing that eased my grief was Clio. She was a good baby. It wasn't until later that she started giving us fits. Most of the time Clio was sassy and full of mischief, but she could get down in the dumps sometimes. She'd let her hair go and not take a bath, and every once in a while she'd act plumb crazy. She got it after Macon's people. He had a great-aunt that took a notion to fly and jumped off of one of these clifts around here. Sometimes Clio'd go to hollering and clawing at her face and slapping at her head. Some of the church people thought she was possessed with devils, but I knowed what it was. She just couldn't stand to be pent up. She was worst in the winters when we got hemmed in by snow. She wanted to be out running the roads and if she couldn't get to town it done something to her mind. One time, when she was seventeen, it came a bad ice storm, so slick even Macon wouldn't venture out. He tried to go to work the second day, but he'd done fell down three times before he ever got to the truck, and there wasn't no digging it out. We had a good fire going in the kitchen woodstove and he was setting there beside of it whittling. I set down at the table with him to drink me a cup of coffee. Not long after that I heard Clio's naked feet on the floorboards. If it wasn't for that, I would never have knowed she was there. She'd crept up to the kitchen like a haint in her long white nightgown. When I turned around it scared me half to death. I knowed she didn't look right in the face, standing there not making a peep. It gave me an awful feeling in my belly. "You better put some socks on them feet," I said, just to be talking. "You'll get the sore throat." She stared at me but it was like she didn't really see me. Then she looked over my head at the kitchen window, frosted over with ice. "I can't stand it," she said.

"What?" I asked, but I knowed. The snow was about waist deep. There was great long icicles like fingers with claws hanging off of the eaves. Walking out to the woodpile was a mess and even with a shawl wound around my head, my face'd get so numb I couldn't hardly talk until I thawed out some by the stove. Wasn't noplace to go and if we wanted to stay warm we had to crowd together around the stove. All we had was each other and this little house. I had tried since I was fifteen years old to make it pleasant, weaving my rugs and tatting lacy curtains and crocheting doilies. Back in the summer I'd hung flowerdy wallpaper in Clio's bedroom, but I knowed she still hated it. She was gone somewhere every minute she could be, one excuse to get off of the mountain after another. I didn't believe she was studying with her girlfriend or practicing for the school play or selling raffle tickets for the church fund-raiser, but I let her go. I knowed she had to be free, and free to her was flying off every chance she got, away from this house and from me and Macon, too. She couldn't help it. She took them itchy feet after me. It was her nature, and you can't hardly fight nobody's nature.

I reckon I always knowed what would happen if Clio got hemmed in for too long. That's why I followed her when she turned around and padded out of the kitchen on into the front room. I couldn't see her feet for that gown being so long and it seemed like she was floating. Seemed like she wasn't even my girl no more, like there was something in the house with us that ort not to be. The front room was quiet and still, lit up cold and gloomy by the snow still falling outside. Clio stopped and stood in front of the window. Neither one of us moved. I was scared to say anything because it was like she was sleepwalking. I've heard tell if you wake up one that's walking in their sleep they'll die. I don't know how long Clio stood there in front of the window that way. Then Macon came in to see what was the matter, with the whittling knife still in his hand.

"What's wrong, girl?" he asked. His voice

was like a firecracker going off.

Clio reached around before I knowed it and snatched up the straight chair Paul used to set in when I fed him his breakfast of the mornings. She took that chair and raised it up over her head and smashed out the window pane. At the same time she let out a scream that liked to froze my blood. It was the awfulest crash you ever heard, too, seemed like that racket rung in my ears for a week after it happened. Macon run to Clio, standing in her nightgown with the cold flooding in, and wrapped her up in his arms. I reckon he was so addled he had forgot to drop his whittling knife and she tried to take it away from him. They scuffled over it for a minute and I didn't know what was going to happen. I was scared somebody was going to get cut, but finally it was like she gave out all at once. She fell and the knife clattered to the floor. Macon picked her up and carried her like a baby to the bed. She slept that whole day away and part of the next. I couldn't sleep a wink myself, or eat a bite of nothing. I paced the floor outside her room until Macon made me rest. When the sun came out and the eaves started dripping Clio finally perked up some. I swear, we liked to froze to death before that window got fixed.

The spring after that was when I lost Clio for good, even before she died. Soon as the ice melted and she could get down the mountain, we hardly ever seen her no more. She'd still mumble out one of her excuses, but they got feebler and feebler. Even when she was home to eat supper, her eyes was far away. We'd let Clio get by with just about anything, but Macon used to be hard on her about running off to town. Many times he'd held his ground and made her stay home, even though she'd sulk around and pout and look at him like she hated his neck. But after she busted that window out, he let her go. Me and Macon both was scared she'd go out of her head for good the next time.

One day after it got warm I was going across the yard with a bucket of eggs, headed for the kitchen door, when I heard a loud car come up the hill. I stopped and tried to see who it was, but the sun was in my eyes. That old car pulled up next to the barn and blowed the horn two or three times, had the dog barking and the chickens running all over the place. Sounded about as loud as Clio busting out the front room window, and give me the same awful feeling. Next thing I knowed, Clio came flying out the door with her purse on her arm.

She didn't look left or right, just ran across the yard to that car with her hair blowing back. I had a pretty good idea who was driving it. I'd heard from some of the church people that Clio was down at the pool hall in Millertown with a boy named Kenny Mayes. I was hoping it was just rumors because I knowed of the Mayeses. I reckon nary one of them has ever set foot in a church house, but they sure do spend plenty of time in the jailhouse. About every week you'll see one of their names in the paper, picked up for drunk driving or writing bad checks or shoplifting. Macon said they was lazy, too. He worked with Kenny's uncle down to the filling station, said he wouldn't strike a lick at nothing. I knowed Clio and me both was in for trouble, soon as I heard she was courting a Mayes. That was the first time she took off without asking me if she could go, even if she made up the place she was going to. I watched her moving away from me and felt the tie that bound us since she was born stretching out too thin. She slammed that car door and it finally broke in two. The way I see it, that was the end of me and her. Kenny Mayes stole Clio away from me and there was nothing I could do about it.

She came back in the middle of the night,

but it never was the same. Them few weeks she stayed on at the house it was like she was checking in and out of a motel. But to tell the truth, she was happier than I ever seen her. Her eyes was bright and she was taking better care of herself, all of that long hair clean and glossy around her shoulders. Then one Saturday Kenny Mayes came to the door to get Clio instead of blowing the horn for her. I'd done figured out something was up, because Clio had hovered around all morning acting skittish. Besides that, she'd took it on herself to make a cake and she hated to cook. It was about noontime that Kenny knocked and Clio wanted me to open it. "Go on, Mama," she said. I went to the front of the house with a heavy heart because I knowed what was coming. I opened the door and there he stood, with a big old mealy-mouthed grin. I can't say he was handsome, but his eyes was blue as the springtime sky.

"Hidee," he said.

Clio went to him and pulled him in the front room. "Mama, this here's Kenny Mayes," she said. It looked like her cheeks was on fire.

"Clio said I ought to bring you something," Kenny said. He fished around in his britches pocket and dug out a string of dime store beads with the tag still hanging off of them. I never wore such a thing in all my life, and didn't aim to start. I took them beads and laid them on the table beside of Macon's chair.

"Take you a seat, Kenny," Clio said. "I'll go get us a piece of cake to eat so you and Mama can get acquainted."

Kenny flopped down on the loveseat with them gangly legs sprawled out and his arm slung across the back like he owned the place. I didn't make no effort to talk, but he didn't seem bashful about it. "It's right pretty up here," he said, looking out the window we'd just got fixed, at the blooming trees and the mowed green hill rolling down to the creek branch. "But it kindly stinks, don't it? Must be the hog lot."

We didn't keep hogs no more, but I didn't say it. I kept my mouth shut. Macon was gone since he worked every other Saturday at the filling station trying to earn an extra dollar, so the house was quiet besides Clio clattering around in the kitchen.

"Well," Kenny said when Clio came in with the cake on one of my tole trays. "I aim to take good care of Clio, Miss Lamb, so you ain't got a thing to worry about."

"Dangit, Kenny," Clio said, handing me a saucer of chocolate cake and a fork to eat it with. "I ain't told her yet. We was supposed to do it together."

"Shoot, I forgot," Kenny said, and grinned at me.

Clio set down beside of Kenny on the loveseat. He shoveled in cake, crumbs falling all over the floor for me to clean up later. "Me and Kenny's getting married," she said. Her voice cracked some like she might be nervous, but she still sounded sassy as ever. "I didn't want to tell it in front of Daddy cause I figured he'd pitch a fit."

"When?" I asked.

"Well . . . I figured I'd go ahead and settle in this evening over at Kenny's mama's house. Then I reckon we'll go on down to the courthouse Monday morning."

"What are you telling me for?" I asked. She looked surprised. I couldn't help but speak my mind. Them was the first words I'd said since that old weasel came to the door, and I didn't aim to pussyfoot around. "Why didn't y'uns just run off and do it?"

Clio couldn't think of nothing to say for a minute. "I don't know, Mama. It didn't seem right, I guess."

I headed for the kitchen with my piece of cake, to rake it in the trash. "Well, I reckon I ort to be thankful for that," I said. I went back and stood in the front room doorway.

"Y'uns best be getting along." Clio hadn't took but a few bites of her cake, and Kenny stuffed the rest of his in fast. "You can come back and get your things later."

"Mama . . ."

"It's what you been aiming to do since the day you was born. Might as well get it over with."

"Now, I never meant to hurt your feelings, Mama. . . ."

"I'll put your clothes in a bag, if you'd rather do it that way, and send them down with Macon when he goes in to work Monday morning."

"That'll be all right," Clio said. She put down her saucer hard on the end table. The dirty fork rattled off and fell on the floor. "I done got my things packed."

She stood up and we looked at each other. Her eyes was cold as that snow she hated. She stomped off to the bedroom and left me and Kenny Mayes by ourselves.

"That sure was some good cake," he said.

"Clio made it," I told him.

"Well, then," he leant over and whispered at me, "somebody's going to have to learn that girl to cook, if she's fixing to be my wife." He winked and laughed like a mule. Then Clio came stomping in with her traveling case and took him by the arm.

"Come on, Kenny," she said, and they left without saying good-bye. I sunk down in Macon's chair feeling like somebody had laid a rock on my heart. I seen them beads on the end table and it was too much to bear. I snatched them old things up, like a string of shiny black snake's eyes, and took them and throwed them in the kitchen garbage. Then I leant over the sink and squalled for a long time because my last living youngun was gone.

Clio left with Kenny Mayes when she wasn't but seventeen. If he ever seen her act crazy like she did that day she busted out the window, he never let on to me. But Clio didn't ever love this place like me and Myra do. I believe she needed off of this mountain, because she perked up once Kenny took her away from me. Now, Myra's John Odom had me fooled at first, but I knowed Kenny Mayes was no count from the start. He didn't beat on Clio or nothing like that, but he was shiftless. She had to keep them both up, working on the assembly line at one of them factories in Millertown. I know she had to been tired of it, standing on her feet all day, but she was too stubborn to let on.

Myra was better off not knowing her daddy. I didn't tell her nothing about

Kenny, not even good stories, like how he always tried to buy me and Macon something nice at Christmas. When he was working he liked to treat Clio, too. He'd buy her perfume and take her out to the restaurants. He'd blow every penny he made, but I reckon he meant well. Course there wasn't no use telling Myra about her daddy's mean streak, either, how he liked to scare Clio driving. He'd laugh fit to split, her holding on to the dash and me stomping the brakes in the backseat, them few times I let him take me to the store. I quit going with him after I learnt better, that heathern. Then him and Clio got hit and killed by a train. Nobody knows for sure how it happened, if the car quit or he tried to beat the train or what, but I'd bet anything he was trying to scare Clio like he did.

Something queer happened the night Kenny and Clio got killed. I was taking care of Myra again. I never would say it out loud, but I don't believe Clio was cut out to be a mama. She never meant to be expecting in the first place, and she was always leaving the baby with me. I had rocked Myra to sleep and fell off to sleep myself with her on my shoulder. I was stiff as a board from setting so long in that chair and I was fixing to get up and take Myra to bed with me when

I heard a train whistle off down the mountain. I had the windows open to catch the breeze and that noise made the hair stand up on my arms. I thought, how in the world am I hearing this? Them train tracks is plumb in town. I put my hand on Myra's little back to feel it going up and down. The house was quiet and dark besides the light of the moon. I don't know if I was ever more blue in my life, it was the awfulest feeling you could think of. The next morning Bill Cotter knocked on the front door and said Clio had got killed on the train tracks in Millertown. He was a volunteer fireman and helped them pry her and Kenny loose from the car. It liked to killed me to hear it, my last child was gone, but I can't say I was surprised. Clio died on them same tracks that runs by where Myra lives right now, with that devilish John Odom.

Doug

Myra and I grew even further apart after that day at the creek. The kiss we shared didn't seal anything between us, it severed something instead. Myra was only a few months younger than me, but she was growing up faster. Overnight, it seemed, she was full-breasted and long-legged and almost as tall as me. Last summer, before our senior year started, Daddy let me take Myra to town sometimes in his truck. We'd walk across a diner parking lot or step out of a matinee blinking in the sun, and men passing on the street would crane their necks and call out to her and whistle. Myra just laughed but I was always embarrassed and a little bit angry at her, even though it wasn't her fault.

One Saturday I'd been to the drugstore for Mama and saw Myra coming down the sidewalk with a girl from our church, smiling and whispering behind her hand. She froze when she saw me standing beside the truck, holding Mama's prescription. She was wearing makeup, I could tell, and it was like being slapped in the face. I stared at her red lips for a long time, until she said in a flustered way, "Don't you like it?" She puckered up, trying to make me laugh. When I didn't, she gave up. "Don't tell Granny, okay?" she said. "It's not mine. I'm just trying it out." Then she walked on without saying goodbye. I guess that's when I knew it wasn't my imagination. She was slipping away from me.

By the end of the summer she was spending more time with her girlfriends than with me, but I tried not to worry. I thought when school started up things would get back to normal between us, and I did see more of her. But she didn't wait anymore in front of her house so we could walk down the road and catch the bus together. Without explanation, she began taking off early and leaving me behind, already standing at the bottom of the mountain by the time I got there. I couldn't make it any earlier myself because I had chores to do on the farm. When Myra and I got on the bus each morning, it was like she wasn't even really there in the seat beside me. For most of the ride she looked out the window and whenever I spoke she turned to me startled, eyes cloudy and far away.

I thought about her all the time. Pouring water into the troughs, filling the drum-shaped feeder with grain, mucking out the barn stalls, I was devising plans to win her back. I'd find a way to break Wild Rose and come galloping into Myra's yard. I'd sweep her up onto the horse's bare back and we'd ride off somewhere together. One morning at breakfast, I looked up from my daydream and realized Mark was staring at me. He had graduated the year before and was supposed to be helping Daddy on the farm, but most days he took off and went to the pool hall. Daddy had already told him to shape up or ship out. It was around that time he started talking about joining the service, even with Mama begging him not to because of the war going on. Vietnam had seemed a long way off until a boy we knew from church was killed over there and the newspapers started reporting protest marches in Knoxville, less than an hour away from us. There was a draft but Mark didn't want to wait for it. Sometimes I could see on his face how angry and desperate he was to get away. That morning he was sitting across the table from me drinking black coffee, looking hungover. "Hey," he said, with a glint in his eye. "Guess who I seen the other day?" I lowered my head and stared at my plate. Mark still had a way of getting to me. "Your girl, Myra. She was hanging around with some long tall feller, looked a lot older than her. They seemed to be awful cozy. If I'd stuck around, there ain't no telling what kind of show they would've put on." I gripped my fork and swallowed a lump of grits that had turned to paste in my mouth.

Later on the bus I tried to ask Myra about it, but when she turned her distant eyes on me I couldn't go through with it. I didn't want to hear the truth. Months passed, the weather got colder, and I never mustered the courage to confront her about the rumors I was hearing. I figured her granny didn't know and wondered if I should tell her. Maybe she could put a stop to it before something broke forever between Myra and me. Even though she'd been my best friend since first grade, I could barely stand to look at her anymore. But it wasn't all her fault that we drifted apart, and things probably wouldn't have been any different if I'd fought for her. All winter we still sat together on the bus, but for Myra it was out of habit. I looked past her profile, half hidden behind a dark curtain of hair, at clots of ice rushing down roadside creeks and gullies swollen with melted snow.

Then one day in March, Myra didn't get on the bus after school. I asked the driver to wait a few minutes, but she never came. I didn't want to think about who had given her a ride home. I sat in her empty spot with my forehead pressed against the window, mailboxes and ditches racing by in a blur, remembering again what Tina Cutshaw had said. I was cursed to have known Myra, more cursed to have loved her like I did.

As usual, the bus driver didn't go all the way up the mountain. He let me off at the bottom of the dirt road and I couldn't stop thinking of Myra as I began walking the rest of the way home. She had made my life a misery since the minute I saw her jumping out of the churchyard tree. Some nights I lay curled on my side, the things I couldn't tell even Mr. Barnett aching like bruises in me. When I did sleep it seemed Myra sang to me, her breath trembling against my ear. I'd wake up thinking she was in my bed and find a moth batting its wings against my face. Or I'd dream of her warmth on my back and wake to find one of Mama's cats purring there. Many times I fled my room and went outside to look up at something bigger than Myra and my love for her, something that might make it feel smaller, but it didn't work. The same God who made that sky full of stars had made this love and I couldn't wrap my brain around the bigness of either one.

As I walked, scuffing up dirt with the toes of my boots, I was struck by the unfairness. I had been loyal to Myra our whole lives and now I was left behind, like that chimney swift we found floating in the cistern. I felt a pang of sorrow for myself and then blinding anger. I threw my schoolbooks into the road, papers flying everywhere, some of them landing in the creek branch. I tore up the mountain looking for Myra, not sure what I would do if I found her, breaking off saplings and ripping the undergrowth out of my way, briars grabbing at my pant legs and rocks throwing me down.

All the way up the mountain a storm raged in me, until somehow I made it manifest in the world outside. A keen wind rose out of nowhere and shook through the trees. By the time I reached the place where Myra's rock jutted high over a bluff the wind blew so hard that all I could hear was its screaming whistle. I stepped into the clearing and there she was, hair whipping wild, crouched like an animal on the ledge where she had read to me so many times. All the rage deserted me. The way she was poised on the edge of the rock, I worried for an instant that she might jump. I saw it happening, how she would spring, how she would spread her arms and fly. I thought of a story I'd heard long ago, how one of her ancestors leapt from a cliff on Bloodroot Mountain. I had hated her only minutes before, but if she had jumped right then I would have gone flying after her, caught her in the air, and positioned myself to cushion her fall.

I shouted to Myra, screamed her name so hard it felt like something ruptured in my throat. If she hadn't heard me I might have gone crazy. But she turned around and smiled when she saw me, even though her eyes didn't light up the way they usually did. She said something and the wind tore the words from her lips, as if she were already fading away, as if she were already half gone. She climbed down from the rock and came to me holding her shoes in her hands, barefoot even though the ground was cold.

"Doug," she shouted over the wind. "What are you doing here?"

"Looking for you," I said.

"What?" she said. "I can't hear you!"

"It's true. You are a witch."

"I can't hear you!" she shouted again.

"Nothing," I said.

She tugged at my arm, smiling. "Come sit with me!"

I didn't move and Myra's smile faltered. I thought a moment of sadness passed across her face, but looking back she was probably already too wrapped up in John Odom to care. Since that day, I've been thinking about the anger that took hold of me. I didn't even know it was in there. Now I know it always was and always will be. But I could never have hurt Myra, or gone through with poisoning Wild Rose. I can't turn my anger loose, even on a horse. I guess it will poison me instead, maybe for the rest of my life.

Byrdie

Even with Myra there to love, them first few years after Clio died liked to done me in. I volunteered me and Macon to clean up the church and take care of the graveyard so I could at least stay close to her body. Saturdays we'd head down the mountain and while Macon scraped chewing gum off the bottoms of the pews I'd pull weeds from around the headstones with Myra crawling over the grass. Summer evenings I'd drag my lawn chair out of the truck bed and set in front of the graves of my children, watching lightning bugs rise out of the ground like sparks going up in the dark. They was all lined up together, small markers for the babies and a bigger one for Willis and a double headstone for Kenny and Clio. I'd think about their bones down yonder, scraps of the clothes I buried them in still clinging on, and try to feel close to what was left of them. But I couldn't reach none of my children that way, no matter how long I set there. I couldn't even picture their bones after a while. Macon wouldn't come out to disturb me. He waited inside after he was done cleaning the church. I know he thought I was taking comfort, but for a long

120

time being in the graveyard didn't do me a bit of good. Then one evening I was listening to the tree frogs, thinking about heading back up the mountain, when I felt Myra's hand on my arm. She was three years old, standing on the grave of one of her aunts that never even made it to her age. She was alive and solid and there with me. I took her fingers and studied them, rubbing over the dirty little fingernails with my thumb. She looked at the graves, decorated with the wildflowers I had brung, and asked, "Is this Heaven, Granny?" I took a big breath of night air and drawed her close. "No, honey," I said. "It's not." I buried my face in her neck and thought, You are.

Me and Macon suffered a lot of heartbreak, but at least we had one another to lean on. I ain't going to say it was always peaceful between us, but it was always loving, even when we fought each other. I never cared to fight. In school, I scrapped with boys and girls both. When me and Macon first got married we'd get mad and scrabble around in the floor, smacking each other and pulling hair and grinding our heads together like billy goats. To us, that was all part of being married. There wasn't no hate in it.

Once we got older we didn't fight like that

no more. Neither one of us had the stomach for it. We figured it was time to rest in our old age. We didn't talk much either, but it wasn't out of hatefulness. We just got to where we liked the quiet. We'd set back and watch Myra dart through the house, long red hair ribbon streaming out, chattering like a magpie and pretty as a doll. It was her time now, we'd done had our own.

Macon didn't show it, but he loved Myra from far off about as much as I did close up. He was always leaving gifts on her pillow, like that red ribbon she wore all the time. When she found it she took it right to the mirror and tied up her hair. Then she ran to find Macon smoking by the stove. He stood there pretending not to wait for her. She throwed herself at his legs and asked, "Am I pretty?" He stroked her head and said, "That red suits you, Myra Jean." Times like that, I wanted to bust, seeing how much Macon loved to please our grandbaby. He'd stand in the kitchen door while I cooked supper and watch her play in the yard, letting in flies to pester me. In the summertime it was hotter than a firecracker in here, with grease popping and splattering on my arms. I'd finally get plumb ill and say, "Macon, let that youngun alone. How's she ever going to

122

grow up with you stifling her down?" But I never could get Macon to give that child rest. I knowed what it was. We'd lost so many, he was scared to let the last one left out of his sight. If Macon was out of the bed at night, I knowed he was standing over Myra watching her breathe.

I struggled with them same old demons. It was hard to let Myra loose when I wanted to keep her with me every minute. She was wild, but not as bad as her mama. Sometimes the schoolteacher would send home a note saying Myra wouldn't set down at her desk. She'd stand up to do her lessons, or wander over to the window and stare out. But she settled down in the later grades. The most trouble we had out of Myra was when she took it in her head to climb to the top of the mountain. She'd slip off and Macon would have to go find her. He'd pepper her legs with a switch but she'd head right back out. Thank goodness she quit doing that, but she never did lose that old restless nature. She didn't run off once she got bigger, but she'd set on the back steps and chew her fingernails to the bloody quick, looking off in the woods like she didn't even know she was doing it. I'd feel like squalling, watching her gnaw at herself that way, because I knowed what it meant. Still, Myra was a good girl. She didn't give me too much grief, but I made up plenty for myself to worry about. If I found a tick in her ear I'd mark the date on the calendar and watch her real close for that spotted fever I'd heard tell of. First sign of a sniffle and I'd have to go off somewhere and collect myself before I let Myra see my nerves all tore up. Only thing that got me through her childhood, with all them croups and stomach bugs and sore throats, was going to the good Lord daily in prayer.

Sometimes Myra tried to tear away from me when I held her, but she'd always come back to be petted and loved on because she knowed how bad I needed to do it. But Macon showed his love in different ways than mine, like buying them trinkets to leave on her pillow and whittling things for her. He carved up a whole set of animals for her to play with, and brung her home I don't know how many puppies and kittens over the years. I'd get mad enough to wring his neck when I'd see him carrying another mutt up the hill. Sometimes people would set out a dog or cat at the filling station just because they knowed he'd take it home if he found it hanging around the pumps looking hungry.

In 1969, the summer Myra turned twelve,

me and her left Macon working in the yard one day and walked up to the Cotters. Oleta Cotter had had female surgery and was laid up for several weeks, so me and Margaret Barnett took turns going up yonder to see about her. The Cotters live the furthest up the mountain and keep the most to theirselves. They don't poke their nose in nobody's business, but they'd give you the shirt off of their back if they knowed you was in trouble. I learnt that after Clio got killed. Oleta came down the mountain every day to cook for Macon and take care of Myra until I could stand to get out of the bed. That's how come I didn't care a bit to see to her worshing and make sure them boys was fed when she was laid up. It was hot that day and I had sweat dripping in my eyes by the time me and Myra got halfway up to the house. Them two youngest Cotter boys, Douglas and Mark, ran out of the woods to meet us like wild Indians. They stopped in the middle of the road plumb out of breath.

"Hidee, Miss Lamb," Mark said, pushing his shaggy hair out of his eyes. I don't believe I ever seen them two that they didn't need a haircut. Mark was the only one of them boys that'd talk. I don't reckon I ever heard Douglas say a word. Myra said he knowed how to talk, he was just real quiet. Douglas was in Myra's class and Mark was two years ahead of her. Both of them boys was struck on Myra and tried to court her all through school, but she never would go with either one of them. Mark and Douglas was nice-looking fellers, even when they was little, had big old brown eyes and gold hair, but I reckon they seemed like brothers to Myra. They was always into something. That day it wasn't even dinnertime yet and looked like they'd already been rolling in mud. Myra always kept right up with them, climbing trees and shooting marbles and whatever else it was they done. Mark held out his BB gun to show Myra and said, "Let's go shoot cans." Then they tore off up the hill ahead of me like their britches was on fire.

I took my time following them on towards the house. Bill and Oleta have a tiny little place with a stone foundation and a covered porch. Not too long ago Bill had put on some cheap gray cardboard siding, supposed to look like brick. He'd poured a cement walk up to the porch, too, but grass had growed over most of it. There was trees and bushes crowded against the house and a line of fence posts sticking up behind it where Bill kept a few cows.

126

Bill gets rid of his cows every few years, until he takes a notion to buy up some more, but he never does get tired of that horse he bought from a man in Dalton, Georgia. I swear that's the orneriest creature I ever seen, but Bill loves her like somebody. Now, she's beautiful, I can't deny that, and you can see her spirit burning like fire in them blue eyes. She's a paint mare, and the first time I seen them eyes I liked to jumped out of my skin. I never knowed a horse could have eyes like that. They was just like Myra's, and that might be why my grandbaby was so fixed on her from the beginning. I knowed that was why she always wanted to go up to the Cotters' with me, to see Wild Rose. That's the name the horse had when Bill bought her, and it suits her. His old fence never could keep her in. I don't know how many times Rose came tearing down the mountain with her tail up, trampling through our garden and leaving manure in the yard. Sometimes I wondered if she was looking for Myra. It was eerie seeing them together. Myra would stand at the fence and Wild Rose kept her distance, but she'd stare Myra straight in the eye, neither one of them moving a muscle. Then Rose'd take off like she was spooked across the hills. Wild as Myra was, I guess in a way them two was sisters.

When I got up to the house I could hear Douglas and Mark and Myra at the barn calling for Wild Rose, but I couldn't see them. As I was walking up on the porch Bill Cotter opened the front door and came out. I said, "Hidee, Bill." He tipped his cap at me and went on down the steps to his truck. Bill don't say much, but he's a good man.

I went in the front room and seen the linoleum needed mopping. Bill or them boys had tracked mud in. Oleta was laying on the couch and her head nearly wringing wet with sweat. Poor thing looked like she was roasting so I opened some windows for her.

"Where's that Bill headed off to?" I asked, gathering up some pieces of newspaper he'd left by his chair.

"Laws, I don't know. He don't never tell me nothing. Why, he don't even tell me bye no more when he leaves the house. Does Macon do you thataway?"

"Well," I said, but Oleta was done off on another subject before I could answer.

There was quite a bit needed doing. I swept and mopped and put a pot of beans on the stove. As I was tidying up, somehow or other I got to feeling funny. I got to studying on what Oleta asked, did Macon

128

do me that way. I reckon the answer would have been yes if she had give me time. He'd head out for work every morning without saying a word, but he didn't need to. We knowed each other so good after all them years of marriage, there wasn't no use in saying much. I'd fix his dinner and put it in his bucket and we'd drink us a cup of coffee beside of the stove, then he'd get up and leave. I didn't see nothing wrong with it, but the way Oleta said it sounded bad. I tried to remember if I said goodbye to Macon when me and Myra left the house that morning. The whole time I was worshing Oleta's breakfast dishes and sweeping off the back stoop I was retracing my steps, trying to decide if I told Macon bye. In my head I was waking up before first light, Macon already setting on his side of the bed getting his boots on. I was walking across the dewy grass toward the barn to gather eggs. I was frying the eggs in my old iron skillet and calling for Myra to get up before she slept the day away. I was eating breakfast in the kitchen by myself because Macon and Myra was done before I ever set down. I was bringing in some tomatoes before they rotted on the vine. I was telling Myra if she wanted to walk up to the Cotters' with me she better come on. I was passing Macon on my way down the hill with Myra as he was headed for the barn. "Did you see them dadburn Japanese beetles on my rosebush?" I asked him. "I was fixing to spray," he said. That was it. I never did say bye. I reckon he knowed where I was going, because he probably heard me holler at Myra, but I started feeling bad just the same.

The longer I was at the Cotters', the more anxious I got to get back to the house. I allowed to Oleta I better get on home and fix Macon a bite of supper. I had to stand in the yard and holler for Myra a long time, until she finally came out of the woods looking like she'd rolled in the mud with them Cotter boys, sticks and leaves stuck in her hair. I thought how I'd have to check her head for ticks before she went to bed that night.

Since I'd turned seventy-one, I didn't get around as good as I used to. I was wore out by the time we got home, but Myra never ran out of wind. She took off for the house soon as we made it up the hill and beat me to the door by a mile. She went on in while I was still dragging across the yard. I seen where Macon had done a little bit of weeding around the steps and there was a mess of wood shavings in the grass, too, so I knowed he must have been whittling. He was getting on in years hisself, nearly eighty by then, and couldn't take the sun for long at a time. He'd take a break and set down if he got too hot working in the yard, but Macon never could stand for his hands to be idle.

I didn't think nothing of it and went on in the house. First thing I seen was Myra, standing in the middle of the floor with her back to me, hair ribbon hanging crooked where she'd been playing. It took me a minute to see she was looking at Macon. He was slumped over in his chair, the same way he took a nap of the evenings, but it still didn't hit me that something was wrong. I reckon I was so hot and weary my head was addled.

"What in the world are you doing?" I asked Myra.

She turned around and I never will forget the look in her eyes. She said, "Is Granddaddy sleeping?"

That's when I knowed. I walked over to his chair and seen how still he was. "No," I said to Myra. "He ain't asleep." I ran my finger across that island birthmark one more time. Then I sent Myra down to the Barnetts' for Hacky to get word to the coroner. I hated for her to have to do it alone, but I couldn't bring myself to leave Macon's side.

I was setting at Macon's feet waiting for the people to come when I noticed this little wood box, about the size of my hand. It was on a piece of newspaper on the end table beside of his chair, looked like the varnish was still tacky on it. He must have been working on it for a while out in the barn when I thought he was making another birdhouse. Once I seen it I smelled the varnish, but I hadn't even noticed it until then. The lid was laying separate and it was the prettiest piece of carving I ever seen. It was carved with a bloodroot flower, all by itself. I could tell he'd took time with every petal and every vein in the leaves. I figure he made it for Myra's birthday to hold her trinkets, and meant to hide it someplace once the varnish dried. Then he'd leave it on her pillow without saying nothing and stand off somewhere waiting for her to find it.

I knowed what it meant that he would give Myra that bloodroot flower. I knowed everything he was trying to say to her. I took Macon's hand and wet it with my tears, wishing I never left him alone that day. After all me and Macon went through together, for him to die by hisself broke my heart. It took a little bit of work to pull that blood-red ring off of his poor old finger, stained black with the oil of all them engines he'd fiddled with down through the years. His knuckles had swole with arthritis as he got older. But then it was in my palm, like I dropped it in his that day in the cornfield. I put the ring in that fine box he whittled like it was a casket, the last thing he ever done. I took the box and Macon's whittling knife to the back bedroom, where me and him had started sleeping after Clio got killed by that train so we could feel closer to her. I made a cut in the mattress and hid the box before anybody came to see about Macon's body. I didn't want Myra to have it before she knowed how to appreciate it. She was too young to understand the preciousness of that bloodroot flower, no matter how pretty it was, and I didn't know how to tell her. I slept on top of that ring for four years, until the day I gave it to Myra for that snake John Odom. Now I'd do just about anything to have it back.

Doug

Myra and I didn't talk again after that day I found her crouched on the rock. She stopped riding the bus and I knew it was about that tall boy Mark claimed he had seen her with. One night near graduation, Mama and Daddy were talking over supper about how Frankie Odom's son was struck on Myra. They said he'd been taking her to and from school and coming up the mountain to get her every Saturday night. I recognized the name Odom from a long time ago. We used to stop in at Odom's Hardware when I was small, but Daddy had stopped trading there after Odom raised his prices. I looked across the table at Mark, his cheeks fat with mashed potatoes. He had lost interest in Myra. All he thought about was joining the service and fighting in Vietnam. I wondered how he could eat when my stomach felt like a cauldron of acid. I guess in my heart of hearts I knew he didn't love her, but I never thought how quickly he'd move on.

After supper we stood having a smoke out behind the barn, hiding even though we were grown, because we didn't want to hear Mama's mouth.

"What do you think about Myra and that Odom boy?" I asked, trying to be casual.

Mark pitched his butt into the dark grass. "Shoot, I gave up on that'n a long time ago. If a man's not crazy, he'll finally get the picture." Mark grinned and slapped me on the back. I pitched my butt with shaking fingers and followed him inside.

The next day, for the last time, I went to

see Mr. Barnett. He was in the garden pulling weeds. When he saw me he took off his cap and wiped the sweat from his brow. He didn't ask what I was up to. We stood for a while in silence, looking toward the woods at the edge of the yard where we had walked together so many times. "You were wrong," I told him at last. "She won't ever come around." Then my knees came unhinged and I sank down in the black dirt. Mr. Barnett knelt with me and hugged me tight. "You're the one she ought to be with, Douglas," he said. "You and me both know it's the truth. But Myra's got a choice. Everybody's got a choice. She just made the wrong one."

A week or so later, I saw Myra and John Odom together. He was waiting for her in the school parking lot, leaning against his car. Girls stood around giggling about how pretty he was, but he looked like the devil to me. Long and lean, tall and dark as a shadow, eyes black as pits. It was like he reeled her across the parking lot by an invisible hook in her perfect lip. I was standing close enough to smell her hair as she walked by, but she didn't even see me. He did an odd thing when she got to the car. He put his hand on the top of her head. I couldn't believe what I was seeing. It was like a

135

stranger walking up and saddling Wild Rose, swinging up on her back, and riding off across the hills.

John Odom was the one Myra was looking for all along. I guess somewhere there's somebody that could ride Wild Rose, too. It was Mama who told me that Myra was married. Until I heard it, there was hope she might come back. But the minute the words left Mama's mouth last night, I knew I was leaving. I haven't decided where I'll go, maybe Canada to escape the draft and the memory of her voice. This morning I walked out the back door at first light, duffel bag over my shoulder and a book Myra left behind in my hand. I dropped the book in the trash barrel to be burnt on my way to the pasture. I want the embers to disperse and the words to find her somewhere, in a house beside of the railroad tracks, according to Mama. I picture her standing in some sooty yard looking up at the moon, a flat world with no shine where the trees are black outlines, with a hint of smoke in her nostrils. I know it's not true, but I want some sadness to enter her when she thinks of me and the mountain. I want her to suffer for my sake. Myra might get back one day up Bloodroot Mountain, but if she does I won't be here.

After I dropped the book into the trash barrel, I ducked under the fence and went across the pasture to where Wild Rose was grazing. Standing with my bag over my shoulder and bus-ticket money in the breast pocket of my shirt, I got closer to her than I've ever been. Now her breath snuffs out in white clouds as she sniffs of me. Maybe she's letting me close because she knows it's goodbye. I think she's not mad about what happened out in the barn last night. I might have won her respect. Or maybe she smells my acceptance of the truth she's tried to tell me all along. Some creatures are just meant to be left alone. They can't be held on to, even if we love them more than anything.

Byrdie

After Macon passed on, I vowed to give Myra some room to stretch her legs. That's some of the reason I let John Odom court her when she got to be seventeen. She was the same age as Clio was when she ran off with Kenny Mayes, but Myra was different than her mama. I thought she had a better head on her shoulders. I know now I should have been more careful. But it was plain how Myra loved that man and there wasn't no use fighting her. I didn't want to lose my grandbaby so I let her go, and ended up losing her anyhow. But I don't see what I could have done to hang on to her. She was bound and determined to have John Odom, same way I was to have Macon, and Clio was to have Kenny. If Macon was still living he would have went down to them tracks with a shotgun a long time ago and got her out of there. Matter of fact, he wouldn't have let her go off with John Odom in the first place. Macon might have had it right all along, not letting Myra out of his sight. I guess sometimes a body just don't know what to do.

I had me a good garden last spring, when John Odom first started coming around. I always plant by the signs. Things that grows in the ground like taters I do on the dark nights of the moon, and things that grows on top of the ground I plant on the light nights. Last year I growed the best sweet corn I ever put in my mouth. I'd planted it earlier than usual and it was real warm weather, so the corn was already high. I was out yonder gathering it in, had my tin tub about half full, when I heard car doors slamming shut. I already knowed Myra was struck on somebody because she told me. She wasn't one to keep secrets like her mama done. Ever since I knowed it, I'd been dreading the day she'd bring some old boy up Bloodroot Mountain for me to see, and now the day had come.

I didn't go around the house to meet him and her. I just closed my eyes for a minute, so fagged out it seemed like I couldn't stand up. I figured it was going to be like it was with Kenny and Clio, and I didn't know if I could take it this time. I should have knowed to expect more out of my grandbaby. She came around the house pulling John along by the hand. I turned around holding a good ear of corn, the silky tassel hanging down. It was just about sunset and John Odom was the prettiest thing I ever seen, walking across the yard towards me with the light in his eyes. The devil can fool a body that way. Looked like a movie star, with that shiny black hair and them good white teeth. I had feelings standing with him in that garden that I thought was dead in me a long time ago. That's how the devil works. I knowed right then there wouldn't be no fighting him and Myra. Neither one of us could have resisted him. I can't blame her. I fell for it, too.

Myra showed him off to me like a prize she'd won. "Granny, this is John. You know his daddy, Frankie, that owns Odom's Hardware."

139

"Why, is that your daddy?" I said. "Me and Macon done a lot of business with him down through the years." I hate to admit it, but it crossed my mind that Myra had snagged a good one. I figured she'd be set if she married into the Odoms. I thought when Frankie Odom passed on that store would fall to his boys and she'd be taken care of.

John Odom reached out for my hand. I dropped the corn in the tub and wiped dirt on my apron. His hand was so clean and white, I didn't want to sully it.

"Daddy speaks well of you and Mr. Lamb. Said you all was good people."

"Well. We always tried to be."

John looked down in the tub at my feet. "You got an awful good-looking crop of corn this year, Mrs. Lamb." He reached out and plucked an ear, held it in his hands. "I like the smell of a garden," he said, turning to Myra, "don't you?" She took an ear herself and said, "Let me and John help you get this in, Granny."

I started to tell them to go on and have a good time, but I didn't want them to leave me. All of a sudden I felt old and lonesome. It was good to have them working alongside me, the evening sun pouring between the cornstalks and the smell of garden dirt, even the smell of sweat. It had been a long time since I smelled a man's sweat.

When the tub was full, me and John Odom went to pick it up at the same time. We bumped heads and got tickled. When we looked at each other across that tin tub, there was something about his black eyes that bothered me. I tried to ignore it. I wanted him to be good for Myra. But I should have listened to that small voice inside of me.

Next evening I came upon Myra setting on the steps as I was headed from the barn with a bucket of eggs. "Where you been, little lady?" I asked, gumming my snuff.

"For a walk."

I looked at her for a long time with my hand on my hip. I could tell her whole self was yearning toward town and the hardware store where John Odom was working. I put my bucket down and she made room for me to sit. I touched her cheek with my finger. Next to the smoothness of her young skin, I seen how old and crooked it was. When she turned to me I searched her eyes for the words it seemed like she couldn't find.

"Your face is hot," I said. "Reckon you've caught a cold?"

"No. I'm just sitting here thinking."

"What about?"

"Something I got to tell you."

"All right," I said. But I wished she wouldn't say anything. I looked out across the yard at the shadows gathering under the apple tree.

"Me and John are getting married."

"Well. I figured you would."

She smiled and leaned into my shoulder. "How'd you figure?"

"Honey, you look about as lovesick as anybody I ever seen, except maybe for me when I first laid eyes on your granddaddy."

We both got quiet. I knowed what I wanted to do. I wanted to give Myra her granddaddy's ring, but I hesitated. Sometimes I still worry it's what caused this whole blamed mess. Stealing was the worst thing I ever done and for most of my life taking that ring had been my secret. Now I had to tell on myself, because I couldn't give it to Myra without warning her what came with it. But it felt right for her to have. I seen how deep in love she was. I got up before I could chicken out and said, "Set still here a minute."

I went inside, the kitchen door slapping behind me, and came back out carrying the box Macon had carved. Myra had never seen it before, but she must have knowed right off it was her granddaddy's work. I could tell by the way her eyes lit up. Then she got real solemn and traced the blood-root flower on the lid with her fingertip.

"Open it up," I said. The wedding ring was inside. I'd seen it many times but it looked different off of Macon's finger, like a living thing, a beating heart. "I want you to give it to John," I said. Myra looked up at me with her blue eyes. She opened her mouth to talk but no words came out. She settled her head on my chest and I stroked her hair for a while, the red ribbon Macon bought her a long time ago flowing through my fingers.

"Now I've got to tell you a shameful thing," I finally said. Myra raised her head and I was nervous, because if my grandbaby was to think less of me I didn't know what I'd do. "I stole this here ring off of a woman I worked for." I studied Myra's face close but there was no change in it that I could see. "I never believed I could do a thing like that. But I loved your granddaddy in such a hard way, I didn't know up from down."

She just kept looking at me. I couldn't tell how she was taking it.

"That ain't no excuse," I went on. "It's something I'll have to answer for on Judgment Day. I'm just saying love can be too deep. It'll make you do crazy things."

Myra smiled at me then in a way that made my belly sink down to my feet. "Don't be sorry, Granny," she said. "You don't have to explain. I know why you did it."

All of a sudden I wanted to snatch Macon's ring back and my blessing, too. I wondered what she had already done in the name of that deep down love.

It was two weeks later, in June of last year, that Myra and John Odom got married. They was in too big of a hurry for a church wedding, so they went down to the preacher's house and got married in his kitchen without telling me about it until the next day. I hated for Myra to leave me, but I was relieved at least she was marrying into some money. Macon had done well enough for us and we never went hungry, but it was a struggle sometimes. I wondered if Myra was ashamed, going to school with other boys and girls that had more than we did. I knowed Odom's Hardware hadn't got as much business after the Plaza was built, but it seemed from the look of things that Frankie and his sons was still making a good living. That's part of how come I was so surprised when I seen the house he had Myra in. I rode down yonder with them before they moved in their furniture and I guess it showed plain on my face what I thought of the place. Right off, Myra went to making excuses. She said times was lean at the hardware store and Frankie couldn't afford to pay his boys as much as he used to. But I still believe John Odom could have done better by my grandbaby than that old dump by the railroad tracks. It had rained the night before and the yard was pure mud, with no trees or flowers. Soon as we stepped out of the car a train went by, big and fast enough to rattle the ground. It was all I could do to keep from squalling, thinking of Myra living in a hole like that.

Back at home without my grandbaby, the mountain looked different to me. The woods was dark and sometimes it seemed like they was creeping up closer to the house. At least when Myra and John first got married they'd come and eat dinner with me every Sunday after church. They'd set across the table and look at each other until it just about made my face red. Sometimes I'd get jealous over how much they loved one another. I'd get sad thinking about how my own youth was gone and my loving days was over.

It wasn't long, though, before I seen John Odom turning quiet. Wouldn't hardly look up from his plate, and every once in a while, if me and Myra got to laughing and carrying on, sharing a little bit of gossip, he'd shoot us the evilest look anybody's ever seen. It made me uneasy, but to tell the truth, I was still trying to ignore it. Like I said, I wanted him to be everything Myra thought he was, for her sake and mine both.

Then John stopped coming to church and Myra would be there by herself. She'd slip in and set on the back pew. I could tell she was troubled. One afternoon she came up to the house looking peaked and her hands shaking. She tried to help me worsh the dishes and they kept slipping back down in the sink. Finally I said, "What is it, honey?"

She said, "John's started drinking beer."

"Well," I said, trying to make me and her both feel better, "I never knowed a young man that wouldn't take a nip every once in a while."

"I don't know, Granny," she said, and wouldn't look at me no more.

By November, Myra had quit coming up Bloodroot Mountain altogether. I cooked a ham for Christmas dinner but she never showed up. I set by myself beside of the tree Hacky Barnett drug in and put up for me, worried sick. Her and John Odom didn't have no phone in that house by the tracks, and me and Macon never had one put in

146

either, so I didn't know what in the world happened to her. I had Hacky to drive me down yonder but seeing her didn't make me feel no better. She acted spooked, kept looking at the door the whole time like she was afraid somebody was coming. We tried to talk but seemed like she couldn't concentrate enough to carry on a conversation. I wept all the way back home and Hacky tried to comfort me by letting on like it wasn't all that bad. He patted my shoulder and said, "She looks all right, Byrdie. There ain't no places on her." But I said, "Hacky, the places might be on the inside." He didn't have no argument for that.

Then two months passed without seeing Myra because Margaret Barnett fell off the porch and twisted her back. Hacky's had a time taking care of her, and I hated to ask him to drive me to town. I thought of asking Bill Cotter, but since his boys are gone it's all he can do to keep the farm running. This morning I couldn't stand it no longer and asked Hacky to take me to Myra right away. We didn't talk in the truck. I guess we both had a lot on our minds. We pulled up in front of the house under a big black storm cloud. It had been spitting ice rain off and on all morning and it was a mess trying to get across that old yard. I climbed up on the stoop huffing and puffing and when I finally did get situated to knock on the door, it took Myra a long time to open it. Soon as she seen me, her mouth fell open. I was shocked myself, to see my grandbaby in such a shape. She was skinny as a rail and looked like she hadn't combed her hair in a month of Sundays.

"Granny," she said.

She walked into my arms and we stood there for a long time with tears in our eyes. Finally I heard Hacky clearing his throat behind me. We went on in the house and I never seen such a clutter. I taught Myra better than that, but I reckon she just didn't have no gumption left in her. She cleared a place on the couch for us. Hacky set there the whole time holding his cap with his ears red, looking like he'd rather be anyplace else.

I told Myra, "I would have come sooner but you know I ain't got no way around."

"Have you been getting your medicines?" she asked. I could tell she was worried about me as much as I was about her.

I said, "Hacky runs to the drugstore for me. Him and Margaret's been so good to me. I don't know what I would have done."

Myra smiled at Hacky and looked sad at the same time. I know she wants to be the one taking care of me. That might be why John Odom's got her trapped someway.

"Honey, why don't you come home with me?" I begged her. I hadn't been meaning to say nothing but it just came out. "Don't let him do you this way."

"I can't, Granny," she said. "I made my bed." About that time we heard a car out in the driveway and Myra's eyes got big. It was nearly twelve o'clock and John Odom had come home for dinner. He busted in like an old bull and it was a sight how he had changed in such a short time. His hair was still black and shiny as ever, but he had a gut hanging over his belt buckle and bags underneath his eyes. I could tell Myra was scared to death of what he might do because me and Hacky was there. I wondered myself how he was going to act, but he just looked around at me and Hacky right hateful and didn't say a word to us. He pitched his car keys on the end table beside of Myra's chair and knocked off a bunch of clutter. It made a loud racket and she flinched like he'd shot at her. "Fix me something to eat," he said to Myra. Then he stomped off to the bathroom. Directly Hacky said, without looking at me, "We better get on up the mountain, Byrdie."

"No, wait here for a minute," Myra whis-

149

pered. She dashed off and I could hear her rummaging in the hallway. She was back quick as lightning and I couldn't make out what she had in her hands at first. When she got close I seen she had that box Macon whittled for her. She leant over where I was setting on the couch and put it in my dress pocket. "I want you to keep it safe for me, Granny," she said. "This is no place for it."

Ever since I seen Myra that way, it seems to me I can hear my grandbaby moaning outside in the dark. It's like when I heard that train whistle blowing the night Clio got killed. I've thought many times of putting the law on John Odom, but I don't know what to accuse him of. Far as I know, he ain't been beating on her. I never seen no bruises. But like I told Hacky that day in the truck, there's other ways a woman can get beat up on. All I can do right now is to pray for Myra, that she gets herself out of this fix someway. I might not be around much longer to help her out of it. I'm heading toward seventy-seven years old next month and I'm tired. The doctor says I've got congestive heart failure. Here lately just walking around the house wears me out. My eyes has got so weak these old glasses don't do me much good no more. It's hard to believe, but a time will come when I

won't be in this house on the mountain. I
made Hacky promise to look after Myra if
anything happens to me and he said he
would. He said he's always stood by me and
Macon and our younguns, and he don't aim
to quit now. That made me feel some better, but I still don't know how to get my
grandbaby away from that devil John Odom.

So all my kids are dead and gone and
Myra might be lost forever. People probably
wonders how I kept from losing my mind.
Seeing one youngun go before you, much
less five, is enough to ruin any mammy. I
reckon I am ruint in a way. I can't think
straight no more. I forget the names of the
craziest things, like flowers and biscuits and
chairs. And you know I've buried five
children and seen their dead bodies,
watched them get sicker and sicker and not
been able to help them a'tall, but the picture
that vexes my mind the most is Myra when
she opened the door of that house by the
tracks. That's the thing that's done broke
my heart in two, because she's the one that
saved me after all them others was gone.
She's how come me and Macon to get out
of the bed all of them years. Myra's the one
I love the best of all, it don't matter that I
never bore her. She was mine anyhow.

■ ■ ■ ■

Two:
Johnny Odom and
Laura Odom
Blevins

■ ■ ■ ■

Johnny

I spent a long time trying to forget the first eight years of my life. For some it might be easy to shake loose their earliest memories, but not for me. No matter how hard I tried, there was always some reminder of childhood. Today it was seeing my mama's blue eyes on a baby I was holding for the first time. Over the years there have been other things that took me back, the smells of loam and moss and ferny ground, the taste of ice-cold water. It's been a while, though, since I saw the mountain outside of memory.

In 1990, when I was fourteen, I went up Bloodroot Mountain again after six years gone. It was a long walk, with Marshall Lunsford behind me and neither one of us saying a word. The mountain looked different than when I was small. A sawmill had carved a bald place in the land and the road was paved where it used to be dirt, but I knew we were getting close when we passed Mr. Barnett's. His house was nearly buried behind a briar thicket, just a rusty roof with a stub of chimney poking out of the tangled green. The flag was up on his mailbox and the same dented truck parked in the weeds, glinting in what was left of the sun. He was probably too old to drive it anymore. I wondered if he would come out and if he would still know me, but his place was quiet and still.

We kept climbing and it was almost dark by the time we made it to the witch's house. That's what Marshall called it. "There's a witch's house up yonder," he said. He caught up and stood panting in the road, head down and eyes shifting toward every sound, but looking up at the house I forgot about Marshall and only remembered. Behind the posts of a ruined fence the creek branch rushed downhill over chunks of rock, between thorny vines and flowering bushes. The trees were parted just enough for me to see it up there, like a toy I could hold in both hands, a dirty white box with black window holes and the roof a flake of blood. It did look like a witch's house, a haunted place, the hill leading up to it bumpy with stumps and boulders. I could see a cross of fallen trees in the yard and a weathered barn where nothing lived but the smell of hay and animals.

Something splashed in the creek and Marshall jumped. "We better get on before it's too dark to see the road," he said.

"You can go by yourself if you want to."

Marshall grew quiet, shuffled his feet. "They say she killed a man."

"Is that so?"

Back then, I could have told him I'd guarantee she killed a man. I could have told him the witch was my mama, too, but I kept my mouth shut. I looked at the house and wanted to burn it to the ground, or run up there and find her axe still lodged in a stump and chop the whole place to pieces, barn and all. But first I would tear through the rooms to see what was left, scour the lot for any trace of her and Laura and me, a stray bobby pin or a lost shirt button or a length of fishing line, anything to prove we lived for a time between those trees, with that mountain under our feet and that creek water rushing over us. Then I would burn the whole place down and dance in the light of the flames.

"For real, Johnny, let's go," Marshall whined, and it was like a spell was broken. I didn't need to look anymore. I had seen it one more time. I turned to go with Marshall but he was frozen in the middle of the road, staring into the woods across from the house with his mouth hanging open. Between the crowded trunks there was a greenish glow, a faint ghost light hovering close to the ground. "It's her spirit," Marshall whispered. Then he took off running down the mountain, shoes slapping hard on the pavement. I knew it was foxfire but I stood there for a long time anyway, looking into the trees.

Laura

I had some friends up on the mountain. Sun shined down through the leaves and made fairies for me to play with. I didn't get sad whenever Johnny went off roaming because when the wind blowed them fairies came alive. If I laid on the ground they darted across my body like minnows in the creek. I miss them now when nighttime comes. I'm a grown woman with a child of my own but I still get lonesome in the dark. I try to remember good things, like how Mama was before she changed. I think about that time she was scaling fish. She dropped a bluegill back in the bucket and held my face in her slimy hands. I walked around the rest of the day wearing that slime on my cheeks. I felt touched by some magic creature, like a

158

mermaid out of one of Johnny's storybooks.

Once I watched Mama take a bath in the creek when the sun was orange, naked breasts and fuzzy legs and a swarm of gnats around her head. I stood on tiptoe and reached out to touch her long, black hair. It poured down her arms like oil. When she bent to lift me I was draped in it. One time she made us blackberry cobbler. We walked to the Barnetts' after sugar and I rode on her hip. When I asked Johnny about it later, he said it never happened. He pretended not to remember Mama before she was different. But I can still see our teeth and tongues stained dark with juice. I tried to remember for him, how she turned the radio loud and danced us around, and the chocolate cake she made when we turned six. I reminded Johnny of those things, but he always said I dreamed them.

He didn't even remember the day we walked down the mountain picking up cans and seen a school bus. There was a child's face in the window and I asked Mama where they was going. She said they was going to school. Johnny wanted to go with them but Mama said she could teach us all we needed to know. Later she showed us how to read with her finger moving underneath the words. I forgot fast but Johnny loved the storybooks. He read them over and over. She taught us other things, too, like how to dig up the ginseng we sold to a fat man down the mountain, and how to can what we growed. There was hot days in the kitchen washing jars and standing over pots. I liked canning but Johnny didn't. He wanted to be outside hunting. Mama showed us how to kill rabbits and squirrels and possums with her granddaddy's rifle. I was no good but Johnny could shoot and him just a little boy. Once he got a deer and we had the meat for a long time.

When she quit paying attention to us, I missed her bad. I thought I must have got too big to fit in her lap. If I tried to climb up she didn't put her arms around me. Pretty soon I gave up. I still loved her, though. I know Johnny loved her, too. But he got mad when she took herself away. One time he hacked down her little patch of corn with a stick but it didn't do any good. It was like she didn't notice. Then he set her scarf on fire, a lacy one that hung on her bedpost and used to belong to her granny. He took it out in the grass and held a match to it. Mama went out to stand with him and they watched it burn together. When the fire dwindled down to ashes she walked away and left him there. I went to him but

160

he jerked away. Pretty soon Johnny gave up like I did.

I know why Johnny didn't want to remember the good things. Once she started acting different, it was easier to remember the bad. But even in them last two years there was nice times. I got to share her bed whenever I found her there. I'd wind myself in her hair and curl up in the littlest knot I could make against her back. One morning she turned over before I crept off. We stared at each other and I seen all the shades of blue in her eyes. I understood how she loved me the only way she could. If Johnny was ever that close to Mama's face, smelling her skin and feeling her warmness, he might have been different. I wish I could remember what it was like inside of her. I picture her belly like a moon and me and Johnny living in it. The three of us was a family then, bound up together in her skin. Them nine months is why it don't matter where we go or what the years turn us into. We'll always love each other. For a while, we was all part of one body.

Johnny

Some of what happened on Bloodroot Mountain has grown foggy in my mind, but most of it I remember well. For a long time, my twin sister Laura and I didn't know to fear anything. We'd play in bat caves and climb the highest trees and let spiders walk up our arms. Once, a bear came lumbering through as we knelt in the pine needles searching for arrowheads. It stopped a few yards from us and sniffed the air before moving on. We must have smelled familiar. Our mama always said we had inherited a way with animals.

I'll never forget how she cried when I saved Mr. Barnett's dog, Whitey. It was the fall Laura and I turned five and we had gone down to the Barnetts' with our mama to trade apples for a bag of cornmeal. While she was in the house with Mrs. Barnett, Laura and I stood watching Mr. Barnett work on his truck, the three of us bent together under the hood. There was a sudden commotion in the woods and I could tell right away that it was Whitey, yelping over a din of wild barking and growling. Mr. Barnett dropped his wrench and Laura and I went running with him into the trees. Whitey was lying on her back in the middle of a dog pack, all of them fighting her. People in Polk County let their dogs roam loose and they ran together sometimes, causing trouble all over the mountain.

Mr. Barnett lunged at the dogs to scare

them off, but they weren't afraid. He threw a rock but that didn't work either. I knew those dogs meant to kill Whitey. I could hear Laura crying over the racket, eyes squeezed shut and hands clamped over her ears. While Mr. Barnett looked for something else to throw, I walked without thinking toward the fighting dogs. Mr. Barnett yelled for me to get back but it was too late. He ran to dive in and save me, but I didn't need his help. The dogs scattered to make a path for me as if someone had fired a shotgun. They slinked off, leaving Whitey shivering and bleeding on the leaves. Then the woods were quiet. Mr. Barnett stood frozen as I knelt beside Whitey and picked her up in my arms. She was so big and heavy that I could hardly rise up with her. That's when I saw my mama standing at the edge of the trees with tears running down her face. I still don't know if she was crying out of pride or sadness.

Laura and I were always bringing animals into the house. Once we found a nest of baby skunks in a brush pile and it was the only thing our mama didn't let us keep. Anything else we could catch, we could bring inside. Once it was a red-eyed terrapin that crawled all over the house until one day it just wasn't there anymore. I don't know if it found a way out or if my mama set it free. She let us keep the animals but it troubled her. She said wild things belonged outside and not to forget their true nature. I should have listened to her. One summer morning, when I was seven, I got too brave. Rain had been pouring for two days straight and the sun had come back out hot and bright. The yard was soggy and rainwater splashed up my legs when Laura and I ran into the trees. I can still see her stopping to balance on a mossy log, the dark shawl of her hair parted down the middle and sunburn tracing the bridge of her nose. Even though we were born five minutes apart, we didn't look alike besides our black hair and eyes. Laura was plainer than our mama but had the same long face and high forehead, features I didn't inherit.

I chased after her, flushing rabbits out of the brush and sending frogs plopping into the creek. We knew where we were going without saying anything. Further up the mountain there were two big tables of rock in a clearing, one slab like a step leading down to the other, jutting high over the bluff. Both were scabby with lichens and scattered with piles of damp leaves. Sometimes I would read to Laura up there, but she couldn't be still for long, so that rock step became my spot to sit and think.

On the way up to the rock something caught Laura's eye in the woods, prisms of light filtering down through the trees. The way they moved along the ground when the wind blew, she always ran off after them, arms outstretched and head thrown back to let them play across her face. I didn't like her drifting too far out of sight, but when I wanted my twin I could call her back without words. I didn't question how it was possible. I remembered a time when we were smaller that we didn't need to speak at all. I could read the set of her mouth and the line of her shoulders and know what she wanted to say.

I went on to the rock, but when I stepped into the clearing I stopped in my tracks. In the place where I usually sat there was a snake. I walked closer for a better look. He wasn't long but he was fat, a lazy S shape soaking up the heat. I had seen snakes before but this was the prettiest, sun shining on his banded back, patterned with rounded spots. When I hunkered down, he lifted the coppery-red triangle of his head. My heart thudded. I stretched out on my belly to look him in the face. Staring into his eyes, it seemed he knew everything about me. I thought if he could speak, he would call me by name.

Slowly the snake began to coil, scales undulating like magic. I wanted to show Laura, because back then my sister and I shared everything. "Laura, come and see!" I shouted, reaching out for the snake. Just as Laura came into the clearing, he shot up and bit me on the back of the hand. I saw the plush pink lining of his throat, the thin black line of his tongue. Then I felt the pain, hot and fiery, shooting up my arm. I was surprised, but I didn't feel betrayed. I should have known that he was untouchable.

I woke the next day with a headache, hand bloated and bruised nearly black. The stiffness worked its way up my arm to the shoulder and the throbbing lasted for weeks, but it wasn't all that bad. I couldn't find the words to tell Laura, but there was something good about it, driving out the other aches inside that vexed me all the time. When I got better I thought that copperhead might have turned me into what he was, like vampires and werewolves do. The idea didn't trouble me. I almost wished it would happen.

Laura

I've had a long time to think about what made Mama how she was. I know now she never was like other mamas, but them last two years with her was harder. I figure it had something to do with that day in town when me and Johnny was six. It was the only time we ever left the mountain with her. We'd walk to the bottom of it selling ginseng, but she always made us hide in the weeds. The fat man leaned over the rail of his porch and counted the money down into her hand. She never set foot on his steps that I can remember. Sometimes we rode up and down the dirt road in the back of Mr. Barnett's truck with the wind in our hair, but she wouldn't let him take us anywhere else. I never wanted to go off the mountain anyway. I seen Mama's fear of whatever was down there. I figured out she was trying to hide us from something dangerous. Johnny probably did, too. But he was different than me. He always wondered what else there was to see.

It took until we was six for Mama to give in. The leaves had fell and she was building fires in the stove. That meant it was time for Mr. Barnett to go to the co-op. Mama gave him money and he brung things back for us. Mr. Barnett was our good friend. Mama didn't talk to him much, but I could tell he didn't make her nervous. Not like that Cotter man we bought fresh milk from up the mountain. His wife would stand at the door with her arms crossed and look down at our dirty feet. Mama would hand over the money and take the milk fast as she could. Mostly we had powdered milk. That's one thing she bought before winter. Powdered milk, flour, sugar, and cornmeal in big sacks. That year, when it was time for Mr. Barnett to go to the co-op, Johnny begged Mama for us to go with him. She said no at first but he started to cry. Worried as Mama was, she loved Johnny more. I believe it hurt her to deny him anything he wanted so bad.

Mama wouldn't let us go by ourselves with Mr. Barnett so we all piled in the truck together, me and Johnny crowded between Mr. Barnett and Mama. Mr. Barnett smelled like liniment and dampish flannel. I liked riding in his truck with the heater blowing on my face. Mr. Barnett must have seen Mama shaking. He said, "You remember where the co-op is, honey. It's in Slop Creek, not all the way to town. They won't be many there this time of morning." He put his big hand on top of my head. "These younguns need to see a little piece of the countryside anyhow. Don't you?" I nodded, even though I didn't really think so. I was nervous when Mr. Barnett first turned his truck right at the bottom of the mountain, but after a while I got excited. There was long fields with pinwheels of hay and silos and bridges over rolling water. I looked out the back window and seen the mountain getting left behind. But I still felt safe. Johnny and Mama was with me.

Then we was at the co-op and it was the most people I ever seen in one place. I stood still with Johnny, watching the men with caps and coveralls on, buying things for their farms. The lights there was a dirty color and sometimes they buzzed and blinked. There was heavy sacks stacked nearly to the ceiling and people rolled them out on long carts. I stayed close to Mama's legs. After she paid, Mr. Barnett bought me and Johnny a bag of candy. We stood in the parking lot sucking peppermint while he helped Mama load the truck. A man got out of the car beside us and stopped to light a cigarette. When he seen Mama his eyebrows flew up. Then they growed together like he was angry.

"Hey there," he said to Mama. I felt Johnny's body get stiff beside me. Mama put a sack of flour in the truck like she didn't hear.

"I said hey there, gal." The man's voice

169

was loud and ugly. "You going to let on like you don't know me?" Mama lifted her face then and looked at him. The red spots went out of her cheeks. "It's been a long time," the man said, "but I knowed it was you the minute I seen all that damn hair."

Mama stared. It was like she couldn't move. Mr. Barnett put down his dog feed and stepped toward the man. I knowed Mr. Barnett would protect Mama.

"What's wrong, Myra?" the man asked. The way he grinned at her made me feel funny. "Do I look too much like my brother?" Mama didn't say anything. He turned his mean eyes on me and Johnny, like he just noticed us. His face got white as Mama's. "What's this?" he said in a different voice. "Are these your younguns?"

"Get on in the truck, honey," Mr. Barnett said to Mama. Then he looked at me and Johnny and said, "Y'uns, too."

"If I recall, you was a churchgoing girl, Myra," the man said. He stepped toward the truck and it was like Mama woke up from a dream. She opened the passenger door and got in fast, just as me and Johnny was climbing in the driver's side. Mr. Barnett said, "Watch it there, feller," but the man kept on coming. I squeezed close to Mama. She was pressed up against the window staring straight ahead.

"You ever read that part in the Bible," the man asked as Mr. Barnett got in behind the wheel, "that says your sins will find you out?" Mr. Barnett pulled the door shut but I could still hear the man's voice. "I know what you done!" he hollered, slapping the hood as Mr. Barnett backed out of the parking lot. "I know what you done to my brother!"

Looking back, it don't make sense about that man being at the co-op the first time Mama ever let us off the mountain. She probably figured it was the Lord punishing her, but I don't think He works that way. Sometimes the world is just hard to understand. I don't believe it was seeing that man that ruint Mama. I think it was her worst fear coming true, of that man seeing Johnny and me. On the way back from the co-op she whispered, "I knew better." It was the last words she spoke for a long time. After that, I never wanted to leave the mountain again. I seen what she had tried to hide us from.

Johnny

In the early spring of my eighth year, I ended up with ringworm. We kept a few chickens and Whitey had puppies, but

171

wherever the fungus came from it was ugly, traveling up my leg in big scabby loops that looked like burns. That morning while my mama was sewing a rip in Laura's dress, she happened to glance up and notice. It was one of those days she would come to life and see what needed replacing in the pantry and picking in the garden and what needed to be washed. Those were the times she would silently note the holes in our shoes, slip off for a day or so, and come back with new things in a brown paper sack for us to take whenever we found them. Laura and I seldom got sick or hurt in those last two years on Bloodroot Mountain, but when we did we looked after ourselves. She never made mention of my copperhead bite, as if she didn't even notice how bad off I was. It was up to me to get better alone. Later that same year, when Laura ate the wrong berries and got sick to her stomach, I was the one who took care of her. But for some reason, my mama happened to see the ringworm that morning and it must have reminded her of the way her granny used to cure ailments like mine.

She finished sewing Laura's ripped dress and slipped it back over my sister's head. We followed her out the back door and up behind the house where the mountain was steeper and wilder. It was hard to keep up with her, ducking under branches and climbing over fallen trees. Now and again her hair would get hung on a twig or bush and she would push on without caring. I tried to help Laura along and we both slipped a few times on the wet, slimy rocks. More than once we came across swampy puddles and trickles of ice-cold water running down the mountain because it was early spring and the woods were thawing out. By the time we reached the spot on a slope where she wanted to stop, we were all three briar-scratched and muddy. There were shreds of low fog and the air was colder so far up the mountain. It hurt my throat to breathe, but it tasted sweet.

Our mama pointed to a scattering of white flowers along the ground, peeking up through a leftover litter of winter's dead leaves. She got down on her knees and dug one up with a trowel she had brought in her dress pocket, then held up the root for us to see. It was thick and fleshy, like a finger under a mess of thin, wiry hair. She snapped it with her long, strong hands and I was scared when I saw the red sap because it looked like splattered blood. I didn't know much better than to think she had wounded a living thing, made a sacrifice for my ringworm. "The Cotter boys used to gather up this bloodroot and sell it," she said. "But it might die out if we take too much. Granny used bloodroot to treat everything. Warts, headaches, sore throats. When Granddaddy's gums would bleed she'd put it in his toothpaste. You know he still had most of his teeth when he died, and him an old man. Granny said, too, the Indian warriors used to paint their faces with it."

Laura took hold of my shirttail. We hadn't heard our mama speak so much in a long time and didn't know what to make of it. If we stayed close while she hung sheets on the line or split wood or scaled fish we could hear her reciting verses sometimes that I thought might be from the Bible. Otherwise, we seldom heard her voice anymore. I held still and willed Laura not to move either, afraid of breaking the spell. Then our mama turned on us with those wild blue eyes and I had a crazy fear that she was going to eat us up. But she just reached out her fingers, stained red with bloodroot sap, and smeared some high on my cheekbone. She did the other side, too, and I must have looked funny because she laughed. I'd heard my mama laugh before, but that day it felt like a miracle. She knelt in the leaves and dipped her finger in the sap again and again until my whole face was painted. It tickled and soon all three of us were laughing, scaring up birds from the trees. Then suddenly it was over, her laughter dried up like turning off a spigot. She went back to the business of gathering bloodroot as if nothing had happened.

On the way back to the house I fell behind and stopped to look at my reflection in the creek water. She had given me the face of a warrior, anointed my cheeks with birds in flight and marked my forehead with snakes coiled to strike. I thought, "She must know that I'm a copperhead now." Or maybe she knew I was bitten all along.

Laura

I might never know for sure who that man at the co-op was, or what Mama done to his brother. Me and Johnny was little then and didn't talk about it much. All we knowed was how Mama changed after she seen him. First she started forgetting to make me and Johnny breakfast. The house didn't smell like ham and eggs anymore when we woke up. Mama would still be laying in the bed with her eyes wide open and the covers pulled up to her chin. When I touched her shoulder she'd flinch. I cried because she looked at me like she didn't know who I was anymore. Johnny said, "It's okay. I'll fix you something." He tried to make biscuits but they was flat and hard like crackers.

Them first weeks after the co-op it was like Mama was waiting on somebody to come. She'd pace the floor and look out the window. One evening we was setting in the front room listening to the radio and heard a bump at the side of the house. Then the lilac bush by the kitchen door started rustling. Mama jumped up and went after her granddaddy's shotgun. Me and Johnny stood in the kitchen holding hands. She went out and the gun shot off. Me and Johnny ran down the back steps and seen one of the Cotter man's cows had got loose. It ran back in the woods bawling and Mama turned to us with the shotgun still in her hand. Johnny said, "Don't worry. It was just a cow." But Mama started crying so hard she couldn't stop. All me and Johnny could do was stand in the light of the kitchen door and stare at her. We didn't know how to make her get better.

The winter was even harder. It came a storm and I found her laying in the snow, so cold her lips was blue. I throwed myself across her to warm her up. "What's wrong, Mama?" I asked, but she didn't say. After that she got worse. Some days she acted more like her old self. But on the worst days she stood in one place for hours without moving. It was like her soul flew off some-place. Mama never had talked much, and she always liked being outdoors better than indoors. But after that trip to the co-op she hardly ever said a word. Sometimes she even slept outside in the woods under piles of fallen leaves.

Me and Johnny did the best we could for ourselves. Mr. Barnett and his wife was worried about us. He brung us food and clothes and one day he said they might ought to tell somebody how Mama was acting, but I knowed he didn't want to get her in trouble. It got so bad on the end that Johnny's ribs was poking out. I hated seeing him so skinny. He was the one that held me when I was hungry and made me laugh when I got scared.

It was good to have Johnny but I needed Mama. One time she was gone all day and I slipped off from the house and went far up the mountain to Johnny's rock. I pressed myself flat and stretched out my arms. The rock was smooth and cool and a wind was blowing, raising bumps along my arms. I closed my eyes and prayed hard for Mama to come home. I still had my eyes shut when

I heard feet coming. My heart went faster. I never had a prayer answered the minute I said it before. I was afraid to look. Somebody was standing over me. I heard breathing and knowed it was Mama. It seemed like something magic was about to happen. Finally I got the courage to look. It was a big brown and white horse with Mama's blue eyes, staring down at me. I never seen anything so pretty. I didn't know what to do. I couldn't move. I just laid there and shivered. Whatever it was, God sent it to me. I opened my mouth to say something, but before I could get out any words, the horse had done walked off in the trees. That's one memory I never told Johnny about. I didn't want him to say it was another one of my dreams.

Johnny

I watched my mama sometimes at night, peering around the doorjamb into her bedroom. There was no door and she used to tack a ragged blanket up, but eventually it fell down and she never bothered to put it back. She would kneel by the bed with her back to me and though I couldn't see her mouth moving, it seemed I could hear the creak of her tongue, the snap of her opening and closing lips like dry twigs underfoot.

178

I always bowed my head and prayed with her, asking God for the same thing every night. I wanted my father to come for me. I realized at some point that I must have one. I only asked my mama about him once. She was rolling out dough and I was sitting at her feet, flour sifting down on my head as I cut pictures from an old catalogue. I asked, "Do I have a daddy?" Her rolling pin stilled. "Of course," she said. "Everybody does." I thought for a second. "What's his name?" When she answered, her voice was small and hoarse. "John. His name is John." It didn't occur to me until later that I had been named after him. Then I asked, "Where did he go?" She put down the rolling pin and stared at the dough. "Far away," she said. "Across the ocean, to another country where there were children who needed him more than you do." She stood there for a second longer before turning and walking out the kitchen door. I was sorry without knowing what I had done. I never brought it up again. But even as small as I was, I didn't believe her. I had my own idea of a father, one who was closer to home and easier to find. Hiding there in the dark I saw him best, a taller version of me with black eyes like mine and nothing like the wild blue of my mother's. Sometimes I saw him sitting behind a desk in an office wearing a tie. Sometimes I saw him bent over a hoe tending his garden, at a house in the valley where the mountains were a distant, smoky dream. He lived alone, waiting, preparing a place for Laura and me. When we got there, he would let us sip strong black coffee before we left for school on a yellow bus. At night the three of us would sit together watching a television set like the one the Barnetts had in their living room.

One summer I hid in the woods and watched a man walk up the road, shirt off and slung over his shoulder, naked back gleaming with sweat. From a distance I couldn't distinguish his features, and some object I couldn't make out dangled from his hand. As he got closer my mouth went dry. I thought maybe God had answered my prayer.

The man stopped in the road near my hiding place to wipe sweat from his brow. He didn't look the way I had imagined, but I thought he could still be my father. I wanted him to be so badly that I couldn't keep quiet. I burst out of the trees and skidded down the embankment. I stood panting before the man and he took a few step-backward.

"Hey, buddy," he grinned, eyes wide.

"Where'd you come from?"

I wanted to answer but my tongue was numb. I was convinced that I had been saved. The man waited for me to respond. When he saw that I didn't intend to speak, he held up the big can in his hand and shook it.

"You know where I can get me a little gas? My pickup quit on me back yonder."

That's when all the hope drained out of me in a puddle at the stranger's feet. Standing there in the middle of the road, staring sorrowfully up at the empty gas can, I had no idea how soon I would find my father, or at least a piece of him.

The moon was full that night and I could see everything in my mama's bedroom, long curls of flowered wallpaper coming down in places and the corners netted with cobwebs, a rocking chair with missing slats. There was a rag rug on the floor, like others scattered all over the house that she would take out and beat in the sun, dust flying around her head in a brown swarm. Under the window was a bureau with yellowed glass knobs that held her nightgowns and the few graying shifts she wore every day. Sometimes I watched her slip them over her naked body before she left the house to wander the mountain or fish along the creek and I never knew when she would be back.

So many nights I had watched my mama kneeling beside the old iron bed, but this time she leaned her back against it so that I could see her face, bowed and silvered in the moonlight. I can only think she must have wanted me to know about the box. I couldn't tell much about it in the shadows, a small, blackish square that she held open in her hands. Then she turned and looked in my direction. She seemed to stare straight through me. If she had spoken a word, I might have bolted away from there and never gone back. I'm still not sure whether she really caught me spying that night, or if my mind was just playing tricks on me. Even then, with cold shivers running down my spine, I was making plans. The minute I knew she was gone in the woods, I would steal back into her room. I would take the box and look inside. Finally, I would know something about her.

Laura

At the beginning of our last summer on the mountain, I was outside trying to catch a salamander with a blue tail that kept disappearing under the back steps. It was getting dark and Johnny came to me with a peaked face. I got up quick and dusted off my knees. It worried me if Johnny got upset. My eyes was stinging before he said anything.

"Is she still gone?" he asked.

I nodded.

Johnny's throat clicked when he swallowed. "I was spying on her last night."

I balled up my hands into tight fists. Part of me wanted to hear more but the biggest part wished he'd turn around and go back in the house without me.

"I found something," Johnny said. I couldn't bring myself to ask what it was. He stood there for a minute trying to work up the nerve to tell me before he finally gave up and said, "Just come on." I followed him because that's how it was with us. I would have followed him anywhere. The house was full of gold twilight, brown shadows in the corners. I shivered because it seemed like this was a stranger's house and not ours anymore. We went in Mama's bedroom and it felt wrong being in there. I was a little bit scared of her ever since she had changed toward me and Johnny, even though she never hurt us. I thought about her shadow moving in the yard at night. I thought about her arms splitting wood and her teeth tearing at whatever needed tore, fabric or thread or a sealed-up bag.

I snuck with Johnny to her bed. He knelt down like he was fixing to say prayers. I was already crying when I got down beside him. For a minute I couldn't see where his hand disappeared to. It was gone inside Mama's mattress. Then I seen there was a slit, puckered around Johnny's wrist like a mouth with thread teeth. The whole time he was rooting around in the mattress I was begging him in my head not to show me. Sometimes we could hear each other that way, maybe because of being twins. But this time he didn't hear, or else he ignored me because he didn't want to know whatever it was by hisself.

His hand came out holding a wood box. It was whittled and I knowed who made it. It was Mama's granddaddy. She had a whittled bear and a turtle he made setting on the kitchen windowsill that she showed me and Johnny one time. Johnny held out the box to me. I shook my head, so he opened it hisself instead. I didn't understand at first what I was seeing. It was three hard yellowish pieces pushed through a red ring. I swallowed and my tongue tasted like pennies, like that blood-colored ring was in my mouth.

"What is it?" I asked Johnny. My voice sounded muffled to my ears like when I covered them with my hands. Me and him looked at each other for a second.

"It's a finger," he said.

A choking sound came out of my throat. I wished it was possible for Johnny to lie to me, but in my heart I knowed he was telling the truth, even though I'd never seen a human bone. There was a rotted scrap of somebody in the house with me. It had been there before I knowed about it, maybe before me or Johnny ever drawed breath. The whole room was filled with it, a little piece broke off of death. I screamed and Johnny about dropped the box. I scooted back but he put his hand out to keep me from going.

"I think it's our daddy's," he said. I covered my eyes and peeked through the cracks. I couldn't stop staring at that bone. I had never thought much about our daddy. His face was dark in my mind. Once I was sleeping in the little room Johnny and me shared and a shadow shaped like a man was sitting in the straight chair in the corner. I laid there all night beside of Johnny not moving a muscle, wishing it would go away. To me that was our daddy. But now I imagined him a flesh and blood man without a finger.

"She killed him," Johnny said.

185

"Don't say that!" I yelled. Johnny got quiet, but I knowed he still believed it. I was mad at him for thinking she could do such a thing. But later that night I laid there looking at the wall wondering if he was right. I started thinking maybe there's times when you have to kill somebody. But if she didn't do it, that meant he was alive someplace. Then the man from the co-op parking lot came into my mind. I got to feeling like our daddy had something to do with whatever Mama was hiding us from. I started worrying he might be coming back, as a ghost or a real-life person. Either way, I figured he meant to do us harm. I don't know if it was something I picked up from Mama or something I made up in my mind, but I didn't like thinking about mine and Johnny's daddy, whether he was dead or alive. I tried not to whenever I could help it.

But right then, standing in Mama's bedroom, I didn't know what to think. We heard a clang under the window and Johnny clapped the box shut. He stuffed it back through the slit in the mattress and tried to smooth the mouth hole and its raggedy thread teeth to look like it hadn't been bothered. We went to the window and watched Mama drag out the tin tub. She had caught a catfish and was fixing to scald it. Johnny wiped off my runny nose with his shirttail and leaned over to press his forehead against mine.

Johnny

Sometimes in the heat of the day Laura and I slept naked in the musty shadows of the house, wherever we found a cool spot. We liked the rug in the front room best, one of those woven by our mama's granny, its bright colors faded by years of dirt and sun. Before she fell silent our mama had rocked us, one on each knee, and told stories about our great-granny and other ancestors from Chickweed Holler, who called birds down from the sky and healed wounds and made love potions and sent their spirits soaring out of their bodies. When I asked if it was all true, she said, "It's not for me to tell you what's true. It's your choice to believe it or not." I know now it was more than just stories she was talking about. It was a whole world of things I could choose to believe or not.

Our mama used to show us family pictures and I always wished as she turned the pages of the photo album to have known my great-granny, to have met her at least once. There were pictures of other relatives, too, posed

187

portraits that must have been made in town. Like the one of my grandmother Clio, who died when my mama was still a baby. She had a solemn face with haunted eyes that I didn't like. It was almost like seeing a ghost. Nobody smiled in the old pictures, except for my mama when she was a little girl. She seemed to have been much happier then. When I was around five, I noticed for the first time the blank squares in the photo album, empty corner pieces where they had once been tucked. I knew there were pictures of my father somewhere, maybe even of my parents together. That's when I began to imagine him, to think of him almost all the time.

I didn't like those blank spaces, or the haunted eyes of my long-dead grandmother, but I took the album down to look at my great-granny again and again. In my favorite picture she was standing on the back steps, squinting against the sun with her hands on her hips, her mouth a sunken line. I liked to imagine that same old woman weaving her rags as she watched my mama playing in the yard, never knowing that one day Laura and I would sleep on her rug and wake up with its pattern printed on our skin.

We were curled on that rug like cats when the church ladies came. It was during our last summer together, in early August, when we were still eight. I thought I was dreaming the sound of their car and the murmur of voices approaching the house, but then there was a loud knocking. I sat up fast, sweaty and dazed in the hot sun streaming through the windows. Laura rose beside me, a silvery thread of drool on her chin. I felt her fear in my own stomach. Our mama once said that I was born first, so I was the oldest. I knew it was my duty to protect Laura, no matter how small I was myself.

"Hello," a woman's voice called out. "Is there anybody home?"

Laura got to her feet but I jumped up and held her back. I looked to the room where our mama was sleeping and thought of waking her up. But after finding that finger bone in her box, part of me was more afraid of her than I was of these strangers.

"Don't," I said to Laura, and the church ladies must have heard.

"Hello?" one of them repeated, rapping sharply.

My mama stirred, the bedsprings groaning. I turned toward the gloomy opening of her room, wanting so badly for her to come out that for an instant I saw her there, arms held open like wings for us to hide under. But it was only a shadow on the wall. When

I looked back there was a face in the front room window, with little stone eyes under a mound of stiff gray hair. My stomach dropped. The woman caught sight of Laura and me, holding hands in the middle of a dusty room strung with cobwebs and littered with humps of sad-looking furniture, wearing nothing but underpants. Her stone eyes widened and she pecked on the window glass. "Is your mama and daddy home?" she hollered. I shook my head, alarm bells going off inside me. She stared for a minute more and then was joined by another face, younger and leaner with bright orange lipstick. The second one took us in, painted-on eyebrows raised, and shouted through the glass, "Where's your mommy at, honey?" I shook my head again and the two women turned to each other, maybe considering what to do, before finally disappearing from the window.

Laura wanted to look outside but I stopped her. I could still hear them out there in the yard, talking about us. There was a scuffling sound on the stoop and Laura's grip tightened on my fingers. Then we heard their ugly voices going away and the slam of doors and the hum of a car starting up. We went to the window and watched it lurching down the hill. When the car was out of sight, I found Laura's dress pooled on the floor and tossed it into her arms, then pulled on the blue jeans Mrs. Barnett had sent in a trash bag full of her grandson's outgrown clothes. Laura and I opened the door carefully and went outside. There was a stack of pamphlets on the top step, weighted down with a rock. We stood for a long time looking at them, thin manila papers with crosses on the front, but didn't touch or move them. Then we stepped around the rock and went into the yard.

The sky was bright blue with fat clouds sailing over. A squirrel darted across the clothesline into the weeds. It all looked the same but everything had changed. I imagined I could see brown foot shapes where our grass had died under the trespassers' shoes.

Laura and I walked halfway down the drive to where their tire tracks stopped in the muck. They had only made it part of the way, the dirt path still nearly impassable from the last rain. I couldn't understand why they would go to such trouble to bother us, or how they even knew we were there. Looking up the hill toward the house it seemed abandoned, one shutter hanging crooked and a vine growing up the soot-blackened chimney. The grass was almost knee high, overrun with dandelions and purple clover. There was an old wringer washer beside the back steps and a rusty tub filled with rainwater under the apple tree. It chilled me to think of those coiffed and powdered ladies creeping like monsters up to our window. I stood for a long time examining their tracks. When Whitey came sniffing into the yard she startled me so that I whirled and chucked a rock at her without even thinking. She yelped and ran off and I was sorry.

I looked for Mr. Barnett to come along behind her, but there was no sign of him. It would have made me feel better, the way he always smiled down at me with his kind eyes. I used to sit on the porch for hours waiting for him to come walking with a bag full of clothes or oranges or candy. Mrs. Barnett was always sending him up the hill with something she thought we needed. The Barnetts were good people and Laura and I had love for them, but we never trusted them completely. Sitting next to Mrs. Barnett on their living room couch as she read us picture books, I always made sure no part of us was touching. Even Laura remained guarded. I think both of us were afraid of betraying our mama by learning too much about the world she had tried to hide us from. Now that world had come knocking on our door, and we didn't know what to do about it.

We tried to play. Laura found a funny-looking toad and we sat on the ground beside the stoop poking at him with a stick, making him jump in the grass between us, but our hearts weren't in it. Our eyes kept returning to those papers on the step. When our mama opened the front door at last, our backs stiffened but our faces turned to her. She stood in the doorway looking down at the pamphlets with eyes that didn't belong on some rawboned mountain woman with sleep-tangled hair. Then she bent and lifted the rock, crumpled the tracts in her hand and tossed them into the weeds.

She went down the steps, probably meaning to disappear into the woods, but I couldn't let her this time. As she stepped onto the grass and turned her back, I reached out to her. I would have said "stay" if my voice had worked. She turned back and looked down at me without expression. Then she stooped to pry my fingers loose with no more feeling than if her dress had been caught on a nail. Laura and I watched as our mama walked off into the trees. Later, when she finally came to gather us close, it was too late.

Laura

Three days after them church ladies looked in our window, two other cars came up the hill, one with a light on top. The man who got out looked a little bit like Mr. Barnett so I thought he might be nice. Johnny grabbed my arm and said, "Let's hide." He tried to drag me off but I was hungry. I stayed in case that man had oranges like Mr. Barnett brung at Christmastime. There was a heavyset woman with papers, too. I watched them walk toward the house. Johnny stood beside me. The man went up to the front door and knocked. Then he noticed us and came over. I seen too late his hands was empty.

"Is your mother home?" he asked, bending down to talk to us.

Right when he asked, I seen her stepping out of the woods with a string of fish. Her legs was wet and specked with grass. There was a leaf stuck to her ankle. When she seen the car she froze in her tracks. The man followed my eyes and turned around. He asked, "Are you Myra Odom?" That's the first time I knowed our last name. When Mama didn't answer, he went on talking. "We're with the Department of Children's Services, ma'am. I need to speak with you for a minute."

Mama let the fish slither to the ground. Their bellies flashed in the sun. Then she was running toward us. "Don't let them touch you," she said to me and Johnny, her voice jogging up and down. Before them people knowed what was happening, she had took me and Johnny by the shoulders and herded us in the house. The man and woman tried to follow us but Mama was too quick. She slammed the door shut in their faces.

Mama knelt on the floor and gathered me and Johnny up. I could feel her shaking. We watched the door as the man pounded on it. "Open up, Mrs. Odom. I got an order here from the court." We knelt for a long time in the front room with the furniture left from some life Mama had without us. We hardly ever set on that couch or them chairs but they was ours. Someway it felt like that knocking was taking our things away from us.

It was the longest I could remember Mama holding me and Johnny in a long time. Her body heaved up and down. Her smell, like fish and creek water, filled the room. When the knocking quit she got still between us. Her arm clamped tighter around me but Johnny slipped out of her grip. She snatched after him but he didn't come back. She stayed on her knees with me. He stood at the window, white and thin with hair like a pile of blackbird wings. I asked, "Are they gone, Johnny?" He said, "No," and that was all. We waited some more. Johnny finally came back to wait with us. He crouched beside Mama, but not close enough to touch. I don't know how much time went by. But the knocking came again, then another voice. "This is the police, Mrs. Odom. You'd better come on out." For a while it was quiet again. This time I didn't ask if they was gone.

Mama stood up and started walking back and forth. Her bare feet creaked on the floorboards. She cracked her knuckles and tore at her fingernails with her teeth. After a while she got to muttering under her breath. I couldn't make out the words but she didn't sound like a person anymore. Johnny and me hugged each other. Her voice got bigger and bigger. Slobber strung down her chin. She walked back and forth faster and faster until she was just about running. Then she was yanking at her hair. Clumps of it trailed from her fingers. I wanted to close my eyes but someway I couldn't. I called on the fairies but they didn't come. Johnny got mad and screamed, "Stop it! Stop it!" He covered his eyes like I wanted to. But my eyes kept following Mama back and forth.

Then the loudest pounding came. A different voice hollered, "This is the Polk County Sheriff's Department. Open the door!" Mama rushed at me and Johnny and swooped us up, one under each arm. She ran with us to the back room. She put us down rough and my sides felt sore. She throwed open the window. The smell of outside and birdsong came in. "Go on," she whispered at Johnny. Her eyes was red and her mouth was wet. I thought Johnny wouldn't go. He was shaking his head but he must have got scared not to mind Mama. He climbed up on the dresser. He looked back at me once and disappeared out the window. I was bawling out loud then. The pounding hurt my ears.

Mama turned and knelt down by her bed. She reached into the mattress and pulled out the box. A puff of dirty stuffing came out behind it. She shoved the box in my hand but my fingers didn't want to close around it. Mama made them. She pressed them so hard around the wood it hurt. That's when I heard the front door breaking open. She lifted me under the arms and pushed me towards the window. "Run," she said.

Johnny wasn't gone. He was crouched under the window. I knelt down with him. We listened to Mama's screams and things breaking as she fought. We couldn't leave her, even if she had left us so many times. After the fighting was over, it didn't take them long to find me and Johnny huddled there. By then, Mama was gone from us forever.

Johnny

All that happened after we were found under our mama's bedroom window is like a blur in my memory. A social worker took us to a house in Valley Home, about ten miles from Bloodroot Mountain. She left us with a couple named Ed and Betty Fox and their two children. The man owned a carpet-cleaning business and drove a white van with a fox painted on the door. The woman was obese and Laura and I couldn't stop staring at her. She asked us to call her Mother Betty as she led us to the kitchen, where it smelled like cookies baking. We stopped in the doorway gaping at the shiny appliances, the row of cabinets, the plants hanging in the window. The bright rooster wallpaper hurt my eyes.

Laura and I never ate the cookies. We stood at the table staring at the plate while the Foxes talked to the social worker. When we were sure they weren't paying attention we slipped out through the sliding glass doors into the street-lit yard. Laura said, "Let's run away," but our feet didn't move. We stood paralyzed with fear of the houses on both sides and the cars passing by and of being unable to see the mountain. That's when it sank in that we were stuck, maybe for a long time. Laura whispered, "Look." She raised her blouse and showed me our mama's box, stuffed behind the waistband of her corduroy pants. She glanced back at the house and asked, "What if they take it away from us?"

I looked around in a panic until I saw the garden, its tomato-vine stakes rising up in the dark. I took Laura's arm and we ran across the cut grass into the rows, trampling the plants under our shoes still caked with mud from Bloodroot Mountain. I dropped to my knees and dug with my fingers the best I could, rocks jabbing under my fingernails. Laura put the box in the ground and we used our hands to cover it over. I stamped the mound down and Laura tried to hide the spot with a curling green cucumber vine. She was panting, a mess of sweaty hair in her eyes. I reached out to touch her back. "We'll come back in the daylight and do it better," I promised. Then I looked to the house and saw a silhouette in the glass door. We ran back across the yard with black dirt on our hands and staining the knees of our pants. Mother Betty opened the door to let us in.

I never closed my eyes that first night, lying in the top bunk above the Foxes' fat son. All I could think about was Laura's face when they led her away from me to sleep in another room. For most of the next day Laura and I stood silent and wide-eyed in the hall. Sitting down made our situation seem more permanent so we stayed on our feet, lurking in corners and hidden spaces, hoping to be forgotten about. Mother Betty was talking on the kitchen telephone as she cleared the breakfast dishes. I heard her say we were found living like animals in the woods and our mama was locked up in a Nashville crazyhouse. I prayed Laura hadn't heard, but when I turned her face was pale and still. "Is that true?" she whispered. "What she said about Mama?" I couldn't answer but she knew anyway. A light went out of her eyes then and never came back. I had the urge to destroy something, like the time I burned my mama's scarf. I took a pair of bronzed baby shoes from the console table and flung them against the wall but they didn't break. Mother Betty came thundering, rattling dishes in the cabinets, the phone still in her hand with its long cord stretched tight. When she saw my face her plump cheeks reddened. She stood staring, mouth hanging open. I stared back at her. Neither one of us said we were sorry.

At least there was plenty to eat at the Foxes' house. At the edge of the backyard there was a high bank overlooking a newly built gas station, with the main road running in front of it. Not long after Laura and I moved in, the Foxes' children, Pamela and Steven, asked us to climb down to the gas station parking lot with them. I wouldn't have gone if Laura hadn't wanted me to. I went to protect her, but standing inside among the aisles, the racks of powdered doughnuts and fruit pies and cakes, the humming dairy case against the wall, my palms were sweating. We had gone hungry so many times on the mountain, unable to sleep at night for the pain in our empty stomachs. Pamela and Steven offered to share what they bought. We followed them out and stood facing each other in the hot parking lot, stuffing candy into our mouths. Laura's cheeks were packed tight and when she smiled around a mouthful of wet chocolate I couldn't help smiling back. Soon

201

Laura and I were going to the gas station by ourselves with the quarters we earned doing chores. It was a ritual with a meaning only we could know. The Foxes' children could never understand how it felt to be Laura and me, what a relief it was to eat until we were full.

Almost a month after she left us with the Foxes, the social worker came back to visit. Her name was Nora Graham. Her hair was a frizzy tumbleweed and she wore half glasses low on her nose. She sat between us on a green glider out by the garden, as sloppy and disheveled as the night we were taken from the mountain. "We're trying to find your father," she had told us then, searching for something in a folder on top of her cluttered metal desk. "Are you sure you don't know where he is?" When I shook my head she had smiled at me. "That's okay. We'll find him." She was trying to be comforting, but if my father was dead, I hoped she was wrong. Now she sat with us beside the garden, asking questions to determine how well we were getting along. After a while Laura spoke up. "I reckon you never found our daddy." I stopped breathing and Nora's pen stopped moving on her clipboard. There was a long silence. Then she said, "No. We never found him."

That night in the bunk bed with Steven snoring over me, I thought of my father, the imaginary man whose presence had been with me on the mountain. I realized I might be close to where my mama had once lived with him, to where they had made Laura and me together. Even if he was dead, there might be a way to know something about him. I might find another piece of him and of myself. I wasn't like Laura or my mama. In my heart, I knew I was like him. I had other people than the ones in my mama's photo album and I could look for them. The question was whether or not I wanted to. I had a chance now to leave behind the mountain and my missing father and my crazy mama for good. I shut my eyes, trying not to picture her locked up somewhere dark and far from home.

When summer ended Laura and I started elementary school. It was a long brick building across a two-lane highway from a patch of deep woods. Seeing Laura among the other schoolchildren, silent and awkward with her pale skin and black hair, I understood that I must look the same way to my classmates. They didn't laugh at me. They only stared. I made myself look back until they dropped their eyes, but I was scared of them.

Sometime during those first days of school, my fear turned into hatred. I taught the other children not to stare. I bent back fingers and twisted arms and pinched tender baby fat. It didn't hurt when the teacher paddled me. Nothing did after my copperhead bite. If they had fought back I wouldn't have felt it. I never got used to being among them, but Laura had an easier time. She was different away from the mountain. My separation from her began long before what happened with Steven. I could see in small gestures how she was adapting. The way she fastened her hair back with barrettes each morning before school, how she chewed with her mouth closed and clipped her toenails and said please as she had been taught by Mother Betty. I knew she wanted to play with Pamela and Steven. I tried to make them leave her alone. I hid behind the living room curtains and chopped up the windowsill with a knife. I threw rocks at the carpet van's windshield, leaving pings in the glass. I tore the heads off Pamela's dolls, smashed Steven's model cars. I warned them but they wouldn't stop reeling Laura in.

Then one evening it was my turn to wash the supper dishes. When I was finished, I felt Laura gone from the house. I checked outside and the yard was empty, no sister sitting in the garden glider. Finally, I heard her voice and forced myself not to run toward the sound. It was coming from the old doghouse near the edge of the yard, grass still worn away and a metal stake where a beagle had been chained. Pamela and Steven said he was given away because he warbled all night. I knelt before the doghouse and what I saw knocked the wind out of me. Laura was wedged between Pamela and Steven in the dog-smelling shadows, crowded close to them with her knees gathered up. The smile died on her face when she saw me. Pamela said, "We got a clubhouse." Laura said, "Come on. You can fit." But her eyes said something else. I sat on my knees in the dust staring in at her. The others kept playing but Laura stopped. For her it was ruined and I was glad.

When I finally lost Laura, it was like my mama prying my fingers loose from her dress tail all over again. We had been with the Foxes for a year and another summer had come. I still remember how it felt, watching Laura's back disappear into a downpour. She was holding Steven's hand, water running down their faces. Sneaking off with him, the shelter of rain meant to keep me out. To see her fingers laced in someone else's, not her twin, not her blood, was too much. If I had caught up to them then I might have killed him. Whether or not my nine-year-old hands were able, my heart was capable of it.

I followed them, moving through the rain toward the white haloes of the gas station floodlights. They were running and I hurried to match their pace. When I reached them they were sitting at the edge of the grass, looking as if they were planning to slide down on their bottoms. I thought how fast it would be and how much fun. I pictured Mother Betty's neck turning blotchy and red when she saw her mud-streaked boy, her disgust for Laura and me showing plain on her face for an instant before she hid it again.

I watched Laura and Steven from a few yards away, cold drops tapping my shoulders like slugs from a slingshot, plastering my shirt to my skin. Their heads were bent close, water dripping from the ends of their hair. I could hear them laughing under the beat of rain. Then she put her hand on his cheek and left a muddy print there. Such an intimate gesture made me sick. I charged at them, feet tramping in standing water. Laura leapt up, face a white smudge in the misty light. Steven knew they had betrayed me. I saw it in his eyes. I covered the mark Laura had made on his face with one hand and shoved him backward. He went over the edge of the embankment and Laura screamed. It was a fairly long drop to the parking lot below. She stared at me open-mouthed, disbelieving. Then we went to the edge and looked down. Steven was at the bottom, slick with mud. After a moment he sat up and blinked at us. Then the blubbering started, loud and panicked. He struggled to his feet, slipping and sliding in the muck. I had a sinking feeling when I saw how his arm was hanging. Not because I was sorry, but because I knew it was over for Laura and me. I stood there watching him struggle to climb up as Laura went to get Mother Betty. When she joined me at the edge of the bank she froze for a moment with the rain wilting her beauty-shop curls. Then she pressed her hand to her throat and burst into tears. Laura and I ran off to hide in the musty dark of the doghouse while Steven was at the hospital having his dislocated shoulder moved back into place.

Mother Betty wanted us gone as soon as she got back from the emergency room with Steven, but it took nearly a week for the state to find homes for us. On our last day together we sat in the garden, rich with the smell of loam. Many times over the past year we had slipped off to look at the spot where our mama's box was buried, with the ring and our father's finger bone hidden inside. Now Laura sat across from me in the red dress she would wear to the new foster home. We were both leaving, but she was going first.

"We have to run," Laura said. "Mother Betty won't see us if we go right now."

I stared down at the ants crawling over her knuckles. "We can't."

"Yes we can. We can go find Mama. We're bigger now and you're smart."

I shook my head. "You heard it the same as I did. They've got her locked up in Nashville. And even if they let her out, I don't want to be with her."

"Johnny, hush," she said. "Don't you love Mama anymore?"

"You know there's something wrong with her."

Laura's fingers curled into fists. "No there ain't."

"She didn't take good care of us. She's not able to."

Laura fell silent. "We can still run away," she said after a while, but with less conviction. "We don't have to find Mama. We can just go off someplace else."

"Laura," I said. "I can't take care of us either."

Her shoulders sagged. "What about Mama's box?"

"You keep it. She gave it to you."

She looked at me then, studied my face. "Okay," she said. But it wasn't.

When Nora Graham came, I followed Laura down the walk to the curb where the car waited, keeping my eyes on the ground. If I looked at her my heart might stop beating. I stared down at her feet, small and square in the dress shoes Mother Betty had bought her. I would never know them again that size. I saw through the patent leather, through the sock to her toes, the nails outlined in dirt because the mountain was never scrubbed out of them. I made myself examine her face, the curve of her nostrils, the wet rims of her eyes. I unwrapped a piece of bubble gum from my pocket and stuffed it into my mouth. I didn't know what else to do with my hands. "Bye, Johnny," Laura said. She knew me better than to say anything more. She was letting me go because she thought I wanted her to. I swallowed and strangled on the sweet juice. A cough rose in my throat. Laura looked at me one last time before she got into Nora Graham's car. When she was gone, I spat the gum onto the sidewalk. From then on, the taste of candy sickened me.

Laura

At school, me and Johnny started out in the same classroom. I was scared but my brother was in the desk in front of me. The way he held up his shoulders made me feel better. Then we started having to take these tests in a little room. There was a woman with coffee breath. She figured out how smart Johnny was and put him two grades ahead of me. I seen right then he might be gone from me for good someday, just like Mama. When they made us live in different houses, I asked Nora Graham if I could go with Johnny. She claimed it's hard to keep siblings together in foster care, even twins like us.

That's how come I went to live with a preacher and his wife. The preacher's name was Larry Moffett and his wife was Pauline. They was Church of God people. I put on the dresses they gave me and let my hair grow long like they wanted me to. I didn't mind. It made me more like Mama. When I looked in the mirror it was easier to remember her.

But it was hard at first getting used to living there. I had chores to share with other foster kids. The house was crowded and always loud. The only quiet place was the basement. I went down there to do laundry. It had a washer and dryer under a dirty little window. There was a moldy carton of dishes shoved back in the shadows beside the washer. I took Mama's box from where it was hid under my mattress and carried it down to the basement in a basket of towels. I pulled the dishes out of the shadows and sorted through them, bowls and gravy boats and teacups with the husks of dead bugs inside. I put the box in a big blue willow soup tureen and shoved the carton back against the wall.

I didn't get to know the other foster kids that came and went. None of us made friends. We hardly ever talked to each other. We just did the chores and tried to get along with Pauline. I didn't get to know the preacher either. He didn't have much to do with us foster kids. We mostly answered to Pauline. She had the longest hair I ever seen, brown and thin with jaggedy ends, and her eyes was two different colors. One was green and one was brown. She had two different ways of acting, too. Sometimes she was nice and sometimes she was mean. One time she was making pies for homecoming. I dropped them trying to put them in a box. Pauline hit my arm with a wet dishrag until it bled. She drove me in the corner calling me names. I thought she wouldn't quit, until Larry asked where his dress socks was. She turned around and hollered, "They're on the bed with the rest of your clothes! I swear, Larry, you're blind as a bat!" I hurried to clean up the mess. When she came back from finding Larry's socks it was like nothing ever happened.

Pauline said the Lord had laid it on Larry's heart to take in orphans, not hers. She said she wasn't sorry she married him, but she never asked for the foster kids, or his mama, Hattie, having a stroke and moving in with them. I felt sorry for Pauline over Hattie. Hattie thought Larry was too good for Pauline. She said it all the time. She talked out of one side of her mouth where she had a stroke. She was real fat under her housecoat. Her belly had puckered white lines all over. I seen it because I had to wash her sometimes. It was scary to go in Hattie's room. The first time I almost turned around and ran right back out. She was watching her black-and-white television set with rabbit ears, fussing at the people on her stories. Her words was hard to figure out because of the stroke, but not the mean-ness of them. I was standing there with her tray. She said, "Well, bring it here, dingbat. I'm fixing to perish." I was shaking so bad the glass rattled against the plate. "Where'd they find you?" she asked. I couldn't answer. I just stared. "Take a picture, it'll last longer," she said. Her belly shook when she laughed. I froze. "They laws, girl, you're dumb as a post, ain't you?" I couldn't think. I nodded. She laughed again. Then she turned back hateful. "Get along," she said. "I can't stand somebody watching me eat." I backed out of there as she was slopping soup down her chin.

After that I was taking care of Hattie all the time. Pauline taught me how to give her permanents. The smell burnt my nose. I hated rolling her greasy hair. Her scalp was yellow and scaly. The first one came out bad. She called me a little hussy. She would have hit me if I hadn't got away. I had to cut her toenails and shave her legs. They was like white tree trunks. The one time I cut her she hit me upside the head so hard my eyes watered. I never could do anything to suit her. She hated all of us foster kids, but not more than Pauline. I don't know how Pauline put up with her. I guess be-cause they both loved Larry. That was one thing they had in common. The other thing was Percy.

Pauline told us how they found him. Back when Hattie still got around on a cane, they was having coffee in the kitchen. It was early and still half dark. They heard a meowing sound outside. They went out the back door and found him in the bushes beside the steps. He was shivering in the dew. Pauline wrapped him in her sweater while Hattie warmed him a saucer of milk. For a while there was a truce between them. But the next day they went back to fighting. Now they just had one more thing to fight about. They couldn't agree on what to feed him or what kind of litter to use or what to name him. Hattie won that fight. Percy was short for Percival, after Hattie's ancestor that was a hero in the Civil War. Pauline said Hattie was a liar. Her people was white trash and always had been. Pauline lost that one, but there was others. They still fought over whether or not to have him fixed. Pauline said it keeps a cat from running off. Hattie said it was cruel. She asked Pauline, "How would you like it if somebody cut off Larry's balls?"

I hated their fighting, but I understood how come they loved Percy. He was heavy and warm like a baby in my arms. Sometimes he got out of Hattie's room if she left the door cracked and came to me. He hopped on the bed and curled up under my chin. For the first time since Johnny I didn't feel alone. There was another heart beating close to mine. Percy was my only friend. All of us girls in the house spoiled him. Pauline brushed him every night. Hattie fed him off her plate. I made him aluminum foil balls to play with. The other foster kids liked petting him, too. He gave us a kind of love we needed.

Then one day we was getting supper ready before the evening church service and Hattie screamed, "Oh Lord! Percy's fell out the window!" Me and Pauline ran in. The window was open and the screen was gone from it. Percy had leaned against the screen and pushed it out. I ran to the window and seen the screen on the grass but no sign of Percy. He must have got scared and darted off. Hattie was bawling and carrying on. "Oh Lord, Pauline, you know he can't make it outdoors! Quit standing around and get out yonder!" I didn't waste a minute. It wasn't far to the ground. I dropped right out the window myself. Pauline ran out the front door and we started calling for him.

My heart was flying. I couldn't lose Percy. I knowed Pauline was thinking the same thing. We searched all over the yard. We got down and looked under Larry's church van. We looked under the house and turned over the wheelbarrow. We looked in all the empty boxes on the carport. Even Larry came out for a while because Hattie made him. Then he had to go back in and study for his sermon. Me and Pauline spent a long time in the shed going through the junk. We was both wet with sweat. Pauline was crying. I was sorrier for her than I was for myself. I knowed what Percy meant to her. It was getting dark. Larry came out to holler for Pauline. "We got to go," he said. "I can't be late." Pauline stopped and looked at me. We both knowed Larry wouldn't let her miss church over a cat. "Reckon I could stay?" I asked. I could tell she was relieved. "Okay," she said. "It won't hurt you to miss this once. Go in and get a flashlight."

They piled in the van and took off. The house got quiet besides Hattie sniffling in her room. I went to the kitchen drawer and found the flashlight under the phone book. I turned it on to test the battery. Then I closed my eyes and prayed the Lord would guide me to Percy. I went down the back steps. The stars was out. I tried to open my eyes and ears. I didn't call for Percy so I could hear every noise. I walked around the yard moving my flashlight over the chain-link fence. I knowed I was going to find him. I had faith. I knelt and poked around in the azalea bushes. I looked up in the trees. I walked around the whole length of the fence and checked the carport again. Must have been two hours passed without me finding Percy. I was getting discouraged. I decided to stop and take a deep breath. I thought about the mountain and how quiet it was in the woods. I pretended I was laying on Johnny's rock over the bluff. Then I started hearing a little ticking in my ears, like what a cat's heart might sound like. I went to the shed again and stood for a minute. I moved the light up and down the side of it. I seen the flash of eyes close to the ground. The shed was up on blocks and Percy was underneath it. I got down on my knees and shined the light. I seen him crouching there. There was spiderwebs in his whiskers. "Thank you," I said. "Thank you, Lord." I got down on my belly and reached for him. He hissed and bit me on the hand. I didn't draw back. I was worried he would get away. I dragged him out by the scruff of the neck. He was growling and wrestling. I seen an old feed sack under the shed. I drug it out with my other hand and put it over him. He was wrestling too much to put him inside of

217

it. He calmed down after a minute under there. I carried him across the yard bundled up in the sack. My hand was hurting. I opened the front door and hollered to Hattie, "I found him!" It was the first time I ever talked to her on purpose. "Praise Jesus!" she hollered and started crying again. Percy wrestled loose and darted off. About that time Pauline opened the door with the others behind her. She took one look at me and knowed. She came to me and hugged me tight. I didn't know how to act. I hadn't been touched that way in a long time. "Where's he at?" she asked.

"Under the couch."

"Well," she said, "I guess he'll come out when he's ready." We looked at each other one more time. Her eyes was shiny. Then she went about getting Larry's coffee. I could tell by her humming that she was happy. The next day when my hand swelled up she let me stay out of school. She took me to the doctor. After that we had milkshakes and she bought me a purse. From then on, it was easier to live at the Moffetts' house.

Johnny
After what I did to Steven, I was sent to the Briar Mountain Children's Home. It was a

218

red-brick building with a bell tower behind iron gates, nestled in a grove of pine woods. On the highway there, past fields and gas stations and through dark tunnels, I felt home receding. Our empty house, my mama in the asylum, my father's finger bone, and most of all Laura. It was like I didn't fully exist without her. I drifted among the other boys and girls, around the main building where we slept in a dorm, the chapel where we sat through the sermons of the pastor who ran the home, the fellowship hall where we ate tasteless meals, the room with folding chairs where the pastor's son counseled us in groups. I spent the whole hour looking out the window at the mountains wreathed in fog. They were not the same mountains I had grown up with. I was almost certain somewhere among those hazy blue ridges was Chickweed Holler, where my great-granny had come from. I pictured shady thickets and cool ledges of rock, tree bark wriggling with bugs. Soon I began skipping the counseling sessions and disappearing into the woods outside the iron fence for hours at a time. Whenever I came wandering back, the pastor's son always took me by the arm and asked if I wanted to be living there forever, if I never wanted to have a real home. I didn't say what I was thinking, that there's no such thing.

Some of the boys whispered that the grounds were haunted, telling ghost stories after the lights went out. They said it was once a Civil War hospital where many soldiers had died, but I never saw or felt the presence of anything there. The main building was the oldest, its corroded pipes spitting brown water when we washed our hands. All night in the dorms we heard the drip-drip of the leaky showers down the hall. In the summer opening windows gave no relief from the heat and in winter the boiler always went out, leaving our teeth to chatter on frozen mornings, making the other children sick so that I couldn't sleep for their coughing. But I never caught their croups and colds and bouts of bronchitis. I was an outsider among them, made of something different than they were.

In the five years I lived at the children's home, I saw my sister twice. Nora Graham said visits were hard to arrange because we lived in separate counties. On our twelfth birthday, she drove Laura an hour from Millertown to see me. She left us alone on the playground behind the main building, a patch of worn grass with swings hanging limp at the ends of their chains. Laura was taller and her face was longer. She had grown up behind my back. Sitting on the swings together, I was reminded of things I'd tried hard to forget. I heard my mama's screams, saw Laura's handprint on Steven's cheek. When she gave me the present she had made, a drawing of our house on the mountain, I crumpled it in my fist. She studied me with sad eyes. Then she reached out and guided a lock of my hair back into place. For a long time I could still feel the brush of her fingers on my brow.

When Laura was gone I climbed the iron fence and got lost between the pines. I ran through the woods half blind with unshed tears, clambering across gullies and over rises, tripping and falling again and again. It was almost dusk when I came to a bluff of stacked rock shelves with more pines perched high on top. Near the ground I saw a crack under an overhang. When I ducked inside, the cave smelled of algae and minerals and wet stone. Within the sun's reach the limestone walls were mottled with moss, shaggy near the top with russet-colored roots like the pelt of some mythical forest animal. Farther in, I found what looked at first like three old trash barrels leaning on uneven piles of rock. On closer inspection I realized it was an abandoned moonshine still. There was a tin tub with a pipe running down from its rust-eaten lid into a weathered barrel made of rotten gray boards, and from it a length of tubing coiled into another metal barrel, brittle and fiery orange with rust. Not far from the still, I noticed something glinting on the ground. I bent down, startling a lizard up the stone wall, and found a silver cigarette lighter. I held it in the sun falling through the cave's opening and saw initials engraved on one side. I stopped breathing. The initials were J.O., like mine. But I didn't think of my own name. I thought of my father's. It was like somebody had left the lighter there for me to find.

A few months after I discovered the cave, a girl named Libby came to live at the children's home. Boys and girls ate together in the fellowship hall and one morning at breakfast I caught her staring at me. She had brown hair and green eyes and a chicken pox scar on her forehead. I learned later that she was fourteen but she was built like a woman, breasts straining at the buttons of her blouse. When I saw her later at the middle school, I almost didn't know her. There was a dumpster out back where I went to smoke. She was standing with a group of boys wearing blue eye shadow and blowing smoke rings through the shiny oval of her lips. She asked how old I was. When I told her, she smiled and said, "You don't look no thirteen." On the bus back to the children's home she was the same plain girl from breakfast again, no trace of teased bangs or lip gloss.

That afternoon she followed me into the woods. I heard her footfalls on the pine needles behind me but I didn't turn around. I let her trail me all the way to the cave. When we reached the opening I turned and she almost bumped into me, face flushed and pulse fluttering in her throat. I took her by the arm and we ducked into the crack in the rocky bluff. For what seemed a long time, we knelt facing each other in the murky gloom. Then her hand slid up my thigh. My muscles tensed under her touch. The black holes of her pupils widened to draw me in, opening to show me what was inside of her, heaps of cinder and mud and things left out in the rain, wells where living things fell inside and drowned. I pulled her close by the nape of the neck, kissing her so hard I tasted blood. I twisted my hands up in her hair, bit her shoulders, sank my fingers into her flesh. She didn't pull away. She was drawn to me in spite of or maybe because of my darkness. She was only there for a month, but after her there were others that I lay tangled with on the cool dirt floor of the cave, pinning them down with my body, pulling their hair until they cried out. Like Libby, they always wanted more, as if they craved my meanness.

Not long before I left the Briar Mountain Children's Home, when we were fourteen, the state arranged another visit with Laura. It was an overcast day in March so we sat at a table in the fellowship hall, where the windows faced the mountains. I wasn't prepared for how much she looked like our mama. She was wearing a skirt down to her ankles and had hair to her waist because her foster parents were Church of God people.

"You look skinny," she said.

"So do you," I said.

She smiled. "I learnt how to make biscuits. I wish I could fix you some."

I turned my head. "I don't like biscuits."

There was an awkward silence. We sat listening to the clanking radiator, smelling the dampness of the long, drafty room. She pulled her cardigan tighter around her. When she spoke again it startled me. "What's it like in here, with all these other kids?"

I thought about it. "Like being by myself."

She fidgeted in her folding chair. "Are you

lonesome?"

"No," I said. "I don't mind it."

She got quiet again. I felt her studying me and looked down at the floor tiles, the same dingy color as the weather outside. "I guess there's something I ought to tell you," she said. "I meant to keep it to myself, but I can't do you that way."

I waited for her to go on, not sure if I wanted to hear.

"There's a store in Millertown with our name on it."

My eyes moved to her face. "What?"

"There's a building on Main Street that says Odom's Hardware on the side. I seen it when I was downtown with Pauline. The woman I stay with."

I leaned closer to her. "Did you go inside?"

Laura shook her head. "Pauline don't trade there. But she knows who owns it. She said his name's Frankie Odom." She bit her lip. "I reckon he's our granddaddy."

I blinked at her. "How do you know that?"

"Pauline said so."

"Then how does she know?"

Laura looked down at her scuffed shoes. "Everybody knows it."

"You didn't go in the store and ask any questions?"

She shook her head again. "Pauline said

Frankie Odom ain't in his right mind anyway. She said he's got old and senile. His boy runs the store now."

My stomach dropped. "His boy?"

"Not our daddy," Laura said quickly. "Our uncle. Pauline called him Hollis."

"Hollis," I repeated, so I wouldn't forget.

Laura twisted her hands in her lap. "Pauline said the Odoms are bad people and I believe her, Johnny. I don't want any part of them. For Mama to do something like what she might have done to our daddy, he must have been mean."

My eyes began to sting. "We have people who knew our dad and you don't care?"

"Can't we talk about something else?" she asked. "I been missing you so bad."

"You want to find our mama, though. You'd talk to her, after the way she did us."

"I don't know about that, either," she said. "I used to want us to run away and go find her but I've give up on that. I've quit believing we'll all be together again."

"Don't lie," I said. "I know how it is. You'd go to her right now if you could."

"What do you mean, how it is?"

"I mean you're just like her."

"How's that true? I don't even know her anymore."

I clenched my teeth trying to keep in the

words, but in the end I couldn't stop them from tumbling out. "You walked off and left me, just like she did."

Laura's eyes widened. "Johnny, you know I never wanted to be away from you."

I looked down at the floor again. "I don't know anything."

Laura spent a long moment thinking. Then she said, "I guess I can't help being something like Mama, on account of having her blood. But so do you."

I grabbed her arm. "Don't say that. I'm not like her."

Laura looked into my eyes. "Okay, Johnny," she said. "I wish you'd let me go."

I took my hand away from her arm and stared down at it. Laura turned her face to the window and the distant blue chain of the mountains, where Chickweed Holler was hidden from us. She rubbed at my fingerprints fading on her skin. I was sorry but I couldn't take it back. Then Nora Graham cracked the door of the fellowship hall and my time with Laura was over. I didn't know it would be five years until I saw her again.

Laura

For a long time I looked forward to Johnny getting out of the children's home. Nora

Graham said she'd place him with a foster family as close to me as she could. I thought even though I was still in middle school and he was starting high school, we might at least get to ride the same bus. When he finally did get out, he lived for a while at a foster home in Millertown and went to the ninth grade. He was on the other side of town so we didn't ride the same bus, but Nora Graham arranged a visit. Then, before I even got to see him, she said he done something bad and got sent off again. My heart was broke in two. No matter what Johnny thought of me, I loved him better than anything.

When I started high school myself, the girls there was still talking about Johnny. They said he done them wrong in the short time he was there. He'd go with one until he got tired of her and then move on to the next. It wasn't just the girls Johnny left his mark on, either. This boy named Marshall Lunsford asked if I was Johnny's sister. He claimed Johnny was his best friend and had been to his house. He said Johnny had lived with his mama's cousin so they was like family. I couldn't see Johnny being friends with anybody. He said when Johnny got out of jail they was going hunting together. I figured that boy would be better off to never see Johnny again. It was a sad thing to think about my own brother, but I knowed something was broke in Johnny, the same as it was in me.

I didn't like high school. The only good thing about it was Clint Blevins. A bunch of us used to stand around and wait for the bus to take us home. One day I felt a finger winding up in my hair. I whipped around and Clint said, "Sorry about that. I couldn't help it." Clint was in some classes with me and he was always getting called to the office. Seemed like every week Clint Blevins was in a fight. One time I walked up right after the gym teacher pulled him off of a boy. There was blood all over the hall. It made my belly hurt. I thought Clint was just another mean boy. But when I turned around, I knowed he wasn't. He had eyes like Mama's and his hair had fat yellow curls like rings of sunshine. Then I seen something peeking out of his shirt collar, flashing in the sun. He had a chain around his neck, a silver rope. I didn't know I was fixing to talk until I opened my mouth.

"Your name is Clint," I said.

"Yeah, but I can't remember yourn."

"Laura Odom."

"You're a pretty girl, Laura."

"I favor my mama some. But she has blue

eyes like you got. Not black like mine."

"I like black eyes the best," Clint said, and followed me up on the bus.

He sat down with me. He said he'd moved back in with his mama, that's why he rode my bus now. He said, "Me and Daddy was living in a little green trailer beside of the lake. I don't get along too good with Mama, but Daddy finally drunk hisself to death. She thinks I ortn't to live out yonder by myself and me still in school." Clint looked out the window. I felt sorry for him. I could tell how sad he was. "You should've seen poor old Daddy there on the last. He was shrunk down to nothing and yeller as a punkin where his liver was bad." Clint looked up at the bus ceiling. I moved my hand closer to his on the seat between us. I think that made him feel better.

"Where'd you get that silver necklace?" I asked to change the subject.

"From Louise," he said. I got jealous. Later I found out she was just the gray-headed cashier down at the grocery store where he worked.

Clint got off the bus at a house behind the laundrymat. After that, we set together every day. He told me all about his life. I seen the stories in my mind. Clint couldn't remember things being any different. His daddy held down a janitor job before he started drinking, and his mama worked in the school lunchroom before she went on welfare. When he was a baby they rented a farmhouse beside of a pond. But the first thing Clint remembered was living in that house behind the laundrymat. When he talked about it, I could smell warm clean clothes drifting across the yard. He said when he was real little it was like being wrapped in a blanket. But later on the smell of laundry got to where it gagged him. Too many times Clint had set in the weeds out behind the house, with the cinder blocks and busted glass, smelling that laundrymat and listening to his mama holler and carry on. Then after while he would see his daddy plod off down the street holding a whiskey bottle with a cut place over his eye where she throwed something at him.

Clint said sometimes he used to slip in the laundrymat and watch the clothes float in them glass portholes. He'd listen to the blue jean buttons and loose change clinking around. He'd watch that round and round motion and get sad, thinking about a circle that kept going and didn't end up anywhere. Sometimes his daddy found him and bought him a Coke in a glass bottle and a pack of peanuts to pour in it. Then Clint said that old laundrymat life was finally over, at least for a while. His daddy got a job driving the garbage truck long enough to put back some money. One day he came out of the house with a paper sack in his arms. Clint's mama was screaming and throwing his things out behind him. Clint followed his daddy in the street and asked, "Where are we going?" His daddy said, "I got us a little spot by the lake." Clint said when they got down to the water, it was the prettiest place he ever seen. Him and his daddy was happy there from the start.

Clint spent every day he could in the lake until it got cold, trying to be a fish. He'd sink as far as he could and stay down for as long as he could hold his breath, because he knowed it was all going to end. He said it was like time stopped when he was under the water and he wanted to stretch it out. He could see his daddy getting sicker and sicker. He remembered what his mama said when his daddy left. "That's all right. You're just slinking off to die, like a dog does. Mark my words. It won't be long." Clint hated his mama having the last laugh, about as bad as he hated that his daddy was fixing to die.

But while his daddy lived, they had a nice life by the lake. Clint came and went as he pleased. He didn't have to do homework.

He failed three years in a row. Only reason he went to school any was because the truant officer threatened to put his daddy in jail. He never had to take a bath either and got dirtier and dirtier. He said them dirty smells was the ones he liked best, greasy hair and black feet bottoms and most of all fishy lake water. I thought that might have been what brung us together, the way we both loved fish. We must have seen each other's secret scales glinting under our skins. There was something the same inside of us. Clint talking about his life always made me think about my own. I seen we could take care of each other in a way our mamas didn't know how to.

After Clint went back with his mama he thought every day about running off. But he said there was a part of hisself that would always be afraid of her. It was like her shrill voice froze him up, especially with his daddy gone. Clint told me, "If it wasn't for Daddy, I never would have been brave enough to get away from her in the first place."

She made Clint go to work at the grocery store and help pay the bills. He didn't mind about that. The store wasn't as good as the lake, but it was still someplace to go. He said he liked the people there. He looked forward to going to work at night, but during the day at school he'd set around in class and get mad at his mama. It was like she won, and he couldn't stand it. He'd beat up other boys the same way he wanted to beat on his mama. He was sorry after he fought them, but he said he couldn't help it until he met me. "All that black hair of yourn looked like a big old pool of lake water," he leaned over and whispered in my ear one day. "When I was standing behind you out yonder, I just wanted to dive right in it." Hearing him talk that way made me feel like I was worth something.

Clint told me all them things on the bus. Then he started bringing me presents, mostly barrettes and combs. I knowed he wanted them done up in my hair. I'd fix myself in the school bathroom and take it down before I got off the bus. I figured Pauline might not like my hair done up that way, but Clint sure did. Before long, we loved each other.

Johnny

After my visit with Laura, I made up my mind to attend the counseling sessions, as much as I hated the pastor's son. Seeing her took something out of me. I couldn't stand being at the children's home any longer. Each meal at the fellowship hall soured on my stomach and the smell of wet limestone began to hurt my head. I was too tired to climb the iron fence anymore. I knew the only way to earn my freedom was to do as I was told, so I sat with the others in a circle of folding chairs and pretended to listen. The summer before I turned fifteen, the pastor's son decided I was ready to have foster parents again. Nora Graham took me in late August to Wanda and Bobby Lawsons' old clapboard house outside of Millertown. They worked long hours at the gas station they owned and when they got home they went to bed. They seemed more interested in the check the government provided for my upkeep than in being my parents and I was grateful for it. At the end of five years living among so many strangers, all I wanted was to be left alone.

Like the children's home, the Lawsons' house was ringed in woods. It wasn't the same wilderness I was used to, with craggy bluffs and limestone caves. These woods were flat and crowded with tall, skinny trees, the ground humped with snaking roots. I could walk for hours without the scenery changing, save a random piece of rusty junk here and there. Once I saw an old stove on its side, half buried in kudzu, and once a car bumper shaggy with honeysuckle. I traveled so far that I came out behind the high school, standing on a rise overlooking the football field. I saw how close I was to Millertown, how easy it would be to find Main Street and Odom's Hardware. But I still didn't know whether I wanted to forget who I was or go looking for the man I came from.

Then I met Marshall Lunsford on the first day of high school and everything changed. At lunchtime I went through the line and took my tray to the first empty seat. There was a boy sitting across from me eating a greasy square of yellow cornbread. He was gawky and long-necked with dirty fingernails and a head full of cowlicks.

"You're lying through your teeth, Marshall," the fat boy beside him was saying. "There ain't even no coyotes around here." He looked across the table at me. "You should've heard what all this retard said."

"I ain't retarded," Marshall said. "Me and my daddy went hunting up on the mountain and I seen a coyote."

"That ain't all he told," the fat boy piped up. "Why don't you tell him the rest of it, see if he believes you any more than I do."

Marshall's face turned red. "It ain't no lie. Me and Daddy got separated. Then I heard this growling noise. There was a female coyote coming out of a cave. I guess it must've had pups. Well, I stood right still and it kept coming at me." Marshall was enjoying himself, getting carried away. He leaned forward. "I figured I ort not to run, cause if I fell it would've ripped my throat out. I stood my ground and the next thing I knowed, that coyote was jumping at me. Then I caught hold of its head and gave it a twist. That thing fell down dead with its neck broke, hit the ground like a rock."

"You're full of it," the fat boy said, shaking his head.

"What mountain was it?" I asked.

Marshall's eyebrows shot up. He seemed startled that I had spoken to him. "Blood-root Mountain."

"You live on Bloodroot Mountain?"

"Down at the bottom of it," he said, and went back to stuffing his mouth with great hunks of cornbread.

"You really believe this retard killed a coyote?" the fat boy asked smugly, as if he already knew what my answer would be.

I looked Marshall over, cold settling around my heart. "He might have."

Marshall looked up from his tray at me with surprise and gratitude. I could tell that he thought I was an ally. It was just what I wanted him to think.

After school, I walked into the late summer woods with Marshall Lunsford on my mind. If I befriended him, I could go home whenever I wanted. I knew he'd be glad if I asked to sleep over. I had seen the hero worship in his eyes. He even claimed to know the Lawsons. He said Bobby was a distant cousin of his mother's. But I remembered how hard it was seeing Laura. It would be even harder to see our house on the mountain.

I walked a long way under the rustling green leaves, head down and hands in my pockets. After a while, I came to a wire fence with a sign that said "No Trespassing." I slid under and kept going. The terrain was mostly the same except for the evergreens crowded now among the leafy trees. I topped a rise littered with pine needles and saw, not far off in a clearing, a leaning shack no bigger than an outhouse. My heart sped up, some crazy part of me wondering if this was my father's house. Maybe he would even be waiting there for me. I walked fast, breathing hard, but when I reached the shack I was afraid to look. The woods had grown eerily silent. I held my breath and peeked inside. I saw a mildewed blanket and piles of damp leaves rotting in the corners. In the middle of the floor were three water-swollen books. Like the lighter in the cave, they seemed to have been left there for me to find. I stepped inside and knelt to pick them up. They appeared to be old poetry books. I stacked the volumes in the crook of my arm, leaving square shapes in the grime where they had been. I walked back to the house and crawled under the porch to read by the diamond-shaped light through the lattice until dark.

My fingers shook as I turned the mold-spotted pages. It was like hearing my mama's voice in my head, the lilting way she recited her verses, the rhythm and music of all those poems bringing her back to me. Then, about halfway through the last volume, I dropped it in the dirt. I'd seen my mama's words, those she whispered so often I thought they were from the Bible or maybe something she made up, printed there in smeary ink.

"These beauteous forms, through a long absence, have not been to me as is a landscape to a blind man's eye, but oft, in lonely rooms, and 'mid the din of towns and cities, I have owed to them, in hours of weariness, sensations sweet, felt in the blood, and felt along the heart. . . ." I picked up the book and read the poem over and over. It had been written by William Wordsworth about a place called Tintern Abbey. I whispered it out loud and my mama's presence came creeping over me. I looked down and saw a dark blot with crawling tendrils like long, black hair spreading over the dirt and pooling around my feet. I know now it must have been my imagination, but it seemed like she was more with me there under the Lawsons' front porch than she had ever been on Bloodroot Mountain.

I crawled out from under the porch and went inside, holding tight to the books from the woods. Wanda had left my plate wrapped in a dish towel on the stove. I ate in the darkened kitchen and put my plate in the sink and took the books to my room along the back of the house. I switched on the naked bulb overhead and wrote my first poem sitting on the bed. I scribbled until pale light seeped under the window shade and my fingers were numb and the arm once stiffened by a copperhead bite sang with pain. It was clear now what I needed to do. This was a sign I couldn't ignore. I had to see our house on the mountain one more time. Then, whether he was alive or dead, I had to find my father.

When I went to Odom's Hardware a week later, I didn't have to fake being sick to get out of school. The Lawsons left for work at dawn and I waited in my bed, thinking a hardware store wouldn't be open so early. I brought my notebook from under the mattress and wrote again until my mind was empty and the sun was higher in the sky. Somehow getting the thoughts out calmed me. My hands were steady as I pulled on my shoes and ran a comb through my hair. I left the house and cut through the woods until I came out behind the high school. It wasn't a long walk from there to Main Street. The buildings were abandoned looking, display windows crammed with junk, some cracked and repaired with tape. When I saw Odom's Hardware, my own name painted on the dull red bricks of the building, my stomach clenched. It felt like someone or something else piloted my body down the sidewalk to the propped-open door. I stepped inside and the floor was made of wide, grimy planks that creaked under my feet. Once my eyes adjusted to the gloom I saw long aisles of shelves holding dusty cardboard boxes spilling bolts and screws and hinges. By the dirty light of the smeared plate-glass window I saw him perched on a stool behind the counter, just inside the door. It seemed as if he'd been waiting for me all along. I walked closer to see my uncle better, a smallish man with cigarettes in the breast pocket of his shirt, sitting in a shaft of whirling dust. He was unremarkable, with slicked-back hair, a plain, ruddy face, and ears too large for his head.

"Help you?" he asked.

"Maybe," I said, taking another step closer. He rose from the stool and placed his hands on the counter, leaning forward. The way his eyes narrowed made my heart race.

"What are you looking for today?" he asked. I could see his mind working as he took me in, trying to decide where he knew me from.

"My father," I said.

He stared at me hard for a long moment, face strangely still. He touched something metal hanging from his neck, gleaming dully in the gloom. I saw that it was a pair of dog-tags. He rubbed his thumb over them as if for comfort. Then he laughed but his eyes didn't change. "Your father, huh? Are you pulling my leg?"

"No."

The man stopped laughing. That's when we remembered each other at the same time. I could see the light coming on in his eyes. In my head, he was standing in the parking lot of the co-op all over again. I

could hear the slap of his palm on Mr. Barnett's hood. I stepped closer and put my
hands on the counter so we were almost
nose to nose.

"What's your name, boy?" he asked softly,
although I suspected he already knew. I
could smell cigarettes on his breath, in his
clothes.

"Odom," I said. "Just like yours."

The redness crept up from his neck to set
his lined face on fire. "I know you," he said,
calmly enough. "I knowed your mama, too."

I pressed my palms harder into the
counter and stared at his throat, imagining
how it would feel between my fingers. My
voice was surprisingly even when I opened
my mouth. "You said you knew what she
did to your brother. Is he dead or alive?"

"You think I'd tell you a damn thing about
my brother?" Hollis Odom asked through
gritted teeth. A dot of spittle landed under
my eye. It burned there but I didn't move
to wipe it away. "Hell, you probably ain't
even his. I didn't know that whore had any
babies. I would have called the human
services on her after I seen you all at the
co-op but I figured they'd come around
with their hands stuck out, wanting us to
take responsibility. We don't owe you nothing, boy. You been signed over to the state a

long time ago. You ain't no Odom. And you ain't got no business sniffing around here, so you might as well get along, before I put you out."

"What was it you called her?" I asked, jaw clenched so tight my teeth ached. My hand shot out to seize his throat as if of its own volition. His eyes bulged and his face went plum. He pried at my fingers and I dug in deeper, the dogtags pressing into his flesh. I can't say when I would have let go if he hadn't scrambled around with one hand under the counter, knocking things onto the floor, and come up with a gun. He thrust its long barrel into my face. It didn't even look real. I let go of his throat and watched, heart drumming in my ears, as he whooped and coughed and spat, leaning on the counter for support, still clutching the gun in his hand. When he was finally able to speak he croaked between hectic breaths, "You get out of here before I shoot you right between the eyes. I ever see your face in here again I'll have you throwed under the jail. You hear me?"

I backed out of the store and into the sun. I stood looking at the building, breathing hard, thinking what to do next. It was only then that I realized I had somehow ripped the dogtags from around his neck. I was squeezing them tight in my hand, their notched edges biting into my palm. I opened my fingers and saw how old the tags looked, maybe from the Second World War. The name pressed into the metal was Franklin J. Odom. I knew they had belonged to Frankie Odom, my grandfather. I didn't wonder what the middle initial stood for, either. It was John, like my father. It was Johnny, like me.

Laura

I told Clint things on the bus, too. He's the only one I ever told what happened to Mama. It was hard to say out loud. I told him about the mountain and our old house up there. The only thing I didn't tell him about was Mama's box with a finger bone inside. I'd look out the bus window and talk about how I wanted to go back. I told Clint first I'd visit the Barnetts and their dog, Whitey, and thank them for being so good to me and Johnny and Mama. Then I'd go in the house and lay in Mama's bed, like she used to let me of the mornings. After that I'd wade in the creek and try to catch minnows like me and Johnny used to do. I'd climb up to Johnny's rock where he got snake bit and look off down the bluff. Then I'd go high enough to find that white ghost flower and show Clint how it bled. One time he asked, "What about your mama?" I didn't understand. He said, "Don't you want to go visit her in Nashville?" I wanted to answer but I didn't know how to say I'd got to where I'd just as soon see her dead than to see her locked up. I believe he felt bad for asking. I knowed he didn't mean anything by it. He never brung it up again.

Clint understood how bad I missed the mountain. He said, "Soon as I get me a car, I'm driving you there." I knowed he was saving up money from his job. Going home seemed like something way off in the future that might never happen. Then one day Clint came to me grinning after school. It was spring already, close to the end of my freshman year. He led me out to the parking lot and there it was, a long green car with a busted place on the windshield. First thing Clint said was, "Now I can take you home." I knowed he wasn't talking about Larry and Pauline's house. I hugged Clint tight and felt like crying, but not with happy tears. My heart was beating loud in my ears.

That Saturday I told Pauline I was going to the library to write a paper for school. I hated to lie, but she never would have let me go off with a boy. I walked to the end of the street. It was a nice day. The neighbor

246

kids was out playing with water guns. I ought to felt good, but I was scared. When I got in Clint's car, he pulled me across the seat and kissed me. Then he leaned back and looked me over. "What's wrong, baby?" he asked, starting up the car. It was loud and the exhaust just about made me sick. I couldn't say anything. When we got to the stop sign, Clint asked, "Which way?" I started getting even more tore up. I never thought about it before, but I couldn't remember how to get there. I was just eight when I got took away. Clint must have seen the worry on my face. He said, "That's all right. We'll just head for the country until you see something you know."

We drove for a long time, past the city limits. We went down the two-lane highway, through Valley Home and Slop Creek. I had lived in them places. I should have knowed my way around. The mountains got closer but nothing looked familiar. I set against the door twisting my hands. Every once in a while Clint would pat my knee. "See anything you know?" he'd ask, and I'd shake my head. Finally when we got to Piney Grove he said, "Let me pull over here to this store and ask somebody." It seemed like he was in there a long time. I kept looking at the mountains, getting hotter and sicker.

I don't know how long I set there until Clint came back. He opened the door and grinned at me. "That feller said we ain't got far. Just hang a right here at the corner and keep going about five miles, then hang another right and I reckon that road goes straight up the mountain. Won't be long." He rubbed the back of my hair and I tried to smile, but my belly was hurting. I needed to use the toilet but I didn't want to get out of the car.

After Clint took that first right, it seemed like we was driving forever. It was the crookedest road I ever saw. There was thick trees on either side and a lot of dead groundhogs and possums along the ditch. I wanted to be happier about going home, but I kept seeing Mama in my head, how she pulled out her hair and slobbered and screamed like a wildcat when she was fighting them people. I don't know how long it was before we came to that second right, and a sign that said "Bloodroot Mt. Road." Beside of the turn there was an old white house with a man in the yard fixing his truck. He looked up when we slowed down. He had a long, stringy beard and mean eyes. He didn't wave back when Clint lifted his hand. I had a bad feeling. Clint turned onto the road and it looked like new blacktop. The road to our house was dirt, that much I remembered for sure.

We started the climb up and Clint's car was laboring. Leaf shadows fell across the road and right away I knowed something was wrong. First I seen a trailer set back in the hill, so new it didn't have any underpinning. The trees had been cleared to make room for it. Big muddy gashes had been cut in the ground for a driveway. On the other side of the road there was a house under construction. Men without shirts was hammering on the roof. There was a yellow machine parked in the mud beside a heap of dirt. Then there was a long stretch of bald land with just a few scattered tree stumps here and there. Cold started spreading over me. It was like we had took a wrong turn into some hainted place.

"This ain't it," I said to Clint.

"Huh?"

"This ain't the right mountain."

"Baby, it said so on the sign."

"Sign must be mixed up," I said. I didn't want the tears to come out but what I was seeing didn't look a thing like home. The mountain I came from was wilder than this.

"This ain't it," I said again. I couldn't hold back the crying any longer.

"It's got to be," Clint said, real quiet.

"But it ain't!" I hollered. I couldn't hardly see out the window through my tears. We was passing a place that seemed like the Barnetts', only it was growed up with briars and weeds. It couldn't have been the same house or the same land, rundown as it was.

"Stop the car, Clint!" I screamed at the top of my lungs, so hard it hurt my throat. "Stop the car and turn around!"

Clint didn't hardly know what to do. "Okay, okay," he said, looking over at me with big eyes. "Just quit that squalling, honey. You're fixing to make yeself sick."

He backed into the driveway of the place that looked something like the Barnetts'. I cried even harder, thinking he meant to take me there. When he seen how worried I was, he turned the car around and drove off so fast the wheels slung gravel everywhere.

Before long Clint had to pull over for gas, at the same store where he got them bad directions. While he was pumping gas I thought of my real home. I felt better when I closed my eyes and seen it how it really looked, cool and green and wild with no trailers and no muddy gashes in the land, no chopped-down trees and scruffy bald patches, no half-built houses peeking out of the trees with satellite dishes on their roofs.

When Clint went in to pay, I watched him

walk across the parking lot. Just looking at him, tall and lanky with all that sunny hair, made me feel safe. He came back and opened the door real careful, like he was afraid of what he might find. He poked his head in and looked me over, trying to judge what kind of shape I was in. He tossed something wrapped in plastic across the seat and it landed in my lap. It was chocolate cupcakes with cream in the middle. He knowed how much I liked them. I smiled and tore them open. He squinted at me to see if I was okay before he got in the car. I pulled him close and hugged him tight. I don't believe I ever loved anybody that much, even Johnny. I scooted next to him. We set in the parking lot of that store while I ate my cupcakes. We never did talk any more about going home. I reckon I was scared we'd get lost again.

Johnny

In my cell at the Polk County Juvenile Detention Center, I relived many times what I had done to get there. The night I burned down Odom's Hardware, I was carrying a rock and a whiskey bottle stuffed with a gas-soaked rag in a duffel bag I stole from Bobby Lawson, the fumes traveling with me through the dark. In front of the

251

store, I stood before the dirty plate-glass window and tested the rock's weight for a moment before launching it through the stenciled letters of my last name. There was a satisfying shattering sound, a spray of shards that glinted in the streetlight. Somewhere distant, a dog began to bark. I waited for an alarm to go off or someone to come into the street or a car to cruise by but there was only silence. I pulled the bottle from under my arm and reached for the silver lighter in my pocket. When I lit the rag, the flame was sudden and hot. I lobbed it through the hole I had smashed and stood there waiting. For what seemed like hours, there was only a faint orange glow. I stepped closer to the window and saw a line of flame dancing across one floor plank. I watched hypnotized as another branched off and then another. After a while, I could smell the fire. Smoke began to rise, thick and black, behind the broken window. I was too tired to wait and see what happened. I turned and walked off, down deserted streets and back through the woods to the Lawsons'.

A few days later, crossing the parking lot of the detention center handcuffed, I still wasn't sorry for what I had done. If I thought of my mama's face when she saw

Hollis Odom at the co-op, or of his voice calling her a whore, or of those two years we spent suffering on the mountain over the wrong he must have done for the sight of him to have driven her out of her mind, I wanted to burn the place down all over again. That building was the representation of everything I had wanted to destroy since our mama took herself away from us. But when I saw my cell, a closet-sized room with chips and gouges gone from its dreary beige cinder blocks, a metal toilet and a bunk with a thin mattress bolted to the wall, I almost went mad like she did. I thought I wouldn't make it four days locked up, much less four years. I worried if Laura would be told where I was. I needed her to know, but I made it clear that I didn't want to see her. Not in that place.

I seldom looked at the other boys there. I can't remember their faces, even though I sat with them on crowded benches for hours in the classroom. I only had to fight once, when a boy tripped over my foot and rounded on me with his fists. I aimed for his throat with the sharpened pencil I was holding and missed, skidding it along the hard ridge of his jaw to tear through the soft pink meat of his earlobe. I spent two days on lockdown and after that I was left mostly alone. I kept my head down and did as I was told, the way I had learned at the children's home. I saw what happened to some of the others who made trouble, the boy whose eardrum was busted when a guard kicked him in the head, the one whose nose was broken when he was slammed against the wall, the one I heard crying when they came after lights out to beat him with their sticks. There was only the library for escape, and my poetry books from the woods. I read them over and over. But it was my notebook that saved me. When my thoughts of home and freedom were too much, I emptied them onto the pages, containing them like poison. They did no good inside my head, memories of Laura and my mama and the mountain. It was better to hide them under my mattress, to sleep on top of them as my mama had done, keeping a piece of her old life to take out and examine from time to time. That part of her I understood.

I wrote the ink out of hundreds of pens, a callus forming on the middle finger of my right hand. Sometimes rubbing the callus while I sat trapped in the classroom was enough to settle me. By the end of my time at Polk County I had filled stacks of notebooks, most of them thrown out so they could never be read. I was glad to see them go. I might have burned them if I had been allowed to strike a match. It was a way of purging that the others didn't have. Fights broke out over nothing among them. The detention center was old and not big enough to house forty of us, a tall fortress of dirty white brick with banks of dark windows behind chain link and razor wire. Even the basketball court was claustrophobic, enclosed on three sides by the building's outer walls. In all weather but hard rain we went outside in the afternoons, a guard leaning in the door keeping watch. That's where I first noticed the one who didn't seem to belong there.

The basketball goal was a netless rim with a flaking backboard, rotten and graying in the shadow of the building. The boys dribbled and shot the ball, chuffing and grunting as brown birds hopped on the pavement around their feet. One afternoon I noticed a boy trying to catch one, stalking it along the edge of the court. I understood his need to hold a bird. I stood against the wall admiring his stealth. He had a harelip and a lumpy skull under dirt-colored bristles of hair. His orange jumpsuit hung on the broomstick of his body, arms and legs poking out of its folds. I'd seen him hunched

255

over his lunch tray as the others slapped the back of his head. There were rumors about what he had done. Some said he had raped a little girl, some said murdered. He didn't look capable of either.

At the start of winter I saw him sitting on a slat bench patterned with crystals of frost, snow flurries blowing over the pavement. He was talking to a boy who stood a head taller than the rest of us, with pockmarked skin and an undershot jaw. When he strode among the others with his hands in loose fists, they dropped their heads and gave him room. It seemed unlikely that he would befriend the harelip. I stood as close to them as I could without being noticed, hands numb in the pockets of my jumpsuit. After a while, the tall boy bent and untied his shoes. They looked brand-new, stark white in the gunmetal light. Then the harelip slipped out of his own, the shabby color of dirty mop strings. Even from a few yards away, I saw how the rubber sole was coming loose. They made the switch, the harelip tying on the new shoes as the tall boy, wide shoulders bent, wedged his feet into the old ones. Later, when the tall boy had taken the basketball to shoot, the others keeping a respectful distance, I approached the harelip for the first time. I stood over him, my shadow falling across the bench where he sat. He looked up and waited for me to speak. My voice, when it came, was rusty. I had seldom used it there.

"How did you do that?" I asked.

"What," the harelip said, "you can talk?" His own speech was strange and nasal, the repaired cleft of his lip like a razor slash.

"Why did you trade shoes?"

The ugliness of his smile startled me. "His was better than mine."

I studied him. Up close, his eyes were glittering slits.

"His mama lives down at the end of my road."

"So?"

"So I know his family." He glanced over at the boys playing basketball. The snow had begun to flurry faster, dotting the bristles of his hair and the shoulders of his jumpsuit. "I'm getting out of here next week. I told him I'd kill his little sister."

My fists clenched inside my pockets. "Why would he believe that?"

The boy flashed his ugly smile again. "He knows what I'm in here for."

"You killed a little girl?"

"Naw. I just burnt some of her hair off. But I would have if she hadn't squealed that way. It made the neighbor man come out of

257

his house."

I stared at him, speechless. After a while, he turned to watch one of the brown birds pecking at a crack in the pavement, as if he had forgotten I was standing there.

That night I lay looking at the shine of the metal toilet in the dark, thinking not of the harelip but of the tall boy. I decided it was his blood that had made him weak in that moment on the bench. His love for his sister had given the harelip power over him, and maybe I was no different. It was my kin that had landed me where I was. If I hadn't cared what Hollis Odom did to my mama, I wouldn't have burned down his store and he could never have had me locked up. But I couldn't take hearing my mama disparaged, as much as it felt like I hated her. I couldn't let him get by with ruining her the way he had. He was the reason for what happened to us on the mountain and the reason I was in a cell. He had seen to it that I was put away for a long time. But my own moment of weakness had passed. I would be smarter when I finally got out of Polk County, more in control of myself. I wouldn't give Hollis Odom power over me. I hadn't forgotten that day in the hardware store, the panic in his eyes and the feel of his throat in my hands. I kept all of it with me. I grew even more determined to know about my father because Hollis Odom didn't want me to. As soon as I got out, I would go back to Millertown, maybe to my grandfather's house this time. I would only have to look up his name in a phone book to know his address. I would only have to call and hang up to find out if he was still alive.

I learned on the day before the harelip was to be released that the tall boy's moment of weakness had passed, too. It happened so fast I only saw the aftermath. He was being wrestled away by two guards, another running to them across the basketball court. He knelt over a twisted body, lips skinned back and mouth leaking ropes of foam. It was the harelip, lying facedown, arms broken and ears bleeding onto the pavement.

Laura

Them years Johnny was at Polk County, I couldn't sleep at night. I had nightmares about him and Mama locked up together in the dark. Sometimes it seemed like I was stuck in a cell myself. I could still feel my brother every day, even after all of our time apart. I wanted to go visit him, but he sent word for me to stay away. I didn't much want to see him like that anyhow, same as I couldn't have stood to see Mama.

Me and Clint decided not to stay in school and graduate. I found out I could quit when I turned seventeen, so I done it as soon as my birthday came. With Johnny gone and not coming back, there was no reason for me to be there anymore. I never had fit in right anyway. I still lived with Pauline and Larry. I didn't tell them I dropped out. I hated lying to them, but Pauline wouldn't have let me quit. So I took a job at a hamburger place and Clint still worked at the grocery store. We knowed one day we would marry, but we never talked about when.

At the end of April, we was at the breakfast table and Clint drove up. He didn't have to tell me he was coming or why. Someway I already knowed. I didn't make him wait. I got up from the table and flew out the back door. I ran across the ground to the driveway without any shoes on and none of my things except Mama's box. I had took to carrying it in my skirt pocket because I was afraid I was starting to forget her face. Just like school, there was no reason to stay. Percy was gone. Ever since he fell out the window he kept trying to get away. It was like he got a taste of freedom and wanted more. Every time the door opened he darted out. Then one day Larry came home from visiting the sick and found Percy dead in the street. Pauline and Hattie hugged each other and cried. I never thought I'd see them loving on each other. I remembered how Percy felt like a baby in my arms. We buried him out behind the shed. I pictured him under there with spiderwebs in his whiskers. Pauline and Hattie never was the same. They both got quiet. They didn't fuss much anymore. It was a sad house. Clint was the only one left that loved me. Percy was dead and Mama was gone and whatever love Johnny had for me was buried deep. I'm not dumb as everybody thinks. I went where love was and that was with Clint.

When I got in the car his blue eyes was shining. He pulled me on top of him and kissed my face all over. Backing out of the driveway he seen my feet curled up on the seat. "Lord, baby," he said. "You ain't got no shoes on." The way he laughed made chills all over me. He turned up the radio and we drove off. That was the best day of my life.

"Clint," I said halfway down the road, "what made you finally come and get me?"

His ears got red. He tapped his fingers on

the steering wheel. I didn't know if he ever was going to tell. Finally he said, "Well, Mama found this set of hair combs I bought for you. I had my eye on them for a long time, ever since I seen them down at Belk's. They was carved real nice with these jumping dolphins." Clint cleared his throat and wiggled around in the seat. I could tell he was embarrassed. "When I come in from work I seen Mama had busted them combs all to pieces. Soon as I walked in the door, she went to beating me over the head and shoulders with the box they come in. She said . . . she said, 'You ain't spending another cent on some old girl and us needing groceries.' "

I knowed Clint had cleaned up what his mama said. There was no telling what all she really called me. I didn't care. All I cared about was me and Clint being together.

"She claimed I'm just like Daddy," Clint said. "Why, I'd rather be like Daddy than her any day of the week. I swear, Laura, I bellered like a bull, I's so mad. I snatched her up by the hair of the head and for once she didn't have a thing to say for herself. I got to feeling sorry for her then and let her go. I reckon I couldn't hurt a woman, even one as mean as her. But I ain't never going back to that house."

"You don't never have to, Clint," I said. I put my head on his shoulder. "There ain't a thing to worry about." I believed what I told him. I thought our worries was over.

We drove straight to that green trailer beside of the lake. The trees was thick and the water lapped right up to the grass of the yard. Clint carried me down to the sand at the bottom of the hill because I didn't have any shoes on. He held me there for a long time looking out across the lake. "I ain't got to swim since Daddy died," he said. "I stayed in the water so much he said I ort to been borned a fish." I felt sorry for him. I knowed he was missing his daddy. Then we went up to the trailer. Clint opened the door and the carpet stunk where it got damp and mildewed. We spent most of the day cleaning out garbage. A lot of it was beer cans his daddy left behind. Whenever I seen Clint getting sad I snuck up behind him and tickled the back of his neck. That always made him smile.

Mr. Thompson, the manager at the grocery store, had a cousin that's a preacher. He said me and Clint could get married at his house, on the back porch overlooking a creek. I asked Larry to perform the ceremony first, but him and Pauline didn't approve of what I was doing. Clint's mama didn't want us to marry either, but I was eighteen and he was twenty, so we didn't need anybody's permission. It didn't matter what they thought.

Me and Clint decided to have the wedding on the first of May. It took a while to get to Mr. Thompson's house, little and white at the end of a long driveway. Mr. Thompson's wife met us at the door. She said, "You can call me Zelda, honey." She led me through the hall to the bedroom. It was cool in there, with thick carpet and roses on the wallpaper. There was a dress laid out on the bed. "Now, this is new with the tags on it," Zelda said. "I bought it for my daughter-in-law to wear to church, but she was too big for it." She held it up to me and frowned. "It might be loose, but we could safety-pin it." It was long and cream with scratchy lace. I didn't care if it was loose. I liked it anyway.

Louise, the cashier from the grocery store, set me down on the toilet seat and fixed my hair with a curling iron. She put some lipstick on my mouth and rubbed a little on my cheeks to make them rosy. She dusted my face with powder and said, "Your skin's so pretty, you don't need much." Then Zelda and Louise led me through the kitchen out to the deck, where Zelda had arranged her begonia pots in a circle. All of Clint's friends from the grocery store was gathered around. Somebody had brought their children, two little girls and a boy dressed up in bright colors. They whispered and giggled when I came out but they got shushed. All the talking stopped. Clint was standing with the preacher, a short man with glasses. When I stepped out on the deck in them too-big shoes that belonged to Zelda, Clint turned and looked at me. His face lit up with a grin. Then he did something I didn't expect. He busted out with great big sobs. They was like sobs of relief, the way somebody might cry if they made it through a bad accident. The preacher patted Clint on the back while he tried to hush. I was embarrassed, but I was happy.

I didn't cry myself because I wanted to be tough for Clint. I went to him and wiped his tears while his hiccups went away. I tried to listen to the preacher when he read from his book, but all I could hear was blood rushing in my ears. I looked at Clint in that ring of begonias and all them people crowded around to watch us get married. The sky was so blue and the grass so green, and down at the end of the yard a creek was running over rocks that was round and furry with moss, like the ones I used to step on at home.

We had to use the Thompsons' rings, but that was okay. Clint was saving up for the rings we really wanted. When the ceremony was over, we had a kiss that seemed too short for the mountains that was moving inside of me. Zelda took pictures and the flash was bright. Clint led me down the deck steps and everybody else poured into the yard behind us. The kids chased each other off looking like butterflies in their summer clothes.

Mr. Thompson was done firing up the grill for hamburgers. I closed my eyes and drunk in the charcoal smell of the rolling black smoke when he opened the lid. The others gathered up for a game of horseshoes. I drifted down the creek a little ways, to where I could breathe and take it all in. The wind picked up and blowed the smell of the grill toward me. The children came running along the bank and before I knowed it one of them, a girl with plaits, crashed into my knees. The shock ran all through me. I looked down and her face was like a little sun. She hugged my legs hard before she ran off. I shut my eyes and felt hot tears. I hadn't been touched by a child in a long time. Someway it made me think of Johnny.

It seemed like the Lord's way of saying the day was blessed.

It was getting evening by the time I walked back toward the house. Clint had left me alone, even though I seen him looking for me. He knowed I needed to take it all in by myself for a while. Everybody else was full but there was plenty of food left over. I was too tired to eat. I sunk down in a lawn chair on the grass beside of Louise. Me and her watched Clint up on the deck. He was talking with Mr. Thompson and drinking iced tea out of a plastic cup. I could tell Louise cared for Clint by the way she looked at him. "That boy's had a hard time of it," she said. "But he's been better since he found you." Louise reached out for my hand to squeeze. Her fingers shocked me, like the touch of that child had done. She looked back at Clint and said, "He's like one of my own sons. You know, I gave him my youngest boy's clothes after he got killed on that motorcycle. It makes me cry just about every time I see Clint wearing something of Randy's."

I didn't say anything, but I hated the thought of Clint in a dead boy's clothes. I wondered which ones belonged to Louise's son. Was it that knitted sweater I loved to see in winter, with deers leaping in a line across the front of it? Or them corduroy pants with a tiny hole in the knee that gave me little peeks of Clint's curly leg hair? It bothered me something awful to think about. All of them fabrics, wools and flannels and cottons, that I touched and pressed and ran my hands over when I kissed Clint, wasn't even his. They belonged to a dead boy. Then I thought of the worst thing of all. Clint said that silver rope chain I loved came from Louise. He wore it all the time, even in the water. I loved to see it shining on his collarbone. Now that chain would make me sick every time I looked at it, like a noose around Clint's neck. I wanted to throw it away and burn all them clothes. Maybe he was even wearing some of them right then. That white dress shirt that was yellowed at the armpits, them jeans that was faded at the knees, that old belt threaded like a poison snake through the belt loops might have belonged to Louise's dead son. I didn't want to ask. I couldn't stand to know. Clint was the only one that ever loved me right. Then I seen him laughing under the porch light with moths in his hair. His eyes shined whenever he smiled. I couldn't believe I was his wife. Finally, I had a family again.

Johnny

I hitchhiked from the detention center to Millertown with everything I owned in a duffel bag, the books from the woods, my notebook, the silver lighter, and an address written on a scrap of paper. On the highway I watched the shopping centers and motels and rest stops go past, taking in how the scenery had changed while I was gone. When the man who had picked me up let me out of his truck, I paused in the street to look at the Odom house. It was tall and weathered and seemed to be leaning. A spring wind picked up and flapped the shingles, a few scattered over the rotten roof. I went up the porch steps and stopped at the door listening for movement. I heard the slow creak of floorboards somewhere inside. I had decided on the way to the house that if nobody was home I would break in, but it sounded as though someone was there. I reached toward the doorbell and then changed my mind. I went to a moldering couch under the window and sat down to rest instead, dropping the duffel bag at my feet. I had waited a long time. I could take another minute to catch my breath. I leaned my head back and closed my eyes.

When I opened them there was a station

wagon pulling up to the curb, its engine dying with a rattle. A heavy woman struggled out from behind the wheel with a grocery bag in her arms. She came up the walk breathing hard, frowning up at me. She was wearing what looked like hospital scrubs, the top patterned with teddy bears. I couldn't see her eyes for the shine off her glasses. I rose from the couch and looked down at her.

"Didn't you see the sign?" she asked.

"Pardon me?"

"Sign right yonder over the doorbell. Says no solicitors."

"Oh," I said, putting on a smile. "I'm not selling anything."

She smiled back, still sizing me up. "What do you want then?"

"I'm looking for Frankie Odom. Is this the right house?"

"Depends on what you're after him for."

I came down the steps to her. "Let me get that for you, ma'am," I said.

"I can get it," she said, letting me take the bag. "What do you want with Frankie?"

"We're kin," I said, climbing the porch steps ahead of her.

"Kin? I been taking care of Frankie two years now and I never laid eyes on you. You're awful handsome. I believe I would've remembered." She snorted laughter.

"Are you Frankie's daughter-in-law?"

"Lord, no. I wouldn't have none of them turkeys. I just set with Frankie while his boys are gone to work. Name's Diane."

"It's nice to meet you, Diane," I said, shifting the bag to offer my hand. She looked down at it, flustered, then gave my fingers a quick, moist squeeze.

"What kind of kin are you?"

I smiled again, standing close. "I'm Frankie's grandson."

"Huh. I thought I done met all of Frankie's grandkids."

I only paused for a second. "Did you ever hear of Frankie's son named John?"

Diane stepped back and studied me. "I've heard tell of him. From what I know, none of the Odoms has seen hide nor hair of him for going on twenty years now."

"Yes," I said. "That's him." I willed the smile to stay on my face.

"You saying you belong to John?"

"That's what I'm saying."

She looked at me for a long time, lips pale and nostrils flaring. "Now, you didn't come over here meaning to cause any trouble did you? I reckon they had trouble out of some of their people back a few years ago, before I started coming around."

"No, ma'am," I said. "Did Hollis tell you something bad about me?"

Her face flushed. "I don't pay much mind to anything that comes out of that man's mouth. I reckon I can judge anybody for myself."

"All right," I said. "Can I see Frankie then?"

She paused, looking me over again. I tensed, waiting. "If you start anything, I'll put the law on you in a heartbeat. County jail is right down the street."

"I promise you," I said. "I just want to visit my grandfather one time."

"Well," she said, eyes softening behind the glasses. "I reckon anybody can understand that. If you're John's boy, Frankie will want to see you. But I ought to warn you, he's been getting senile these last few years. He might go to talking out of his head."

She pushed open the door and we stepped into a dim foyer onto humped and scarred linoleum. There was a stack of damp-looking newspapers against one wall and a smell of ancient cooking grease. I followed Diane down the hall into a kitchen with a ceiling so bowed it looked in danger of caving. In front of the sink there was a hole in the floor showing chewed-looking boards. Sun-faded curtains hung limp and mildewed on the window above it. Sitting in a wheelchair near the table was a birdlike man with tufts of hair standing up in corkscrews, wearing a yellowed undershirt and a pair of boxer shorts that bagged around his skinny thighs, holding a cigarette with a long ash.

Diane said, "I brung you somebody, Frankie."

Frankie Odom blinked at her and coughed wetly. "Did you get my cigarettes?"

"There's somebody here to see you," she shouted. "This here is John's boy."

I gave Diane her grocery bag and crossed the floor to stand before the wheelchair. His eyes were black and somehow familiar. Closer up, I saw dark threads left in his hair.

"John?" he said, bushy eyebrows lifting.

"Yes, this is John's boy. Your grandson," Diane said.

"I didn't bet on you ever coming back."

"He ain't never been here before, Frankie," Diane shouted patiently. "This is the first time you ever seen him."

"Some of them thought I might ort to report you a missing person but Hollis reckoned you didn't want to be found."

"See, I told you," Diane said to me. "He ain't all there."

"Eugene and Lonnie wanted me to call the sheriff," he went on. "Said she might

273

have done something to you."

"Now, Frankie," Diane scolded. "You're talking about this boy's mother."

"It's all right," I said, not looking away from his eyes.

"She was a pretty girl. Sweet little old girl. But some of them that come in the store said it might surprise you what a woman will do."

"Yes," I said.

"Frankie," Diane said, "this is your grandson. This ain't John. If you don't behave, you ain't getting these cigarettes." She put the bag on the counter.

"It's all right, ma'am," I said. "Can I ask you a favor?"

She paused, brows knitting together. "I reckon."

"Do you know if Frankie has any pictures of John?"

She hesitated. "Let me think. They're not much of a picture-taking family. I believe he might have some pictures in a box back here in one of these closets."

"Would you mind finding me one?" I asked. "Not to keep, or anything. It would mean a lot to me just to see what he looked like."

I waited, careful to keep my face relaxed. "Okay," she said. "There might be one of all the brothers together. But it'll take me a minute to locate anything in this mess."

"Thank you, ma'am. I'll just stay here and wait."

I watched her leave the kitchen, footsteps heavy on the rotting floorboards. Then I went to Frankie Odom and knelt before his wheelchair. The stench of him was powerful.

"Dad," I said. "It's been a long time."

"Hollis figured you run off, but some of them said you might be killed."

"What did you think?"

"I never did think that little old girl would kill anybody."

My jaw tightened. "So you thought I was alive somewhere."

He took a puff from his cigarette. "She made good coffee."

"Where did you think I would run off to?"

"She always done a good job on the bathroom, made them faucets shine."

"Where did you think I was for all these years?"

He plucked a shred of tobacco from his fat, purplish tongue. "I figured you went up north. You always did think you was borned in the wrong place."

"Did you ever try to find me?"

"No, I never did try to find you. None of

the rest of them did neither. They probably figured they'd divide your share. Greedy sons of bitches."

"What about you?" I asked softly. "Why didn't you look for me?"

"Shitfire, boy," he said, fumbling at the baggy lap of his boxers where the ash of his cigarette had fallen. "You know you always was the meanest one of the bunch."

I heard the creak of Diane's feet and turned to see her watching us warily from across the room, holding a square of picture. "This is the only one I found," she said. She came to me and I reached up from where I knelt to take it. I paused for a long time staring down at the creased black and white, a young boy with pitch hair and eyes, not smiling. I couldn't tell if he looked like me. I tried to hand it back but she said, "You can keep it."

"Thank you," I said. "I appreciate it." When I tucked the picture into my pocket I felt something else there, carried with me for a long time, its metal warm against my hip. "There's something I'd like to give Frankie before I go. I believe it belongs to him anyway." I pulled out the dogtags. "The chain was broken but I had it fixed." I rose to my feet, the chain dangling suspended between us, and dropped it over Frankie

Odom's head. He blinked up at me with owlish surprise. The dogtags hung limp from his neck, down his stained and rumpled undershirt. He stared at me for a long, uncomprehending moment. Then he said, "You can't let a woman run over you, son. She gets to acting up, you got to straighten her out, just like we done your mammy." He paused, still blinking up at me. "I ain't never told nobody what we done to her. By God, you better not either."

Laura

Clint's daddy was right. He should have been born a fish. I never knowed before how Clint loved to swim because we started out so far from the lake. All summer long, he swimmed every morning before work at the grocery store. At night when his shift was done, he pulled hisself with long strokes under the moon. Once me and Clint went out to the lake and took off our clothes. We got in the water and sunk like rocks. I wasn't scared, even though I can't swim. My hair floated up like a sea plant. I opened my eyes and it was dim. Clint had murky light all around him. His long legs and arms waved like tentacles. I wanted to live down yonder with him forever. Finally he took my hands and we floated back up. I was sad when we

277

broke the surface. I could tell he felt like plain old Clint again, sputtering water with his hair plastered down. I missed him when he was out swimming, but I never made any fuss about it. I knowed he needed his time in the lake, like Mama needed her time in the woods. When he was ready to come in he'd dry off and climb in our bed smelling like fish and muddy water, the smells I like best in the world.

At the end of June, Clint asked me to quit my job at the hamburger place because he wanted to take care of me. We made out all right on his salary and I didn't mind staying home. While Clint was at work I buried Mama's box under a cedar tree in the woods beside the lake. I didn't want to risk Clint finding it in the trailer. I hated keeping a secret from him, but showing anybody that box would have seemed like betraying Johnny and Mama. Sometimes I'd take the shovel and dig it up because holding it made me feel closer to Mama. Them's the times I'd cry for her and Johnny. But then Clint would come home and we'd wrestle all over the trailer. He'd make me laugh so hard I couldn't breathe.

Pretty soon, summer was gone and fall had come again. At the end of September, when it was too chilly to swim, Clint got nervous. Every night after work he paced around the edge of the water. When Mr. Thompson said he had a junked car for sale, I told Clint he ought to buy it. It was three hundred dollars, but I thought fixing it up might occupy his mind. It was an old orange Pinto that barely ran enough for Clint to drive it back to the trailer, but he loved it. He was always coming home with a new part for it. He'd stay under the hood some nights until way after dark. I'd get bored while he was working on the Pinto. There was a sadness growing in me and I couldn't pick one thing that caused it. I'd set on the cinder-block steps for hours looking out at the water, feeling lonesome.

Then one morning, I got sick. I hung over the toilet wishing for Clint, but he was gone to work. After a few minutes it finally dawned on me. That whole time I was lonesome, mine and Clint's child was already with me. I seen what had been causing my sadness. I just needed a brand-new little baby. I already knowed it was a boy, too, the way I know things sometimes. Later being pregnant was like a dream, because I couldn't touch or see him. It was like my womb was another planet off in the sky. But right then he was real to me. I closed my eyes and thought of Mama. I wondered if I was ever this real to her when me and Johnny was in her belly. I imagined my baby, warm and heavy like Percy in my arms. Me and Clint was close, but it would be even better to have a child inside my body. I needed to be that close with somebody. I wanted a chance to be the kind of mama mine wasn't to me.

When Clint got home from the grocery store I was standing on the trailer steps. He came up whistling and jingling his keys. He stopped as soon as he seen me, halfway across the grass with a big patch of yard still between us. I blurted out, "I'm fixing to have a baby." Clint turned white and dropped his keys. We had a time finding them later. Then he came to me like he was sleepwalking. He fell down on his knees and hugged my belly for a long time. I looked out across the lake. His hair smelled like the water.

Them first weeks, Clint would lay his sunshiny head on my belly and try to hear the baby's heart beating. Louise from the grocery store gave us a book of names. We stayed up late looking but never found one we liked. He'd rub my feet and we'd try to think up what the baby was going to look like. Clint wanted him to have black eyes, I wanted blue. Sometimes we'd even fight about silly things like that. Clint would get mad and stomp off. He'd slam the door so hard things would fall off the walls. I knowed he was going to swim, even though it was fall and getting cooler outside. He seemed glad about the baby, but someway it made him nervous, too. I figure he was thinking about his parents, and the bad times he had when he was a little boy. He always came back in the trailer and said, "I'm sorry for being hateful. I don't know what's wrong with me." Sometimes he was happy but sometimes he got quiet. He started staying outside more, working on his car. It helped Clint having something to work on. He still loved that Pinto.

Then one afternoon while he was at work and I was getting ready to cook supper, I heard a car door slam and a loud shrill voice. "You come on out of there, Clint!" the voice was saying. "I swear I'll burn that place to the ground with both of y'all in it!" I knowed right away it was Clint's mama, even though I never met her. I rushed around in a panic, looking for my shoes. "You ain't no better than that sorry daddy of yours!" Clint's mama was hollering. "I always knowed it!" Her voice was getting closer. I hurried through the living room and opened the front door just as she was fixing to pound on it.

"Where's Clint?" she screamed at me. She was swaying on her feet. I could tell she was drunk or maybe on pills. She didn't have any teeth and there was blue tattoos all over her arms. Her eyes was nothing like Clint's.

"He's gone to work," I said. I pulled the door shut behind me. It was a chilly day outside and I hugged myself, wishing I had put on a sweater.

"You're a liar," she said.

"No. He's at the store." I came down the steps and she backed up. "He'll be home around five-thirty if you want to come back then."

"Listen to you," she said. Her words was hard to make out for the slurring. "Trying to run me off from my own property. This place belongs to me, not you."

I didn't say anything, just stood still hoping she'd leave. She stared at me. Then she went to crying. "People's always doing me this way," she said. It was even harder to understand her words through the tears. "I ain't never had nobody. When I was little they was always passing me around. Didn't none of them want me." She wiped tears away with the back of her hand. "D'you know they took my first babies I had away from me? Put them with my ex-husband's

282

people and they never would come back to live with me. Then I had Clint and he picked his sorry old daddy over me every time."

I didn't know what to say. I wished I could make her feel better. I reached out my hand to her. I opened my mouth to ask her to come on in the trailer, but she went back to mad again. I never seen anybody act so mixed up since I left Pauline behind.

"But I'll fight for him this time, little girl!" she hollered. "You better believe it!" She stumbled backward into Clint's Pinto and fell. It was pulled up close to the trailer so he could work at night by the porch light. He never took it to the store. It was still in bad shape, so he drove the green car. "I been fighting people my whole life!" she screamed, spit flying off of her lips. "I been in fights all over this state!" When she got up I seen there was something in her hand. It was the jack handle Clint used to change the Pinto's tires. "I always win, too," she said. Then she raised the jack handle and I thought she was going to come after me with it. She crashed it into one of the Pinto's headlights instead. Then she beat out the other one. I couldn't stand to see her hurting Clint's car. I ran at her faster than I thought I could move. There was noises coming out of my throat that didn't seem like me. Clint's mama had her back to me, busting out the Pinto's windshield. I jumped on her from behind and grabbed hold of her face. My fingers was hooked into claws. They dug at her cheeks. I yanked her backward until she dropped the jack handle. She tried to sling me off but I hung on tight. She pried at my fingers but I wouldn't turn loose. She dropped to her knees and tried to crawl away. I couldn't let her go. I beat her head and bit her shoulders, put my whole weight on top of her. I wanted her to bear it all. "Don't you hurt Clint's car!" I yelled in her ear. "Don't you ever hurt Clint's car!" That's all I could make myself say, even though there was a lot more that I wanted to.

Pretty soon I felt tired and rolled off of her. I laid in the yard breathing so hard it hurt my throat. She stumbled up and started limping to her car. "You crazy little bitch!" she tried to holler, but her voice was nearly gone. "I'll call the law on you!" I laid there in the grass shaking for a long time after she took off. I couldn't believe what I had done to her. I asked the Lord to forgive me. I was sorry but most of all I was worried about my baby. I thought something had broke inside me, the way it broke in Mama.

Johnny

I left the Odom house in a daze, duffel bag over my shoulder. I had meant to search for my father after seeing Frankie Odom, but there was a weight on me when I walked out the door. I didn't know what to make of all I had heard, especially the last thing my grandfather had said to me. I wandered down the street and paused at the stop sign to look around, head heavy and muddled. I noticed a house on the corner that seemed out of place in such a seedy neighborhood. It was white with two stories, set back from the curb on a manicured lawn. Urns with ivy topiaries flanked the front door and a sign above it read "Imogene's" in fancy script. It was obviously a shop, not a residence. I crossed the grass thinking dimly of calling a cab to somewhere. When I opened the door I was standing in what looked like a living room crowded with musty-smelling furniture, price tags dangling off everything. A woman appeared out of nowhere, small with dyed hair and a powdered face. I assumed that she was Imogene. When I noticed the book in her hand my whole body tensed. Like always, a sign. But this time I would rather not have seen it. She was holding a slim volume, forefinger marking her place. It was a book of poems like one I had

285

found in the woods but in better condition, not swollen with moisture or specked with mildew. She smiled at me. "Can I help you with something?"

"What's that book you have?" I asked, buying some time to collect myself.

She looked at her hand. "Oh," she said. "I have a friend by the name of Ford Hendrix who travels all over the place hunting old books. The ones he doesn't keep, he brings to me." She paused, maybe deciding if I was dangerous. I must have passed inspection because she smiled at me again. "I've got more upstairs if you're interested."

I thanked her then excused myself and hurried up the stairs. At the end of a narrow hall there was a room with books shelved from floor to ceiling. I ran my fingers over the spines, closed my eyes and took in the good smell. There were no others like those I found in the woods, but if I hadn't been broke I would have bought one anyway.

I went quietly back downstairs, meaning to sneak out, but a square of door in a nook behind the stairwell caught my eye. It looked inviting with light falling through its cracks. I glanced over my shoulder as I turned the knob, feeling like an intruder even though the shop was a public place, and stepped out into the sun. There was a deck with garden furniture and more topiaries in pots. At the edges of the property a tall wood fence blocked out the neighboring duplex on one side and hid an overgrown lot behind it. I stood there among the plants, pots crowded under glass hothouses and bell jars, ivy and fern leaves trailing everywhere, and had a moment of disbelief that I was free. I would never see my cell at Polk County again. I needed to think about finding work and a place to stay, but the deck was so peaceful, I couldn't resist sitting down for a while in one of the flaking wicker chairs. My whole body sagged, my arms and legs going limp with exhaustion. I hadn't realized how bone tired I was, not just from that morning at the Odom house, but over the past four years locked up in prison. I looked at my duffel bag resting on my lap and thought of my notebook inside. If I could clear my head, maybe it would come to me what to do next. I took out the notebook and a pen, but after only a few lines my eyelids grew heavy. A cool wind stirred through the plants and blew over me like a spell from a fairy tale. I felt my fingers loosening on the pen as I nodded off. I don't know how long I dozed before Imogene's voice jerked me suddenly awake, the notebook sliding off my lap and landing at my feet.

"Didn't find one you liked?" she asked, standing in the doorway behind me.

I jumped up as if I'd been caught stealing. "Not this time," I said.

Imogene smiled. "Well, my friend said he'd probably be by sometime today with another load of books. You ought to come back later and see what he brings."

I had no intention of going back. But when I left the shop, I still didn't know where I was headed. I could have tried to find Laura, but I wasn't ready to see her yet. It would have been like facing up to all I had done and seen since we were together last. I thought of the Lawsons, who had been good to me when I lived with them. Not far down the street from Imogene's, I saw a phone booth outside a convenience store. I hesitated and then went inside to buy cigarettes first, a habit I'd picked up at the detention center. There was a long line at the counter and the cashier was slow. I stood under the buzzing fluorescents shifting from foot to foot, something nagging at me. After paying for the cigarettes, I walked out to the phone booth, tucking the pack into my breast pocket.

I was looking up the Lawsons' number

when it hit me that I'd left my notebook behind. I froze, dropping the phone book to dangle at the end of its cord. I ran all the way back to Imogene's with my heart threatening to give out on me. When I got there, throat raw and side aching, I barely registered the red truck parked at the curb. I didn't bother to go inside the shop. I went around the house to where the garden deck was, praying the notebook would still be where I'd left it. I stopped in my tracks on the bottom step. There was a man sitting in the wicker chair, with long white hair under a greasy baseball cap. He was holding the notebook in his hands, so absorbed in his reading that he didn't notice me. It took a second to comprehend what I was seeing. Then I crossed the deck in a few leaping steps, knocking over a flower pot, and snatched the notebook away from him. The man stared at me with wild eyes. I was assaulted by the stink of his sweat.

"Hey, sorry," he said, holding up his hands as if to prove they were empty. I saw that his ring finger was missing, a smooth, pink nub where it should have been. I backed off a few paces. "I assume that belongs to you," he said. Standing, he was a striking figure in spite of his dirtiness, tall with broad shoulders and a sunken belly. His hair was white but his face was smooth. It was impossible to guess how old he was.

"You should mind your own business," I said over the thud of my heart.

"I know, I know," the man said. "But I had a good reason."

I looked down at the notebook, gripping it so tightly my fingertips were purple. Slowly, it sank in that someone had read the words between the covers. "You had a good reason," I repeated. I thought of lunging at him again, but the image of that smooth, pink nub on his hand held me back. "What the hell are you talking about?"

"It'll take some time to explain."

"Explain what?"

"I needed to read your poems."

I stared at him blankly, unable to speak.

The man grinned, teeth bright in his sun-browned face, and stepped toward me. I tensed, prepared to fight. "Listen, are you hungry?" he asked.

"What?"

"Let me buy you a hamburger and I'll tell you all about it." He thrust out his hand but I didn't take it. "Name's Ford Hendrix."

"Do you know me somehow?"

"You could say so."

My mouth went dry. I looked at his damaged left hand, now dropped at his side, and back at his bloodshot eyes. "What do you want with me?"

"I want to help you, that's all."

"What makes you think I need helping?"

"I had a vision," he said. "You were in it."

I stood gaping at him for a long time, wondering if it was possible that I was having a dream. Then I followed him like a sleepwalker to his truck, because he had read my poems. He knew me better than anyone else on earth now, even Laura. But there was another reason I went. It was the missing ring finger. I needed to know how he lost it.

We didn't speak as he drove with the windows down, bits of trash whirling everywhere. I couldn't have carried on a conversation if he'd tried to talk. I still wasn't sure if all that had happened since I'd left the detention center that morning was real or one long hallucination. He took me to a bar and grill on the outskirts of town and we went inside where it was dim and hot. He stood at the counter and ordered cheeseburgers from a man in a stained apron. Two men drinking coffee by the window nodded as we passed. We sat down and stared at each other across the table. A fly buzzed between us.

"You say you had a vision about me."

291

"Yes."

"What does that mean?"

"I take after my grandfather. People called him the Prophet of Oak Ridge."

"So you're a prophet?"

Ford grinned like all of this was funny. "I was born fifteen years after he died, but my mother told me stories about him. He was always roaming the woods and one day, after he had been missing for a few weeks, he showed up at the general store in town and told his neighbors he'd seen a vision. Said a voice told him to sleep with his head on the ground for forty days and nights and he'd see the future. He predicted Bear Creek valley would be filled with factories that would help this country win the greatest war ever fought. People thought he was crazy. They locked him up for a while at the county farm, but now they know he was right. Twenty-eight years after he died, the factory was built in Bear Creek valley where they made the uranium for the first atomic bomb."

"What's any of that got to do with me?" I asked, working to keep my composure. The man in the apron brought our food on a tray and left without speaking.

"Nothing, except he's the reason I see visions. It never happened until after I lost this finger." He held up his hand. "That's when I found God and the voice started speaking to me." He took a bite of cheeseburger, mustard squirting down his chin. My food sat untouched on the table. Smelling it turned my stomach.

"How'd you lose it?" I asked.

He raised his eyebrows. "You mean my finger? It happened while I was noodling for catfish. Some people call it grabbling. That's where you wade out in the water and feel along the bank for holes where catfish go to spawn. The female lays her eggs in there and then the male moves in to guard them. If you stick your hand in his hole, he'll bite it and you can pull him out. I was in the lake up to my neck, water so cloudy I couldn't see a thing, even when I ducked under. The trouble with noodling is you never know what you're going to get. That time it was a snapping turtle, bit my finger clean off."

I felt a vein pulsing in the middle of my forehead. I knew that he was lying. It was something about the way his eyes shifted. "That's not what happened," I said.

"Well, I wish that's what happened." He grinned again in that maddening way.

For a while I watched him eat in silence, smearing ketchup on his plate with his french fries, looking out the window as if I wasn't even there.

"What did you see?" I asked.

"Hmm?"

"In the vision."

"Not much. Just that you were coming to us."

"Who's us?"

"Me and my wife, Carolina."

I shook my head and laughed for what felt like the first time in years. "You're one crazy son of a bitch."

"Maybe," he said. "But so are you. Because you believe me."

He was wrong. I didn't believe him, but I felt like I needed to know who he was. When we finally walked out of the bar and grill, it seemed we had been there for decades. Ford fished around in his pocket for his keys and asked, "Where can I drop you off?"

I thought about it. "I don't know. Just take me back to town."

"Where you staying?"

I took out a cigarette. "Nowhere right now. But I'll figure it out."

Ford fell silent, leaning on his truck. I lit the cigarette and smoked, watching cars pass on the road. Finally he said, "Why don't you come and stay with me for a while?"

I turned to him, startled. "Huh?"

"I've got a shed with electricity. It's quiet out there. No kitchen or toilet, but all you have to do is walk across the yard. You can eat with us."

"What about your wife?"

"She's expecting you." I pretended not to notice another allusion to visions.

"I'm not going to sponge off of you and your wife."

He laughed. "I don't expect you to. I've got trees that need trimming, a tractor to fix, tobacco to set out. Me and Carolina can't handle all that land by ourselves. I was planning on hiring a man this summer. It might as well be you."

I shook my head, part of me still not believing what was happening. I wondered if he would be inviting me into his home if he knew I was fresh out of prison. "I can't."

"Just for a while. You can't get any writing done without somewhere to stay. I'll give you a few minutes to decide. You can let me know when you make up your mind."

"Well," I said, taking a last draw from my cigarette and pitching it into the parking lot gravel. "If you're a prophet, I guess you already know what I'm going to do."

Ford smiled and opened the truck door. "Carolina will be glad to see you."

295

Laura

As time went by, Clint got more and more nervous about the baby. Every chance I had, I told him how happy our son would be. "He's going to grow up right here in the fresh air, beside of the water." Clint acted like he believed me, but I knowed he was worried because of his mama. I didn't think she'd ever come back after what I done to her, but I was wrong. Every once in a while she'd get mad about Clint leaving her and drive over to the trailer to let him know about it. Once it was the middle of the night. We was in the bed asleep. Next thing we knowed, she was out in the driveway laying on her car horn. Every dog for miles was barking. It scared me and Clint half to death. He jumped up and ran outside with just his drawers on. I got up to look and there was Clint's mama, yelling at the top of her lungs. "Clint," I called out the front door. "Are you all right?"

"It's okay," he said over top of her screaming. "Go on in the house."

I was real proud of Clint. He came back in and left her out yonder cussing by herself. Before she went home she drove over in our grass and spun her tires. She tore the yard all to pieces. I held Clint in my arms the rest of the night. He was shaking like a leaf.

Next time she came, me and Clint had been to the store to buy ice cream. It was dusk, and she was setting out by the water in the December cold, waiting on us when we got back. We had been laughing all the way down the road, but when we pulled in and seen her there, our day was ruint. Clint said, "Just stay in the car. I'll run her off."

I rolled the window down so I could hear them fussing. "Me and your daddy never was divorced," she hollered in Clint's face. "Every last thing that son of a bitch had belongs to me." Clint took her by the arm and started steering her back to her old beat-up car. "This place belongs to me!" she shrieked, trying to get away from him.

After he forced his mama back in her car she finally drove off, slinging mud and gravel everywhere. I got out of our car and Clint went on to the trailer with his head down. One of his arms was bleeding where she'd scratched him. I took the ice cream in and made us each a bowl. We set down at the little kitchen table to eat. Clint wouldn't speak or look at me. I didn't want to make him feel worse, but I was too worried to keep my mouth shut. "What your mama said, about this place belonging to her . . ."

"Don't pay no attention," he said, staring into his bowl. "She's all talk." I could tell he wasn't too sure, but, like always, he kept his worries quiet.

After that run-in with his mama, Clint quit eating as much and started losing weight. I'd take hold of his sharp hipbones and say, "I got to fatten you up. I can't get big as a house all by myself!" I acted like I was kidding, but he went around with dark rings under his eyes not smiling near as much, and I didn't know how to make him feel better. It should have been a happy time for us. One night I couldn't help crying beside of him in the bed. He knowed why I was upset. He said, "I'm sorry. I can't help it."

I asked if he didn't want the baby, but he swore that wasn't it. He said it was hard to say out loud what was wrong. I realized laying there I didn't want him to tell, because what if it was me. But looking back I don't believe it was. Clint loved me and the baby.

Then one night he went swimming and didn't climb back in the bed smelling like fish and muddy water. I woke up and his side was empty. Dawn was coming under the curtains. I put on my coat and went down to the water with my hands on my belly. I looked across the lake, like me and Clint did when we first came there. Fog hung over the still blue. Everything was quiet. Me and the baby knowed he wasn't coming back.

I set by the water for two days like a sailor's wife anyway, hardly ever going back in the house. I wanted to believe Clint was just holding his breath extra long this time. Pretty soon he would break the surface, hung with algae and sputtering water. I had a blanket to wrap him in just in case. It was cold outside and I'd have to warm him up.

On the third day, not long after the sun rose, I saw red and blue lights twinkling through the trees on down the shore. I tried to get up but I was too stiff. I stumbled around for a long time on the sand. When I finally got to where I could walk, I followed them swooping lights, dragging Clint's blanket behind me. I picked my way along the edge of the water, climbing over fallen trees and rocks. Seemed like the blanket got snagged every few feet, but I kept going. Weak and cold as I was, I don't know how I made it. Them lights got brighter the closer I got. Finally the woods thinned out and it got easier to walk. Not far ahead, I seen the neighbor man's dock and people standing on it. Me and Clint didn't know him too well. I couldn't have picked him out of a lineup. I came out of the trees and onto his grass. I meant to ask him what the lights was for, if I could figure out which one he was. That's when I seen the police cars and the ambulance with its back doors throwed open. Two men was rolling a stretcher across the yard with a lumpy shape strapped to it. Even under a wet-spotted cover, I knowed the shape well.

I wandered toward the people standing around. I didn't have any more questions. I just needed help for my baby. I was fixing to fall down.

"Hey, little gal," the neighbor man said, coming to meet me. He had a toothpick in his mouth. He didn't look too tore up about what was going on. "I found that feller there drownded under my dock, skinny boy with right longish hair. Had a silver chain around his neck. Reckon you know him?"

"I know him," I said. Then my legs gave out.

Johnny

It was a long drive with the windows down, subdivisions and warehouses and restaurants turning to long stretches of farmland. The farther we went, the more the spring smell of cut grass replaced the stink of factory smoke. We traveled west for at least an hour on a two-lane highway, the afternoon heading toward evening. Then he turned off the highway onto a narrow back road that wound and twisted through a patch of thick, dark woods, onto another stretch of cracked asphalt that led us through the trees and petered out, turning into a dusty gravel lane with rolling hills on both sides.

The whole time, Ford talked about his life. He said he was born on a farm outside of Oak Ridge and all those years hearing about his grandfather's visions had given him a lust to see things for himself. He got an inheritance from an aunt he'd never met and ran off to travel the world. He claimed he had seen it all, the Highlands of Scotland, the pyramids of Egypt, the Great Wall of China. He said he'd lived on just about every continent and in every state of the union but nothing he saw satisfied him. "What I really wanted to see," he said, "was the future. Like my grandfather did." I didn't ask about his visions, although he probably wanted me to. I kept quiet, waiting for him to slip up and reveal who he really was. He said that even as he roamed, he knew he'd return someday. When he finally went home to the farm where he was born, his parents had been dead for three years and the house they had left him was falling down. He demolished the remains by himself, breaking off chunks of crumbling plaster, tearing off shingles, knocking down walls with a sledgehammer. Then he mentioned the books he found in the rubble.

"I moved some rotten boards I was hauling off and there they were, had been hidden in the house for who knows how long, waiting for somebody to find them. They weren't rare or valuable, just old. One of them was *Great Expectations*. It must have been a gift to somebody, because there was a name written on the inside cover and a date, June 20, 1889. Well, it was the twentieth day of June in 1957 when that book turned up. I think finding those books got me reading and writing. I know it's what made me a collector."

I looked out the window, trying to keep my face neutral. He couldn't have known about the poetry books, hidden in the duffel bag at my feet. It felt like proof that we were connected. He went on talking, telling me how he camped out on the farm until he had enough money to buy a trailer. He did all kinds of work, pulling tobacco, roofing houses, cleaning chimneys, mowing yards. It took a while to save enough and during that time he built bonfires in the field and read and wrote and played his guitar every night under the stars. He said an odd thing happened while he was living outdoors. One by one stray dogs had come out of the woods into the light of his fire and by the time his year of camping was done he had six of them, sleeping at his side and sharing the meat of the animals he hunted. "I still keep a pack of dogs around," he said with a smile. "They seem to like my company." He also claimed he had finished the first of several novels he'd written that year. I wasn't sure if I believed any of what he was telling me, much less that he was a writer. He never let it slip how he really lost his finger, but I knew I had to find out.

After what seemed like miles of bottom-land with not a house in sight, Ford grinned and said, "I bet you thought we were never going to get here." From the road I saw his trailer at the end of a dirt driveway, sur-rounded by hills and woods and grassy fields. It had been built onto, with a long porch across the front hung with plants and wind chimes. When we got out of the truck, a pack of dogs just as Ford had described came running. There were at least eight of them, mutts of all sizes and colors, tongues hanging and tails wagging. Ford patted their heads as they jumped on him, muddying his jeans with their paws. Then I looked across the yard and saw the wife, Carolina.

There was no way to hide my surprise. I had been expecting a graying older woman but this was a girl of no more than eighteen, wearing a floppy T-shirt and cutoff shorts. She was standing barefoot in the balding grass by the clothesline. She paused to watch me cross the yard and her eyes never left my face, even as Ford went to kiss her cheek. "He looks different than I imagined," she said.

It was hard to stop looking at Carolina as she went back to the laundry. She wasn't beautiful, but there was something about the geography of her face. She had dirty blonde hair, olive skin, and light eyes under heavy brows. Climbing the porch steps behind Ford, I nearly stumbled looking back at her. Then I was inside the trailer and the clutter was hard to walk through. There were books everywhere, spilling out of cardboard boxes, piled on the matted shag carpet, stacked against the dark paneling walls, their dusty smell mingling with mildew and woodsmoke and cooking grease.

Ford showed off his collection proudly, like a father. "Look," he said, holding up one of the books. "This is a first edition, John Steinbeck's *Burning Bright*. It's in good condition, still got the dust jacket. It's probably worth around two seventy-five, but I couldn't part with it." He replaced it carefully and took the next book off the pile. "Here's another first edition. Harriet Beecher Stowe, *We and Our Neighbors.* I had somebody offer me eighty dollars for this one." I began picking through the books myself, turning them over, enjoying the weight and heft of them in my hands. Finally, I lifted a thick hardcover from the coffee table and saw Ford's name on the spine.

"You really are a writer," I said, tracing the faded gold letters.

Ford laughed. "You mean you didn't believe me?"

Then Carolina was standing in the door with a clothes basket on her hip. "He's been nominated for a Pulitzer Prize," she said.

Ford went to her and took the basket. "Carolina likes to brag on me, don't you, honey?" He sat down on the flowered velvet couch and began folding clothes. I felt awkward, standing there with my hands in my pockets.

"Do you want something to drink?" Carolina asked, heading into a small kitchen divided from the living room by a bar with mismatching stools.

"No, thanks," I said.

"Have a seat and I'll fix you boys some

supper."

Ford looked up from the clothes basket. "You don't have to cook, Carolina. Me and Johnny had a bite to eat in town."

"That was a long time ago," she said. "I bet Johnny's starving by now. I've got some pork chops thawing out anyway." Reaching into an upper cabinet for the frying pan, she looked over her shoulder and smiled at me. A tingle raced along my spine.

I moved a stack of books from an old recliner and sat down. It was so comfortable that I nearly dozed, listening to the sound of pork chops frying and Carolina talking about her garden and the fruit trees she was nursing. A contented feeling washed over me, an ease sinking into my limbs as she talked and Ford sorted through his books, dividing them into piles according to those he would keep and those he would sell.

When Carolina called us to supper, we ate around a small table with our knees and elbows touching. Carolina lit candles and passed around a cheap bottle of wine. "We're not always this fancy," she said. "This is a special night." It took a minute to realize she meant because I was there. I wondered how long it would take her to slip me a note or brush against me or make some excuse to get me alone, like girls at the children's home and at school always had. I waited for the greediness in her eyes, but it never came. She was only friendly and comfortable with one leg tucked beneath her in the chair.

At some point I noticed that Carolina wasn't eating her own cooking. When I asked about it, she said, "I can't hardly stand to eat meat." Ford claimed it was because her heart was too tender. He reached out to touch her hair. "It doesn't bother me for other people to eat it," she said. "I just can't hardly stand to myself." I wondered what she would think if she knew that I had skinned rabbits and squirrels for my mama to cook, ripped the greasy flesh from their small bones without a pang of remorse.

When Ford's plate was clean, he pushed back from the table and said, "I've got to go check my mole traps. They're tearing the garden all to pieces this year. Carolina, will you show Johnny where he's bunking tonight?"

I followed her across the grass with my duffel bag slung over my shoulder. She carried a blanket and pillow in her arms. It was turning dark and the yard was a chorus of crickets and tree frogs. There was no sign of Ford checking his traps and the dogs were gone. They had probably followed him to the garden. It seemed Carolina and I were the only people for miles. There was a light burning in the shed and the door was propped open. It was tidier inside than I had imagined, the concrete floor swept with cardboard boxes and gar den tools moved to one side. There was a lone army cot in the corner.

"Ford brought this bed out here a long time ago," Carolina said, her voice startling me. I wished she hadn't mentioned Ford's vision. There was an awkward silence.

"Was he really nominated for a Pulitzer?" I asked.

"Twice. I seen it in a magazine. People don't believe it because of the way he lives, but this is the life Ford chooses for hisself. Sometimes people come out here and ask him to sign a book. Once there was a man from the newspaper who wanted to write an article. Ford talked to them, but he doesn't like being found." She paused, looking down at the blanket and pillow she was holding. She seemed tired, and maybe sad. "He's got an agent that sends him letters sometimes. She wants him to write another book, but Ford's stubborn. You can't make him do anything before he's ready to."

We fell silent again, standing in the middle of the shed looking at each other. I wondered what she was doing there with some crazy old man. I couldn't imagine what she was thinking about me. Finally she said, "Well, here's you a pillow and blanket." She delivered them into my arms and then, without warning, her hands were on me, moving quick and fluttery over my abdomen and ribs like butterflies. My scalp prickled at her touch. I couldn't move. Her face was still, as if nothing unusual was happening. It was the manner of a doctor giving an examination. "You got a pain somewhere, Johnny," she said. I could smell her hair, like the woods after a thunderstorm. Then the small hand settled on my chest. She nodded as if she had suspected all along. "It's right in here."

I opened my mouth, tried to think what to say. "No. I'm all right."

"Since I was a little girl," she said, "whenever I lay my hands on somebody, it's like they know right where to go to help that person."

I was about to tell her that I didn't feel any different when I noticed a loosening in my chest, a lightening, as if someone had taken a rock off it. I took a deep breath and it was like I hadn't been breathing at all before. Then immediately I felt foolish and weak, having fallen so easily for some kind of hypnotic suggestion. It wasn't as much of a mystery anymore what this girl was doing with Ford. She was every bit as crazy as he was. I plucked her hand off my chest but she didn't seem to notice. She smiled and said, "I guess I'll go on and give you some privacy." She paused and turned back before closing the door. "Sometimes in the spring it still gets chilly at nighttime. I've got a little heater I can bring out if you get to needing one." Then she was gone. I stood in the middle of the shed for a long time, wondering what I was doing there myself.

Laura

People said Clint did it on purpose but I think he was just trying to stay down where it was peaceful a little while longer. Maybe he sunk too far and couldn't get back up before he ran out of breath. But I don't believe he wanted to leave me. I think he wanted to see our baby get born and be a good father to him. Right after he drowned, I worried things had been passed down from Mama that I didn't want. I thought I might be cursed to live out the same awful things that happened to her. I knowed from the stories she told there's been a lot of sad-

310

ness in our family. Bad times seem to follow our people around. For a minute I wished I was born to somebody else. Then I got to thinking about Mama and cried again. It wasn't her fault that Clint drowned. It wasn't anybody's.

Not long after they found Clint, there was a knock on the trailer door. I snuck a peek out the window and seen Clint's mama smoking a cigarette on the step. I opened the door and looked at her. Since Clint was gone, I didn't hardly have any feelings.

"Well, are you going to let me in?" she asked real hateful. She came in and looked around. "This place looks like a hogpen." I didn't answer her. I just wanted her to leave. "I'll get right down to it," she said, tapping ashes in her palm. "This place never did belong to Clint. When his sorry old daddy died, it fell to me. You can't stay here."

I could have told her that I didn't care. Clint might have wanted our baby to live by the water, but the lake scared me now. Instead I asked Clint's mama, "You're going to set your own grandbaby out?" Not because I wanted to stay, just because I didn't understand what kind of person she was. I couldn't figure out how anybody could be like that.

"I ain't setting out my grandbaby," she

said. "I'm setting out you."

"But the baby's inside of me."

"It won't always be," she said. She had a glint in her eyes that made me feel sick.

"What do you mean by that?"

"Nothing," she said. But I seen a smirk at the corners of her mouth. She was wary of me since that time I jumped on her, but she must have hated me so bad she couldn't resist saying something else mean. "You ain't fit to raise no youngun."

I took a step toward her. I felt something coming loose in me again. It was a bad feeling, like somebody else taking over. "Don't you say that," I warned her. Even my voice didn't sound right to my ears. She took a step back and I seen her hand searching behind her for the door handle. "Don't you say a thing like that to me."

I put my hands on my belly and balled up the cotton shirt stretched across it. She opened the door and I followed her to it. She backed down the cinder-block steps, keeping her eyes on me. "You better be off my property by tomorrow morning," she said. "If you ain't, I'm coming back with the law." It was all I could do not to take after her. I couldn't stand to be threatened that way. I seen what happened to Mama. She hollered before she got in the car, when she was too far away for me to come after her, "You ain't fit!"

Like I said, I didn't care to leave the trailer. It was too sad without Clint. I couldn't quit thinking about them fat yellow curls I'd never touch again. I didn't care if I ever seen water again the rest of my life. I was too tired to care about much of anything. The next day, I took the shovel out to that cedar tree in the woods. It was early and fog hung low to the ground. No birds was singing. I dug up the box's grave. The ground was soft under the cedar tree needles, easy to loosen up. The sound of the dirt sifting was like Clint whispering to me. Then it turned into Clint's baby whispering inside my belly. Then it turned into Mama whispering to herself all them miles away, wherever they put her. I couldn't make out the words. It didn't take long to reach the box. It wasn't buried deep. I knelt and took it in my hands. This time it didn't comfort me. At least I had Clint's baby. I was sad, but I wasn't alone.

I took one scratched-up suitcase with some clothes and Mama's box in it. I walked to the bait shop and called Mr. Thompson to pick me up. I hated to, but him and Zelda and Louise was the only friends I had. We didn't talk much in the

313

car. We'd never been together by ourselves before. It was a pretty long drive down the interstate, back toward Millertown, before I was at the house where me and Clint got married. I was glad the baby could be there. Maybe while he was inside me he could see through my eyes. I tried to send him a memory of me and Clint standing on the deck in a circle of begonias. Zelda came out to the car to walk me across the yard. "Now, I ain't staying long," I told her.

She laughed. "Surely me and Ralph ain't that bad."

"I just mean me and the baby will have our own place, soon as I get a job."

Mr. Thompson took my suitcase as we climbed up the porch steps. He reached across my shoulder and held open the front door for me. "You know you can stay as long as you want. Clint Blevins was like a son to me. But I've already got the job situation figured out for you. We've been short-handed over at the store for a while now. I've just been putting off hiring anybody. Louise can show you how to work the cash register."

Mr. Thompson stood there with my suitcase holding the door open as Zelda put her arms around my shoulders and tried to comfort me. I wished I could explain to

314

them what it felt like to know kindness like that, after all the bad times I'd lived through.

I stayed with the Thompsons for two more months. I slept in that room with roses on the wallpaper where my wedding dress was laid out on the bed. When it was warm enough I stood out on the deck and looked off at the creek. Seemed like I could feel Clint beside me, slipping a ring on my finger all over again. When the ache in my chest got too big, I'd go back inside. I worried it wasn't good for the baby, for me to hurt like that.

Mr. Thompson had sweet eyes and a nice face, and being around him made me think it might be all right to have a daddy. When he noticed a hole coming in the toe of my shoe he said to Zelda, "Get that youngun something decent to put on her feet." One day he got worried because Zelda's blood used to get low when she was expecting. He made me liver and onions and I choked it down to ease his mind. He made sure I got plenty of milk, too. My belly growed bigger and marks striped my breasts. Sometimes I seen the baby's fist or foot ripple across my middle. I talked to him in my head, about his daddy and Mama and Johnny. I told him all Mama's stories about our people, even about the curse and the haint blue eyes. One time Mama had said, "Granny thought I broke the curse." But I wondered if she had. If there was any such thing as curses, I knowed this baby would be the one to break it. He'd bring an end to the suffering all of us had lived through, going all the way back to them great-aunts Mama used to tell us about. Whatever it was in our blood that brought bad things down on us, this baby would chase it away.

It was all right working at the grocery store, even though my ankles swelled up from being on my feet. It made me feel closer to Clint, spending my days how he did when I wasn't around. Mr. Thompson had hired a new bagboy after Clint drowned named Roy. His face turned red when I stared at him. I liked to watch him work because I knowed it was what Clint used to do. There was sad times, but mostly it was a comfort being there. Louise and Mr. Thompson and the other cashier Debbie was always cutting up. It was a happy place, with people bustling around. I seen why Clint liked working there.

One day Louise hollered at me from her cash register. "Hey, Laura, I just about forgot. There's a house come open for rent right down the street from me. It's little but it don't cost much, and you and the baby won't need a lot of room." That evening me and Zelda rode out with Louise to take a look at it. Right off I knowed it would be fine, even though one of the front window-panes was cracked. It was bright yellow, my favorite color in the world. Down the bank from its yard there was a car wash. Louise said, "Now, it might get noisy over yonder during the day." I didn't mind because I'd be at the store and the baby would be there with me. Zelda had offered to fix up Mr. Thompson's office in the back with a bas-sinet and a playpen. She said she'd keep him in there while I worked. She liked to hang around the store anyway, and she didn't have any grandbabies yet. When I tried to say no, she said, "Please let me do this for you." So the noise from the car wash wouldn't bother the baby's naps. Another good thing was Louise being my neighbor, we could ride to and from work together and I'd help pay for the gas.

My only worry was the high porch. It had a trellis around it but I could see junk and weeds underneath. Climbing up and down them steps might be dangerous for a tod-dler. But I'd been saving a little bit of money out of my paycheck since I'd been working. It wasn't much but I hoped by the

317

time the baby was walking I'd be able to rent a better house for us, maybe something away from town. The door was locked but I cupped my hands around my eyes and looked in the window. There was spots on the carpet but the room looked all right. I could picture my baby playing there on the floor. It was next to a car wash but not a laundrymat. I thought Clint would be proud of me.

Johnny

I couldn't get my mind off what had happened with Carolina. I pulled the chain on the lightbulb overhead and lay listening to the sounds outside. The blanket and pillowcase smelled like rainwater and I imagined that's what she washed them in. The cot was more comfortable than it looked. I didn't know I was asleep until a knock on the shed door woke me up. I rose and looked around, disoriented in the dark. Ford opened the door without permission and stood on the threshold like something from a dream, a tall figure with white hair flowing out. He looked clean for the first time since we'd met. He was holding a guitar, his dogs circling behind him. "Sorry to wake you," he said. "I got me a good fire going. Thought you might want to come out and sit for a while."

We walked to the mowed field on the other side of the trailer, dogs slinking at our heels. In the middle, a fire writhed and popped. There were three lawn chairs pulled close to the flames. Carolina sat in one of them with her legs drawn up. She looked up and smiled, face bathed in orange. We took our seats and Ford strummed absently at his guitar. "Something about a fire helps me think," he said. Ford's fire had the opposite effect on me. It helped me not to think. I leaned back my head and looked up at the stars and my mind was clear. Ford played and for a while Carolina sang along in a high, sweet voice. Then she trailed off, seeming to drowse, and there was only the clumsy music of Ford's guitar. The two of us talked softly over his strumming, and all the while I looked at his left hand moving on the guitar's neck, the smooth pink remains of his ring finger.

"So what really happened to it?" I asked.

He smiled, still strumming. "My finger? Well, I was staggering home from this country bar at the crack of dawn one morning. I was getting sleepy, so I slipped off the road into a cornfield. I passed out and when I came to it was later in the day. First the sun was glaring in my eyes but then something blocked it out. A bird came swooping out of the sky. Looked like a crow but I swear it was at least the size of a condor, maybe bigger. All I can figure is that it wanted my wedding ring. You know how crows like anything shiny. It swooped down and pecked off my finger, ring and all, and disappeared with it."

I laughed. "You're full of it."

He grinned down at his guitar and went back to strumming.

"You said it wanted your wedding ring."

"Yes."

"So you were married once."

"I'm married now."

"I mean before Carolina."

"There was nothing before Carolina."

We looked at her together. She was sound asleep in the chair, lips parted and head resting on her knees. "Where'd you find her?" I asked.

"Close to Asheville, North Carolina. About this time last year, I was out book hunting. There was this tall blue house with a sign next to the road that said 'Antiques.' Carolina's dad was selling junk out of his barn. I had an odd feeling when I pulled in the driveway, like before one of my visions comes. I knew something was waiting for me."

320

Ford said it was like being pulled along the dirt track to the barn by some invisible line. Tied in the shade of a chokecherry tree near the barn door there was a white German shepherd barking with its ears laid back. Ford had never seen a white German shepherd before. It seemed like an omen. He entered the musty shadows of the barn looking for something remarkable, but there was only junk, trunks and battered picture frames and chipped dishes stacked on a plywood table. He was about to climb a ladder to the loft in search of books when the dog's barking dissolved into whimpers. He turned and there she stood in the barn's opening with radiant light all around her. In a way, it was a kind of vision. But Ford had never experienced one so vivid. "It was awful hot in there," he said, "and I'm no spring chicken. I thought maybe I was having a stroke." Then she stepped into the barn and he saw that she was human, a barefoot girl in a swaying sundress eating a wedge of watermelon, the juice pinking her lips and fingers. Ford didn't say what happened next, only that he went back for Carolina at dusk of the following day and found her standing at the road by the "Antiques" sign with a folded-over grocery sack at her feet. He stopped the car and she got in. She had been with him ever since.

Right away Carolina began taking care of Ford. On their first morning together she trimmed his hair out on the porch, lathered his face and shaved off the coarse veil of his whiskers, drew his head into her lap and massaged his temples until he fell asleep. She was goodness, she was rest. Carolina, like the images her name evoked, of high mountains and cool hollows, mists rising off of slow-running creeks, acres of rolling green farmland, and sometimes, carried on the wind, the tang of ocean salt.

Ford insisted he had never taken an interest in young girls before. He swore he wasn't a dirty old man. "This is different," he said. "It's Carolina. I know it sounds like an excuse, but she's ageless to me." It was unsettling the way he talked about her. He claimed to have seen her walk through a flock of birds that descended on the yard without even disturbing them. According to Ford, Carolina had her own special gift. He called her an empath. "One time the dogs got to fighting in the yard and Carolina doubled over in pain. Then we saw a woman hit her baby in the grocery store. On the way home Carolina wept so hard I thought she was going to be sick." Ford believed he and Carolina had some divine purpose together. "Before long," he said, "God will reveal it to me."

I looked over at Carolina, still sleeping, and felt sorry for her, to have been so idealized. Then I saw that the fire was dying to embers and the dogs were stirring, preparing to follow Ford back to the trailer. He put down his guitar and the night was over. It was time to go back to bed, but there was something I had to know first.

"What did you think?" I blurted out, heat rushing to my cheeks.

"Of what?"

"My writing."

"Oh," Ford said. He looked at me for a long moment before rising stiffly out of his lawn chair. "I think the whole world should read your poems."

Walking across the field, breathing in the night air, my chest felt light again, as if Carolina had placed her hand on it. I went back to the shed and wrote in my notebook all night long. When the sun came up, I had to step outside to cool my burning hand.

Weeks passed and the days grew hotter. At the end of May, Ford and I fixed his old tractor together and I learned to mow the field. We set out tobacco, repaired a fence in the woods, and trimmed the trees crowded close to the trailer. My muscles grew sore and my skin turned brown. The shed became a sanctuary for me. Carolina brought out an old rug for the floor and a metal fan to make the heat more bearable. In the mornings sun flooded through the shed's cracks and at night moths circled and bounced off the lightbulb overhead. There was always the sound of crickets and tree frogs and dogs panting outside. I went with Ford to flea markets and auctions but mostly I stayed home with Carolina. I helped her paint the porch posts and plant flowers by the front steps. One day we made birdhouses out of gourds. On the weekends Ford built a fire and the three of us talked until the wee hours. Soon I came to trust them both. I began to feel a contentment that I didn't know if I deserved. Maybe a life like theirs wasn't meant for me. Sometimes it felt wrong being there, like I was fooling them. I would think as I worked with Ford in the field or helped Carolina in the garden how they'd hate me if they knew what I had done and who I really was, what kind of curse had been passed down to me in my blood.

Then Ford walked into the woods one evening and didn't come back. I knew he was gone when I stepped out of the shed the next morning because the dogs had vanished with him, leaving the yard silent and empty. I found Carolina pulling weeds in the garden, wearing Ford's big work gloves. "He didn't come back last night?" I asked.

She glanced up at me, the sun in her eyes. "No."

"Aren't you worried?"

"Not really. He does this sometimes. He might not be back for a week or two."

"He stays gone that long?"

"He has before."

"Do you think he really has visions?"

"I know Ford makes up stories," she said, "but I've seen a lot of his visions come true. Like when he said you was coming into our lives." She smiled. "Ford's not like everybody else, Johnny. He's closer to God. You ought to hear him pray sometime."

"Did he ever tell you what happened to his finger?"

She laughed. "He said he went to a whorehouse in New Orleans and met this voodoo woman. She gave him a concoction to drink that got him so high he didn't even feel it when she cut his finger off. Said she needed it for a spell. Every time I ask about his finger, he tells me another made-up story. I guess I'll never know."

I knelt down beside her in the dirt and we

pulled weeds together for a while in silence. After a while, I asked, "Do you think . . . does Ford have any children?"

"I don't know a thing about Ford except what he's told me," she said. "He might have kids all over the country, for all I know." Then she went back to weeding.

For the first couple of days and nights, I watched the woods at the edge of the yard for Ford and the dogs to come walking back. But it wasn't long before I forgot that he was gone. It was peaceful being alone there with Carolina. Sometimes I stood at the shed door and watched her for long stretches sitting on the top step of the porch, looking straight ahead at nothing in particular. She didn't wiggle her feet, which must have been falling asleep, or shift to a more comfortable position. She didn't move so much as a finger to scratch her nose. She was utterly still. The more time I spent with her, the easier it was to see why Ford was so taken with her. She cooked for me, in the mornings biscuits and gravy and in the evenings fried green tomatoes and potato cakes and greasy chicken legs. One Sunday morning we made a chocolate cake together, rain drumming on the trailer's tin roof. I taught her to play poker and she taught me gin rummy. Sitting on the porch one afternoon, she spent almost an hour drawing a splinter out of my palm. When she left to take a bushel of beans to the neighbors down the road I found myself standing at the end of the driveway watching and waiting for her to come back, like that white German shepherd tied outside her father's barn in North Carolina. I didn't want those days to be over. But then Ford was home again, as suddenly as he had disappeared.

The first sign of his return was the dogs. They came straggling out of the woods before him, as if to signal his coming, and loped to the porch where Carolina and I sat playing cards. We stood watching the trees expectantly and when Ford finally came into view there was a strange sensation in me, of mixed relief and disappointment. He walked slowly down the wooded slope and into the grass, a bedroll on his back, shirt hanging almost in shreds. Carolina and I hurried across the yard to meet him. He was weak but smiling. He kissed Carolina and leaned against her small body as if for support.

"What did you see this time?" she asked as we headed back to the trailer.

His smile faltered. "Something I didn't want to," he said. Carolina and I exchanged a glance but didn't press him. Once he was

clean and fed I expected him to tell, but he
didn't. I felt ashamed for wanting to hear,
when Carolina seemed not to care. I realized then how much I wanted to stay
there, how much I longed for nothing to
change.

Laura

Before Clint died, when I first figured out I
was expecting, Zelda got me an appointment at the Health Department. When you
don't have much money, there's not a lot of
choice where you go to the doctor. I sure
didn't like the one I seen there. That first
appointment he didn't look at me, not even
when he was telling me things. I felt like he
was there just because he had to be. Zelda
said that was probably true, because sometimes the government lets new doctors work
at places like the Health Department to pay
back their school loans. I missed some of
my appointments after Clint drowned because I was too tore up over him to remember anything. Then I got kicked out of the
trailer and it felt like everything was upside
down. But soon as I got settled in the yellow house, I went back for my appointment.
It was the same doctor. This time he did
something he called an ultrasound. He
squirted warm jelly on my lower belly and

moved a wand around. I didn't like him standing over me, with my shirt up and my pants down around my hips, but I liked seeing the baby's dark shape on a television screen. His heartbeat filled the whole room. I was proud my baby was strong. I wanted to laugh and clap my hands but the doctor had a stern face. After the ultrasound the nurse left. He set down on his stool and talked to me. "You know," he said, "you should have kept your appointments, Miss Blevins. It's important for both mother and baby to have the proper prenatal care." He looked at me over the top of his glasses. "You're lucky there are no complications."

"The baby's okay?" I asked. He was making me nervous.

"Fortunately, yes. But it was very irresponsible of you. Any number of things could have gone wrong."

"But they didn't?"

The doctor's face didn't change much but I could tell he was getting miffed. "I don't think you understand the potential seriousness of your negligence, Miss Blevins."

That word "negligence" gave me a bad feeling, like when I found out Clint had been wearing a dead boy's clothes all along. "But the baby's okay, right?" I asked again. The doctor gave me another hateful look over his glasses, then he got up and walked away. I felt sick as I gathered up my purse and went to the waiting room to find Zelda.

On the way home she kept asking what was wrong but I couldn't talk. It seemed like somebody was always threatening to separate me from my baby. Zelda let me out and I went up the steep porch steps, straight inside to the bathroom. I splashed cold water on my face and neck. When I seen myself in the medicine cabinet mirror with my face dripping and my eyes big, I looked more like Mama than ever. All of a sudden that scared me more than anything. I rushed to the kitchen looking for scissors but I came to a butcher knife first. I couldn't stand having Mama's hair for a second more. I stood right yonder at the sink and sawed it off. It looked awful. I could tell by how everybody stared at me at work the next morning. But I didn't care. My head felt lighter. I was still worried but it made me feel better to have the weight of Mama's hair off of my shoulders. Louise said she used to cut all of her kids' hair. She asked if she could come over later and shape mine up some. When she was done it was like seeing a new person in the mirror.

But my nerves was still ragged. The bigger my belly growed, the worse I felt, and the more I worried over how I was going to raise a baby without Clint. Zelda said I could get help if I needed it. She offered to get me an appointment to talk to somebody about welfare but I couldn't hardly stand to think about it. The state had been keeping me up just about all my life and I wanted to provide for the baby on my own. That's why I didn't quit working, even though Louise and Zelda thought I needed rest. They made me at least take a day off. It was the third of March. I was laying on the couch when the twinges came low in my belly. I should have got up and called the hospital but I couldn't face the thought of that doctor. I decided I'd wait and see if it got to hurting any worse. It was mostly cramps. Then all of a sudden I felt the baby weighing down like I needed to use the bathroom the worst I ever had to. I got afraid I had been stupid and waited too late. I made myself call the ambulance. I'd seen enough books with pictures to know there was going to be a mess if the baby came before they got there. I climbed in the bathtub to wait for them. It was cold in there. I was more scared than ever in my life.

I don't remember much about the ambulance coming. The ride to the hospital was like a dream. The first thing I remember is being in the delivery room with my baby moving out of me. I heard myself hollering but it was like somebody else's voice. He was gushing out fast between my legs. When the doctor put him on my belly, the first thing I seen was his hair. Even matted down, I could tell what color it was. There was a lot of it, too. It was just like Clint's. Then something crazy happened. My eyes was so blurry, I got to seeing things. They came back to me, them friends I had on the mountain. There was a window in the delivery room. That's where they came from. They was pretty as ever, flitting across my belly on their shiny wings. Them fairies danced a crown around my baby's head, dropping their blessings and kisses. That's how come I named him Sunny.

It was nice in the hospital, with everything white and clean. I got to stay longer because Sunny was born three weeks early and they had to make sure we was okay. I was happy there with him. I liked the sounds of nurses' shoes and carts rattling up and down the hall. I didn't even mind when they took my blood. I tried to mark every minute of it, even the parts that hurt. I'd take Sunny to the window and show him the parking lot two stories below. I imagined he would like cars, maybe even work on them when he growed up. I wondered what kind of man he would make. But even though he looked like Clint, I'd let him be his own person. I knowed he was Sunny, with a life of his own.

The nurse showed me how to swaddle him. I slept with him in a bundle in the crook of my arm. His yellow curls always peeked out of the blanket. When his eyes started opening more, I seen they was the color of Mama's. Clint had blue eyes, but there was no other blue like Mama's anywhere. I knowed Sunny took his eyes straight from her. He was a content baby. He only cried when he was hungry or wet. I'd lean close to his open mouth to smell the newness of his breath. I liked them tiny pearls on the roof of his mouth and all the pink ridges and folds inside it. I even liked when his diaper needed changing, after that sticky black tar went away. The nurse called it meconium. I liked the sound of it, even if it was trouble to wipe off. I liked every part of being Sunny's mama.

The only thing I didn't like about the hospital was when the doctor came around. It wasn't the same one from the Health Department but I didn't like him any better. He looked at us funny. He'd set on his stool with his leg crossed and his pants riding up, showing his long sock. He'd ask

me slow questions, like I wouldn't understand if he didn't form the words real careful with his mouth. I knowed he thought I
was dumb, like the teachers at school did.
Whatever I said, he'd lift his eyebrows and
write on his chart.

Louise and the Thompsons and Debbie
and Roy came to visit me. They brought
flowers and some chocolate cupcakes with
cream in the middle. That made me cry a
little bit, thinking about Clint, but I was
glad to see them. They all thought Sunny
was beautiful. Louise cried, too, and I
knowed she was thinking about Clint like
me. They stayed for quite a while, until I
got too tired. I fell asleep with Sunny in my
arms.

The only other visitor me and Sunny had
was Clint's mama. When I seen her peeking
around the curtain I covered Sunny's little
ears. I thought she might go to screaming
and carrying on. I didn't know if she meant
to cuss me out or what, but she just walked
across the room and leant over the bed. She
smelled like cigarettes. When I seen she
wasn't going to make a fuss, I pulled back
the blanket so she could see Sunny better.
She jumped like a snake bit her. "They
laws," she said. "He looks just like Clint."
Then she busted out crying. I didn't know

what to think. As mean as she was, I felt sorry for her. After a minute I asked her if she might pour me a cup of water, to get her mind on something else. She gave me a drink and switched the channel on the television for me. She stayed for about an hour. I was relieved that she didn't ask to hold the baby.

For that short time at the hospital, it was like there was a truce between me and Clint's mama. Then she got her purse and stood up to go. She stopped at the foot of the bed and stared hard at Sunny. I didn't like the look on her face. I seen it had been a mistake to ever let my guard down with her. "If they wouldn't put me in jail," she said, "I'd snatch that baby up this minute and run out of here with him." My blood turned into ice water. I opened my mouth to scream for the nurse but all that came out was a tiny squeak. "You finally killed Clint but you ain't getting this one. It might not happen today. But if it's the last thing I ever do in this life, I'll get that baby away from you."

Johnny
There was a change in Ford after those two weeks in the woods. He was quieter and sometimes I caught him staring at me. As

we worked together on the farm and spent time peddling books and selling produce from Carolina's garden, it was hard to ignore the strain. Before long, nights in the shed grew cooler and Carolina brought a heater out. Ford and I helped her with the canning because it was more than one person could handle, the windowsills lined with half-rotten tomatoes and the kitchen floor crowded with tubs of corn and gallon buckets of green beans. When the canning was done, I helped Carolina plant the garden with fall greens, kale, spinach, turnips, and mustard. Once the tobacco was curing there was brush to clear from the fields and wood to split. I worked harder than usual on my birthday, not telling them when it came and went because I didn't want to think about Laura. On Thanksgiving, Ford cooked a wild turkey he had shot in the woods. After we were full and Ford had fallen asleep on the couch, I left Carolina washing dishes and stepped outside to smoke. The ground was glittering with frost and the dogs huddled together for warmth, barely raising their heads when I came out. After a while the door opened again and Carolina came to sit on the top step, drawing her knees up into Ford's coat. I lowered myself beside her and thought we would be silent together. Then I startled myself by saying, "My mama's locked up in the state mental hospital." For a second I wasn't sure I had spoken out loud. I looked at Carolina and her face hadn't changed. I tried my voice again. "She didn't love me." I hadn't known how badly I wanted to say it. I told Carolina everything and she listened with her calm face. When I finished she put her hand on my forehead then moved it down over my eyes. In the darkness under her palm I felt healed, if only for a minute. I took her hand and held it in both of mine. There was no ring. She wasn't married to Ford, not really.

The next day, Ford and I helped Carolina decorate a store-bought Christmas tree. She said that back at her house in North Carolina, they always put up their tree the day after Thanksgiving. She strung some popcorn but we ate most of it, and I helped her cut out chains of white paper doves. It was a good day, but after that the weather grew colder and Ford grew even quieter and more preoccupied. I suspected he was trying to convince himself that his troubling vision had been wrong. One morning after breakfast when he had gone off to the dump, his truck bed loaded with garbage bags, Carolina said, "I think he's hearing the voice again. I wish he would wait for warmer weather." But he didn't.

At the beginning of December, I stepped out of the shed and saw that the dogs were missing. I knew Ford was gone again. I walked across the yard, up the porch steps, and opened the front door without knocking. The trailer was dim, lit by the colored lights of the Christmas tree in the living room. Carolina was sitting at the bar in her nightgown, peeling an orange. She had the same placid look on her face as when she sat on the step and I couldn't resist going to her. I climbed onto the other bar stool as silently as I could. I wanted to be still with her, to think about nothing in particular. I focused on her long, thin fingers pulling off strips of orange skin. She separated the sections and brought them to her mouth one by one. We didn't speak of Ford and the tree lights blinked and outside snow flurried and the morning was gray and silent. She looked down at her feet on the bar stool rung. For a minute we examined them together, ridged with small bluish veins.

"My toes are ugly," Carolina said.

"I like them," I told her.

She looked up at me and smiled. Then she slid her hand across the bar counter and slipped her fingers between mine. I looked down at our laced fingers. Hers felt just like I had imagined they would. "You might as well move in here with me," she said. "It's too cold for you to be out yonder. I've been having bad dreams about you freezing to death." But I could see in her eyes that it wasn't just me she was worried about.

She put a clean sheet on a mattress in the junk room at the end of the hall. It was so cluttered that I could barely squeeze through the door when it was time for bed. I liked the shed better, but I wanted to be closer to Carolina. I wanted to sleep under the same roof as her, where I could hear every cough, every creak of the bedsprings when she turned over in her room at the other end of the trailer. The next day I brought in kindling and kept a good fire going in the stove. Sometimes I saw Carolina shivering, teeth rattling, when the trailer was almost too hot for me to stand, but I knew she was just feeling the same cold that was freezing Ford. We tried for a while to play cards but her mind was too far away. When the wind howled she glanced toward the window with big eyes. "I can go look for him," I told her. "No," she said, shaking her head. "There's acres of woods. You'd never find him. Besides that, you know he doesn't want to be found."

On the fifth night that Ford was gone, I heard Carolina weeping and couldn't help going to her, feeling my way to her room in the dark. I climbed into the bed she had shared with Ford and took the curled ball of her body into my arms. As much as I wanted her, I didn't try to make anything happen. She was nothing like the girls I had been with on the floor of the cave. I couldn't even remember their faces, but I knew every inch of Carolina's. I held her until her sobs quieted and we both fell asleep. Then there was a scratching sound on the porch, dragging me out of a dream. I opened my eyes and sun was shining through the curtains. Carolina rose, too. We looked at each other bleary-eyed for an instant before scrambling out of bed. We ran to the front door and it was one of Ford's favorite dogs, an ugly dachshund mix. There were two others whining and circling in the yard, looking from us to the wooded slope at the edge of the snow-dusted grass. Carolina wanted to go right then in her nightgown, but I made her stop to put on a coat.

The dogs moved fast and we hurried to keep up, a thin layer of white powder gritting under our shoes. We walked for what seemed a long time, over a hill into thicker woods, the dogs stopping once in a while to look back at us. Then suddenly they were running forward, tails wagging. I saw Ford lying on his face under the trees, with the rest of the dog pack huddled close around him. When they rose to greet us, there were melted spots in the snow where their bodies had been. Carolina made a strangled noise and ran to Ford, falling on her knees at his side. I followed and when I knelt down with them I could see that Ford's hair was frozen to the ground, a stiff white ring around his head. I was sure that he was dead. The dogs barked as we turned him over. The sound of his hair tearing free sent shivers racing over me. Carolina cried out when she saw his face, taut and gray and covered with sores. Then his eyes opened. They were. glazed but somehow still aware. I saw that his mouth was working. He was trying to speak. I leaned close, my ear almost touching his cracked lips. "What?" I asked. "What is it, Ford?" He said in a broken voice that was barely there, like the scrape of a pencil stroke on paper, "You will be a great man." For a long second I couldn't move, even though Carolina was begging, "Help me, Johnny, help me, we've got to get him down from here."

Somehow we carried him between us, panting and struggling, out of the wooded hills. We took him inside the trailer and lowered him into bed. Carolina said, "Where's the truck keys, I've got to get to a phone," but Ford shook his head, even in his delirium. "Don't you do it, honey," he mumbled. "Don't you get those doctors after me." Maybe it was because he was so much older, or because in her heart she believed that he wasn't human, but she didn't call anyone. I told her that he needed an ambulance, that he might have frostbite, but she wouldn't go against Ford's wishes and I wouldn't go against hers. As Carolina ran for blankets I stood over him and prayed for the first time in years.

Carolina sat in a straight chair at his side for the rest of the night. As worried about Ford as I was, I was surprised to find myself jealous of the attention she gave him. But there was something else on my mind, as I made coffee and soup and tried to feed them both. I couldn't stop thinking about what Ford had said when he opened his eyes. I knew that Ford only saw in the visions what he wanted to see, but some part of me wanted to prove him right. There was an old desk in the bedroom and a manual typewriter. I'd never used one before and it took me forever to pick out the right letters. The keys were loud and I worried that the noise would disturb Ford's rest, but Carolina said it was okay. She thought it would be good for him to know that I was close by. Hunched over Ford's desk, I began typing up the poems from my notebook.

In the night Ford seemed to grow even sicker. The dogs sat outside the bedroom window howling until the sound was too terrible to stand. We had to let them in, even though their stink was suffocating in the small room. Ford sweated under blankets and ice rain pattered against the windows and by morning he was struggling to breathe. Carolina placed her hands on his chest and throat and burning forehead, but couldn't make him well. I told her that we should take him to the hospital, that he was too weak to fight us, but she refused to betray him, even if it meant risking his life. She began to look sick herself, ashen and glassy-eyed. For a week she stayed in her nightgown, the knobs of her spine and the points of her hipbones poking at the worn flannel. She wasn't eating, and it was hard for me to watch. But it was even harder to see how much she loved Ford. Somehow without knowing when it happened, I had come to wish she loved me instead.

Then one morning, nearly a month after we'd found Ford sprawled on his face in the woods, Carolina woke up beside him and placed her hands on his chest. "He's getting better," she said. As if on cue, he propped himself up and asked for coffee. It was the first thing he had wanted. The dachshund mix curled at Ford's feet lifted its head and thumped its tail. Ford asked for a few of his books and flipped through them as he sipped the coffee. He was too weak to sit up long, but I knew Carolina was right. He was getting better. The dogs knew it, too. They went to the door and scratched to be let out. Carolina opened it for them and we stood watching as they chased each other off across the yard.

Later that day, I typed the last word of the last poem in my notebook. I pushed back from the desk, feeling light-headed. I was about to go for a walk in the cold when Ford sat up and said, "What's that racket? Sounds like machine-gun fire."

I smiled and turned to see him leaning back on the pillows. He was pale and there were still scabs on his face, but he looked much stronger. "Typing my poems," I told him.

"The ones I read?"

"And some you haven't."

Ford glanced at the desk, at the stack of white pages. "Can I see them?"

"I want you to have them," I said. "I did this for you." My hands shook when I took the pages from the desk and dropped them into his lap. I wanted to say something, but I was too tired. I walked away, out of the hot trailer into the cold. The dogs stood, wagging their tails. There was a new one among them, long-haired and skinny with ticks behind its ears. I knelt down and held out my hand. It sniffed and licked at my fingers.

I walked out to the field, bare and dead under a hard blue sky. I sat in one of the lawn chairs where the burned spot was, imagining bonfires rising up toward the stars and Carolina's sweet voice singing over the notes of Ford's guitar. I stayed in the field for what seemed like hours, getting colder and colder, watching brown winter birds peck around in the grass, until Carolina came. She put her hand on my head, my cheek, the side of my neck. My heart stopped and for an instant the copperhead that still existed in me, even here, with Carolina, was disappointed that Ford had lived. I folded her into my coat and pressed my lips against her temple. I couldn't tell her how much I loved her.

As the weather grew warmer and Ford grew stronger, I moved back into the shed.

I didn't like hearing Ford and Carolina murmuring to each other in the night. I should have gone back to Millertown but I couldn't bring myself to leave. Another week passed and I began to imagine that Ford and Carolina wanted me gone. I sat huddled in the shed for a full day, not even walking across the yard to eat. They didn't come out to check on me, which seemed to prove my suspicions. The next morning I heard their voices outside but they didn't knock on the shed door. After a while, I stepped out into the sun. There was no sign of Ford but I saw Carolina kneeling by the front steps with her back to me. She was pulling up the dead things of winter, ripping up the ruins of what we had planted together to make room for the new growth of spring. I crept up on her, not sure exactly what I meant to do. I knelt down and slipped my arms around her from behind. She stiffened at first, but then she melted into me. I could feel her heart beating under my hands. "Why didn't you come out to see about me?" I asked into her hair.

"We thought you wanted to be by yourself." She turned around in my arms and her face was inches from mine. She smelled like dewy grass.

"You want me to go," I said, trying to

control my breathing.

"No, Johnny." There was an eyelash on her cheek, a tiny black crescent. I raised my hand slowly between our bodies and Carolina caught her breath. I brushed delicately at the eyelash with my finger. Then her eyes widened a little. She was looking over my shoulder. I stood up and turned to see Ford standing there, holding the gas can he kept under the trailer. It was March and time to mow. The look on his face was not one of anger but of fear. Carolina stood up, too, and moved away from me. I reached out and took hold of her arm instinctively, pulling her back, not wanting her to leave my side.

"Let go of her, Johnny," Ford said. When I didn't release Carolina's arm his eyes hardened. My possessive gesture must have said it all. Carolina looked down at my hand on her arm and then up at me, her face sad and pleading at the same time.

"What have you two been doing?" Ford asked.

Carolina turned to him, shocked. "Nothing, Ford."

He stared at me. "I saw in a vision you'd betray me. I didn't want to believe it."

Carolina looked stricken. "He never betrayed you, Ford."

Ford took a step toward me. "I've treated you like a son," he said.

I was stunned when he launched himself at me, knocking my breath out against the porch. We grappled and fought and it was strange to feel him on top of me, to be that close, the stink of his sweat, the heat of his breath, and the weight of his bones. As much as I had always wanted to hurt someone, it was no good. We couldn't best one another. He was surprisingly strong for an old man, especially one who had been so sick. We wrestled in the yard for what seemed an eternity, the dogs barking and snarling all around us, and Carolina wailing like a wounded animal herself. I don't know which one of us caught sight of her first, but she was the reason we both gave in at the same time. She was crouched by the porch steps, hives like bright red welts covering her face and neck and chest. I had the thought that we were killing her. We staggered to our feet, panting and spitting blood. She gaped at us, clutching at her middle, and then ran into the trailer.

Ford and I stood in silence for a long time. The dogs circled around our legs, growling and snapping at each other. "Shit, Johnny," Ford said at last. "I can't blame you. I know better than anybody what it's like to be around her."

I took off my shirt and wiped my throbbing face with it. I looked down at the blood smeared there. When I raised my head and saw the look in Ford's eyes, I knew he'd answer me this time. "How'd you lose it?" I asked. "How'd you lose that finger?"

"All right, Johnny," he said softly. "Here's the truth. I was working at a furniture factory down in Oliver Springs. Damn drill press cut it off. That's all it was." We stared at each other for a few seconds. Then he turned and limped across the yard, back into the woods with the dogs at his heels.

I watched Ford's sagging back until he disappeared from view. Now I knew the story of his missing finger, the one I had hoped might somehow be rotting to yellowed bone in my mama's box. Like always, the truth had turned out to be disappointing. But in that moment I didn't care who my father was or what kind of curse I carried in my blood. I turned around and walked back to the trailer. As soon as I opened the door, I knew that it was empty. There was a note on the kitchen table. It said, "I can't stand this. Don't forget I love you both." I heard Ford's truck starting up and bolted outside. She was pulling out of the driveway as I leapt off the porch and skidded in the grass. I ran to the road and watched as her taillights disappeared around a curve. The land looked deserted for miles. I had a familiar feeling that the whole past year had been a dream, one long hallucination. Maybe I had been there by myself all along, having a vision of my own.

Laura

I still don't know if the hospital or Clint's mama sent that woman. As soon as I seen her, I knowed what she came for. I had gone to the door with Sunny in one arm and a wet dishrag in the other. The house was a mess where I'd been feeling bad them last few weeks of being pregnant. The day that woman came I had been working on a pile of dirty dishes in the sink.

I was expecting Louise. She'd cooked spaghetti and was bringing me the leftovers. She was always dropping off food for me that way. She knowed how tired I was. When I opened the door my belly was growling, but soon as I seen that woman I got sick. My legs got weak. The only thing that held me up was Sunny in the crook of my arm. If I fell it might have hurt him. Right off that feeling of going wild came over me. She said, "Are you Laura Blevins?" I didn't answer. My mind was racing, trying to

350

figure out what I was going to do. There was black spots in front of my eyes but I still seen her badge necklace. She had on a blue pantsuit. There was a big purse on her shoulder and a clipboard in her hands. She looked hard and rocky. Not like creek rocks, but jaggedy ones. Her eyes was empty. I could tell she didn't care about me and Sunny. She wouldn't notice how cute it was when he sucked his fingers. She wouldn't see his cheeks like two fuzzy peaches. "I'm Pat Blanchard, with the Department of Children's Services," she said. "We had a call that you might be having some trouble taking care of your baby."

If she said anything else, I never heard it. Because that's when she turned her eyes on Sunny. She moved her hand toward him, the one not holding a clipboard. Looking back on it now, she might have just meant to touch him. Maybe she wanted to tickle his foot that had come out of the blanket. Or she might not have been meaning to touch him at all. She might have just been gesturing toward him. But her movement broke something inside of me that was loose for a long time. It's hard to tell exactly what happened. I wasn't in my right mind. I just wanted her to go away. From what I remember, I did the best I could to drive her off with the arm that wasn't holding Sunny. I raised up the wet dishrag and started whacking her with it. I slapped that woman Pat Blanchard over and over, across the face and hands and arms. I believe I was screaming and crying. She tried to cover her face. There was a big red welt across her nose and cheeks. Then the worst thing happened. She stumbled backward trying to get away from me and fell down them steep porch steps. After that, it got quiet. She laid there groaning at the bottom, like she wasn't all the way awake. It's awful, but I wasn't worried if she was okay. I was just worried about how to get out of there with Sunny and where to go.

The first person that came to mind was Louise. I went down the porch steps and stepped over Pat Blanchard. I headed down the street toward Louise's. I don't remember how long I ran with Sunny, both of us crying, before Louise's car slowed down and stopped beside of me. She rolled down the window and said, "Lordy mercy, what's happened?" I yanked open the door and nearly set down in the spaghetti she was bringing me. I said, "Take me to Zelda's." It was a comforting place where the best day of my life happened. I'd think better if I could stand on that deck where me and

Clint got married. Louise didn't ask any questions. She just drove me there. I cried the whole way, still half out of my head. Sunny slept in my arms, even though Louise had a car seat in the back she'd found at a yard sale. I couldn't stand to let go of him. We pulled up in the Thompsons' driveway and Louise had to help me to the door. Zelda answered it with her hair rolled up in pin curls. I seen all the color go out of her cheeks. Louise said, "She won't tell me what's wrong." They led me inside to set down with Sunny. Zelda brought me a glass of water. I told them as much as I remembered about Pat Blanchard coming to the door and what I did to her. They looked at each other with big eyes. Mr. Thompson had come in from somewhere. He was standing in the doorway between the living room and the kitchen. He said, "Somebody's got to call an ambulance for that woman."

Zelda said, "We can't, Ralph. She'll get in trouble with the law."

Mr. Thompson said, "Think about what you're saying."

Louise said, "He's right, Zelda. She might be hurt bad."

Zelda said, "Laura heard her making noise. I bet she's all right."

"Why don't you talk sense?" Mr. Thompson hollered. I'd never heard him raise his voice that way. It made me feel like crying again. "We can't let somebody lay over there with bones broke and their head busted and no telling what all else."

Zelda turned to me. I seen her trying to be calm. "Listen, honey. I believe you're in shock. Why don't you take Sunny in my bedroom and rest until you're feeling better."

I didn't want to rest but my head was too addled to argue. I let her lead me down the hall to the bed with Sunny in my arms. I gave him to her while I climbed on the bedspread with roses on it. She put him down beside of me and he snuggled up to my belly. He was rooting around for my breast in his sleep. I pulled up my shirt for him. Feeding him made me calmer. It was almost like nothing bad had happened. I dozed off looking at the scissors on the nightstand, where Zelda had been clipping coupons in bed.

I must have slept quite a while. The room was dark when I woke up. I heard a strange man's voice in the living room and switched on the lamp. I got out of the bed, careful not to wake up Sunny, and cracked the door to hear better. He was saying, "I'm sorry, but I'll have to take her in. Miss Blanchard is pressing charges."

"She's resting right now," Zelda said.

"Will you have to use the handcuffs?" Louise asked. I could tell she was crying.

"She's a good girl," Zelda said. "She was just scared for her baby."

"I can't help it, ma'am," the policeman said. "I've got a warrant."

I looked at the window and then at Sunny. It was too high off the ground and I might drop him. I would have to go out the kitchen door, onto the deck. I thought of the children at my wedding, fluttering down the steps like butterflies. I wanted to cry but there wasn't time. I got Sunny up from the bed. He whined a little bit, but he was a heavy sleeper and he didn't wake up. I opened the door as quiet as I could. It was going to be hard because it was a small house, but I could go through the dining room to get to the kitchen. It was right across the hall from the bedroom. I crept across the hall and into the dining room. The mahogany hutch was shining in the dark. I headed for the light of the kitchen. I could already see the black panes of the door leading to the deck with the kitchen's reflection in them. If I could make it there, me and Sunny would be free. But as soon as I stepped on the kitchen tiles I seen Mr. Thompson by the sink. It was like he'd been expecting me. My heart dropped to my feet. He said, "Honey, you won't get very far with that baby. It ain't no kind of life for him anyhow, running from the law."

That's when I heard another strange voice in the living room, a woman that sounded so much like Pat Blanchard I thought for a second it might be her. Then I figured Pat Blanchard wouldn't be in any shape to get out and take somebody's baby after what I done to her. I knowed they'd sent somebody else to take Sunny. There was probably twenty more just like her. Zelda asked, "Can the baby stay with me or Louise until we get this mess straightened out? We're the only family Laura's got."

"I'm sorry," the woman said. "In a case like this, the baby always goes to a blood relation. The paternal grandmother will be taking him."

She might as well have shot me through the heart. It was all I could do to keep from sinking down right yonder in the floor. I had to make myself get moving again. I lunged for the door but Mr. Thompson stepped in front of it. I crashed into his belly and bumped my head on his chin. Sunny started crying so loud it hurt my ears. It hit me that Mr. Thompson was probably the one that called the police on me. Then all of a sudden they was in the kitchen, the policeman and the woman that sounded like Pat Blanchard and looked something like her, too. I was still trying to get around Mr. Thompson. I'll never speak to him again, even though I know he just wanted to do the right thing. The policeman was moving toward me saying, "You'll have to come with me, Miss Blevins." Zelda was begging, "Now, wait just a minute." Louise was standing with her hands over her eyes, bawling out loud. I was looking around, trying to find an escape route and hold on to what was left of my mind at the same time. Then the policeman had ahold of my arm that wasn't holding Sunny. I hollered out, "Wait, he's hungry! He's hungry!" trying to be heard over Sunny's and Louise's crying. It was all I could think of to do.

The woman came forward and said, "We have formula."

"I'll just take him back here to the bedroom and nurse him right quick," I said.

"You can sit down here and do it," she said.

"Please," I said. "I need privacy." I turned to the policeman. He had kinder eyes.

"All right," he said. "Go on." Then he

looked at her. "I'll wait outside the door."

I was fixing to bust out fighting again. But then I remembered how awful it was for me and Johnny, seeing Mama go wild. I didn't want to mark Sunny like Mama done me. I forced myself to be calmer. The policeman followed me down the hall. I thought of the window again, wondering if I could make it to the ground without hurting Sunny. But Mr. Thompson was right. I couldn't go on the run with such a small baby. I was cornered. My mind went blank. I went in Zelda's bedroom and shut the door in the policeman's face. Under the lamp on the nightstand, Sunny's hair was even more yellow. I held him and gave him my breast. At home I nursed him all through the nights. I didn't wear anything so he could find my breast in the dark. I knowed they'd put a bottle in his mouth, after I had tried to make sure no rubber nipple ever touched it. I knowed my breasts would get hard and leaky when he was gone. I vowed not to cry in front of them people.

Then I seen the scissors glinting on the nightstand. They was laying on top of a stack of bright colored coupons. I reached over and took the scissors in one hand. The other hand was curled around Sunny's bottom. He was sleeping as he drunk from me.

358

His long eyelashes made shadows on his soft round cheeks. I dipped my head to smell of him and went to the end of the bed. It creaked when I set down. That's the same sound the bed made at home when I bounced Sunny. We'd bounce up and down when he got fussy, until pretty soon both of us was smiling. The scissors shined when I brought them close to Sunny's head. He liked anything shiny. I looked at all that pretty yellow hair. I could hear the policeman pecking on the bedroom door. I knowed I would have to do it fast.

Johnny

After I left the farm, I went back to Millertown. The Lawsons gave me a job at their gas station, a sooty building with pumps out front and a room over the garage. Bobby rented me the room while I saved money and decided what to do next. I couldn't stop thinking about Ford's prophecy. Sometimes I heard the scrape of his voice saying the words in my head. "You will be a great man." A week after I got back, I was having a cigarette in the rocking chair on the gas station's porch while Bobby was gone running errands. When a hatchback with missing hubcaps slowed down and turned in, I thought it would pull up to the pumps but it came across the dusty lot and parked in front of the porch instead. I remembered Marshall Lunsford as soon as he got out of the car and shuffled up to me grinning. His face hadn't changed much but his eyes seemed older.

"Bobby said you was around."

"Yes."

"I ain't seen you since the ninth grade."

"I know. It's been a while."

Marshall looked down at his shoes. The morning was warm and the old T-shirt he wore had dark rings at the armpits. "I just got back in town not long ago myself."

"Huh."

"I took off on the Greyhound, lit out for Texas. I always did want to see Texas."

I took a long draw from my cigarette. "How was it?"

"Not how I thought."

I smiled. "It figures."

"Yeah. I stayed in a hostel down yonder while I was looking for work. I swear, all I could think about was getting back home. I wouldn't have bet on that, would you?"

"No," I said, "I guess not."

"I always wondered if you'd be back."

"I didn't think I ever would."

Marshall looked down at his shoes again. "Neither did I."

We were quiet for a while, watching a bag float end over end toward the used car dealership across the highway. Then he said, "Well, I come to tell you something."

I pitched my cigarette, still smoking, over the porch edge. "What's that?"

"I seen your sister."

I stopped rocking and sat there frozen.

"I remembered her cause of how she favors you."

"Where did you see her?"

"That's what I thought you'd want to know. She was down at the county jail. Some man claimed Daddy was trespassing, digging ginseng on his property. I was in the office trying to bail Daddy out when they brung her in."

"What did she do?"

"I don't know. I didn't ask. I had other things to tend to."

The wind freshened, flapping the faded plastic pennants strung over the parking lot and blowing dirt across the planks at my feet. I sat thinking, listening to the hum of the drink machine, as Marshall watched patiently. Then I stood up. "Can I get a ride?"

At the county jail, I was shown to a place where there were booths with phones and windows. I sat on a stool between cinder-block walls. It seemed I was floating outside myself, watching from above, when the door opened and a guard let Laura into the room on the other side of the glass. She was swallowed up in a blue jumpsuit, rail thin and ghastly pale, her skin like curdled milk. Worst of all, her long black hair had been cut off. I couldn't bear knowing she had spent even one night in a cell like the one I was in for four years at Polk County. I thought in those first seconds I would get up and leave. But when she approached the window to sit on the stool opposite me, the feeling passed.

Laura took the phone and I looked at the one on my side without picking it up. I had forgotten what I could possibly say to her after so long. The guard who had opened the door for Laura crossed the room behind the glass and let himself into where I was. Without speaking, he brought a white envelope and handed it to me. Then he walked out another door, the one I had come through, where there was an office with a desk and filing cabinets and a water cooler. I sat blinking after him for a second and then turned to pick up the phone. "I told them I wanted to give you a letter," she said. At the sound of her voice, an unexpected warmth bloomed in my chest. It was filled with images of home, high cliffs and light-gilded leaves and groundhog holes on the muddy creek bank.

"Are you okay?" I asked at last. It was a stupid question, and not what I wanted to say to her, but there were no words close enough to what I was feeling.

Laura smiled weakly. "They're always trying to lock us up, ain't they, Johnny?"

I tried to smile back but couldn't.

There was a silence. Then she said, "Where have you been?"

"I guess I could ask the same of you."

"Well, here lately I been in jail."

"Laura," I said. "What did you do?"

"I done a lot of things since I seen you last."

I glanced around the room, toward the office where the guard was, down the line of empty booths, at the polished floor reflecting the lights overhead. "Yes," I said. "Me, too." Then I made myself look back at her. "I don't have enough money to get you out."

She took a ragged breath. "There's a way you can get some more."

I gripped the phone tighter. "How?"

"Go to my house on Miller Avenue. It's bright yellow, beside of a car wash. I got a key hid in a watering can under the porch."

"A yellow house?"

363

"Yes. I want you to go in yonder and get that ring from out of Mama's box."

I only hesitated for a second. "Where is it?"

She smiled her tired way again. "You know where I would keep it."

"All right," I said. "I'll find it."

Then her smile faltered. "Johnny."

"What?"

"I throwed that finger bone away."

I opened my mouth and closed it again. I didn't know what I wanted to say.

"Wasn't no use hanging on to it."

"No," I said after a moment. "I guess not."

"It don't seem right for that box to be empty, though."

"No," I said.

"There's something I want you to put in it for safekeeping." She looked at the envelope still in my hand. "I wouldn't quit squalling until they gave it back to me."

I looked down at the envelope, too, the sweat on my forehead turning cold.

"Open it," she said.

I fumbled at the unsealed flap and reached inside. What I found there wasn't paper. It was a lock of glossy hair, yellow as the sun, tied neatly with a length of string.

"I had a baby, Johnny," she said. "I named him Sunny."

For a few seconds I thought I hadn't heard her right. I closed my eyes, trying to make sense of her words. I didn't know if I could stand to hear more. If I was going to turn my back on her, now was the time. But I didn't leave.

I bent closer to the window and asked, "Where is he?"

Her eyelids reddened. "He got took away from me."

"No, Laura," I said, even though I already knew it was true.

"I got to get him back," she said.

"We will." My voice cracked. "We'll get him back."

I opened my fingers and we looked down together at the lock of yellow hair in my palm. It seemed I could feel some old part of myself dissolving into smoke and ash.

After a while, Laura asked, "Do you still believe there's such a thing as curses?"

I didn't have to think about it. "No," I said. "Not anymore."

"I don't either." She looked up into my face. "I'm ready now, Johnny."

"Ready for what?"

"To go see Mama. Let's get Sunny and leave out of here for good."

I looked into her eyes. They were like they used to be, only sadder. But I saw something alive in them that might be rescued. She didn't belong in that room so I put her back in our woods, shrunk her down and grew her hair into long black sheaves again, stood her on a mossy log with her arms held out for balance. I was beginning to see then what I have learned now. It's not forgetting that heals. It's remembering. I swallowed hard, wetness blurring my eyes. I hadn't felt tears in so long I barely knew what they were. "Okay," I said. "We'll go see her." I knew Laura was right. We were both ready. She looked startled. Then she smiled and I couldn't help smiling back. I leaned over to press my forehead against the glass. I shut my eyes and pretended we were high on a rock over a bluff again, my tongue singing with the tartness of the berries she brought me.

■ ■ ■ ■

THREE:
MYRA ODOM

■ ■ ■ ■

I can't stand to hold them. I have to let them go. I don't want to leave too many marks behind. There were fingerprints all over me when I came back here, and it's taken a long time to wash them off. I hardly remember the names I gave them. That was another time. I think of them now by their real names. Silver like how her eyes glint in the dark. Cinder like how his eyes look in the white of his face. Woodsmoke, the way he smells passing by me in fall. Lacy, the way leaves pattern her shoulders as she moves under the trees. Their old names mean nothing now. Neither does mine. I am whatever I say I am. Rainy, when I come in dripping after a storm. Bird, when I climb to the ledge and sing down the mountain. Alive, now even more than when I was a child living here. I squat where I please and watch the water I lapped up from my hand run back out of me, spreading and mixing with the dirt of this place, swirling with pine needles as it heads down the mountain toward the creek where it came from. I am part of this place like never before. When I was small, there was always something hindering me.

Granddaddy was too protective, but I believe Granny's instinct was to let me go. She would allow me to stand for a while in the rain, hair parting soaked down the middle, before making me come in. Once she found me stripped naked facedown in the dirt. She stood watching for a long moment before she pulled me up by the arm, wiping at my blackened tongue with her apron and brushing sow bugs from my chin. "Lord, youngun," she said, "you're going to be sick as a dog." All I wanted was free. Granny seemed to understand. After Granddaddy was gone she let me roam. But every minute in her presence it seemed she was touching me, stroking my hair, pulling me onto her lap.

I still miss her every day. Time is different on the mountain. It stretches out longer. I used to always know what year it was, and how old I would be on my next birthday. But, like names, it seems less important now. There's a calendar hanging in the kitchen, yellowed and stiff as if something was spilled on it. It has been there on the same rusty nail since before Granny died. It's a calendar from 1975, the year I came home and my babies were born. If I mark time, it's by their birthdays. Not the exact date, because I forget sometimes. But I can tell by the weather, how it smells outside and what's growing out of the ground. One day I'll wake up and there's a charge in the air and I'll know it's the anniversary of their birth. I'll get up and see what I have to make a cake for them.

Today I woke to a chill wind blowing colored leaves through the window, scattering them across my bed. I sat up and plucked one from the blanket. I smelled what day it was, a scent I can't describe. I went to the kitchen knowing they are six. The house was empty. They rise early and go into the woods because morning is their favorite time to play. The floor creaked as I brought flour down from the pantry shelf. My back prickled like there were eyes on me. I froze, sure it was all over, my time with them. It came back to me then, how it felt in that house beside of the railroad tracks with John, listening for the creak of his boot on the floorboards. But I stood still, counting backward, and nothing happened. No arm snaked under my throat, no fingers snagged my hair. I tried to hum as I made the cake, but I was rattled. I couldn't shake the feeling of an end coming. Not the end of the world that our pastor at Piney Grove preached about, but the end of my world, the one I've made on Bloodroot Mountain for my twins and me.

I'm not sorry for the way I live, even when I see how Mr. Barnett looks at me sometimes, and Mark Cotter when I go up the mountain to buy fresh milk from him. He owns the farm since his parents died. I've only spoken to him once, when his wife was gone to town. I asked about Wild Rose. He claimed she spends most of her time loose in the woods now. "I don't even try to pen her up no more," he said. "She's more ornery than ever since she's got old." He stared at my babies as he spoke to me, one on each hip, but he didn't ask about them. I know Mark Cotter and I are not friends anymore, but he is still loyal to me. He must remember how it used to be. Whatever Mark and Mr. Barnett think of the way I live, they keep my secret. That's all that matters. For six years, I've managed to hide my twins up here. But stirring the cake batter this morning I couldn't stop thinking, not just about John, but about my whole life. I remembered myself as a six-year-old girl, when I marked time by my own birthdays and not those of my children.

I thought of Granny and how she liked to talk as she worked. There was a wringer washer by the back steps and I can still see her feeding Granddaddy's shirts through, telling stories about Chickweed Holler. She talked most about her cousin Lou Ann, who I pictured as a crone with a hump, putting a curse on our family. I saw her with sores eating at her nose and mouth corners, eyes like holes pecked into her face by crows, standing on her high porch handing down love potions and charms to women desperate to bewitch a man, to have a child or lose one, to be granted long life or for someone else to die. I imagined powders in twists of paper, left hind feet of graveyard rabbits, snakeskin bags with toad's eyes inside. They walked up the holler with their darkest desires and she did what she could to make them real. Even one of Granny's great-aunts had gone to her.

"When Della was young and silly," Granny said, "she had dealings with Lou Ann herself. She got struck on an old boy that came around selling Bibles, not that he ever cracked one open. Nothing do her, she had to have him. But he wouldn't look twice at her. Well, Della went to see Lou Ann, with

Grandmaw Ruth and Myrtle both begging her not to. She came back looking peaked. They all still lived at home and she asked her mammy if they could have chicken for supper. Said she'd be the one to cook it. Their mammy said she reckoned so. Della went out in the yard and caught her one right then, wrung its neck and plucked it and took it in the kitchen. She pulled out the innards and Grandmaw and Myrtle thought she was fixing to make chicken livers. But that ain't what she was up to. She found that chicken's heart, popped it in her mouth, and swallowed it whole. Grandmaw and Myrtle seen her do it. She hacked and carried on, but she kept it down. Lo and behold, the next day that Bible salesman came calling. Him and Della ran off and got married. It didn't last long, though. Grandmaw said he beat Della like a mule. I reckon he got shot six months later, messing around with some other man's wife. Della wouldn't talk about it much, but she told me all the time, 'Be careful what you wish for.' "

Granny was always telling stories like that, about Grandmaw Ruth and the great-aunts and Mammy and Pap. I know she was trying to teach me something, but that wasn't her only reason. After so many years, she still missed her family. As much as she loved Bloodroot Mountain, she talked sometimes about going back to Chickweed Holler and seeing the old homestead again. It belonged now to distant cousins who wrote her letters. Once she went so far as to ask Granddaddy if he would drive her over there, but when the day came to travel she changed her mind. "I reckon I better stick close to home," she said. "I'm too old to be running off. I used to dream about crossing the ocean on a ship and seeing the world, but it never happened. Your granddaddy scratched that itch."

But it seemed nothing could scratch mine. The soles of my feet itched so hard in the night, they almost burned. Whenever Granny saw me squirming, she looked troubled. One night I asked her to scratch my feet. She said, "No use in me scratching them. You took that after me. Ain't but one cure, and I dread the day that itch gets satisfied."

"What day, Granny?"

"The day you run off from here."

"I won't ever!"

"I don't know if you can help it," she said, reaching under the quilt to take one of my feet in her warm hand.

She was right about me. I've done a lot of

things I never thought I'd do. When I was a little girl, I always figured I would marry a mountain man, who knew the sting of briar scratches, the teeth-rattling shiver of cold creek water, the black smell of garden soil that made you want to roll in it. But John was the first thing I ever saw that was prettier than my home. The first time I laid eyes on him, we had gone to Odom's Hardware after seeds. Granny usually ordered them from a catalogue, but that Saturday we were working in the yard when Mr. Barnett stopped to drop off a red velvet cake from Margaret. He was headed to Millertown for nails and snail bait. He asked if we wanted to come along and I was surprised when Granny said, "Why, I believe I will. Let me run in the house and get my pocketbook." I could tell by the way she turned her face into the summer wind as we rode down the mountain that she just wanted to go for a ride. I was always up for a trip to town myself. The high school was usually the closest I got, unless I hitched a ride with Doug or Mark or went along with one of my girlfriends. Granddaddy had left behind a truck when he died, but it was rusting in the barn because Granny never learned how to use it. Sometimes it was like being stranded on an island. But I felt free as we drove past the red brick school building, making waves with my arm out the window.

There were only a few people milling the streets downtown. I drifted behind Granny and Mr. Barnett as they browsed the dim aisles of the hardware store. I was ready to go after we'd picked out the seeds, but Granny and Mr. Barnett stopped to make small talk with the man behind the counter, about weather and farming and inflated prices. I asked Granny if I could walk to the dime store and Mr. Barnett handed me his bag of nails. "Will you put these in the truck on your way down the sidewalk, honey?"

I stepped into the sun holding the wrinkled brown sack, sharp with nail points, and stopped in my tracks. A boy and girl stood outside the door in a patch of shade, kissing each other in a hungry way I'd never seen before. A tingle darted through me. I couldn't see much of the boy's face but I could see his hair, black as pitch, and her pale fingers digging into the dent between his shoulder blades. Then the girl cracked her eyes and noticed me. She broke away from him with a start. He turned around and I dropped the sack, nails spraying everywhere on the cracked cement. I knelt to pick them up, cheeks on fire. I'd seen his face, both sinister and beautiful. Before I could register what was happening, he was coming to kneel beside me. "Let me help you with that, miss," he said. His voice was like a silk ribbon unrolling. Our fingers touched and when I glanced up, I thought I saw a flicker of interest in his eyes. Then the girl was saying, "I'd better get on back to work, John. My dad will skin me alive." He rose and went to her as Granny and Mr. Barnett were coming out of the store. "I'll walk you," he said. When he looked back over his shoulder at me, my legs felt made of something unreliable.

I watched them go, taking in the shape of his body, tall with narrow hips and wide shoulders. "Who was that?" I asked, following Granny to the truck.

"That's John," Mr. Barnett said. "One of Frankie's boys. You don't want nothing to do with him. I reckon he's tomcatting around with that Ellen Hamilton now. Her daddy's got a drugstore down here on the corner. But you ort to hear the stories John's brothers tells on him. They claim he's got a girlfriend for every day of the week. I reckon it's pitiful how he does them girls. They was one tried to kill herself over him."

I was so quiet on the way home that Granny asked if I was sick. It didn't matter what Mr. Barnett had said about John. I couldn't stop seeing his eyes, the hair that fell across his forehead when he knelt by me, the beauty of his face, like something carved from marble. I never knew there were real people in the world that looked like him.

Mr. Barnett let us out of his truck at the house. Walking across the yard, Granny said, "Let's have chicken and dumplings for supper." I stood under the apple tree while she killed and plucked the chicken, trying to cool my face in the shade. After a while I followed her up the steps and into the kitchen. When I saw the chicken's carcass laid out on the counter, it seemed like a sign. The instant Granny went to the pantry I tore into the bird's chest and pulled out its heart. I crammed it into my mouth and it was awful, small and slick, sliding down my throat. I coughed and gagged, the heart struggling to come back up. But, like my great-great-great-aunt Della, I was determined to choke it down. When Granny rushed over to pound on my back, I said, "It's okay. I just got strangled on spit."

I felt guilty for betraying Granny. If she'd known what I had done, she would have been disappointed in me. But there was no going back. I didn't know if I believed in Lou Ann's charm, but I knew now what those women had felt. I wasn't worried about Ellen Hamilton or anybody else. I was only concerned with myself and what I had to have. I went to bed early that night, half sick from the chicken heart, but I couldn't rest. I tossed and turned, thinking how he'd looked over his shoulder at me as he walked the blond girl back to work. It was like being possessed. When I finally closed my eyes and drifted down toward sleep, I dreamed his face hovered inches from mine in the dark, his long, sculpted body floating over my bed like an angel or a wraith. I opened my eyes with a start, prepared to be kissed like he had kissed Ellen Hamilton on the sidewalk. I promised myself that if he ever did kiss me that way, I'd kiss him back twice as hard.

Now the ghost of John is different. It has no face or body, just the shine of eyes. Last night, I saw them in a tree and thought he was there. Then something moved along the branch and hissed down at me, a red-eyed possum. But sometimes I wake up smelling sulfur and dead rats and sweet aftershave. My bedroom reeks of him and I know he's been there watching me sleep. Once I walked in and saw him sitting in the rocking chair. I dropped my book but didn't scream. He was there for a long second and

I thought he would say something. Then I blinked and he was gone, the rocking chair empty. These days John could come to me in any form. Long shadows falling across the yard could be the shape of tree trunks or of his legs, claw-tipped branches could be his arms, dripping water could be his tapping fingers, cold drafts could be his breath. But back then, when I was seventeen, I wanted every noise to be John Odom coming after me in the dark.

It wasn't the next day that he came. It was a long four weeks in which I could think of nothing but him. I was guilty about the chicken heart and desperate for it to work at the same time. I had no appetite and Granny kept shooting me troubled looks across the table. I couldn't concentrate on chores. I broke eggs carrying them in from the barn, cut my finger peeling potatoes, singed one of my good dresses with the iron. Then school started back and my life fell into a familiar routine. I still dreamed of John Odom, but I began to feel foolish for believing that swallowing a heart might bring me love.

On Monday of the second week of school, John materialized out of the early gloom as I walked to the bottom of the dirt road on my way to catch the bus, eyes and teeth shining. It seemed he had boiled up from the dust of the road.

"Don't be scared," he said. "I just came to drive you to school."

"How did you find me?" I asked when my tongue came unstuck.

"I been asking around." He fell in step beside me.

"What makes you think I'd take up with just anybody?" I asked, keeping my eyes straight ahead. I should have been scared but I was only excited.

"I ain't just anybody. You've been in my daddy's store before."

"Who's your daddy?" I asked, pretending ignorance.

"Frankie Odom."

"I thought you had a girlfriend."

"I couldn't stop thinking about you."

I stole glances at him from the corner of my eye as we went down the hill, heart slamming against my breastbone. He looked at least five years older than me, maybe more. He was a man, not a boy. He was no less beautiful than I remembered. He looked almost foreign, hair and eyes black as soot. I wondered then if his mother had been someone exotic, but not after I saw pictures of her later. She was scrawny with bleached hair and slit eyes under pointy glasses. I remembered his jug-eared father from the store, and his pot-bellied brothers, plainer versions of him. His beauty was inexplicable.

He wasn't like the boys at school. He kept his hair short while they grew theirs long. He wore creased trousers, they wore bell-bottoms. His old-fashioned ways made him even more foreign and like home at the same time. Living with Granny on the mountain, the old ways were what I knew best. As we walked I took secret sips of him, unable to find a flaw. His one physical imperfection, I discovered later, was invisible. He was deaf in his left ear since childhood, when his youngest brother, Hollis, had shot a cap pistol beside it. I learned this is what saved him from the war. Later I would come to wish that he had gone to Vietnam, that he had been killed over there, and I had never met him.

I didn't let John take me to school. I was too shy to get into his car. I caught the bus instead. But I looked back at him, sitting behind his steering wheel beside the road. All day long I tried to remember the details of his face. After school I had plans to go to the library and study for a test with one of my friends. Her father had offered to pick us up and drive me home when the library closed. I was supposed to meet her in the parking lot but when I walked out the double doors of the high school, shading my eyes against the sun, John was standing at the bottom of the steps. I almost dropped my books.

"I'm here to take you home," he said, squinting up at me.

"I told Granny I was going to the library."

He smiled in a crooked way. "I'll take you to the library."

"No," I said. "Let's go somewhere else."

I climbed into the passenger seat of his car and told him to head for Bloodroot Mountain. It was a risk to have him take me home, but I wanted to be somewhere safe with him. As he drove, I cracked the window to let in the September wind. We didn't talk but he kept glancing over at me. When we finally turned onto the dirt road leading up the mountain, I asked him to pull onto the shoulder so that his car would be hidden in the trees. I led him by the hand along the creek, to a place I had shared with no one else. Not long after Granddaddy died, I had followed the creek up the mountain trying to find its source. I found an abandoned springhouse instead, a little block hut with its foundation covered in weeds and ferns, the arched roof patched with vivid green moss, springwater flowing out the shadowed opening over ledges of rock. Farther up the mountain, I found some rotten poplar logs and the remains of an old stone chimney. When I asked Granny about it, she said Doug Cotter's great-grandfather had once lived there in a cabin.

John didn't ask where I was taking him as we cut a path through the bushes and saplings. We were both out of breath by the time we reached the springhouse. I watched as John hunkered down to drink from his cupped palm. When he looked up at me, chin dripping, all of my shyness disappeared. I got down on my knees in the mud beside the spring, not caring how I would explain my dirty skirt to Granny. We studied each other, a beam of sun lighting his face. After a while I asked, "Why did you come to me?"

He was quiet, looking up into the tree branches. "It was your eyes," he said at last. "I never seen a blue like that." He turned to me and studied them for a long time. He reached out to touch my hair but his hand paused in the air. He was looking at me in a way I had never been seen. I was a girl to everyone else. John Odom saw me as a woman. But I could tell that he was nervous. Like me, he was scared of the spell we were under. "I shouldn't have come up here," he said. "I better go on, before I get you in trouble."

"No," I said. "I don't want you to go." I only hesitated an instant before leaning over to kiss him, as hard and wild as I had promised myself to if I ever had the chance. When his arms came around me I was lost, not thinking of Granny or how to behave. The whole thing happened fast but it felt like slow motion, John pushing me down on the leaf-littered mud, the weight of him pressing the breath out of me. If someone had come upon us it might have looked like a fight, our mouths and teeth clashing so that my lips were sore later, my fingers tangled up in his hair as he kissed where the buttons of my blouse had come undone. It was a helpless feeling, like in dreams of diving off the rock over the bluff, those few sweet moments of flight worth the death that was waiting for me. When I groped for his hand and pushed it under the hem of my skirt, I could feel his heart beating in his fingers, or maybe it was mine. I gasped as his palm slid up the length of my leg. But then, without warning, his fingers clamped down on my thigh. Before I could protest, he was wrenching himself out of my arms. "I should have left you alone," he breathed, getting to his feet. When he rushed off, leaves clinging to his pants, I was too stunned to go after him. I lay on my back trying to catch my breath, the smell of him all over me.

The next day at school, I could think of nothing but the scrape of his stubble, the hot flesh of his stomach under his shirt, the trail of his hand moving up my leg. I had to close my eyes and put my head down on my desk. I didn't understand what had happened between us. If the rumors were true, John Odom was no gentleman. It made no sense the way he ran off and left me. I knew that my feelings for him were dangerous, but after what had happened at the springhouse, nothing could have kept me away from him.

After school let out, I walked over to Main Street. I don't remember getting there. I only remember standing in the shadows of an awning across the street as dark came early, the sky turning sunset orange between the buildings. I watched the door of Odom's Hardware for him to come out and when he appeared, stepping onto the sidewalk and turning to lock the door behind him, my chest went heavy and tight. I crossed the street without feeling the ground underfoot. As I drew close to him everything came into sharp focus, his carved face, his shining eyes, his black hair. He stopped when he saw me and drew in a breath. Somewhere distant I heard voices and traffic, but on Main Street we were alone. We stared at each other for a long while in silence. I felt everything inside me threatening to rise to the surface, but I knew it was important to be calm and still. His coat collar was turned up on one side. Without thinking, I reached to smooth it down.

"What are you doing here?" he asked.

I tried to smile. "I need a ride."

He smiled back. "Mountain's a long way off."

"Yes," I said. "But it's a pretty drive."

He looked past me into the street. "You shouldn't be out here by yourself."

I stepped closer to him. "Why'd you run off like that?"

"I don't know. I guess I came to my senses."

"What does that mean?"

"It means I can't be with somebody like you."

"Somebody like me?"

His eyes returned to my face. "Somebody good."

"Well," I said. "I think you're somebody good."

He paused. "You don't even know me."

I took another step closer. "I don't care."

He opened his mouth to protest but I didn't want to hear it. I took a deep breath, mustering my courage, and did what I had wanted to the minute he stepped out of the hardware store and locked the door behind him. I grabbed his coat and stood on tiptoe to kiss him like before. In those long seconds, something happened that I can't forget. A strong wind came howling down Main Street, a cold blast whirling with dead leaves and trash, whipping my hair and plastering a sheet of newspaper to John's shoulder where it clung before flying off toward the stoplight. I remembered stories of banshees Granny had told me, Irish witches who wailed outside houses at night to warn families of danger. To hear a banshee was always a bad omen. That night in my dreams, when I broke away from John's kiss, the banshee's veiled face floated inches from mine, the wind from her scream taking my breath. But on Main Street it was John who broke our kiss. The wind died as fast as it came, letting go of my hair and John's coattail. He held me for a moment at arm's length. "Are you sure about this?" he asked. "Because once I get ahold of you, I ain't turning you loose." I said yes without a second thought and followed him to his car.

I wasn't ready for Granny or anyone else to know about us at first. John continued to park at the bottom of the road, a little inside the tree line, and we took long walks on the mountain. I was careful to choose paths I hadn't explored. The going was harder, briars clawing at our ankles, but I didn't want to risk running into Mr. Barnett or Doug Cotter. I wanted to climb to the top of Bloodroot Mountain with John, to stand in the secret meadow with him. I hadn't tried since I was fourteen, when I caused Doug to fall. But John and I never made it that far. He always wanted to stop and sit, on fallen trees or rocky bluffs, anywhere he could kiss me. Sometimes I smelled another woman's perfume on his clothes, but I didn't say anything. I knew I hadn't fully claimed him. At first I thought if I could be with him the way those other women were, I would have all of him. But each time we got close, his hands under my dress and mine tearing at his shirt, he pulled away again. Then one day, lying on the ground beside the springhouse, he said, "I've had plenty of whores, Myra. That ain't what I want out of you." His words stung but their meaning made me hope I was different than the ones who left perfume on his clothes. Whenever he got quiet I held my breath, praying that he would propose to me.

Every second he was out of my sight, my stomach churned with worry about what he was doing and who he was with. I sat on the back steps chewing my nails, stood at the bottom of the road and looked for his car even when I knew he wasn't coming, took to my bed sometimes before dark and buried my face in my pillow. I knew Granny saw my misery, but she didn't comment on it. Sitting at the kitchen table, tension hung like smoke between us, choking our conversations. Finally, I couldn't take keeping the secret any longer. As scared as I was that she'd deny John and me her blessing, I had to confess.

At the beginning of winter, we were taping sheets of plastic over the house's old windows to keep in the heat. It was already cold and drafty in the front room. I stood holding the thick silver tape roll for her, realizing how old it seemed she had grown overnight. I tried to memorize the seams and creases of her face, soft and wrinkled as brownish crepe paper. I charted the constellations her age spots made, took in the black brogans she wore for outside chores, Granddaddy's dingy socks rolled down around her ankles, and the faded flowers of her dress, thin from hundreds of washings. I ached for her then as much or more than I did for John, thought of choosing her and the mountain and never getting married or moving away. But she turned to me, as her fingers smoothed a long strip of tape down the window frame, and said, "I believe my girl's got something to tell me." I wasn't expecting to burst into tears. The flood startled me more than it did Granny. She came and held my face in her arthritis-knotted hands. "I've got cataracts," she said with a sad grin, "but I ain't blind yet. Now, I done decided I ain't going to meddle. You'd just end up resenting me for it. But you better be careful, Myra Jean."

I understand what Granny meant. Like her, I let my twins make their own mistakes. I don't make them wear shoes, even when locust thorns have blown among the weeds. I don't stop them from climbing trees or robbing beehives or swimming with snakes. I let them go, as Granny did me, only without warning them to be careful. I know they wouldn't listen. But I protect them from a distance. I used to spend weeks without John or any of the Odoms entering my mind. I saw my twins out from under a cloud. I taught them how to count and hunt and clean fish. One day lying in the grass I flew them, lifting them up with my feet on their hipbones, holding their hands with their hair hanging down and their small faces shining. They took turns, the girl's homemade dress swaying over me and the boy's floppy shirt filling with wind like a sail. They laughed and I laughed with them, until tears leaked out of my eyes. I know they won't remember it. They might never know me again that way. Lately it's been hard to think of anything but the past. I carried a disease with me out of that house by the tracks and pieces of me are still coming off. It's unfair how my fear has grown over time and begun to take me over. Sometimes it feels like John has won. But I'd rather die than trap the twins as I was trapped while I was with him. That's why I'll always give them their freedom.

After my talk with Granny, I didn't hide my relationship with John, but I spent less time on the mountain for the sake of Doug Cotter. I knew he loved me, and I cared for him enough not to flaunt my happiness. John and I mostly went to Millertown. I thought of my mother, running off with my father when she was my age. John showed me places and I imagined her there, the glass-sprinkled lot of a drive-in, the restaurant where I ate pizza for the first time. I wondered if my parents ate it together as John and I did, by the window of a dim place with checked tablecloths and silk daisies in vases.

When spring came, John taught me to drive his car. We spent hours tooling down the back roads of Valley Home and Slop Creek and Piney Grove with the windows down and the radio playing, pulling over for long golden meadows and covered bridges and ponds green with scum. The more time we spent together, the more certain I grew that he would propose. That's why I pushed aside my nerves and took him up Bloodroot Mountain to meet Granny. I was relieved to see that she was charmed by John, but by then nothing could have kept me from being with him, not even my love for Granny.

One Sunday afternoon we were supposed to meet at the springhouse after church. We hadn't walked together in a long time and I missed being on the mountain with him. Granny and I always rode to Piney Grove squeezed between the Barnetts in the cab of their truck and I was quiet all the way down the mountain, dreaming of lying with John once again on the bank beside the spring. After the service I waited in the churchyard as Granny and the Barnetts chatted with the preacher, sitting on my mother's grave with my knees drawn up under my dress tail. I tried to talk to her in my mind. I closed my eyes and conjured her, not bones in a casket six feet under, but the girl I had seen in pictures with somber eyes and long hair parted straight down the middle. I felt closer to her than ever before. I sensed her spirit moving up through the grass and passing over me like a sigh. She of all people would understand how loving John Odom made me feel. She had run off to town with a man herself, left Granny and the mountain behind for him. Now she would lie in her grave beside him forever. I pictured a double headstone with my name carved in granite next to John's. The image filled me with warmth from head to toe.

When I looked toward the church again, Granny and the Barnetts were finally heading for the truck. I jumped up and ran fast enough to beat them. I leapt over the side of the truck bed into the straw and dirt, dress billowing up. I rode home hugging myself against the keen spring wind, knowing I was late and John was waiting for me. As soon as Mr. Barnett let us out at the house, I vaulted over the side of the truck and took off. I heard Granny saying to the Barnetts, "Lord, I don't know what's got into that girl."

I ran all the way to the springhouse with a stitch in my side, but I couldn't slow down. It seemed I could already taste his lips, cold from the water he would drink from his palm. I only stopped running when the block hut came into view on a rise above me. When someone stood up out of the bushes on the opposite side of the spring where he had been squatting, I expected it to be John. But I saw the fair hair and the long, skinny legs and the smile I had carried all the way up the mountain wilted. It was Mark Cotter, holding a cane fishing pole in one hand and a string of fish in the other. For a moment we were both too startled to speak. The woods were quiet and still besides the wasps hovering in and out of the springhouse opening. Then he grinned in his lazy way. "Look who it is," he said. "I ain't seen you in a long time." He came down the slope and splashed across the creek to where I stood. I scanned the trees, heart thudding in my ears, hoping his brother hadn't come with him. "You found my good fishing hole," he said, standing so close I could smell the salt of his sweat. "Don't tell nobody and I'll give you a bluegill." He held up the string of dripping fish, rainbows shining on their scales.

"That's all right," I said, forcing a smile. "I won't tell." It was true, Mark and I hadn't seen each other in a long time. He had become a man since I saw him last. It was more than the scruffy beard he had grown. There was something wiser about his eyes.

"I hope you know you've done broke my little brother's heart," he said after an awkward silence. "He's been moping around the house like a sick puppy dog."

I shifted from foot to foot, wondering how to get rid of him before John came along. "I've been meaning to walk up the hill and see Wild Rose."

Mark shook his head. "Shoot, you'd be just as likely to see her out here running the woods. They never made a fence that could hold that horse."

There was another silence. I glanced nervously at the pole leaning across his shoulder. "Looks like you're on your way to the house. Tell Doug hello for me, okay?"

Mark grinned again, but not with his eyes. "What are you doing up here anyway?"

"Nothing. Just taking a walk."

"Why don't you set down here and watch me catch a fish?"

"I better not," I said, looking down at my dress. "I've got my church clothes on."

He held his hand in front of my face, black with soil from baiting hooks. "Since when was you scared of a little dirt?" He lowered his cane pole to the ground. "Here," he said. "You can blame it on me." He reached out and took hold of my arm, fingerprinting the sleeve of my dress. I tried to twist away but he wouldn't let go. I was surprised to see a flash of anger in his eyes. I had never thought he might have wanted me as much as his brother did. That's when I heard John's footsteps coming up the slope behind us.

"What's going on here?" he said. I turned around and the look on his face made my stomach lurch. His eyes seemed almost inhuman, mean and glittering black like a crow's. I had the urge to take off running for home as fast as my legs would go.

"Who the hell are you?" Mark said.

John stepped between Mark and me. "You better move that hand."

"It's okay," I said, but neither one of them seemed to hear.

Mark let go of my arm. "Watch it, buddy. This is my daddy's land."

"I don't care whose land it is," John said. "You don't touch her."

Mark's face flushed a deep, ugly red. "She's on my daddy's property, too. I reckon I can do whatever I want to with her."

Before I knew what was happening, John had Mark Cotter by the throat. The string of bluegill slid onto the mud at our feet alongside the fishing pole. "You better get on away from here," John said through clenched teeth.

After what seemed a lifetime, he turned Mark loose. Mark stood still for a moment gasping for breath, rubbing at his throat where John's fingerprints were fading. Tears of humiliation stood in his eyes. He looked at me in an accusatory way, as if I were the one to blame. Then he backed off and blundered into the trees, swatting vines and branches out of his path. I looked at the fish he had caught, left behind on the ground to rot in the sun, and felt a wave of pity for him so overwhelming I had to sit down on the bank. John watched Mark until he was gone and then lowered himself beside me.

"You didn't have to hurt him," I said, near tears myself. "He's my neighbor."

John put his arm around me and pulled me close. "I'm jealous-hearted, Myra. I don't like nobody else touching you. I don't even like your granny having you all to herself. It don't seem right for her to be with you more than I am." He took hold of my chin and tipped my face up to look at him. "I want to marry you," he said, growing solemn. "But if you're going to be with me, you belong to me. I can't have it no other way."

My heart leapt, what he had done to Mark forgotten. I stared at him, unable to speak. "I belong to you," I said after a moment. "But it works both ways. I'm jealous-hearted, too. If we get married, you can't have another woman for as long as we live."

John leaned over and touched his nose to mine. "Hell, that's easy," he said. "You've done ruined me. I can't even stand to think about nobody else."

Looking back, we would have said anything to possess one another. If we had known we were making promises we couldn't keep, it wouldn't have mattered to us.

For two weeks, I walked around with my steps unburdened and light. I didn't wonder anymore whether John was seeing Ellen Hamilton or any other woman behind my back. But soon after he proposed, just like that night a banshee wind came screaming down Main Street, I had another glimpse of the darkness to come. Near the middle of June, John picked me up and drove me down the mountain to a part of Millertown I'd never seen.

"Where are we going?" I asked.

"Will you quit asking me that? I said it's a surprise." He smiled, white teeth flashing. He twisted at the radio knobs as we passed pawnshops and seedy restaurants and then the junkyard, big hunks of car metal twinkling in the hot summer sun.

"I hate surprises," I said, studying his profile. It took a second to realize he was turning into a lot by the railroad tracks, gravel crunching under the tires. I looked out the windshield at the tiny, peeling box of a house, the streetlight high on a pole, power lines hanging like black snakes stretched across the yard. I turned to him and waited, thinking he had pulled over to kiss me as he did sometimes, fingers wrestling through my hair.

"What do you think?" he asked, eyes bright.

"About what?"

"The house, goose. I rented us a place."

I blinked hard, my chest going tight.

"Come on," he said, getting out of the car. He dug in his pants pocket and produced a greasy-looking key dangling from a dull silver hoop. I stared out the windshield, mouth open. He laughed. "I got you good, didn't I?"

He came around to open the passenger door and pulled me out, still laughing at my expression. "Let's look inside. I ain't even seen it yet. There was a man came in the store, said he had a place for rent cheap if we knew anybody. I said, as a matter of fact I do know somebody and you're looking at him. He didn't even ask for a deposit."

I followed John across the sooty lot, our feet scuffing up grit. It was so hot it seemed I could hear my skin sizzling. It struck me that these were the tracks where my mother was killed. I thought I might faint. There was no color. I was used to the trees setting the mountain on fire in fall and all the blooming bushes in spring and every shade of green in summer. Even the mountain ground was spotted with shade and light, blanketed with moss and deep trenches of fallen leaves, ridged with cool-colored sparkling rock, springing with mottled toadstools. But this was all still and flat and buzzing with flies. The smell of factory chemicals made my head ache.

There was a chipped concrete stoop and a light fixture beside the door covered in sticky webs. John put the key in the lock and I watched as he jiggled it, turned it, and cursed under his breath. We were both caught by surprise when the door swung in with a whine. In those first seconds my eyes played a trick that I kept to myself but never forgot. I saw the dark shape of a woman standing in the front room, tall and bone thin with wild clumps of hair and no discernible face. I stopped and clutched at the door jamb. John said, "What?" and she was gone. "I thought I saw something," I said, my voice as creaky as the rusty door hinges. I was still shaking when we went into the hot stink of the house.

But once John was touching me again, his warm hands moving over my skin, it didn't take long for me to bury my doubts about the place he had rented. I told myself it didn't matter where we lived, as long as we were together. We got married a few days later in the preacher's kitchen, a coffeepot slurping on the counter. I could barely wait to kiss him. I smelled his aftershave and his clean black hair even over the coffee. I didn't realize, putting Granddaddy's ring on his finger, how fitting it was that Granny had passed it down to me. Like her, I had given in to temptation and done wrong in the name of bloodred love. Outside in the car John and I kissed each other longer and harder before driving away, his flesh hot under the thin white fabric of his dress shirt.

My wedding night was not how I expected. Later on there was pleasure, but that first night alone in our bedroom, it was painful, not just between my legs but in my heart. I would never be Granny's little girl again. I felt the mountain falling through my fingers, but I was foolish enough to think as I clung to him in the dark that at least we belonged to each other. At least the pact we made by the springhouse was finally sealed.

John took a week off work and we spent most of it at home, leaving only to buy groceries. I came to know his body better than my own, from the peak of his hairline to the arches of his feet. I loved the blue veins of his temples, the tender bracelets of his wrists, the intricate folds of his ears. The house was depressing but I forgot when I saw him sleeping late in a stripe of sun or in the bathtub with his wet knees poking out of soapy water. I worshipped everything about him, even how he took greedy bites at supper and there was always a crumb left on the corner of his mouth. In the night he'd tickle me with the ends of my hair, trailing it up and down my naked arms, along my jaw and chin. Sometimes I read poems to him and I didn't mind when they put him to sleep. I kept reading after his eyes were closed. All these years later, watching over my twins as they sleep on Granny's rag rug, I try to remember the first whispers of fear. I try to mark the time when everything changed. It happened the night I asked about his mother. It was almost dawn and the house was still, no trains rattling the bedroom window as they passed. We were lying curled together under the sheet, my head nestled in the hollow of his shoulder, when I realized we had never discussed the thing we had most in common.

"Tell me something about your mother," I said.

He was breathing slow, almost asleep. "Huh?"

"We never talk about it."

"Talk about what?"

"Not having a mother."

He opened his eyes. "I had a mother."

"But you were just twelve when she died."

"Yeah," he said. "I don't remember much."

"How did she die?"

There was a long pause. "What do you mean?"

"I mean, what did she die of?"

He paused again. "They said it was a heart attack. But that ain't what killed her."

I sat up and pushed back the sheet. The

405

air in the room had changed somehow. Even my legs were sweating in the summer heat. I already knew then that the contented feeling of John and me being the last two people on earth was fading away. I began to wish I'd never brought up his mother, but it seemed too late to turn back. "Then what do you think she died of?"

He looked at the ceiling. "I don't think. I know. Because I'm the one caused it."

For a moment I didn't know how to respond. I leaned over him, trying to see his face in the early morning light falling through the parted curtains, coloring our room the dark blue of an ink stain. "A heart attack is nobody's fault," I said at last.

He rolled over to face the wall. "I told you, it wasn't no heart attack."

"Whatever it was, it's not your fault."

He got quiet again. Then he said, "Tell that to my daddy."

"He blamed you for your mother dying?"

"No. He never blamed me for it. It's about the only thing he's proud of me over."

"John," I said, knots forming in my stomach. "What are you talking about?"

A long time passed. I willed him not to go on. Whatever he was trying to tell me, I was afraid to hear it. "Nothing," he said after a while. "I'm done talking about it."

I slipped my arms around him. "I'm sorry I brought it up. I didn't know it would bother you. I just never had anybody to talk about my mother with. Even Granny didn't talk about her much, and she wouldn't talk about my father at all. If I asked about the Mayeses, she said, 'Them people wouldn't piss on you if you was on fire.' It's the closest I ever heard Granny come to cussing." I paused and there was only the sound of his breathing. I rushed on to fill the silence. "I never tried to see them while I was living at home. Now I figure I can go visit them without Granny knowing about it. They might have pictures I haven't seen, or stories they can tell me. Granny said the Mayeses owned a pool hall around here." I stopped again and there was still no response. I began to think he had fallen asleep. I nudged his side. "Do you know where it's at? The pool hall?"

When he finally answered, his voice was cold. "It's over on Miller Avenue."

I hesitated. "Will you take me there?"

"No," he said, in the same harsh voice. "And you might as well get it out of your head. I ain't having my wife hanging around no pool hall. I'd be the jackass of the town."

John was never the same after our talk. The next morning he sat up in the tangled sheets with eyes dead as coal. When I saw the emptiness in his face, I had a flash of Granny and me standing beside the wringer washer. Her story of a black-haired Bible salesman flew over my head like a bird I didn't allow to nest. I draped my arms over his back and said, "Let's go for a drive." He seemed not to hear. "Fix me some coffee," he mumbled. I tried to hum as he sat with his cup at the kitchen table. I made small talk as I fried the eggs and hovered over him while he ate breakfast. My palms sweated and I kept wiping them on my nightgown. Then John stood up. "Say you want to go for a ride?"

I released the breath I hadn't realized I was holding and hurried to throw on my clothes. I ran out to the car with him chasing after me, sure I had imagined whatever cold had crept between us in the night. Riding with the windows down on familiar roads, John began to talk as usual. I thought he would tell one of his funny stories, about pranks he had pulled on his brothers or trouble he got into in grade school. But he looked out the windshield, brow clouded over, and asked, "You ever feel out of place around here?"

I looked at him. "No," I said. "I never thought about it."

He lit a cigarette on the glowing end of the car lighter. "Sometimes I listen to them hicks that comes in the store and wonder what in the world I'm still doing here."

I turned my face to the fields passing by, high with goldenrod and purplish heather, cows grazing behind barbwire fences. "I guess I can't imagine anywhere else."

"You're just like the rest of them, then," he said. "A body can't amount to nothing here. What's a man going to do, if he don't want to work in a factory or shovel shit on a farm, or do like my daddy and scrape together a business that don't make enough to live on. All there is to do around here is break your back and not have a thing to show for it."

"Where do you want to go?"

"I ain't going nowhere," he said. "I'm stuck in this hole."

"How come?"

He turned on me with angry eyes. "You think I'd walk away from that store?"

I fidgeted in the car seat, knees drawn up, wind tearing at my dress.

"People think because I'm Frankie Odom's boy I'm rich, but they don't know how he is. He works us like mules for next to nothing. When he's gone, I mean to have my piece of that place. You know, one time this woman came in with her husband and said, 'Odom's Hardware is a landmark. Buildings like this are the heart of our town.' I wanted to say, 'Why don't you come in here at the crack of dawn and choke on dust and sell nails and put up with hicks like you all day, then you'd think, heart of our town.'"

I studied his face for traces of the John I had known just the day before. I'd never heard him talk that way. "I'd go anywhere you wanted to," I said, desperate to fix him.

He smirked. "You think you'd leave here? You couldn't get along a day without Granny. You ain't like I thought. You was the prettiest girl I ever seen. Looked like you didn't belong around here either. It ain't took me long to figure you out, though."

I wiped my sweaty palms on my dress again. "We can leave here anytime you want to," I said, so low I wondered if he even heard me.

"We ain't going nowhere," he said. "You got to have money to go anywhere. What do you think we'd live on?"

I looked down at the floorboard, heart in my throat. "We could find work."

"I done told you, I ain't put up with my daddy's shit all these years for nothing. But

I don't belong around here. You can take one look at my face and see that."

He drew deep from his cigarette, jetting smoke through his nostrils. There was a long, terrible silence. My chest was so tight I couldn't breathe. We passed a pond with pollen floating on its surface and I wanted nothing more than to get out of the car and stand beside it. "Can we stop here?" I asked. I was relieved when he pulled over to the shoulder of the road and killed the motor. But he sat with his wrists dangling on the steering wheel looking out the windshield and I didn't know what to do but sit there with him. After a few minutes he got out of the car and leaned against the hood with his cigarette. I got out and sidled close to him but he didn't move to touch me. I looked at the pond, feeling frightened and alone. After a while another car pulled alongside us. It was an old man in a junker with mismatching doors. He cranked down his window and called out to John. "Hey there, son." John turned as if waking up from a dream. I saw his eyes darken and his brows draw together. "Having car trouble?" the old man asked.

John stepped away from the hood. "Why don't you mind your own business?"

The man looked surprised. "Why, I was

just trying to be neighborly."

John bent lightning fast, cigarette clamped between his teeth, and snatched up a rock. Mineral flecks glinted in the mid-morning sun. He stepped toward the junker and the old man's expression changed from indignation to fear. John charged forward and let the rock fly just as the old man stepped on the gas, spinning a cloud of dust. "Nosy old son of a bitch," John muttered, breathing hard, smoothing his hair back into place as he stood in the road. I reached out to brace myself on the car hood, spots dancing before my eyes.

Sometimes a week would pass with the John I had first met, sweet and gentle and teasing. Before summer was over he bought an ice cream maker and it took so long to crank that our arms got tired. We stood in the kitchen with the back door open to let in the night air. Our laughter made the tracks and the yard seem not so barren, the smell of homemade ice cream muting the stench of bitter smoke. I still liked making John's coffee and drinking it with him in the early dark of the mornings. We didn't say much, just looked at each other over our warm cups. After he left, I sat on the couch waiting for him to come home. Each afternoon when I heard the car door slam, I ran across the scrubby grass and jumped into his arms, locking my legs around his hips. He would groan, pretending I was heavy, and kiss me all the way to the front door.

But the changes were hard to ignore, like the beer and then the whiskey he started drinking. It altered his breath, his speech, even how he kissed me. When he was drunk he slept so hard it was like he had gone away. I felt alone in the house with the scuttling mice. I came to hate being home while John was at work. Most days I sat in the front room looking at the clock, waiting to make supper. Going outside was no better, the sooty lot and the thundering trains and the smell of burning tires drifting over from the junkyard. All I wanted was to drink creek water from my hand, to catch a fish, to suck the juice from a honeysuckle between my teeth. If I couldn't go home whenever I wanted, I needed at least to get away from that smothering house. Once over supper I asked John about getting a job. He gripped a bottle of beer hard in his hand. "It's my opinion that a woman should keep at home," he said. "It's an outdated way of thinking, I guess, but that's how it is. I'm supposed to take care of you, and that's what I'll do."

I tried to tell myself maybe John was right about how a wife should be. He was older and wiser than me. At seventeen, I couldn't be expected to know. Besides, I'd made my bed. I had swallowed a chicken heart, like that long-dead aunt. This was my penance. By the end of August, he made it known that I couldn't visit Granny so much. He told me I needed to grow up, that even the Bible said you're supposed to leave behind your family and cleave to your husband. I told him the Bible also says you're supposed to take care of your old and that Granny needed us. His eyes grew so black and mean that I thought he would hit me. He said, "I don't know how come you love that old woman better than me." After that, he stopped taking me to church or back up the mountain at all.

It's strange the way time makes things different. Back then I always wanted to go somewhere. Now I have to make myself walk to the Cotters' and the Barnetts' and down the mountain selling ginseng. When I lived by the tracks I might have hopped a train if I'd had the courage. I thought of it sometimes when the rusty beds came squealing by, heaped with coal as black as John's eyes. Now I wish there was never a reason to set foot on any ground outside the house and land where Granny raised me. But in those dark days I would have gone anywhere. The first time John said we were eating supper with his daddy, I was relieved. I even sang to myself as I made a yellow cake to take with us.

I learned that every few months, Frankie Odom called a family meeting. Frankie claimed it was important for kinfolks to sit down at the same table together, but John said it was so he could keep his nose in his sons' business. "Only reason I'm going is because he puts bread in our mouths," John said. "That's how it is when you're under somebody's thumb." I didn't tell him that I was glad to be going. But my enthusiasm waned when I saw the house. Before John told me how stingy his father was, I might have been surprised to see the owner of Odom's Hardware living in such a place. There was a slumped look about it, tall and peeling with black windows and missing shingles. The lot next door was heaped with trash, a neighborhood dumping ground. There were other vehicles in the driveway and John's nephews chased each other in the brown grass. When we got out of the car I almost dropped the yellow cake. There was an odor outside like sulfur and dead rats. I knew the smell. One summer after a man had shot his wife at a house down the mountain, Granny and I were in the creek cooling off when a stink rose all around us, like a giant match had been struck. "Get out of that water," Granny said. "Let's get on to the house." She picked up her skirts and I followed. As we hurried through the woods, she said, "Devil's loose on the mountain, Myra Jean. We better stay in for a while." Now here the smell was again. I had grown up with the Holy Spirit. I wasn't the kind to fear things unseen. But standing before the Odom house, I was afraid.

Nobody met us at the door. When we stepped into the foyer a black shadow darted along the baseboard. I told myself it was a mouse. The smell was even more intense inside the house. John led me to the kitchen where Lonnie's wife Peggy was stirring a pot of soup beans. She looked up, sweat shining above her lip. "Hey," she said. "You can put that down on the counter." Eugene's wife Jewel was filling glasses from a pitcher of tea. I had never seen the other wives before. They were tired and colorless, Peggy rail thin and spattered with freckles, Jewel dumpy with a pockmarked face.

We left the cake with the wives and went to the living room. The curtains were drawn, making the room dark and claustrophobic.

I tried to smile but my chest was tightening. Frankie Odom didn't get up from his recliner. "What do you say, darlin?" he asked. He had always been the friendliest of them. But there was something rotten under his grin, maybe the source of the sulfur smell. The three brothers were sitting on the couch. Only Hollis stood to clap John on the back and tip an imaginary hat at me. I had never seen them outside the store, Eugene and Lonnie both older than John, their foreheads lined and their middles thick. Hollis was the youngest, not much older than me, slighter than his brothers with eyes that flicked all over the room and never landed anywhere. John was strange among them, tall and lithe and ethereal. He was right about not belonging there. The smell seemed to be growing stronger. I counted backward to keep from bolting for the door. Then Peggy called us to the dining room. Most of the chandelier's lights were blown. It cast lurid shadows on the close walls. At the table I thought they wouldn't speak, all of them, including the nephews, bent over their plates and stuffing their mouths. I tried to eat with them, despite the knots in my stomach.

Finally, Lonnie said, "I'll just tell you right off, Daddy. Peggy can't come by and straighten up for you no more. She's took a job at the bakery."

Frankie Odom's fork halted on the way to his mouth. "What?"

"We ain't got no choice. They's bills to pay."

"Well," he said. "It's about like y'uns to let me and Hollis fend for ourselves. I know you boys is just waiting on me to die so you can get this place."

Lonnie grinned around a mouthful of bread. "What would we want with this old place? Looks to me like it's fixing to fall down around your ears."

Frankie Odom slammed his fist on the table. I flinched but the others seemed undisturbed. "That's because you dadburn boys won't help me do nothing. I've worked like a dog all of my life to keep y'uns up, and what do I get for it?"

"Cheapest labor you can find," John said. For the first time, I saw how much his eyes were like his father's. "You think you could get anybody else to work that cheap?"

"Now, Daddy," Eugene said, wiping his mouth with his hand. "You know times is lean at the store. Jewel's had to go to work, too, down at the bank." He pointed his fork in Hollis's direction. "Hollis is setting right there. Why can't he do something?"

Frankie jammed a spoonful of mashed potatoes between his lips, a white blob falling onto the table. He looked at Hollis with disdain. "Why, Hollis can't do nothing."

Jewel spoke up sheepishly, without raising her eyes from her plate. "I reckon there's people you can hire to cook and clean."

"Hire!" Frankie Odom squawked, crumbs spraying. His face had gone a deep red. "You think I can afford to hire somebody? It takes ever dime I get to keep food on your tables and roofs over your heads." After a moment of thought, he said, "I reckon I could take some out of you boys's pay and get a woman to come in once or twice a week."

There was a long silence. The Odoms looked around at each other, the women's faces livened with panic. Then their eyes fell on me. It hit me all at once what they were thinking. I turned to John, hoping he could read my expression. "Well," he said. "I guess Myra could do it. She's been telling me she'd like to get out of the house." Peggy and Jewel sagged with relief. They went back to their food, not waiting to see what I would say. After a while Hollis spoke up. "That'd be all right, wouldn't it, Daddy?"

"I reckon," Frankie said. "If she knows how to fix soup beans. Long as I've got a pot of beans and a pan of cornbread, I'll be just fine."

"Myra knows how to cook," John said. "That's one thing her granny taught her."

I sat there like a stone, unable to look at anyone. The Odoms went on eating, the tension gone from the room. When his plate was clean, Frankie Odom said, "How about a cup of coffee?" Peggy stood up and went to the kitchen, like they all expected her to. I felt trapped, the table so crowded my elbows were touching Hollis's on one side and John's on the other. When I mumbled I'd be right back, I didn't think anyone noticed I was leaving. They had begun to argue about the store. Their querulous voices, John's the loudest among them, chased me out the front door. I sat on the porch steps, grateful for the evening air. I breathed deeply, trying to still my hands. I pictured what Granny might be doing at that hour, reading her Bible, mending old dresses, knitting doilies, eating cornbread and buttermilk. I wanted to forget her warning about being careful what I wished for. I told myself I loved John and it was worth everything to have him. I needed him to come out and check on me. When the door creaked open behind me, I turned around hopefully. But it wasn't John, it was Hollis.

My face must have fallen because he said, "He's a little bit busy right now. Him and Daddy's going at it hot and heavy. I'm like you, I don't like to be in the middle of a fuss." He sat down on the steps beside me, uncomfortably close. He paused, gazing across the yard. Then he turned and studied me.

"You're looking kind of sickly," he said. "You all right?"

I glanced at him. "I'll be okay in a minute."

"You know, I used to get sick a lot when I was little. I always thought it was something in this old house making me puny. But I don't get like that anymore."

I turned my face, hot and flushed, wanting him to disappear. Sweat trickled under my dress even though the sun had gone down, bats wheeling around the streetlights.

Hollis didn't take the hint. "I know what happened in yonder," he said. "Nobody asked you what you wanted to do. But me and Daddy won't be too much trouble." He put his hand on my back. It took every ounce of my will not to recoil from his touch. "Don't you worry about none of it. You got a friend right here. I won't let them run over you."

After that night, John began dropping me

off at the Odom house twice a week. The first time, Frankie Odom answered the bell and said, "Hey there, darlin." I followed him with my purse clasped to my side, holding my breath as I walked into the stench. He showed me to a bag of hairy green stalks on the table. "Do you know how to fry okrie?" he asked. I looked at him for a moment without answering. I had fried okra many times, but never for breakfast. "Well, get busy," he said. "I'm starving plumb to death." He sat there as I tried to cook, not telling me where the iron skillet was or the lard or the flour or the knife, only talking about everything else as I sweated over the stove. He didn't comment when I presented a plate of hot fried okra. He fell to eating and I stood fidgeting, not knowing what else to do. After a while he lifted his head from the plate as if remembering my presence and said, "You can give the bathroom a going-over."

I searched for something to clean with until I found a jug of bleach and a scrap of yellowed shirt under the kitchen sink. I did the best I could with what I had to scour away the mildew and rust stains. When I heard the front door open and close an hour later, I hoped it was John coming back for me. I stepped into the gloomy hall and it was Hollis again, standing in a square of light in the foyer. "Got to work and figured out I lost my dadblame wallet," he said, to no one in particular. Then he saw me and froze, head cocked like a bird of prey. "It's your day to cook and clean, I guess." I nodded. We looked at each other. It would have been impolite to go back into the bathroom and pretend to scrub. I stood still as he came creaking down the hall to me, aware of being alone in that foul house with two men I didn't know and who didn't feel like family.

"Come to think of it," he said, "I ain't seen that pocketbook since yesterday. I bet you it dropped out of my britches when I was out yonder pulling weeds." He paused, appraising me in a way that made my ears warm. "Are you good at finding things?"

"What?"

"Two pairs of eyes is better than one. Come on out here with me and look for it."

I stepped blinking into the sun behind him, out the back door and down the steps into the yard. My feet were heavy as if in protest, the bleach-smelling rag still in my fist. I looked down at it numbly and dropped it in the dirt beside the stoop. He stopped, hands on his hips, surveying the yard. I stood a few paces behind him, waiting for him to go on. Finally, I shaded my eyes against the sun and asked, "Where were you pulling weeds at?"

"Out in the garden."

I saw it across the yard, dry cornstalks leaning over a patch of snarled briars and weeds, a few tomato vines and green bean plants rising out of the ruins. I wondered what good it would do to pull weeds in all that mess. I followed Hollis across the yard and up close it was even more overrun. He stood at the edge and said, "Go ahead, your eyes is keener than mine. A woman pays more attention than a man." When I didn't move right away, he took me by the elbow and guided me into the patch. "A man can't do without his pocketbook," he said. "My driver license is in there." He stooped and began to pick his way across the rows. "It's odd how my eyes works. I can't find nothing when I'm looking for it, even if it's right under my nose." I was relieved when he fell silent. We searched for a while without speaking, but I should have known he wouldn't keep quiet. I was learning fast about his awkward need to tell me things. "But you take any kind of pattern and my eyes will make a picture out of it," he blurted, startling me. "Like when I was little, I got to seeing faces. The worst one came out of this water stain over my bed. Had an open mouth with pointed teeth and the meanest eyes you ever seen. You might say I was dreaming it, except I seen it other places. I seen it in the wallpaper and the spots on the mirrors. It got to where it followed me everywhere. Then one day, I told John about it. He was washing the dishes and I was drying them. I was seeing it right then, in the suds of the dishwater. You know what John said to me? He said, 'I see it, too.' That was all. Not another word about it to this day. But that was all I needed. After that, we was brothers in a way that went deeper than blood." I didn't know how to respond. I concentrated on looking for the wallet, hoping to find it fast. I was beginning to feel frantic, green flies buzzing around my head as I ran my hands over the ground. When my fingers finally passed over the wallet, hidden under the bug-bitten leaves of a melon vine, I almost sighed with relief. I held it up, black cowhide warm from the sun. He laughed and said, "I knowed you'd find it quicker than me. I'm a pretty good judge of people."

We stood up and I handed him the wallet, thinking I would escape. Then he said, "Let me show you something." It was all I could do to remain there beside him, half sick from his closeness and the heat. He opened the wallet and reached in with thumb and forefinger to pull out what looked like a clump of gray hair, pressed flat and bound with a rubber band. "I ain't never showed nobody this," he said. "But me and you can tell each other things." He held his hand near my face. "Did John ever say how Mama died?"

I closed my eyes against what lay in Hollis's palm. "John doesn't like talking about it," I said, wishing he wouldn't talk about it either. But somehow I knew he wouldn't let me go. I wondered if he'd even left his wallet in the garden on purpose.

"We was boys when it happened. John and Lonnie and Eugene was off to the store with Daddy but I wasn't old enough yet to go. Mama was sick with the stomach flu. I heard a thump in her room. I went up the stairs and when I opened the door I seen her laying facedown on the floor. I reckon she had fell out of the bed. I turned her over and soon as I seen her face, I knowed she was gone. I don't know what made me do it, but Daddy had give me a little old pocketknife. I knelt down there and sawed off a hank of her hair before I went in and called anybody." I stared down at the dull gray clump, a gag rising in my throat. "I like to keep it on me somewheres," he said. "Blood kin is worth a lot to me." I looked at his face because I couldn't stand to look at the hair. He stared into my eyes, as always standing too close. "Just like these dogtags," he said, not taking his eyes off mine as he pulled them by the chain out of his collar. "My daddy fought in the Second World War. He killed a bunch of Japs with these right here around his neck. I think family's about the most important thing there is. Don't you?"

He had edged even closer to me. I stepped backward, turning my ankle. "I better get to work," I said. My voice came out no more than a whisper.

Hollis reached and took a strand of my hair, held it without looking at it, his black eyes still boring into me. "You reckon you and John'll have a son one day?"

I didn't say what came to me. I hope not, if he would turn out anything like you.

I wish I didn't remember Hollis so well. I used to believe certain houses were haunted but now I think it's just me. One day not long ago, I saw the tail of Granny's dress disappearing around a bend, walking along the fencerow with a bag looking for greens to cook. She always soaked them in vinegar to kill the poison. One frozen morning last winter I woke to the sounds of squealing, sure I would find Granddaddy at the barn scraping a hog, the ground beneath steaming from its warm blood. But the barn was empty and shadowed and still. I stood listening for echoes but there was only the rushing creek. If this place is haunted, at least it has good spirits along with the bad.

Not like the house where John grew up, the sulfur smell clinging to windowsills and sink drains and doorsteps. Being away from Granny and the mountain wore on me after so long, did something to my mind. I knew it was probably rats, but sometimes I heard voices behind the walls there, like babbling in a foreign language. Sometimes I saw flashes of John as a boy with a mop of black hair, hooded eyes and white skin, crouching behind doors and peering around corners, disappearing when I turned around. There was, like Hollis said, a feeling of being watched. Part of it was the pictures. Dusting the frames I examined John's mother, wiping her face clean with my rag. Her eyes were chilling behind her glasses, dead and vacant as a wax dummy's.

I was less nervous when Frankie left me alone in the house, driving off in his old Cadillac to check on the store. I preferred whatever ghosts or demons there were to my father-in-law, hawking phlegm into his handkerchief and chain-smoking at the kitchen table as he listened to the radio, sleeping in his chair with his mouth open and his head lolling on his shoulder. When Hollis came home for dinner, he leaned on the counter with arms folded and ankles crossed, watching me cook. Sometimes he helped with the dishes and I winced when his fingers met mine under the water, always touching me on purpose.

I had Hollis's full attention, but it was John's that I longed for. More and more he seemed preoccupied, his eyes seldom settling on me. If we had conversations, I started them. Sometimes after work on Fridays he didn't come home and I knew he was at the only bar in town. When his eyes did find me I saw his disappointment. I wasn't what he had expected or wanted. Spending my days in haunted houses, I felt like a ghost myself. By the first of September, I was starving for a little bit of life. That's why when I saw a burning bush sprouting up by the back steps of the Odom house, something moved in me.

The bush was sick and stunted-looking, just beginning to turn red. I had been sweeping the back stoop and stopped to lean on the broom for a closer look, half expecting a voice to come out of it. When a car door slammed somewhere down the street, I woke up and glanced around. The yard was bare, the garden still weed-choked. On impulse, I ran to Frankie Odom's shed, a lean-to with a rusted tin roof like a half-peeled-off scab. I scraped back the splintery door and saw a shovel against the far wall. I climbed over piles of junk to reach it, a nail from a rotten board scratching my leg in the process. I carried the shovel out, looking left and right to make sure no one saw.

Beside the stoop, I stood on the shovel and dug into the hard ground. When the dirt was loose enough I reached into the hole I had made and lifted the burning bush out by a rich-smelling ball of roots and soil. I took it up the steps and into the kitchen, shedding black crumbs I would sweep up before Frankie or Hollis came home. I leaned the bush in an empty mop bucket while I soaked a dish towel to wrap around its roots. Frankie had left a brown grocery sack of half-rotten tomatoes on the counter, the only yield of his miserable garden. He'd said on his way out the door that morning, "Them's for you and John to take home." I unloaded the tomatoes and found the burning bush was small enough to fit inside. One by one I replaced the tomatoes and folded over the sack. I sat for a while looking at my handiwork, feeling guilty and alive. When John came to pick me up I ran out holding the bag by its bottom. "Your daddy gave us some tomatoes," I said. He looked away, switching a toothpick from one corner of his mouth to the other.

The next day I didn't have to go to the Odom house. I watched John eat breakfast, anxious for him to leave. When he was gone I went to the back of the lot beside the tracks where the landlord had a shed much like Frankie Odom's. I didn't have to look far for the shovel. It was leaning inside the door shrouded in cobwebs. Until then, I hadn't tried planting anything where it looked like nothing would grow. But this burning bush was different somehow. If I was careful, maybe it would live. I took the grocery bag around the house, heading for a back corner where John might never see what I had stolen. On the way, I passed the wood stacked under the bedroom window for winter, sprouting fungus and crawling with bugs. That's when I noticed for the first time a squat door in the house's block foundation near the woodpile, made of weathered gray boards and fastened shut with a rusty hasp. I paused to inspect it, the shovel in one hand and the grocery bag in the other. Just as I was about to move on, I heard a noise coming from under the house. I froze, not sure I had heard anything. I put down the bag and knelt before the door. Then it came again, a sly shifting. I hesitated before reaching to unlock the hasp. I pulled the door open, hinges groaning, and lowered myself on all fours. What I saw when my eyes adjusted to the gloom made my stomach turn. Under the house it was moldy and earthen and tomblike. The dirt was littered with broken dishes and Mason jar fragments, pipes close overhead with the protective mummy wrappings of winter still clinging to their joints. Thoughts of closed caskets and burial alive flickered through my head. Then, not far from my hand, I saw something from a nightmare. It was a long blacksnake, coiled around what looked like a rabbit's nest. I gasped and scrambled backward into the light. I sat for a moment catching my breath. I had never been afraid of snakes. Granny had taught me about them. Once I held her hand in a field, looking up at one dangling from a tree branch like a black noose. "It's just an old rat snake," she said. "It ain't poison." I wasn't afraid then because she told me not to be. But lately I hadn't been myself. It felt suddenly important to take another look, if only because I knew Granny would have.

The rabbit's nest was made from a ring of dried grass and puffs of cottony fur. In the middle were the babies, tiny and almost hairless, eyes still closed, noses and ears the color of flesh. One was caught in the snake's unhinged mouth, only its back legs left to be consumed. I backed silently out and rose to my feet without taking my eyes off the snake. I reached for the shovel and chopped at the long rope of its body the best I could, until it lay in raw, pink pieces around the nest. I stood back panting and leaned the shovel against the house. Then I got down on my belly and went as far under the house as I was willing to venture. Looking closer, I saw punctures in one of the tiny bodies. I reached over the snake and prodded with my finger at the baby rabbit, dead but still warm. Then the third one began to squeal, a high, piercing alarm that made me scramble out backward again, bumping my head on the pipes. After a while I crawled back under and took the baby rabbit still screaming into my palm, unable to believe something so small could have such a voice. I held it in the sun begging it to stop, whispering into my cupped palms until the cries died away. I took the baby rabbit inside, the burning bush leaning forgotten against the house, one secret traded for another.

I had to hurry so I wouldn't be late making supper. I put the sightless creature in a shoebox stuffed with strips torn from one of John's flannel shirts. I searched the kitchen drawers until I found an old medicine dropper and climbed on my bed to feed it drips of warm milk. At first it stiffened like it would choke but after a while it was content. When it was close to time for John to come home I took the shoebox and hid the rabbit in the hall closet, behind the water heater with the box Granddaddy carved for me. I had realized long ago the box was something John would despise and might destroy. Now I knew the rabbit was something he wouldn't stand for either, because it comforted me.

All that night during supper I worried the rabbit would cry in its shattering way, but the house was still as we sat at the table over our plates. When John was finished he went to drink in front of the television set he'd bought one week with our grocery money. He didn't question why I was warming milk or why I went to the bathroom so many times. If he noticed me leaving our bed all through the night, he didn't seem to care. As long as I kept the baby rabbit full, maybe I could have something of my own for a while.

For almost a month, I took the shoebox with me to the Odom house hidden in a bag of cleaning supplies. Once or twice I thought Hollis would find me out, the way he always hovered close. But, as if by instinct, the baby rabbit kept quiet when he was around. It was fattening up, its fur thickening, its eyes opening, thriving despite the cow's milk and the dark closet where it lived. It liked to nestle under my chin, still and warm and breathing fast. Granny always said I had a touch with animals. Holding the rabbit close to my heart, I promised when it was strong enough I'd find a way to turn it loose on the mountain. I felt more like myself in those few weeks, having something alive that depended on me, something that knew in its blood and bones what it meant to be wild.

Then Hollis showed up on my doorstep one day near the end of September, while I was feeding the baby rabbit from its dropper. When the knock came, I hurried to settle the rabbit in its bed of rags and hide it behind the water heater. I thought it might cry out because its feeding had been interrupted, but it only rooted at the stuffing of its bed. I looked down at myself on the way to answer the door. It was noon but I was still in my nightgown. I wanted to throw on some clothes or at least a house-coat, but the knocking came again, louder and more persistent. When I opened the door and saw Hollis, my shoulders slumped. He took off his cap and scratched at his flat-tened hair. "I was about to think you was gone somewheres," he said. When I didn't respond, he replaced his cap and sighed. "Well. I was on my dinner break and thought I'd look in on you."

"I'm all right," I said.

He looked past me into the front room. "Shoo, it's kindly hot out here. Looks like we're having Indian summer. Can I trouble you for a drink of water?"

He followed me to the kitchen and sat at the table as I filled a glass from the tap. I remembered my naked breasts under the thin nightgown fabric and stood at the sink with my arms crossed while he drank the water in long gulps, Adam's apple bobbing. Then he put down his glass hard and I jumped. He laughed at me. "What's got you so wound up?"

I glanced toward the kitchen doorway, willing the baby rabbit to stay asleep.

"I bet you thought I was John, coming in for dinner," he said.

"No," I said. "Sometimes he eats in town."

Hollis grinned. "If I had you waiting on me, I'd come home to eat."

I dropped my eyes, face burning.

Then he said in his awkward way, "Most people thinks me and John favors."

I decided to ignore him, hoping the less attention I gave him the sooner he would go away. I went to the table and took his glass, not touching where his mouth had been.

"Do you think me and John looks alike?" he asked.

I turned my back to him and rinsed the glass in the sink. "No."

He fell silent, seeming to think it over. "All right," he said after a long pause, "I didn't mean to bother you. I just thought I'd see if you needed anything."

I turned around and looked at him, waiting for him to leave.

"Hope I didn't bother you," he said.

"No," I said. "It was nice of you to stop."

I thought he would go but he only sat there staring at me, smiling in a way that made my guts draw into a knot, eyes moving over my face, my hair, my breasts, so intent that I almost felt his touch. After a moment he said, "You don't like me much, do you?"

I froze, caught off guard. Before I could think, I blurted out, "No."

His smile died. My hand rose to my throat. For a second I wasn't sure if I had spoken out loud. "You got a smart mouth, girl," he murmured, the shock plain on his face. I thought to apologize, but nothing came out. Hollis's neck and ears turned red. "My brother's run through a lot of women in his day," he said. "Don't think you're any different than the rest of them." Then he got up from his chair and stalked to the front door, slamming it behind him. I went to the window to make sure he got into his truck and left. I stood for a long time gnawing my fingernails, knowing I had made a mistake.

I would like to pretend that year never happened and enjoy the life I have now with my twins. Sometimes when I sit on the back steps the girl climbs onto my knees, long legs hanging down and bare toes poking at my calves. I bounce her as we watch the boy playing in the yard, peeling bark from a stick in ash-colored strips. He doesn't come to me the way she does. I can't remember the last time I held him. In cold months he follows me to the woodpile and takes the heaviest log he can carry, brings it behind me into the kitchen to put in the wood box beside the back door. He lights a fire and stands back as he tosses in kindling, embers shooting out and disappearing like the ghosts of fireflies. Summer nights I put the oil lamp on the table and we eat as moths bat at the blackened glass chimney. In the mornings they come to the kitchen and stand at the stove waiting for a biscuit. I blow on them before setting them down on their small palms.

I wish this was the only life I ever had, light coming in and ceilings high enough to breathe and windows and doors thrown always open. If a lizard skitters in, blue-tailed and fast, I watch him dart up the wall or into a baseboard crack. If the rain blows in, I don't mop it up. I stand in the door hoping the smell will soak into the boards of the house to keep for days when the sun is shining. Even when it's cold I leave the house open, letting snow flurries collect on the rugs. The twins are like me, used to all kinds of weather. They're not sensitive to heat or cold, so I'm not careful with them. I know how it feels to be kept inside and how it will winnow away at your mind until you feel like nothing. Even with the baby rabbit to care for, being pent up in that house by the tracks finally became too much to bear. One gray morning at the beginning of

October, rain beating and wind blowing and leaves plastered everywhere, my restlessness came to a head.

It was cold enough to need a fire and I went out to the woodpile, careful to avoid looking at the door in the house's foundation. I stamped my shoes bringing in the wood and left them on the kitchen mat. John was watching football in the front room. He didn't look at me as I got a fire going in the stove. I went to sit beside him, drawing a quilt around my shoulders and pressing my chilled body against him where he leaned on the couch arm. I needed his nearness to keep me sane. I needed back the loving John I had married. He stiffened, fingers curled around the glass he drank from, not moving to touch me. I kissed his neck, his jaw, his cheek. My heart sank when he wrenched his face away.

"Let's go for a ride," I said.

"Weather's too bad," he muttered.

"No it's not." I bit down hard on my lip. "You just don't want to."

"What if I don't?" He turned on me, eyes bloodshot.

I rose from the couch and began to pace the floor. "I have to get out of here," I told him. It was more a plea than a statement. "At least for a while. Give me the keys."

"Where you going? Back to Granny?"

"I don't know," I said, voice cracking. "But I hate it here."

John put down his drink. He sat forward on the couch. I knew I should hush before it was too late. "What do you mean? There ain't nothing wrong with this place."

"It's too dark in here," I said, unable to help myself.

"We'll fix it up, then. I'll hang you some wallpaper."

"No," I said. "Nothing can fix it."

His jaw tightened. "You better watch yourself, Myra."

I wanted to stop but I couldn't. "I want to see Granny," I said, close to tears.

He slammed his glass on the coffee table. "Quit being a suck baby."

Something snapped in me then. I snatched his ashtray from the table in a plume of soot, white butts fluttering down like confetti, and threw it against the wall. It bounced off and skidded across the linoleum. We stared at it together, a silence descending over the room. Then John blinked up at me in disbelief, mouth hanging open. I thought it was going to happen at last. He was going to hit me. But just as he got up from the couch, the baby rabbit's high squeal shattered the stillness. John's face went pale. He jumped up, knocking over his glass. "What in the hell?" he said, looking toward the sound with big eyes. For a long moment I stood rooted in place. Then I took off running for the end of the hall. John caught up to me at the closet, the rabbit's pitiful cries trapped inside. I plastered myself against the door but he shoved me out of the way so hard I stumbled and fell. He tore open the closet and followed the sound to the water heater. He knelt and pulled the shoebox out of the shadows. I begged him to give it to me but he didn't answer. I watched his back as he stared into the box. After what felt like a lifetime, he stood slowly and turned to me. "Have you lost your mind?" he asked softly.

I thought of lying but there was no reason to. "I found it under the house."

He studied me, face blank and unreadable. "No telling what all diseases you've brought in here," he said at last. "That thing might have rabies."

"It's just a rabbit."

"Looks like a rat to me."

"It's not a rat," I whispered. I tried to get past him but he blocked my way.

"I don't care what it is," he said, dangerously calm. "It ain't living in my house."

Then he turned, raised his foot, and

stomped the box with his boot. The squealing stopped. I stood gaping at it. John passed me, knocking into my shoulder, and walked out of the house. After a few minutes I heard the car start up and spin out of the gravel lot. I went to kneel over the box. Inside the rabbit's back feet were kicking. I took its broken body into my palm one more time. A childhood memory came to me, of standing in a tobacco field plucking worms from sticky green leaves. At the end of the row I found a quivering mouse, sides laboring with rapid breath. It was sick, maybe poisoned, and small like me. I shut my eyes and twisted the baby rabbit's neck until its legs were still.

In the days afterward, I thought more about my mother. I went outside one night when John was gone drinking and saw the dark hump of my mountain in the distance, beyond the scattered twinkle of lights. I stood on the tracks she died on, stretching out of sight before and behind me. I looked down at my feet and saw that the rocks were stained. I knelt to pick one up and imagined it was her blood. I closed my eyes and a cold wind came rushing down the tracks. It was a fresh smell, a breath of woodsy air different than cinders and pollution. I opened my mouth and breathed it deep. My kinfolks were so close. I couldn't go up the mountain, because it would be hard to get back before John came home from work. He might drive up there after me and hurt me in front of Granny. I couldn't stand that. But I could go to the pool hall and try to find some of my people. I was willing to risk that much. I made up my mind to go when Monday came.

There was no money in my purse but I'd been stealing a few dollars here and there from John's wallet when he was passed out drunk. I had folded the bills and put them in a coffee can under the sink. I bathed and dressed and walked to the neighbor's house to call a cab. Pit bulls lunged barking and whining at the ends of their chains when I stepped into the yard. A grizzled man wearing an unbuttoned western shirt opened the door. I asked if he had a phone I could use. For a long, anxious moment I thought he might say no, but then he opened the door wider to let me in. He stood watching suspiciously as I talked on the greasy phone hanging on his kitchen wall. I told the driver I wanted to go to the pool hall on Miller Avenue and went outside to wait in the yard.

The car that came was a dented Oldsmobile with a cracked windshield. The man who opened the back door for me had two missing front teeth. He tried to make small talk on the ride across town, but I ignored him until he gave up. He pulled into a gravel parking lot in front of a low gray building. There was no sign but I knew by the neon inside that this was the pool hall where my parents had met. As I walked across the dusty lot, gravel crunching under my shoes, I tried not to think what John would do if he came home to an empty house. I hesitated for only a moment before pushing open the door.

It was so dim inside after the bright sunlight that I was almost blind. I moved between the shabby pool tables to a snack bar where hot dogs turned in a glass case and fountain drinks gurgled. The man wiping his hands behind the counter had a round belly and great hairy forearms, but little hair on his head. "Help you?" he asked.

"No. Well, nothing to eat. I'm looking for somebody that used to come in here."

He grinned and took a smoldering cigarette from an ashtray on the counter. "A lot of people come in here, sweetheart. What's the name?"

"Mayes. Kenny Mayes, or Clio Mayes. Do you remember them?"

"Let me think." He placed the cigarette between his thick lips and drew deeply.

"There's a lot of Mayeses around here. Now, there's an old woman by the name of Mayes lives down the street, takes care of her uncle. He's the one I bought this place from. But I don't remember no Kenny. Is he a young man or a old man?"

"He died about eighteen years ago. He was . . . my daddy. I was hoping to find some of my family, maybe, to tell me more about him and my mother."

"How about that," the man said. He mashed out his cigarette. "I'll tell you what. I believe that Mayes woman had a boy, got killed down here on the railroad tracks."

"That's him," I said, suddenly hot and dizzy. "Where did you say she lives?"

"It's a little old house down here at the stop sign. You can walk right to it. Watch out, though. Some of these boys around here might holler at you." He laughed at himself so hard that he had a coughing fit. I left him there red-faced, hacking into his fist.

I stepped back out into the autumn sun, the sky overhead a hard, dark blue, and scanned the parking lot. I stopped when I saw Hollis leaning against the hood of his truck picking his teeth. When he saw me he pitched the toothpick into the gravel.

"Looking for ye ride?" he asked with a

snide grin.

I glanced back at the door. I could have gone into the pool hall again but thought I might be more easily cornered in there. I couldn't count on the owner to help, either. I had learned since marrying John and leaving home that men liked to stick together.

"I sent him on," Hollis said, smile disappearing. He uncrossed his arms and began moving toward me. "My brother told me to keep an eye on you and it's a good thing I did. I know he don't want his wife sniffing around no pool hall."

"I was looking for somebody," I said, eyes darting left and right. "My family."

"Why, your family's right here. Ain't I your family now?"

"I've got some errands," I said, taking a step to the side. There was a wooded lot behind the building. If I could make it there, he'd never catch me. "Nothing I can't walk to. You better get on back to the store. John says it gets busy around this time."

"I'll get on back to the store," he said. "But you're coming with me. I'd say John would like to know what you've been up to this morning." He moved forward again.

I took another step sideways. "I'll see John when he gets home."

"You're coming with me, girl," Hollis said.

447

He lunged and before he could close the distance between us I bolted to the left, meaning to buttonhook around the corner of the pool hall and run for the woods. But Hollis was too close. He caught me and wrestled me to the ground. I struggled, kicking and bucking with him on my back. I slung my head and felt it connect with his teeth. He cursed but didn't loosen his grip. He hoisted me to my feet, one arm clamped around my ribs. I looked desperately toward the pool hall door and saw the fat owner watching, eyes narrowed against the light. I squirmed around in Hollis's arms, turning until our noses were inches apart. I hawked and spat into his eyes, wetting both of our faces. Then he drove his fist into my diaphragm, knocking the wind out of me. My eyes flew open and my body went limp. I knew then how it felt to drown. I opened my mouth wide, fighting for breath as Hollis dragged me to the truck and pushed me in. I lay against the seat sucking in whoops of air. "If you try to run off again," Hollis panted, "I swear to God I'll break your neck." I couldn't have run if I wanted to. I sagged against the door, still trying to breathe, as he came around the truck and climbed behind the wheel. He sat still for a few minutes, pulling himself together. He rubbed a finger across his teeth and pulled it out bloody. I rested my heavy head on the window as he started the truck and fishtailed across the parking lot into the street. After a while I tried my voice. "It's none of your business," I wheezed. He spat blood into his hand and wiped it on his pants. "My brother is my business," he said. I didn't say anything else because he was right. I thought of opening the truck door and jumping out. I didn't know what my husband would do to me.

When we got to the store, John was leaning on the counter talking to a man whose bottom lip was fat with snuff. "What say, Grady?" Hollis said to the man, who touched the brim of his hat in greeting. Then Hollis looked at John. "Hey, brother," he said. John glanced up and whatever he had meant to reply died on his tongue when he saw the shape I was in. "Let's step in the back for a minute," Hollis said. John hesitated and then called for Lonnie, who appeared from among the aisles to take John's place behind the counter. I walked between them through the store to the back where there was a stagnant bathroom and one high window lighting shafts of dust like swarming bugs, cobwebs waving in dirty trails from the ceiling tiles. Hollis steered me around the empty boxes on the floor and backed me against a paint-splattered table under the window, knocking off another box spilling styrofoam peanuts. I looked at John but he made no move to stop him. "Why don't you take a guess where I found your wife this morning?" Hollis said.

John stared at me. "Where have you been, Myra?"

"I found her down yonder at the pool hall. I hope nobody else seen her."

John folded his arms. "I told you not to go down there," he said with false patience. I recognized the calm look on his face. "I told you it would embarrass me."

"I know," I rasped, stomach still aching from Hollis's blow.

"Is that all you're going to say about it?"

"I can't live the way I have been, John."

He cocked his head, feigning interest. "How's that?"

"Cooped up in the house."

"You married me, Myra, not somebody else," he said in his condescending way. "You know I expect a woman to keep her ass at home. I done told you that. And I ain't the only one that believes that way. There's a lot of men around here that would laugh at me if they seen my wife at the pool hall. Is that what you want?"

"No," I said. "I didn't mean to be hanging around. I was just in and out." Even as I spoke the words, I knew I was wasting what little breath I had.

"Now, Myra. You're not understanding what I'm trying to say." John and Hollis exchanged a glance that made me cold all over. Then John began undoing his belt. I watched his long fingers working, light glinting off the buckle.

"Hold her still, there," he said to Hollis. I couldn't bear the thought of Hollis's hands on me again. I lurched forward, a guttural sound wrenching out of my throat. John intercepted me before I reached the door. He turned me around and clapped his hand over my mouth. I tried to bite but his fingers were too tight. "Dammit, Myra," he said against my ear, "there's customers out yonder." I screamed around his hand. They carried me together back to the table. "You better shut her up or somebody's going to call the law," Hollis panted. As soon as John's hand was gone I screamed again but it came out more like a croak. "Hold her still," John ordered. I heard his belt slithering free of its loops over their grunting and puffing. Hollis yanked my arms up so far behind my back I thought they would tear loose. My hoarse cries changed from anger to pain, bright flares shooting up behind my eyes. John forced me over the table and Hollis shoved my dress up over my hips. I began to cry hard, snot dangling from my nose. Knowing that Hollis was watching hurt more than the belt licks. When it was over, I fell silent and still, trying to stifle my sobs. Then Lonnie opened the door and poked his head in. "What in the world's going on back here?" he said. "I thought Grady was fixing to call the sheriff."

I summoned the last of my strength and tried to run again but John caught me easily. He held me against his chest and laughed. In that moment, I had no love for him left. "Good Lord, Myra," he said. "You're wild as a buck. I hate I had to do you that way, but I can't let you run around on me. You ought to have more respect for me than that."

From that day forward, my marriage to John was like a fever dream from a time before I could talk. He didn't allow me to leave the house for anything, not even to cook and clean for his father. Sometimes I see the twins building something out of sticks and mud and remember walls I was trapped between. I look down at my fingers once slammed in doors and can't go back inside a house. I have to sit on rocks and climb into trees and stretch out under the arms of flowering bushes. I have to forget Thanksgiving Day of that other life, when I stood at the window wearing the same dress and shoes I got married in, trying to see Bloodroot Mountain through the fog. The sky was steel-colored, the ground frozen hard. John was sitting on the couch. "You'll have to cook something," he said. "We can't go without a dish." He had already been drinking for hours. Lately he didn't go anywhere, even to work, without being drunk on whiskey. He thought I would eat Thanksgiving dinner in that awful house with his mean people, but I had other plans.

"Make some of that banana pudding," he said.

"It's already made," I lied. "I wanted to take a sweet potato casserole like your daddy asked for, but this morning I saw we don't have any pecans."

John rolled his eyes. "You should have put it on the grocery list and I would have got it for you. I swear, Myra, sometimes I think your mind ain't right."

"I could still make it," I said. "It just takes about fifteen minutes for the top to get bubbly. Why don't you let me run to the store?"

He paused, maybe suspicious. "Daddy don't need no sweet potato casserole."

"I don't know, John," I said, not taking my eyes away from the distant outline of the mountain. "Don't you think we ought to stay on his good side? You know Hollis is the pet. It wouldn't surprise me a bit if Frankie didn't leave him everything."

John thought it over. "Daddy ain't got the smarts to make a will."

"Well," I said, turning to look at him. "You're probably right."

John was quiet for a minute. Then he sighed. "Aw, hell. I reckon I can run and get some for you. What is it, pecans? But you better have it ready to stick in the oven as soon as I get back. I don't want them waiting on us to eat. I'd never live it down."

"It's already put together in the refrigerator," I lied again without a pang of remorse. "All I have to do is sprinkle the nuts on top. Be sure to get the chopped ones."

As soon as John walked out, I grabbed my purse and put on my coat. Since he was taking the car, I would have to go back to the neighbor's and call Mr. Barnett to pick me up. I hated to do it on Thanksgiving, but a cab to Bloodroot Mountain would cost more than I had. Besides that, I missed Granny too much to be polite. I went to the door, meaning to peek out and see if John had gone. When I opened it, he was standing on the stoop about to reach for the knob. "Myra —" he was saying. He froze, face falling. "I left my keys." He looked at the purse on my arm. "Where you headed?" I hesitated. The thought of a whipping didn't scare me much anymore. "Home," I said. He stared at me for a few seconds. Then his features transformed into something so ugly I'll never forget.

He grabbed me by the hair and yanked me out the door, pulling me into a headlock. "Don't tell me where you're going," he said against my ear, whiskey breath blasting into my face. "Daddy's expecting you to eat over yonder and that's what you're going to do." My purse fell and one shoe came off as he dragged me backward across the ground. If he hadn't been drunk there would have been no chance, but he stumbled over a rock on the way to the car. I twisted out of his loosened grip and took off running. I couldn't head for the road because he was blocking the way. I swerved around the house, thinking dimly of cutting through the backyard and making it to the neighbor's. But I wasn't fast enough limping on one shoe. John caught me at the woodpile, snagging the end of my hair and pulling me as if by a rope back under his arm. This time, I knew, he wouldn't make a mistake. He forced me to my knees in front of the door in the house's foundation. I shut my eyes, expecting him to undo his belt, but he held me still instead. I could feel him looking around, chest rising and falling behind me, seeming to think over what to do next. "All right then," he said at last. "You don't want to go with me, you don't have to." I glanced over at the door and it dawned on me slowly what he meant to do. I began to beg but it was like trying to reason with a demon. He dragged me closer and unlocked the hasp with one hand. He opened the door and shoved my head down with almost superhuman strength. I resisted but it didn't take long for my body to fold in half. He skidded backward on the seat of his pants and shoved me under the house with his boots. I banged my head hard on the pipes, my hand grating on a shard of Mason jar.

He slammed the door shut behind me with a bang. I flipped over on my back, breathing in ragged shrieks, and beat at the boards of the door with my shoe. He must have been leaning with all his weight against it. Within seconds I heard him locking the hasp and wedging something through its ring, maybe a scrap of wood from the pile. Then there was silence. I called John's name, voice shrill with panic, but he didn't answer. I listened for any hint of his presence outside the door. I pounded at the boards again with my feet and screamed until my throat felt bloody. Then I heard the car start up and roar out of the lot. I went rigid, staring up in disbelief. That's when I saw by the light falling through twin holes in one of the foundation's cinder blocks how close the house was to my face. A yellowed blouse tied to a pipe hung inches from my nose. There was a stench of decaying earth and mildew and moth balls. I turned my head and saw the skin and bones of the blacksnake I had killed. I struggled to calm myself but it was hard to think.

The house was too low for me to sit up. When I tried to raise on all fours my back bumped against the pipes. I inched through the gloom on my belly and hammered at the door with my fist. Then I searched the dirt and found a chunk of block that crumbled to pieces as I pounded with it. Straining to see, I made out the shape of a rake handle near a stack of dishes. I dragged it back to the door and battered until my hands were raw and full of splinters but it wouldn't budge. I dropped the handle and crawled over to press my face against one of the cinder block's holes. I looked out and saw only frozen ground. I fell on my side and huddled in a shivering heap under my coat, unable to stop the tears from pouring out. I wept for a long time, until my eyes hurt and my voice was gone.

Afterward, minutes or hours passed in tomblike silence. My teeth chattered and my bare foot ached from the cold. I dozed and memories came to me of other winters. Once I followed bird tracks to a tree on its side, roots in the air. As I climbed among the branches it began to snow, white drifts piling. For a long time I hid looking up through the branches, watching the flakes sway down. Then I dreamed of another day on the way home from church, sitting between Granny and Granddaddy in the truck. Granddaddy slowed to a stop on the curving road and said, "Looky here, Myra Jean." I peered over the dashboard and saw a red fox crossing, its coat shouting against the whiteness, bushy tail disappearing up the bank and into the roadside woods. Soon it became less like a memory and more like something that was happening. I smelled the exhaust of the puttering truck and felt the seat bouncing under me, snow scurrying over the hood like something alive.

The slam of John's car door snapped me awake. I couldn't tell how long I had been sleeping. I pressed my face to one of the holes again and called to him, begging him to let me out. After a moment I stopped, thinking I heard the approach of his footsteps. I scuttled on stiff elbows and knees for the door, hoping for his fingers to unlock the hasp. Instead I heard the front door slam shut like a gunshot behind him. I could almost follow his progress through the house by the creak of his boots on the floorboards. I scrabbled in the dirt for the rake handle and beat on the moldy wood overhead. Then I heard the muffled groan of mattress springs directly above me, where the bedroom was. My heart sank. I knew he had passed out. He might as well not even be there. But I pounded with the rake handle anyway, until I couldn't feel my arms and shoulders. Finally I collapsed on my side and pulled my knees up under my dress tail against the cold. After a while, I began to drift off again. I wanted to be with Granny so much it was like searching for her inside myself and floating outward at the same time, over bare trees and brown water splitting the fields in two, fencerows like twigs strung together with thread. For a long time I circled Bloodroot Mountain, watching Granny pluck a turkey for Thanksgiving dinner as the Barnetts came up the hill bringing pumpkin pies for her.

I don't remember anything else about being under the house. I think I was there for one day but it might have been more. When John opened the door in the morning I didn't move. I only blinked at him. He knelt there sleepy-headed and rumpled, still half drunk. "Hell, Myra," he said. "I didn't mean to leave you out here so long." When I still didn't come he pulled me out by the ankles, dress rucking up and glass slicing my back. I barely felt it for the numbness. He hauled my body full length into the wintry sun and bent over me as I stared up blankly, like some creature born to live underground.

Back inside, I couldn't get warm. John put his wooly socks on my feet and piled blankets on top of me. He sat on the edge of the bed waiting for me to speak. "What can I do to make you mind?" he asked at last. "I don't understand it. I thought you wanted to be with me. Now you're all the time trying to run home to your Granny. I ain't letting you do me this way, Myra. I never took shit off of any woman and I don't mean to start now." He took a breath and blew it out. "Am I going to have to go up yonder and burn that place to the ground? If that's what it takes to keep you from running off every time I turn around, by God I'll do it."

I looked at his face in the light through the curtains, still sinister and beautiful. I didn't know if I believed him. But I thought if he ever followed me there, he might hurt me and Granny both. I felt more trapped then in my bed with John than I had been under the house alone. At least there I had been away from him.

For days I shivered coughing under the blankets, burning up with fever. Once I woke from a nightmare and saw Hollis and John like goblins at the foot of my bed. John pulled the covers back from my feet and said, "Reckon I should take her to the hospital?"

Hollis spat tobacco juice into a can he was holding. "Nah, she'll be all right."

John peeled off one of the wooly socks. "Does that foot look frostbit to you?"

Hollis shook his head. "That girl's tougher'n she looks."

John seemed uncertain. "She might have pneumonia."

Hollis scratched under his cap and resettled it on his head. Our eyes locked. "She ain't got pneumonia," he said. "She's full of meanness, is her problem."

John still didn't look convinced. "I don't know."

Hollis spat into his can again. "A little bit

of cold ain't going to hurt her. Daddy claimed he used to slip laudanum to Mama whenever she went to messing around."

"Yeah, well," John said. "Mama's dead, ain't she?"

Hollis laughed and took hold of my foot. His touch burned through the numbness. "That laudanum's hard to get these days, but I bet Rex Hamilton would give you some."

John pulled the blanket back over me. "I ain't giving her no laudanum."

Hollis grinned. "You might have to before it's over."

They looked at me in silence for a long moment. Then Hollis said, "I better head out. Just let her lay here awhile. She'll be up again trying to run off in no time flat."

For months I kept a racking cough that hurt my chest. As I cooked and washed dishes I spat gouts of green phlegm into a dishrag. All winter I was weak and tired, face slick with sweat. I was never the same after my time under the house. I began to see things crawling toward me from the corners of my eyes. Once I thought there was a black dog at the foot of the bed but when I sat up it was a pile of dirty clothes. At night I slept beside John under heavy blankets, the fire dead in the stove. I put my feet between his warm calves, unable to hate him in the dark. I pretended he would protect me if a red-eyed thing crept into the room and that he was not the red-eyed thing himself. Sometimes when I heard his boots on the porch I thought of the winter before we got married, when I unwrapped his face from a scarf as if his mouth, his chin, his neck were all presents.

By the end of December, he was seldom home anymore. One morning passing the bathroom door, I heard the splash of him shaving and paused to look in. I stepped behind him and saw a love bite on his naked shoulder, speckles of blood sucked to the surface of his skin. I realized then that I didn't care anymore. It was hard to remember how jealous I had once been of other women. Our eyes met in the mirror. His razor paused in mid stroke, tongue tucked into his cheek. After a while I turned and walked off. When he was gone to work, I wiped up the ring of soap scum and whiskers he left behind in the basin.

I stopped trying to run away, but he wasn't satisfied. My complacence angered him somehow. He began to punish me for walking in front of the television or coughing too loud or spilling sugar on the counter. He threw empty beer bottles at the wall near my head, pressed his cigarettes into my flesh, bent my fingers back, and squeezed my wrists in the vise grip of his hands until I couldn't feel them anymore. At first I fought back, leaving claw marks on his face and spit dripping from his nose. But as time went on, a stillness stole into me. His violence became something I bore, like when Granny brushed the knots from my hair before school in the mornings. I felt nothing anymore besides regret. But he kept trying to provoke some reaction that I was too sick and tired to give.

In the last months of our marriage, all John wanted to do was drink and eat. He had always loved my cooking, so I made big meals for him. I served him steaming plates heaped with meatloaf, okra, pork chops, soup beans, pickled beets, country fried steak, and cathead biscuits. I stuffed him with banana pudding and coffee cake and cobbler, all the things Granny had taught me to make. I kept him full and quiet as I had the baby rabbit. It was a means of self-preservation, but I didn't like watching his once chiseled face softening and thickening, his belly beginning to lap over his belt buckle. I looked at pictures I'd taken of him in summer, posing by the car with an open shirt, standing under the trees with his arms crossed over his lean chest, and hardly recognized the man I saw.

John and I didn't celebrate Christmas. He sat drinking in front of the television and I stood looking out the window at the snow-dusted ground, thinking about Granny. The next day while John was gone, Mr. Barnett drove her down the mountain to see me. It was a relief to feel her arms around me again, but I was too worried John might come home to enjoy her visit. I felt sick the whole time she and Mr. Barnett were sitting on the couch. After that she only came once more, near the end of February. I didn't mean to cry when I opened the door and saw her standing on the porch, but there was no holding it in. As good as it was to see her, I was still shaking, afraid John might come home for dinner.

Each day it grew harder to bear the dark-paneled walls, the rats scurrying back into their holes when I turned on the lights, the whiskey bottles and charred cigarette butts littering the gulley alongside the tracks. Even when I cooked with the back door thrown open there was no relief from the thick smells of fatback and beans and lard because of the chemical tincture of factory smoke and the squall of train wheel on rust-colored track. Someone might ask how I lived through those last weeks married to John. The answer is simple. I wasn't there with him. My body couldn't hold my soul. It left that smothering place and found its way back to Bloodroot Mountain, like when John trapped me under the house. I whispered those magic lines and they took me right back home. "In darkness and amid the many shapes of joyless daylight; when the fretful stir unprofitable, and the fever of the world, have hung upon the beatings of my heart — how oft, in spirit, have I turned to thee . . . how often has my spirit turned to thee." I could say the words and be gone somewhere John couldn't follow. It didn't matter what my hands were doing, washing dishes, peeling potatoes, scouring floors. My spirit's hands were catching minnows darting silver in the shallow part of the creek. John couldn't touch me where I was.

One morning after I heard the front door slam and John's car start up, I went to the bathroom and splashed water on my face and looked up at myself in the medicine cabinet mirror. I was stunned by my reflection. It wasn't just John who had changed. My hair was limp, my face haggard and thin. My eyes had lost their shine. I was still staring at my haunted reflection when I heard a bird twittering outside the bathroom window. It was a strange sound. There were no trees in the yard, so I thought I must have imagined it. I peeled back the curtain to open the window, but it was nailed shut. It didn't matter. I didn't care anymore if the bird was real or not. I saw the sun and knew spring had come. That's when the clouds parted in my head. I began thinking clearer than I had in months. I knew I had to escape, at least for a while. I wasn't willing to brave going home anymore, after John had threatened to burn it down. But the man at the pool hall had told me where I might find some of my people. I could go to the house and be back before John got home from work. There were a few dollars left in my old coffee can under the kitchen sink. I bathed and dressed and walked to the neighbor's house to call a cab again.

The same snaggletooth driver as before let me out at the pool hall. I thought it wouldn't make the right impression to arrive at my relatives' house in a taxicab. There was no waiting to see my father's mother. She was sitting on the blue concrete porch when I walked up. She was old and dark-skinned like an Indian woman, with what appeared to be a large goiter on her neck. The house was white with shutters painted blue to match the porch. It was dull and dirty and smudged, the yard crowded with dark trees and bushes. This was where I had lived with my parents. A cat stretched and rose to greet me on the steps. The old woman squinted down at me where I stood by the mailbox. I thought she would call out to ask who I was or what I wanted, but she only blinked. I went to the bottom step and she still didn't speak. I wondered if she was blind.

"Hello," I said. The cat rubbed against my ankles.

"Hidee," she said. Her voice was deep and flat.

"Are you Kenny Mayes's mother?"

There was a long silence. She looked at me. She wasn't blind. "Who's asking?"

"His daughter. I'm Kenny's daughter, Myra."

She fell silent again. I was sick to my stomach. I pushed back my sweaty hair and tried to smile. "Do you remember me?"

She adjusted herself in the green metal chair. I was careful not to stare at her goiter. It looked like a bullfrog's throat sack. "I reckon," she said.

"I wanted to see where he and my mother lived. And I wanted to see you."

For a long moment she didn't answer, until I thought I would go mad. Then finally she said, "I didn't figure you wanted nothing to do with us."

"Well," I said, flustered. "I always wondered about my parents. . . ."

"Kenny nor Clio neither one was fit to raise a youngun," she said.

I stared up at her, not sure if I had heard right. I waited for her to go on, but she turned her face to the screen door and bellowed, "Imogene!" I jumped. Her voice was startlingly loud. The door creaked open and a slim woman came out. She had styled hair and tailored clothes. She seemed out of place there. She froze when she saw me.

"Imogene," my grandmother said, "this girl claims to be Kenny's youngun."

Imogene looked at me and touched her face. Then she smiled. "Of course she is, Mother. Of course this is Kenny's girl. Look at her eyes."

We sat in a small, dark kitchen that smelled faintly of mellow garbage. I could hear an old man calling and moaning from another room. "That's Uncle," Imogene said to me as she poured coffee. There was a Chihuahua under the table. It trembled and growled at me. "Why don't you see about him, Mother?"

"He's all right," my grandmother said flatly. "He's always carrying on like that."

The dog stood up and barked at me, showing its teeth. "Hush, Peanut," the old woman said, and kicked at his flank with her bare foot. I could see dirt caked under her toenails. The dog skittered away and curled up again out of reach.

I sipped the bitter coffee and studied them in the murky light. They didn't seem related. Imogene's face was soft and pretty. I liked the veined backs of her hands. "Mother, isn't she beautiful?" Imogene asked. The old woman didn't answer. "What have you been doing with yourself, Myra? You were just a baby when I last saw you."

"I got married and moved down here with my husband, John Odom."

"Is he any kin to Frankie Odom," the old woman asked, "has a hardware store?"

"Yes, that's John's father," I said. I was growing impatient. I wasn't there to talk about myself. "I have some questions, I guess. About Kenny and Clio."

"We'll tell you anything we can," Imogene said, smiling over her coffee. "Won't we, Mother?" The old woman just went on blinking at me.

I thought hard but all my questions had suddenly evaporated. My mind was blank. They stared at me across the table. I felt my cheeks burning as I groped for something to say. Imogene looked concerned. Then her face brightened.

"Would you like to see some pictures?"

"Yes," I said, exhaling at last.

"Mother, where are those albums?"

"Under the bed," the old woman said. She grunted and rose to take a pack of sugar wafers from a bread box on the counter. She stood at the sink eating them as Imogene went for the albums. She looked at me, soggy crumbs falling down her goiter. I was sickened that she had given birth to my father and known my mother as a daughter-in-law. Imogene brought the albums to the table and removed one from the top of the stack. She wiped dust off its cover and turned the pages slowly, a parade of unfamiliar faces in grainy black and white. Then she stopped. "Here. This is Kenny and me," she said. Two children stood on a porch with solemn expressions. It was hard to tell how far apart in age they were, but I guessed he was at least six years younger than her. I wanted to feel something. This was my father. But as the pages turned and I watched the progress of his growth from a boy into a young man, I realized I was waiting to see my mother's face. We flipped through the second album and still no sign. It was like she, and I, had been erased from the history of these people. Granny had pictures of my mother but they were all taken on the mountain. I needed pictures of her there in that house, living a life I didn't know or understand. Imogene must have seen my disappointment.

"Don't you have any pictures of Clio around here, Mother?" she asked.

The old woman bit into another sugar wafer. "That girl never set still long enough to make a picture," she said, spraying crumbs.

"Good Lord, Mother," Imogene said, brows knitting together. "Do you have to talk so hateful all the time? Myra's going to think we're awful." She turned to me and smiled. "I know I've got some at my house. Would you like to come home with me and take a look? I might could tell you some stories, too."

"I don't know," I said, thinking of John for the first time since I got out of the taxi. "I told the cabdriver to be back at the pool hall by three."

"I don't live far," Imogene said. "I can have you back before then."

In the car she told me things about my mother that I'd never heard before. The time she let me taste ice cream on her finger and how I suckled with such a funny look on my face. The time she brought me in from the car bundled up and when she opened the blanket inside the warm house everyone saw that she had carried me across the yard upside down. But something bothered me about the way Imogene kept her eyes straight ahead as she spoke, the way she laughed nervously. I grew afraid that it was all lies, or at least only part of the story. We pulled up to her house, a nicely landscaped brick duplex. She lived in one side and kept tenants in the other. Getting out of the car, I realized how close we were to the Odom house. I ducked my head as we crossed the yard. Inside, the windows were hung with trailing plants and curios lined a white mantel. The room was clean but packed with antique furniture. There were mirrors and picture frames propped against one wall and old books stacked against another. "Don't mind my mess," Imogene said. "I'm opening myself a little shop next door, when the remodeling is done." I glanced toward the window, hearing the hammering outside. She followed my eyes and said, "That's my friend fixing the roof. I've been buying things along as I see them. I've loved old things since I was a little girl. It's scary to try something new like this, but I always wanted my own store." She seemed harried and scattered, talking perhaps to hide her embarrassment. We both knew she was keeping something from me. "You can have a seat, honey," she said. "I'll get my albums."

I went to the brocade loveseat, lace doilies draped on its arms. I felt outside myself, in this unfamiliar place with this strange woman who was my aunt. When she came back, we spent a long time looking at the pictures. One of my mother holding me, not smiling. One of her surrounded by other people, a cigarette between her fingers. She smoked. I never knew. These are the things people forget to tell you. When all the pages were turned, we sat in silence. I supposed it was time to go but I wasn't ready. I couldn't stop thinking of Imogene's nervous stories in the car, the troubling sense of being lied to. She waited expectantly, probably for me to say that I should be going, so I said it. "I ought to be getting back." But I didn't get up. My body resisted and when she was getting her purse I couldn't keep quiet any longer. I blurted, "What were they really like?"

She turned to me, startled. "Hmm?"

"All I hear are the good stories. I want to hear all of the stories. Good and bad."

Imogene put down her purse and keys.

She came to sit beside me again. She put her hand on my knee. "Oh, honey," she said.

"I want to know," I said.

She grew quiet, looking down, biting her lip.

She looked back up. "But what good would it do? What does it matter now?"

"I don't know," I said. "Please tell me."

"You're sure."

"Yes."

"All right. I'll do the best I can."

She began at the beginning. "I've always been different than them," she said. "I hated growing up in that filthy house. You couldn't go barefoot unless you wanted black feet. He tracked it in on his boots. We call him Uncle but he's not. I figure he's my grandfather. Grandmother moved in with her sister Lucille, who was married to Uncle. About a year later, Mother was born. I don't know if Uncle raped Grandmother or if she slept with him. Are you sure you want to hear all this?" I nodded and she went on. "Uncle never was any good. I believe that's part of why Kenny turned out how he did. It was in the blood. Now Grandmother and Lucille are gone and Uncle's still kicking.

"We moved in with Grandmother and Lucille and Uncle after Kenny was born. Mother was a bastard, and Kenny and I grew up fatherless, too. But I do remember my father. The three of us lived for a while in a room over a storefront. He had a strong, nasty smell and whiskers. Straggly hair and no teeth, tattoos all over his arms. One of them was a dagger. I don't know what happened to him. He wasn't Kenny's father.

"I was eight when Kenny was born. I doted on my brother, toting him around everywhere and letting him pitch tantrums. But he had the finest blond hair and the sweetest blue eyes, just like yours. He was the cutest little boy, until he got spoiled and hateful. He wouldn't do his schoolwork and Mother didn't care. I was the only one that ever tried to encourage him, but what was the use? She let him drop out in the eighth grade. He laid around for the rest of his life after that, except to go out drinking on the weekends. He'd take a job here and there, but he ended up quitting every one of them.

"Kenny's father, your grandfather, was shot in a bar, I believe. Mother settled down after that. She was still mean as a snake on the inside, though. Sometimes I wonder why I still go over there. I wonder why I still love her. But it's the same reason you love your mother, and will still love her after I say what I'm going to say. Uncle owned the pool hall where Kenny and Clio met. I had married my husband Gerald and moved out, so I wasn't around much at that time. But I did get to know Clio, at least somewhat. She had hair like yours, even longer. She was a fairly nice-looking girl, but not like you. I'll be honest. There was something odd about her eyes, like the lights were on and nobody home. She couldn't stand to hang around the house. She got a job and left you with Kenny. I know you're wondering if she loved you. I think so. She bought you frilly dresses. Put bows in your hair, which you had a lot of, even as a baby. She played with you like a doll. She wasn't a bad girl. Just restless, and liked to drink. Kenny, I don't know. It bothered him when you cried. He wanted to sleep late and you woke him up early. He and Mother didn't watch you very well while Clio was at work. Some days I'd go over there and find you lying in the crib crying with a dirty diaper. You always had diaper rash where they didn't change you enough, and I'd take you home with me."

She paused then and looked down at her hands in her lap. I held my breath because I knew she was about to tell me whatever she had been withholding. I opened my mouth to stop her, to say that she was right, I didn't want to know. But it was too late.

"She dropped you one time," Imogene said, the words rushing together. "She and Kenny both were drunk. I believe she was on something, too. Some kind of pills. She said you just slipped through her fingers. You hit your head on the floor and Clio thought you were dead. She was out of her head when she called me. I could barely understand her. She wanted me to help her bury you. Said Kenny couldn't do it, he was passed out, and Mother and Uncle both worked late at the pool hall on Friday nights so they weren't home. I rushed over there scared to death what I would find. She was standing in the yard pacing back and forth with you, making this awful moaning noise. I jumped out of the car and snatched you out of her arms. I saw right away that you were just sleeping. I believe she would have buried you alive if I hadn't gotten there fast. I begged Clio to let me drive you to the emergency room, but she was scared they might take you away from her. She could have been right. They might have. But I believe she did love you the best she knew how." Imogene pulled a crumpled tissue from behind her watch band and dabbed at her eyes. She didn't look at me. When she began again, her voice was unsteady.

"After a while Mother got tired of babysitting. She wouldn't do it anymore. Clio started driving you up the mountain and leaving you with your grandmother when she and Kenny went out. Thank goodness you were with her when your mother and father got killed. Once Kenny and Clio were gone it was like you were gone, too. Your granny didn't want me to visit, and Mother never tried to. She's a hard-hearted woman, even being her daughter I can't deny it. I went up the mountain to see you once anyway. It was a scary place to me, so hidden up there in the woods. But I saw that you were well taken care of. You won't be able to see this now, and you might be angry at me for saying it, but for you it's a blessing Kenny and Clio died. Your granny was nice enough to me while I was there. We had peach cobbler and coffee. But she asked me not to ever come back. I understood. So, there's all of it. I'm your aunt. And I'm glad to see you again."

I sat staring at her for a long time, unable to speak. A clock ticked loudly in the silence. After a while, it seemed Imogene felt obligated to say something. She looked out the window, where the hammering was still going on at intervals. "You know I told you I'm opening a shop next door?" she asked, voice high with false brightness. I nodded numbly. "Would you like to take a look before we go? These last renters left me with a mess, but it's a world better now." I nodded again, feeling like a sleepwalker. "Oh," she said, glancing toward the kitchen. "I better take Ford a glass of tea. I bet he's burning up out there." I waited while she rattled around in the kitchen and came out with a frosty glass. She gathered her purse and keys and I followed her outside on automatic pilot. I went behind Imogene in a daze, the dress I'd put on that morning sticking to my legs in a heat that was uncharacteristic for such an early spring day. She talked with forced enthusiasm about the sign she would have painted with her name in fancy script, and where it would hang above the shop door. I pretended to listen, but her voice was distant and hazy to me.

There was a man coming shirtless down from the roof. "I brought you a drink, Ford," Imogene said to him. He had long hippie hair, that's what John would have called it. His chest and belly glistened with sweat. He smiled, showing good white teeth, and drank the tea down with long gulps. "Thank you," he said.

"How's it coming?" Imogene asked.

"Nearly finished." He looked at me with eyes like John's, but kinder. Then I noticed his hand on the slippery glass. One of the fingers was missing.

"This is my niece," Imogene said, "Myra Odom. Myra, this is Ford Hendrix."

We nodded to each other. The sun was in my eyes. Birds twittered. I felt far away. "It's funny how Ford and I met," Imogene said. "We were at a garage sale down in Oak Ridge. This woman had a whole table full of old books, and Ford and I were like kids in a candy store. We got to talking and come to find out, Ford has quite a collection. I've been out to see them, haven't I, Ford? You wouldn't believe it. And Ford writes novels, too. He's a regular celebrity these days, had a book signing down at the Plaza."

Ford grinned. There was a silence. I realized he was staring at me, but I couldn't concentrate on him or on what was being said. Then Imogene looked over her shoulder, toward her house. She frowned back at us. "Is that my telephone? I'd better go check. It might be Mother. Myra, I promise I'll hurry back. I know you need to be somewhere."

"You're white as a sheet," Ford said the instant she was gone. "Are you sick?"

I took a better look at him. He was older

481

than me, at least late thirties, a handsome man. Not beautiful, as John once was, but good to look at. "No. I'm not sick."

He wasn't convinced. "It might be the heat. Let's go over here in the shade." When I didn't move, he took my elbow. His touch startled me. I remembered the missing finger. I let him lead me under the trees. We sat down and I was grateful for the coolness.

"I didn't know Imogene had a niece," he said.

"I didn't know I had an aunt," I said. "Until today."

"You and Imogene never met before now?"

"I wanted to know about my mother. She died when I was one."

"I see. Did Imogene tell you?"

"Yes," I said, looking down at the damp print of my dress. "She told me."

"Ah," he said. "She told you too much."

I raised my head, startled. His face was very close.

"You have eyes like my husband's," I said, without knowing why.

"Well," he said. "You have eyes like the Aegean Sea."

"You've seen the Aegean Sea?"

"Yes. It's very blue."

"Imogene says you have a lot of books."

"Yes."

"Do you read poetry?"

"Some."

"Wordsworth?"

"One of my favorites."

"Nature never did betray the heart that loved her."

"Tintern Abbey."

"Yes."

Looking at him, soft hair, soft eyes, all soft, made me forget. Then Imogene was back and we stood up. She seemed hot and nervous. "That was Mother," she said. "Uncle's fell out of bed and she can't get him up by herself."

"Did she call for an ambulance?" Ford asked.

"No, he's not hurt. He does this all the time. Myra, honey, I'm afraid we'll have to run back by the house. I hope it won't make you late."

I remembered John and tried not to show my fear. "That's okay," I said.

"I can drive her back," Ford spoke up. I stared at him mutely.

"Oh . . . are you sure?" Imogene turned to me, brow creased. "Myra, would that be okay with you? I wouldn't dream of it if I didn't trust Ford with my life."

"No, it's fine," I said.

"I'm so sorry about this. Will you come back and see me?"

"Yes," I said. But I didn't mean it.

In his car I looked through the bug-splattered windshield, half sick on the smell of exhaust. When Imogene's words drifted to the front of my mind I snuffed them like candle flames, not ready yet to sort them out. I looked at Ford behind the wheel, long legs in patched blue jeans, unbuttoned shirt blowing, one dark strand of hair trailing across his mouth. When he caught me staring he smiled but didn't speak, somehow knowing I needed silence. I came back into myself with a start when I saw that we were close to the pool hall, turning onto the street that would take me back to John. Panic fluttered in my guts. "Don't stop here," I blurted as we neared the low building. "I don't want to go home yet." Ford didn't seem surprised. He had slowed to turn in but kept on going. I was scared and relieved at the same time. Maybe I would never go back, should never go back, because John would probably kill me. But I didn't want to think about that. I didn't want to think about anything. It was easy there in the car with Ford to push it all away.

"What do you want to do?" he asked.

"I want to see your books."

He looked at me and lifted his eyebrows. That was all. We drove for a long time with the wind blowing. The landscape reminded me of home, farmland unrolling on both sides of the dirt road and the mountains rising up in the distance, but I didn't want to think about that either. I wanted to be someone else in a strange car with a strange man.

It was a long trailer with a muddy yard and cinder blocks up to the door. Dogs followed at our heels and one came inside with us, a small white mutt with matted fur. The living room was flooded with sun, dust motes dancing, and books piled everywhere. Ford turned to me and smiled awkwardly. We stood regarding each other in the middle of the cluttered room. "Home sweet home," he said. I looked him over, so different than what I was used to. John was fastidious, at least in the beginning of our marriage. This man was sloppy, sweaty, and dirty. But he had a good face. "Wordsworth," he said suddenly, and turned to search through the books. I watched his back moving, the chain of his spine under the open shirt. "Yes, here it is." He brought a slim volume with yellowed leaves. "I found this in Pennsylvania." He looked at the table of contents, scanning

485

with one finger, and turned the brittle pages. I closed my eyes and listened as he read. "Five years have past, five summers, with the length of five long winters, and again I hear these waters, rolling from their mountain springs with a soft inland murmur. Once again do I behold these steep and lofty cliffs, that on a wild secluded scene impress thoughts of more deep seclusion, and connect the landscape with the quiet of the sky. . . ."

The words sounded more beautiful to me than ever before. I focused on his voice, taking me away from everything, taking me back to my mountain. By the time he finished I had sunk down on the carpet. The dog came wagging to sniff my face. Then Ford knelt and I pictured his damaged hand when he put his arm around me. "She dropped me," I said, beginning to cry, and he didn't ask questions. He only said, "It's okay."

I kissed him first. For so long with John, I hadn't been loved. I might never have been loved by my mother. If I retaliated against them, it was unconscious. I cared for nothing in that moment. There was no thought of revenge. Ford resisted at first, tried to pull back, but I thrust my whole self against his chest and he gave in. We stayed there on

486

the floor. It felt like there was no time to move to his bed. When it was over we propped our backs against the couch and sat dazed and half naked, sweating in the heat of the stifling trailer. "What if I told you," he said, "that I knew you were coming?"

"Oh?" I said, heart beating hard but slow. "How is that?"

"I have visions sometimes."

We looked at each other. I smiled. "Visions."

He smiled back. "Yes. Do you believe me?"

"No. There are no prophets in this day and age. Except maybe false ones."

I began to gather my clothes around me, reaching for my shoes.

"Do you have to go? Stay with me for a while."

"I can't," I said. "I've done wrong being here."

"Stay with me forever, then," he said.

"I'm married."

"But he doesn't love you."

"How do you know?"

"I told you. I have visions."

"Well. It's still a sin, being here with you."

"He'll hurt you if you go back."

"Probably. But I still have to go."

"Why?"

487

"Because he's got my granddaddy's ring."

Ford reached for me. "Myra. Your life is more important than a ring."

"I'd never leave John without taking that ring with me."

"You could sneak in while he's sleeping and slip it right off."

"I don't know," I said. I had the wild urge to laugh, even though nothing was funny. "John's put on a few pounds. It might be stuck."

Ford grinned. "You could grease up his finger," he said, holding up his left hand. "Or you could do what my ex-wife did. I bet your husband's a drinker, like I used to be. Nothing will pack on the pounds like beer. My ring was stuck, too. One night she got tired of me blowing our grocery money on booze. I came in drunk as a skunk and passed out cold. She got so mad she chopped off my finger, took my wedding ring and everything else of value we had and ran off with it. Haven't heard from her since."

I tossed my shoe at him. "You're nuts."

"I've heard that before," he said. "Are you sure you have to go?"

I nodded. He kissed me and smoothed back my hair. For a long moment he studied my face. "Because in my vision," he said, "we had babies together."

Ford drove me to the pool hall and let me out. I slammed the door before I could hear his goodbye. I used a pay phone to call the hardware store. I knew John wouldn't be there anymore, but I didn't know what else to do. I stood in the parking lot under a streetlight for what seemed like hours, thinking he might come looking for me there. I only prayed he hadn't been up the mountain. Sometime after dark he wheeled into the lot slinging gravel and leaned over the seat to open the passenger door. I was too numb to be afraid. He didn't say anything on the drive, didn't ask where I had been.

When we arrived at home I sat in the car and waited for him to pull me out by the hair, my knees scraping in the dirt. Grunting and puffing, he dragged me across the yard, my scalp screaming. He yanked up my dress and wrestled my legs open. There was no use begging him to stop. I fought hard but I was tired and he was strong. He forced himself on me as I looked up at the stars. I tried to send my soul floating out of my body again, back up to Bloodroot Mountain. Tears ran from the corners of my eyes toward my ears. Whatever wrong I'd done in swallowing that heart, surely this settled the score.

When it was all over, I lay still on the ground, careful not to look at his face. The night was cool. The neighbor's dogs were barking. I closed my eyes and remembered them lunging at the ends of chains. Then it seemed I caught the scent of mountain woods. For a moment, I felt my mother's ghost with me. I took in long, slow breaths of her.

My whole body was limp as John dragged me by the arms back to the door in the house's foundation. I didn't resist this time as he shoved me inside and locked it behind me. I lay on my back quivering in the blackness, spiders crawling over my arms and shoulders. I felt a warm wetness between my legs, maybe some of it blood. After a while my muscles loosened and I rested on the cool, grave-smelling dirt. Sometime during the night, listening to the thunder of a train that shook the house on top of me, the shine of its light flooding through the cinder block's holes, I became sure there was life growing inside me. I wasn't alone in my body anymore. I didn't question how I could know such a thing. The only question was whether the child was fathered by John or Ford. But it didn't really matter how it came into the world. All that mattered was the one certainty, that it was mine. I rested my hands on my womb. This baby had never bewitched John with a chicken heart. This baby had nothing to make amends for. I had to set it free.

John didn't come back and open the door, but I could see better once the sun came up. After I heard his car leaving for work, I kicked with a kind of strength I didn't have before. I hammered at the boards for hours with my feet, already warped from the last night I spent under the house. Finally there was a loud crack as the door broke loose from its hinges and fell forward onto the ground. I slid out into the sun, squinting against the light. I went inside and took a long, hot bath, carefully washing the throbbing place between my legs. I put on an old blouse and a pair of jeans and prepared to wait. It was Friday and I knew John would come stumbling home drunk in the dark. He would fall across the couch on his face as he did every weekend when his paycheck was spent. I went to the front room and sat thinking of the hours I'd spent there away from home, where I had draped myself in mountain laurel, plaited crowns with this flower, wound myself in that vine, stepped out of green tangles smelling of honeysuckle so that Granny scooped me up and drank my hair like sweet tea in the summertime. It was hard to remember exactly how long I'd been trapped in that house with John, ten months or ten years. I saw the bits of me that had fallen off, the chiseled-off curls of flesh and bone like raw wood he had whittled from me. At some point I stretched my sore body out on the couch and slept, hands folded across the baby I now had to live for. When I woke up later, it was night. I sat up, eyes wide, afraid John had stolen into the house. I tensed and listened to the dark. There was nothing but the hum of the refrigerator.

Then I heard his car engine die out in the gravel lot and a deep calm settled in my guts. Sometimes he was too drunk to find his way home but this night he made it. I had willed him down the one-way streets, past the junkyard to this place, when so many times before I had wished his car wrapped around a telephone pole. As he fumbled with the lock until the door swung open, I got up from the couch and receded into the shadows, crouched in the corner to wait. His footsteps were heavy, a floorboard cracking under his boots. He fell across the couch I had just vacated, springs groaning. He didn't stumble to the bathroom as he did sometimes when he came home drunk.

I was glad because it meant he would lose consciousness faster. He lay there, knuckles trailing along the floor, loose fist finally harmless. I watched the stinking bulk of him rise and fall until he began to snore. I slunk across the floor and knelt before him, the stench of whiskey hanging over him like a cloud. I plucked at his fat pink fingers and he didn't stir. I pulled his hand up into the weak light and placed it on the coffee table where I could see it better. I took a long look at Granddaddy's ring and knew that I couldn't pull it off. It hadn't been removed since that night we stood in the preacher's house and I slid it onto the flesh of a hand like carved marble. Now it was part of the ruin John had become.

I licked my lips. My heart began to beat for what felt like the first time in months, blood pumping hot and fast through my cold veins. I slipped into the kitchen and turned on the light and paced back and forth, trying to think. I couldn't let him keep what was left of Granny and Granddaddy and the home where I ran like a horse through the trees. I wouldn't give him the color of bloodroot and true love. It was blasphemy on his finger. It was hard to remember how much I once loved seeing it there, how I nibbled, kissed, sucked at that ring-finger tip ten times a day. Once upon a time, seeing his fingers laced through mine and the dark shine of that bloodred ring sent heat racing all over me.

I caught sight of myself reflected in the kitchen window, a white horror mask with black eye sockets and long snarls of matted hair. It was the wild woman I saw when John first opened the door of that place. There was an exhilarating moment when I knew it would end for me one way or another. That's when I caught sight of the hatchet, leaning against the wood box beside the back door. I stood looking at it for a long time, thinking of the story Ford told about his missing finger. I tried to keep my breathing slow and calm as I crossed the kitchen and picked up the hatchet, its heft comforting in my hands.

I went silently back to the front room. All the time I had spent learning to be invisible was finally paying off. The limp slab of his arm had fallen from the coffee table and I gently replaced it. Granddaddy's ring glittered in the pale streetlight. I raised the hatchet high and brought it down fast. The sound was loud in my ears, the force of the hatchet whacking through fingers and lodging in wood jarring my arms, causing me to bite down hard on my tongue. John bellowed and rose up, his eyes unfocused and searching. Without thinking, I yanked the hatchet free from the coffee table and brought the blunt end crashing up into his chin. There was a crunch of teeth as he fell backward.

I didn't wait to see if he was out cold or dead. I grubbed around on the floor until I found the ring under the coffee table. Somehow it was still wedged on John's finger. After a moment's hesitation, I scooped up both ring and finger and stuffed them wet and warm in the pocket of my jeans. I ran to the bedroom and slung the bag I had already packed over my shoulder. I left out the back door and as I crossed the kitchen I could hear the terrible gurgling noises he made. I thought they might be his death throes and there was only relief. I fled across the barren yard, away from the tracks and the smothering house and the time I spent there. I'll never forget that satisfying whack. It still lives in me, still vibrates through my arms. When I open my box it's not just the ring that comforts me. It's that scrap of finger, like a shaving I whittled off for myself, carved out of all those months. It was only fair, after the curls of me he left scattered. No matter what I'd done to bewitch him, it was only fair that I take a piece of his hide with me.

I walked out into the night with John's finger and Granddaddy's ring in my pocket. I didn't have to change my clothes. Most of the blood was on John, not me. I walked and walked on those trash-littered roads, busted beer bottles, boarded-up buildings, dark houses. For a while a stray dog traveled alongside me, tail down and eyes watchful. He probably smelled John's blood in my pocket. Above was the clearest night I'd ever seen, so many stars it made me dizzy to crane my neck and look up. Seeing them eased the ragged pain in my shoulder. Just when I thought I couldn't go another step, God sent a car to me, a woman coming home from the night shift. She took one look at me and said, "Get in." She asked if I needed help and I told her I only needed to go home.

She had bleached blond hair, permed tight, and some man's name tattooed on her wrist. Her long fingernails tapped the cracked steering wheel as she talked on and on, false teeth slipping. She spoke of her no-good husband and her lazy sons and the arrogant foreman at the plant. I dozed with my head against the car window, her disembodied smoker's voice loud in my exhausted head. She didn't seem to mind or even notice that my eyes were closed, that I was drifting. She drove me all the way to the foot of Bloodroot Mountain without asking any questions. She said, "I can't go up yonder. I've got to get back to the house before my old man wakes up." I didn't mind. I got out of her car and thanked her. It was a fitting way to come home. It was the third day of March, 1975. The sun was rising between the trees, fog low to the ground, the mountain high on both sides of me. I watched the woman's taillights disappear back toward town.

I'd had time to rest in the woman's car but my feet and back still wept. I was still sore between the legs and my shoulder felt dislocated where I'd yanked the hatchet free from the wood of the coffee table. It didn't matter. The mountain looked beautiful, as if dressed up for my homecoming. I could have run when I saw the house. The house of Granny and Granddaddy and me, the house of us at supper in the kitchen, the house of being rocked on Granddaddy's lap and reading books on the steps, the house, the home, of my soul and spirit. As I went up the hill there was no sound, of leaf or animal or even my feet in the dew-damp grass. It felt like I had been gone for a thousand years. Once I made it across the yard I could finally rest. My blood would run easy and warm from my head to my toes, not because of the mountain, but because of Granny and all that she was to me. I wondered if she would have a fire going. Yesterday's warm weather seemed to have fled and it was a chilly morning. I thought of Granny bent over stoking the woodstove at night in the yellow-lit kitchen, potatoes sometimes baking in the embers, and how in the winter mornings before school, nestled under the blankets with my cold nose poking out, I'd hear her bringing in the kindling. All my life, she'd kept a good fire going for me. I imagined her pouring coffee, the wispy curl of her hair, the knotty crook of her finger. No matter the curse, no matter the charm, no matter the sins I'd committed, there she was, behind that door, as if she had been there since the world began.

But the closer I got to the house, the more I began to fear that I had returned too late. The place was so still, and Granny was usually up at this hour. She always said her old bones couldn't rest for long. I noticed there was no smoke from the chimney, no light in the kitchen window. I moved faster to reach the door but hesitated before turning the knob. I pushed it open slowly, not wanting to see. It was like being twelve again, opening the door to Granddaddy's death, only it was Granny this time, slumped in his chair, eyes closed and mouth slack. Beside her on the table was not a carved box, but a cup of coffee that I was sure had grown cold. Gray light crept across the floor toward her slippered feet. I froze as I had that other day five years ago looking at Granddaddy, no breath coming to fill my lungs. I ran to her and dropped to my knees. I gathered her legs in my arms, covered in broken blood vessels like ugly bruises. I buried my head in her lap and wept out loud. Then I felt a hand on my head, fumbling at my hair. I sucked in a breath and looked up. There was Granny, blinking as if she was still half asleep. "Myra?"

"Yes," I said. "It's me. I came home." Her fingers tightened in my hair, tugged at the roots as she stared at me, maybe struggling to comprehend my real presence. Then she said, "Thank Jesus. I thought I was fixing to die up here without you."

We cried together as I rested with my head on Granny's knees, her hand tangled up in my hair. She seemed afraid to let go. When she finally released me, I raised my face and smiled at her through my tears. She opened her mouth, maybe to ask questions, but she must have decided against it. She wiped her cheeks with one shaky hand and said, "You're plumb wore out. Let me put you in the bed and we'll talk about it later."

"I can't sleep," I said. But even as I dragged myself to my feet, I knew it wasn't true. I could sleep, but only if she sat in the rocker for a while watching over me.

Granny pulled herself to her feet with a groan but then she stopped short, eyes growing wide. She was looking at the pocket of my jeans. I followed her stare and saw it, too, a stiff patch of dried maroon. She asked sharply, "What's happened to you?"

"Nothing," I said, still looking down at my pocket. Somehow I had managed to forget what I'd stuffed inside. I reached in and pulled out John's finger. I offered it to her in the palm of my hand, the usual shine of Granddaddy's ring dulled by John's dark blood. We looked at it together. "They laws," Granny said softly. "Is he dead?"

"I don't know," I told her. That's when the reality of what I had done crashed down on me. "I ran off in a hurry. If he's not, Granny, he'll come up here after me."

"Well." She looked toward the bedroom. "I've got your granddaddy's shotgun."

"Oh no," I whispered. "Look what I've got us into."

She took hold of my chin. "Don't you talk like that. I'm just praising the Lord to have you back. Don't matter to me what it took to get you here." She glanced down at the finger. "We've got to get rid of that thing."

"No," I said.

Her eyes flew open wide again. "You can't keep that, and him might be dead. That's evidence, girl! Why in the devil would you want to anyway?"

"I don't know," I said, crying again. "I can't throw it away. Not right now."

"All right." She reached out to caress my cheek. "Don't get wrought up. We'll worry about getting shed of it later. But you can't hold it like that." She grimaced and it was the first time I'd ever seen Granny recoil from blood. It had always been natural to us here on the mountain, slaughtering hogs and killing chickens and birthing babies and treating Granddaddy's various gashes and wounds. But this, I saw, was too much for her.

"Where's the box?" I asked. "The one Granddaddy made me?"

"Myra —" she began, but something she saw in me, maybe the madness I could barely suppress, caused her to give up. "Come on," she said, and I followed her to the back room. She knelt in front of her bed and pulled out the box. We stood in the growing sun as she opened it for me to lay the finger inside, still pushed through Granddaddy's wedding ring. I put both ring and finger into the box and we looked at each other for a long moment across it. Her wrinkled face was blank. It was hard to guess what she was thinking. Then she clapped the lid back on the box and knelt, old joints popping, and replaced it in the cottony grave of the mattress hole. She took me by the arm and led me to the bed. "Get out of them dirty britches," she said. "I'll bring you a nightgown."

"What if he comes?"

"I'll set up with you."

I undressed and climbed into bed. I was already half asleep before she returned with the gown. It smelled like her and my home. I slept for what seemed like days, having nightmares that John had come and hurt Granny and one where he ripped the child I was carrying out of my womb and ran away with it. I roused up and saw Granny sitting in the rocking chair watching over me, Granddaddy's gun across her knees.

"Granny," I said.

She turned to me, startled. "What, honey?"

"I'm going to have a baby."

She stopped rocking. "Have you been to the doctor?"

"No."

"Then how do you know?"

"I just do."

She looked at me, thinking. Then she nodded. "I'll make you an appointment with Dr. Weems. He's old as the hills but he's got a sound mind. He'll take good care of you."

"I'm not going to any doctor," I said, a little too loud. "I want you to take care of me. You used to help Grandmaw Ruth with babies. You know as much as Dr. Weems."

"They laws, girl, it's been sixty-odd years since I seen a baby born."

"But you still know how to do it."

Granny came to sit on the edge of the bed. "Quit talking crazy, Myra."

"I'm not talking crazy. I know what I'm saying. Nobody but you and I will ever lay their hands on this baby. Nobody else will ever even know it's alive."

Granny frowned. "Myra Jean, no baby can live like that, and neither can you."

"It's the only way my baby can live. If John's dead, I'm in a world of trouble. It's a matter of time before they come after me. If you see anybody driving up the hill, you let me know and I'll slip out the back and take this baby somewhere it'll never be found."

"Lord, Myra," she said. "You know I couldn't stand for you to leave me again."

"Maybe it won't come to that. If he's alive, I figure he'll be after me once he's up and around again. I don't know what I'll do then. But no matter what happens, John or his family can't know about my baby. I'd kill it before I'd let them have it."

Granny took hold of my shoulders. "Don't you say that. Don't you ever." Then she drew me close. "Ain't nothing going to happen to this baby. I knowed the minute you opened them eyes miraculous things was going to come out of you." She rocked me back and forth, like she used to when I was a little girl. "I can feel it all over myself."

Granny's faith made me stronger. Days and weeks passed and neither John nor the police came for me. I didn't understand, but I was thankful for those months with Granny. At first, I didn't want anyone to know I was home, but it was impossible to keep secrets from Mr. Barnett. He checked on Granny at least twice a week and brought her groceries on Saturdays. There was no use trying to hide from him. I opened the door when he knocked and he looked stunned. Then his eyes lit up. "It's about time you got away from there," he said.

When my pregnancy began to show, Mr. Barnett eyed my belly but never acknowledged its roundness. I'm sure Granny told him about the baby, but he didn't mention it to me. Soon the Cotters knew, too. Before Bill died, he stopped by to see about Granny because she hadn't been at church. I wanted to hide then but Granny swore it would be all right. She trusted our neighbors, and I trusted her.

It was like being a child again but even better, at least when I could forget about John. Time stood still as the baby grew. Granny and I cooked together, washed clothes, read the newspaper and the Bible to each other. On my eighteenth birthday she made a cake and we ate it sitting on a quilt under the trees, looking into the woods as the summer wind blew over us. In the mornings we fed the chickens, brought in the eggs, and made breakfast. At dusk we picked green beans and weeded the flower beds. When fall came, we made apple butter outside over an open fire, taking turns stirring the kettle. All those months, Granny took good care of me, just as I had known she would. It came back to her fast, all that Grandmaw Ruth had taught her. She went up the mountain hunting roots and brewed special teas. She listened for the baby's heart with her ear pressed to my belly. She examined me so gently I never felt a thing. One day she looked at me as I rolled out dough for a pie crust. "You're getting awful big, not to be any further along than you are," she said. "There might be two of them in there." I put my hands on my swollen stomach. There was a kick, like an affirmation. I imagined two babies curled together inside me. It was comforting to think they weren't alone in the dark of my womb.

Sometimes I thought of Ford's soft eyes and gentle hands. I thought how he would love my babies if they belonged to him and maybe if they didn't. I thought he might even love me, too. But those thoughts fled when I sat on the mattress with a scrap of John rotting inside. I could never be touched and kissed like that again and stay hidden. Sometimes I daydreamed about showing myself to Ford anyway, my growing belly draped in a sundress. I imagined how he might slide the straps down and kiss each shoulder and then the top of each heavy breast, take them in his hands to lighten my load, curl his long body around the babies in my womb and keep them safe with me through the night. Even now I look off the mountain and wish I could see where he is. I wish we could build a fire and sleep in the long field beside of his trailer and fry eggs in an iron skillet when we wake up in the morning. We could live with the twins among piles of books and matted dogs with ticks fattening behind their ears. Sometimes I wonder what it would have been like to grow up on a farm instead of high on a mountain. That's one life I could have given my babies. It would have been easier there, better hidden from the Odoms, and I know I would have loved Ford. Part of me still does. But it was not the right life for my twins and me. This mountain is their birthright. It's what I have to give.

They were born on the fifth day of November in 1975. I was sitting on the back steps with a jam biscuit, colored leaves skittering out of the woods across the yard. I didn't have to read the poems from a book anymore. I had come to know them by heart. I was saying the verses out loud to my babies when the pains came. As soon as the first sharp contraction cramped low in my belly, all my fears came flooding back. I jumped up so fast that I almost lost my balance but I didn't know what to do next. I paced in the brown grass in front of the steps, waiting for another pain. When it came I felt the panic welling up big and dark, threatening to wipe me out. Once the babies were outside of me it would be harder to protect them. Granny opened the door to ask if I was hungry and I stared at her with eyes that strained in their sockets. "Is it time?" she asked. I nodded. She spat her snuff into the dirt beside the steps, still holding the door open. "You sure you don't want to go to the hospital? I can head down yonder and get Hacky right now."

"No!" I shouted, trying to hold back tears.

"Well, okay. Don't get all worked up. We'll do just fine by ourselves."

"What if John comes?"

"If he ain't come after you by now, he ain't going to."

"He's got brothers, Granny. The one named Hollis is awful. He —"

"Straighten up, Myra. This is a good day and we're going to have a big time. Now come on in and put your feet up. It'll be a long wait yet."

It was a long wait, just as she said. I drank tea and Granny rubbed my feet and sometimes my back and sometimes my shoulders. She told me all the good stories again and read to me from the Bible and tried to teach me how to knit but it was hard to concentrate. Then she checked me once more and said, "I believe they're ready."

I was afraid at first, when the worst pains

came, grinding in my abdomen. I couldn't keep still. My fingers dug into the sheet. Everything was more vivid. Colors shouted and sound had the resonance of a bell. I heard my toes crack as I curled them. The mattress creaked under my writhing. Granny told me to push and there was a moment when I was sure the babies would never come out. I would be giving birth forever. I bore down, head thrashing from side to side, hair plastered to my cheeks and neck and forehead. I felt the babies battling to join me in this life. Everything I was, all that I had done right and wrong seemed far and distant. I gave one last shove, determined to have the babies even if the effort split my body in two. Then the first baby cried and Granny was laughing, shouting like she did sometimes in church, running up and down the aisle with her hands held high in the air. I fell back onto my pillow, the headboard knocking against the wall. "A little boy," she said. "Lordy, he's got stout lungs."

I rested while she suctioned his mouth and nose with the same orange bulb syringe she had used on me when I had the croup. Then she wrapped him in a towel and placed him for a moment in a bureau drawer lined with a blanket. She came back to stand at the end of the bed and I gave one more hard push. The other child came and Granny shouted, "Praise Jesus, this'n's a girl!" Both of us wept from relief and happiness.

Then I must have dozed for a while because the next thing I remember is a baby rooting at each breast, their downy black heads poking out of blankets. Granny sat on the edge of the bed leaning back on the pillow with me, sweat glistening on her face. It had taken almost as much out of her to bring my babies into the world as it had out of me. "What will you call them?" she asked, wiping her face with a clean diaper.

"I've always liked Laura," I said, looking down at the baby girl. Granny had found an old pink shawl to wrap her in, so that we could tell the twins apart.

"That's good," Granny said. "Like mountain laurel. What about the boy?"

I looked him over for a long time, his button of a nose pressed against my breast. "Johnny," I said at last. When I spoke the name out loud, it sounded right to me.

Granny was silent. I could tell she didn't like it. Finally she asked, "How come?"

"Because I loved him once," I said, gazing down at my baby boy.

"All right," Granny murmured. But she

still looked troubled.

I never told Granny about Ford, but sometimes I was tempted. I knew it disturbed her to think the twins were John's babies. Maybe she was worried how they would turn out, but I wasn't. I knew it didn't matter who their daddy was. When I held them I didn't think about their fathers. I just looked at them, pink lips suckling, and thought about God.

In the first weeks of their lives, every sudden movement, every creak, every pine knot exploding in the fire made me tense to run or fight. I couldn't understand why John hadn't come for me, and if he was dead, why someone else hadn't. But Granny and the babies made it a precious time. Mr. Barnett brought a crib that had belonged to his own children, cleaned and smelling of beeswax, and moved it into Granny's bedroom where we slept. Those first nights when I was so weary I could barely lift my head, Granny got up and brought the babies to me whenever they cried, singing hymns to them under her breath. As I grew stronger, we tended the babies together while the rest of the mountain slept, burping and swaddling by the light of Granny's oil lamp, the only sounds their grunts and cries and swallows as they drank from my breast.

Sometimes as Granny rocked the babies, one in the crook of each arm, I pretended to be asleep and watched her in secret through the fringe of my lashes. When she thought I wasn't looking, her face always fell into a mask of exhaustion. Her ashen color made me sick with worry. I heard how she lost her breath while she worked in the kitchen and the yard. Sometimes when she spoke I saw the blue of her tongue. For a long time, I knew something was wrong.

Then one night Granny didn't get up to help me when the babies cried. My heart ached with lonesomeness, but she had seemed so tired all day. I told the babies, "We'll let Granny sleep." But when I opened my eyes at dawn and she wasn't making coffee, I knew. The babies were still resting. I crept by their crib into the front room. The house was cold. She hadn't stoked up the fire. I stood for a moment in the door of my childhood bedroom looking at her, knowing this time it was for real. Winter light fell through the window across her face. Her mouth was open. Her arm dangled off the bed. I crossed the room and crawled under the quilts to be with her, to rest one last time on her shoulder.

This winter it will have been six years since Granny passed away. Sometimes when

I think about her, I have to escape the house where she died and take a walk. That's how I knew the present I wanted to give the twins. They spent most of their sixth birthday rolling down the hill all the way to the road while their chocolate cake rose, running back up with beggar's lice on their clothes. I heard them laughing and wondered how I had ever wanted anything or anyone else, how a man could have been so important to me. I watched them pushing together a pile of leaves in the yard and dreamed of hiding with them in their fall-colored mountain. Later I stood on the back steps looking into the woods while they ate cake, the smell of woodsmoke drifting down from the Cotter farm. Everything was quiet indoors and out. The boy was solemn-eyed at the table, eating with his hands. The girl sat on her knees licking icing off her fingers. I went and lifted her out of the chair. She looked at me as I wiped the smears from her face with my dress tail, fine wisps of black hair in her eyes. The boy got down on his own, cleaning his mouth on the too-long sleeve of his flannel shirt. He could read me as they did each other and knew we were going somewhere. I knelt and the girl climbed on my back, arms tight under my chin. I knew she could make it because the twins have been all over the mountain, but I liked the weight of her body. When I galloped across the yard she giggled in my ear.

It would take a long time but we had plenty of daylight. The boy traveled his own way alongside us. I watched his black hair passing under the trees and tried to send everything I felt for him between the tall trunks as I had once sent my soul flying out of my body. I tried to tell him that I knew him, whether or not he knew me. I want to believe his spirit was with me, even as his body ranged out of sight. I saw that he's worn his own paths on the mountain. Maybe he's already been to the top. I know my twins think their own thoughts and have their own lives. Sometimes I wonder what it's like inside of them.

The path's not as treacherous as our elders claimed. For the last half mile the boy came out of the trees and climbed with us. When we passed the springhouse I wouldn't let him stop for a drink. The waters there are poison now. The girl scrambled onto my back again at the place where Doug Cotter fell. The boy went ahead of us through the fog, surefooted as a mountain goat. After the outcropping, the slope leveled off and we reached the summit. The stories were true. There's a meadow at the top. I thought John might be waiting there, his shadow face revealed at last, but there was only grass and trees. Doug once told me they called it Cotter Field. I thought it would be grown over, and it's probably not as open as it once was, but it's still mostly cleared off. Maybe Mark tends this spot where his ancestors drove their cattle to, or Mr. Barnett, who I think of now as the keeper of Bloodroot Mountain. But it could be Wild Rose who keeps the grasses trampled. I could tell she had been there. I could feel it. I knelt and closed my eyes. She's part of the mountain now, a spirit in these woods. I know she's finally free.

The girl slid off my back and went hopping over thatches of grass like dry hair with briars tangled in. The boy bent to chase a cricket over and under the bracken. There was a border of stunted trees, limbs broken and bare, and the hump of a slate-colored rock in the middle of the field like a tortoise unearthing itself. I saw the edge of the mountaintop and moved toward it, remembering a distant relative who had jumped off a cliff here ages ago. My steps quickened until I was almost running for the sky ahead of me, imagining how she might have flown, hair and dress billowing up. Then I tripped over a hole and caught myself on my hands, palms skidding over ridges of rock hidden in the weeds. I stayed on my hands and knees until I felt small fingers parting the black wings of my hair. I looked up and saw the girl between me and the edge. The boy joined her and there was a knowing in their eyes that made them seem old. If I had gone over I would have taken all of it with me, the things I've never spoken of, how the rabbit's back legs kicked and went still, how it smells of grave dirt under old houses, how it feels to bring a hatchet blade down on human flesh. I swiped the hair from my eyes and sat back on my haunches, examining my palms. There were flecks of dirt and shale in the scrapes. I held them up to show the twins. They stepped closer, drawn to my blood.

I struggled to my feet and went to the border of bushes at the brink of the plunging rock face. I could almost see the cows grazing and the Cotter man looking over the fields in neat squares, farmhouses and red barns like toys from a train set, roads and fences dividing the green. The world didn't seem as dangerous from up there. I felt a tug at my hem and saw the boy holding my dress tail, maybe afraid I would jump. For a long time he's been restless. I told him we'd ride to the co-op with Mr. Barnett, but now I'm having second thoughts. So far I've managed not to lose my mind after what happened to me, but I couldn't stand my twins being found by the Odoms. I have to protect them for as long as I can. If they were older, I know what I would tell them. You might leave but one day your blood will whisper to you. You'll hear witches making magic in a holler, healing wind blowing down a swollen throat, the song of the woman who came here in a mule-drawn cart and made it home. One of these days, wherever you are, you'll turn around and look toward the mountain, old and wild and bigger than you. You'll look this way and know it's still alive, whether I am or not anymore. I was only thinking the words but the girl came to me as if she had heard them out loud. She reached up and I swung her onto my hip. "Look, Mama," she said, pointing at the world below. "Can I go down yonder?" I thought of Granny taking my itchy foot in her hand and ached with loneliness. "Yes, honey," I said. But you'll come back. Just like me, you'll always come home.

■ ■ ■ ■

EPILOGUE:
JOHN ODOM

■ ■ ■ ■

Sometimes I get to missing the hills. I never thought I would when I first cut out and headed up north, but here in Rockford there's buildings instead of trees everywhere you look and cars honking even in the dead of night. Living in a motel like I do, I can always hear somebody talking through the walls. It's like I'm alone but I can't ever get off by myself. If I think about the mountain where Myra came from, it don't seem all that bad to me anymore. I understand now why she was so homesick being in Millertown. It's took me a long time, but I've got to where I don't hold a grudge against her. Since I've quit drinking and got a few decades older, I can look back and see how mean and crazy I was myself. I figure I ain't nobody to judge the way Myra acted or where she ended up.

It's lonesome how time passes. The world's ten years into the second millen-

521

nium and it's been more than thirty since what Myra did to me. Sometimes I pass a mirror and expect to see myself whole. I get surprised by what I look like, even after so long. The doctor said I ought to have surgery, she'd busted my face up so bad. But I couldn't hang around where people knew me any longer. Whenever my reflection surprises me, it's like waking up without fingers all over again. I go right back to that night Myra ran away.

I don't know how long I was out before I came to. My head and face hurt so bad I couldn't think. First thing I knew was that I couldn't move my jaw. I remember trying to call Myra, but I couldn't say anything. I was half choking on blood and some of my teeth was broke out. What was left of them wouldn't line up because she'd knocked my jaw crooked. I know how it sounds, but it took a few minutes to see that my fingers was gone. There was blood all over the place and I guess I was out for quite a while because it was tacky, not fresh. It was all over my shirt and the couch and the coffee table. That's when I saw the fingers, one there on the table and one on the floor almost underneath it. It took a minute to understand they was my own fingers. I held up my left hand and saw that only my thumb and pinky was left, with the pinky hanging on by a string. I can't say exactly what went through my head. I lurched around looking for Myra and bawling out in the yard. A train came up about that time and I couldn't even hear myself hollering anymore.

What I kept seeing in my mind was her offering me that red ring like Eve giving Adam the apple, how her eyes was beautiful and shining, how wild her hair was around her face. The day she gave it to me, she led me up the steepest path I ever saw, a narrow dirt trail, and I nearly tripped I don't know how many times over tree roots and rocks. One spot, we had to walk across a rotten tree trunk over a mud-hole and I nearly fell in. I was wore out before she was ready to rest. We came to a clearing where there was two big slabs of rock hanging over the bluff. It was a long way down. I was weak in the knees standing out on that ledge, but it was a pretty sight. It was summer and the trees was bright green. A breeze fluttered leaves around and lifted Myra's hair off of her shoulders. She sat down with her long legs curled under her dress and I sat facing her. She was like a little girl. She said, "Close your eyes and hold out your hand." I said, "It better not be poison ivy."

She said, "Just do it." I put out my hand and she placed something in my palm. What she put there was a heavy lump, still warm from where she held it all the way up the mountain. It felt kind of like a lug nut. I opened my eyes and there it was, stones glimmering in the sunshine. I didn't know if they was rubies or what, but I could tell that ring had cost a lot of money. I looked at her and she was excited, breathing fast and face rosy. "Put it on," she said. "I know we're not married yet, but I want you to have it."

"I ain't had time to get you one," I said.

She said she didn't care, so I went ahead and slipped it on my finger. It was loose but it fit better than I expected it to. She picked up my hand and held it against her cheek.

Standing in the yard that night, covered in blood with a train going by, it was hard to think about what to do next. I did have the sense to go back in the house and wrap my cut-off fingers in a dishrag and take them with me to the emergency room, in case they could be reattached. The doctor told me later it was too late for that, but I didn't know it at the time. I can't say how I made it to the hospital. I don't even remember driving over there. I kind of remember stumbling through the automatic doors at the emergency room and throwing up on the floor. I believe some boys came to help me up. Next thing I knew, I was laid out on a table and someway I had hung on to my fingers wrapped up in that dishrag. There was a young doctor standing over me, had blood on his scrubs, probably mine. I held the fingers out to him. I couldn't talk. My mouth was busted all to pieces. The doctor took the rag and opened it up and stared into it. All of a sudden it came to me that one finger was missing and I understood then why she did it.

The doctor looked in my eyes and said, "What happened to you?"

That's when I knew even if I could've answered him, I wouldn't have. I'd never tell anybody. I was laid up sucking soup through a straw for a long time. I didn't let the hospital call none of my people because I couldn't stand for them to know what Myra did to me. At first I plotted how to kill her and get away with it. I knew right where she'd go, back home to her granny's place. But in my heart, I didn't want her dead or hurt like I was. She crawled under my skin the first time I saw her and she's been there ever since.

Myra probably thinks I was the devil, but I loved her. I used to watch her sleeping and something about her hair against the white of the sheet pained my heart. Looking at her made me think about my mama, the only other woman I ever lived with. Once I stepped on a broke bottle and me and Mama sat on the front steps together while she dug it out. For a long time that was my best memory, her prying something out of me. I remember wishing she'd keep that glass, with my blood on it. I wanted her to have it but she pitched it in the weeds. That's how it was for me. Pitched in the weeds. But after a while I got to where I didn't feel a thing when I thought about that bloody glass, bitter or sweet. I got used to not being touched. She wasn't no kind of mother. One time Hollis and me was wrestling and laughing on the kitchen floor while she was trying to talk on the telephone. She took off her shoe and threw it and hit Hollis right between the eyes. He had a knot there for a long time. She wasn't much of a wife to my daddy, either. Once before city water came through and we still had a well, I remember a man coming in the yard and asking for a drink of water. He went behind the wellhouse to the spigot where Mama was rinsing specks of grass off of her feet after Eugene had mowed. I was outside throwing a baseball up and catching it. After a while I didn't hear Mama or the man talking. I went around the wellhouse and saw them knelt down with the water still running, making a mud puddle under the spigot, and that man with his hand inside of Mama's blouse. I never told Daddy, but he suspected her of running around anyway. One night after she came in drunk he broke down the bathroom door and dragged her out. I was watching on the stair landing. He beat her and kicked her and pulled her out the door by the hair of the head, out through the mud and into the street. He got down and straddled her and beat her some more, slapping her over and over in the face. Then he got up and come on back in the house, not even breathing hard. But after I got older, she quit going out all the time with her perfume on and her mouth smeared up. She got to where she stayed in the bed all day long. Daddy used to snigger and hint around that he was slipping something in her drinks to keep her at home. I still don't know if he was just kidding or if he was being serious. There's a lot of things about them times that I still ain't figured out. Like whether or not my mama died of heart trouble or if I poisoned her.

I remember it was fall in a windstorm, leaves whirling up in little tornadoes and the sky gray with clouds skidding over. Dark was coming and Mama was stumbling around the kitchen trying to make supper, tanked up on nerve pills or whatever she was drinking. Finally she dropped a hot pan out of the oven and I went out the back door. I couldn't stand being around her when she was like that. From outside, the house was cozy looking. Somebody passing on the street might have smelled the supper and seen the yellow kitchen window and wanted to come in out of the cold. But they didn't know about Mama, puffy-eyed and hair sticking up from being in the bed all day, slumped over the stove in her old housecoat smoking a cigarette. They hadn't heard the stories Daddy told at the supper table either, bragging about all the men he killed in the war. He talked about human life like it wasn't worth a plug nickel, not even his own. He didn't want to be stuck in Millertown with a wife and kids, he wanted to be in the Philippines with a gun on his shoulder, hunkered down waiting for somebody else to kill. He'd go on and on about how many arms and legs and skulls he'd shot off. Me and my brothers would just look down at our plates and keep on chewing, trying to be like him and not feel anything.

After I left Mama in the kitchen, I went down the steps and knelt to look under the porch. There was a stray dog under there, a black mutt with a white ruff that had showed up the day before. I thought it might have been hit by a car or something. It wagged its tail when I made kissing sounds but it wouldn't come to me. It just laid down and cowered, ears back and licking its lips when I tried to lure it out. Daddy came over, wiping his grease-blacked hands on a rag where he'd been working on the car. "Is that thing still under there?" he asked. His coveralls smelled like cold weather and kerosene, leaves blowing across the yard behind him. I wanted to say no but he'd already seen it. "You better leave that old thing alone," he said. "It might have rabies." I looked at the dog, huddled beside the gas can, and knew it didn't have rabies. Daddy went off for a minute and came back with a pie tin and a dirty white jug of something. I watched as he unscrewed the cap and poured thick green liquid into the tin. "What's that?" I asked.

"Antifreeze. It's supposed to taste good to dogs and cats. I bet you he'll lap this right up." He pushed the pie tin under the porch. The dog showed no interest at first but I figured it would later, when we was gone. It was probably pretty hungry and thirsty. We went in for supper and the whole time I was eating I kept praying that dog would be able to resist. When we got done I offered to take out the garbage, but Daddy said the can wasn't full yet. I wanted to sneak and throw away that poison before the dog could take it, but Daddy watched me like a hawk all night. He must have suspected what I meant to do. The next morning I went out and looked under the porch. The pie tin was empty and the dog was gone. I don't know if it went off somewhere else to die or if Daddy drug it off, but I knew it was dead one way or another. Just like one of them Japs Daddy killed.

A few weeks later, my mama got sick. She was upstairs in the bedroom hacking and coughing with a fever. She always had a smoker's cough, but this was different. It might have been the flu or even pneumonia but nobody went to the doctor much at our house. It had got to be winter and Eugene and Lonnie was gone. A man had come in the store and offered them ten dollars apiece to saw up a tree that had fell in his yard. Me and Hollis was setting in front of the television when Daddy hollered for me to come in the kitchen. I could hear Mama having another coughing fit upstairs. Daddy glanced at the ceiling and held out a medicine cup to me, full to the top. "Take this cold medicine to your mammy." He shook his head. "That racket's fixing to run me nuts." I took the cup and looked down into it. "Go on," he said. "Before she hacks up a lung." I was halfway up the stairs before I thought about the dog. I stopped and looked in that cup again. The liquid inside was kind of green, just like the antifreeze. My heart was knocking so hard I liked to lost my breath. But I thought about my daddy down yonder, telling me to do something. I'd had my backside striped with a belt enough times to know what would happen if I disobeyed him. So I went on up the stairs in the dark, into their room where the lamp was on. I hated going in there because it always smelled like the perfume she used instead of taking a bath. She rolled her eyes over at me and I saw she looked half drunk besides being sick. When she reached for the cup I held it back. I thought surely it was medicine and that was all. But I knew Daddy was liable to do anything. I had time to turn around and walk out of there. I could have poured whatever it was down the bathroom sink. Daddy never would have known the difference and Mama probably wouldn't even have remembered me coming. Then I looked at her and thought of all the times she was mean to me and my brothers and how she let that man put his hand inside her blouse behind the well-house. She coughed again and motioned for me to give her the cup, like I was trying her patience. I watched her drink it down without a bit of complaint. I'd say she didn't even know where she was, much less what it was she might be drinking.

Next day was a Saturday and I went to work with Daddy and Eugene and Lonnie. For once I was glad to go. I wanted to be as far away from that house and my mama as I could get. I'd heard her stumbling down to the bathroom in the night, back and forth until she finally must have slept down yonder on the floor. At first light I heard Daddy leading her back up to the bed. He made breakfast for us before work, fried eggs and baloney. Eugene was sitting across the table from me, mopping up runny egg yolk with a piece of light bread. "What's wrong with Mama?" he asked, without looking up from his food.

Daddy was wolfing down his breakfast standing at the sink. He said, "I reckon she's got the stomach flu. Hollis, you better keep an eye on her while we're gone." Then he looked at me and our eyes locked. I wish it was my imagination but later on when Hollis called, Daddy said, "You boys watch the store. I got to get on home." Then his eyes locked on mine again. "Something's happened to your mammy." My bowels got hot and loose. He never said a word about giving me that cup. But for as long as I lived at home he'd give me a secret look every once in a while, like we was in cahoots together.

I can't say for sure if I helped my daddy poison my mama, but thinking I might have weighs on me. Not a day goes by, and me getting to be an old man, that I don't think about handing her that cup. I should've snatched it away from her and drunk it down myself. The world probably would have been better off. I know Myra would have been. For a while with her, I thought I could forget about it. I thought loving her could chase off whatever evil there was in me, but I was wrong. Someway, Myra brought out my bad side. I wanted to be good to her, but I didn't know how. I never felt in control of myself around her. I got to drinking just to get my head back on straight. We made a promise before we got married to change for each other. Come to find out, there wasn't no taming either one of us down. She couldn't be the kind of wife

I wanted, and I wasn't cut out to be a husband. You can't fight that old nature, at least that's what I thought when I was younger. I figured there wasn't no use, I might as well give up.

As soon as my jaw didn't have to be wired shut no more I got out of that hospital. I packed my things and burned hers up in a barrel out behind the house and took off, with no intention of ever coming back. I cleaned out the bank account and got me a motel room until I could figure out what to do next. I decided to come up here to Rockford in Illinois, a city I'd been to with Daddy on a buying trip. It was hard to make ends meet at first. Nobody would hire me, looking the way I did and with my hand not working right. Finally a foreigner let me manage his motel. I've lived for decades in this tiny room with just a television for company. The cold has been hard to get used to. My jaw pains me all through the winters. The nights are so long, I don't know whether to curse Myra or wish she was here to warm my back. The only person I let know I was alive was Hollis. I needed some cash so I told him what happened and where I was. He came to see me several times. He wanted to go up Bloodroot Mountain and cut Myra's throat, or at least put the law on her, but I told him to leave her alone. He didn't understand it, but he never fought me on anything. He said Daddy was fixing to call the sheriff and report me a missing person, but I got him to convince Daddy I'd finally dusted my hands of Myra and run off like I was always threatening to. Hollis was the one who let me know when Daddy died and left me a little inheritance. After him holding that store over our heads all them years, it ended up being worth next to nothing. But I needed the money, so I took it.

Running off to Illinois don't mean I got away from the place and the people I came from, though. It ought to be easy here where it's cold and the sky is like a blank slate. But something, maybe God, won't let me forget. I could avoid the mirror. I could wear a glove, but I've learned the past would still find me. Like what happened today. The foreigner I work for subscribes to the national newspapers. Every morning I make a pot of coffee and read the paper in my office behind the curtains. I have to keep up with the world someway, since I don't get out much. I opened the newspaper and saw a face I knew, even though I only laid eyes on it once. Right there above a black-and-white picture I saw my own last name. My hand shook so bad I sloshed coffee on my lap. Hollis told me a long time ago Myra had twin babies. I didn't know what to think when I heard it. Back then, I hoped they wasn't mine. Now the boy has won a prize for a book he wrote. If he was mine, I'd be proud. But I could never get in touch with them. They wouldn't want to look at me and see on my face how bad it was between me and their mother. Besides that, if they are mine, it's sad how they came into the world. Best thing for me to do is let them alone, like I should have done Myra.

All day I've been nervous after seeing my name in the newspaper. Maybe God's trying to tell me that a man can't run away from who he is and where he comes from. It's like when that man came here looking for me once, about ten years after Myra took off. There was an ice storm coming and I was out salting the parking lot. The sky over the motel looked like sheet metal. He came walking across the highway from over at the truck stop. He could have used a haircut and a shave, had on a tatty old coat and a flannel shirt with holes in it. The heels of his boots was run down, like they'd seen a lot of traveling. He headed straight for me. I knew by the way he stared me down that he wasn't looking for a room. I quit salting and we stood there sizing each other up. I figured he was caught off guard by my face, but that didn't seem like all it was. I didn't ask what I could help him with. I waited for him to talk first.

"I been working on the bank building they're putting up downtown," he said finally. I seen he had a rotten front tooth. He looked familiar, but I couldn't place him.

"So what?"

"I heard from the men there's somebody works here by the name of John Odom."

I got to feeling dizzy-headed. I could tell where he was from by the way he talked.

"What if there is?"

"Is that you?"

"Who's asking?"

"Doug Cotter. I believe we come from the same neck of the woods. You ever been to a place called Bloodroot Mountain?" I saw in his eyes that he knew I had been. He took a step toward me. He was tall. I didn't know if I could take him or not.

"Well, what in the hell do you want?" I asked, trying not to show my nerves.

He looked me over again, seemed like he was thinking. Then he said, "I came here meaning to put you in the hospital. But it looks like somebody beat me to it."

I forced myself to laugh. "What, did Myra send you here to finish the job?"

His eyes changed when he heard her name. It took him a second to collect his cool. Then he smiled in a way that hid his rotten tooth. He looked toward the truck stop where he came from. "Why don't you let me buy you a cup of coffee?"

I went on across the highway with him. He didn't seem to want a fight anymore. We sat at the counter and I ordered pie to go with my coffee, since he was paying. We both got quiet. I didn't want to talk first but I couldn't help it. The ice had started ticking on the window of the truck stop. I looked at the weather instead of his face. "I guess Myra left her mark on you, too," I said. "Not on the outside, but I can still see it." I looked back at him. My jaw had started aching. "Have you seen her?"

He shook his head and looked down into his coffee cup. "No. But I know where she is. Mental hospital over in Nashville. I thought you put her there, but now I don't know." I had already been told where Myra was. Before Hollis died, he kept me informed. But I wondered how she was surviving in a place like that, as bad as she'd hated being cooped up. "They auctioned off her house on the mountain," he said. "My brother bid on it." He smiled in his odd way. "I guess she left her mark on him, too."

"What is it that woman does to people?" I said. All of a sudden the pie didn't look good to me anymore. I dropped my fork on the plate.

"It's funny you would ask that." He looked out at the ice rain with me. "I've always thought I was cursed for loving Myra. Everywhere I go, bad luck follows me."

I shook my head. "You and me both."

"I don't know." He turned back to me. "I feel different now that I've seen you."

"Why's that?"

"There's nothing supernatural about what she did to your face, is there? It's not right, what we've put on her. She's made out of flesh and blood, just like anybody else."

I forced myself to laugh again. "Glad to be of service, buddy."

He hung his head for a minute, like he was wore out. "I'm trying as hard as I can to forget about her," he said. "But some-times I still think I'd give anything to have her."

Then he got up and paid the bill and left the truck stop. I never saw him again. Whenever I passed the new bank building downtown I didn't look over there. I didn't want to think about Myra anymore. I doubt he ever did manage to forget about her. I got to mulling over the things he said and wondering myself if I'd ever really get over her. Sometimes it seemed like she was crying out to me when winter storms came. I'd cover my ears to drown out her screams, begging me to rescue her from that old asylum. It drove me out one night into the snow and I fell on the ice in the parking lot. I thought I was dying of a heart attack and maybe I was having one, because the weight on my chest was so bad I couldn't get up. I laid out yonder freezing for a long time, and all I could think was if I died right then I'd never see her again. I knew someday I had to find her.

But I didn't go see her until Hollis had that aneurysm in 1996. I took a week off of work at the motel and went to Millertown to visit his grave. I knew it was time to look for Myra, too, while I was back down south. By then I didn't want revenge for what she did to me, even though seeing her locked up would be the next thing to seeing her in hell. All I wanted from Myra was to look in her eyes one more time before I died.

It turned out I had to stay around Nashville longer than I meant to, since there was only certain visiting days. When it finally came time to see her, my guts was churning all the way up the road to the asylum. There was stone pillars marking the entrance and behind them I saw the shape of the building through a piece of woods. At first it looked like a big brick mansion, but closer up I saw how old and shabby it was, one or two trees shading a little patch of grass in front of the door. The parking lot was half empty, like the patients didn't get many visitors. I could see why. I knew as soon as I passed through the steel doors it wasn't a place I wanted to hang around long. It stunk like piss and bleach and I nearly gagged just walking to the nurse's booth. When I went up the stairs to the third floor, there was crazy people everywhere. It was a din of shouting and laughing and crying and begging. One woman was slumped against the wall with her hair hanging in her face and I had to step over her legs on my way down the hall. Another one kept asking if I had brought her cigarettes. I liked to never shook her off of my arm.

When I found the room they told me was Myra's, I tapped on the door with my good hand. It was quiet in there but seemed like I heard something moving, so I opened the door and went in. There was two beds and somebody curled up on their side in one of them, under the cover so all I could see was a half-bald head with a few strings of white hair. I thought surely that couldn't be Myra. Then I saw her sitting in a plastic chair pulled up to the radiator under the window, looking down at a concrete path in the grass out in front of the asylum. It was a jolt to see how short her hair had been cut. I guess it was hard to take care of, as long as it used to be. It was limp as a dishrag and just a streak of black here and there left in it, even though she wasn't no more than forty then. She had on clean pajamas but they was buttoned up wrong. When I came in she didn't even turn her head. I walked over and stood in front of her and she still didn't move her eyes. Then I knelt down beside of her chair and she turned away from the window with a pleasant look on her face, like she was coming out of a good dream. She might have been doped up, but I don't think so. I looked in her eyes like I had been wanting to for so long. They was still blue, but not the same kind. I thought of my life in Rockford, how I'd stare across the empty lot behind the motel remembering her hair on the pillow and her legs under the sheet and forget what she did to me, wishing things had turned out different.

"It's John," I said. "I didn't die." It sounded stupid, but it was all that came out.

"Are you really here?" she asked. She didn't seem afraid of me.

"Yeah," I said. I couldn't get over the shape she was in. I'd never seen nobody so skinny except in pictures. "Lord, Myra. I used to think I wanted to see you like this."

She smiled a little but didn't say anything.

"How do you stand it in here?"

She looked back at the window. "You wouldn't believe me if I told you."

"I might."

She turned back to me. Her eyes gave me shivers. "I can be anywhere I want to. Even home on the mountain."

I cleared my throat. "You've been here a long time. Why ain't they let you out?"

"I don't know," she said.

We both got quiet. It was a four-hour drive from Millertown to Nashville, plenty of time to figure out what I wanted to say to her, but all of a sudden my mind was blank. Finally I came up with something. "I heard you had a baby after . . . after we was through."

She nodded. "Twins. A boy and a girl. I don't think they're yours."

I felt my face get red. "Yeah. Well. Don't they ever come and see you?"

"No. But I'm waiting."

"What if they don't ever come?"

"They will."

"How do you know?"

"They can't help it. We're bound to-gether."

"I guess I couldn't help it either," I said. "But we was bad for each other."

She nodded again. "It's a shame we're not the only ones who got hurt."

I looked down at my bad hand. "Like Hollis. You might have heard your boy set fire to the store several years back. He rebuilt that place but it took a lot out of him. He never was well after that. Back in July he had a blood vessel to bust in his head. That's what I'm doing down this way. I came home to see his grave. Lonnie claimed there wasn't many at the funeral. He never got married or nothing. It's kind of pitiful."

We both got quiet again. I looked around the room to keep from looking at her face. The ceiling was high with cobwebs in the corners. I figured it was drafty there in the winters. There was flowered wallpaper but it didn't do nothing to brighten up the place. I seen there was a desk between the two beds, bare with a layer of dust on top. It made me think about how long she'd been in there. She wasn't acting all that crazy but I could tell something wasn't right with her.

544

I had the feeling if I'd come another day, she might have been different. I pictured her slumped against the wall with her legs sticking out, or maybe like one of them that shuffled around screaming and crying. My skin crawled, imagining her strapped down to a bed and put in a straitjacket and getting shock treatments. Then she asked, "John?"

I looked back at her eyes. "Yeah?"

"Why didn't you come after me sooner?"

I tried to smile. "I've not come after you."

"I thought you would come after me. I kept waiting. Why didn't you come?"

I thought about it for a second. "Because I loved you once."

She looked away. "Maybe. But it's like you said. We were bad for each other."

I couldn't think of nothing else. I thought surely there was more I could say after driving so far and waiting so long, but I was tapped out. Then all of a sudden Myra reached out with her bony hand and touched my jaw where she had broke it. I quit breathing for a second. Her fingers moving over them lumps and scars done something to my heart. Nobody had touched me that way since I seen her last. It hurt me just about too much to take. I grabbed her fingers to stop them but once I had ahold of her I couldn't let go. I closed my eyes and we stayed still for a while, me holding her hand on my ugly face. Finally she took it away and it was like losing her all over again. "I'm tired, John," she said. "Please don't come back." I was relieved. She didn't have to tell me twice. I never went back. But I know me and Myra will never be shed of each other. It don't matter what I saw in that asylum, she's still in my head with that long, long hair and them heaven blue eyes and legs that are always running away from me. I love and hate Myra Lamb now the same as I did then. There's some things the years can't do nothing about.

After I left Myra's room I went and stood for a minute beside of the front doors under a tree, not feeling like driving. The wind was stirring up a whirl of leaves and the sky was turning stormy. I never thought much about God before what happened in them next few minutes. Some nights I still lay in the dark and doubt I ever saw or felt anything at all. I go back to figuring my life and all that's happened in it has been an accident. But times like this morning, seeing that newspaper, I know it was real and no coincidence.

Standing in the shade beside of the asylum

entrance, I looked out at the parking lot and saw them walking toward me from several yards away. They must have just got out of whatever car they had come in, a boy and girl that favored so much they had to be twins, with black hair and eyes like every other Odom's down through time. Myra said they wasn't mine but that boy was like an old picture of me come to life, only a different me that got out of the hills and made something of myself. I could tell by the proud way he carried hisself that one day he'd shake the dust of the mountains off his coat and walk away from there without looking back, if he hadn't done it already. The girl was like a plainer version of Myra, pale with long hair blowing out behind her. There was a yellow-haired baby on her hip, stretching his arm up over his head to grab at the leaves fluttering down. It was easy to see by the way she smiled at him what kind of a mother she was. When they finally got near enough, that baby looked over and noticed me standing under the tree. His eyes was the same blue as Myra's used to be. Then the hand that was grabbing at leaves reached for me. I wanted more than anything to touch him but I couldn't move. I watched him disappear through the doors and stood there feeling like all that mattered in the world had left me behind. I felt the closeness of another life I might have had.

I used to think I was born worthless, considering the people I come from. But when I saw that blue-eyed baby years ago, it made me wonder. I ain't done everything I wanted to, but looking at the picture in the newspaper today, I know I was right about that boy in the parking lot. He's carried me and his mama off into the world and that girl has been the kind of mother neither one of us ever had, and who knows what all that baby is capable of. Ever since I seen them three, I've had a little bit of peace. The wind don't sound as much like cries anymore. Knowing they're out there makes me feel better about all the wrong I've done. At least some good came out of the mess me and Myra made. Sometimes I wish the boy and girl had seen me but there's nothing I can do now to make them stop and turn around. There ain't no changing what's already been. I know I'll never see them again. They passed me by like they ought to have done. But I was there and nothing can change that, either. I'm still with them, whether they know it or not, part of how they came to be. Before I drove away from that asylum, we was all together there like a family for a while. I wonder if they felt the same thing I did in them few minutes, my blood moving in their veins and passing through their hearts.

ACKNOWLEDGMENTS

Thanks to the Greene, Oler, and McCoy families, especially Adam, Emma, Taylor, Mom, Dad, Stephanie, Mickey, Allen, Arela, Carl, Linny, Sis, Earl, Travis, Dena, Justin, Isaiah, Tommy, Cathy, Brittaney, Colton, Julyanna, and Conner, for love and support.

Thanks to Vermont College and to my teachers and professors, Kathy Levine, Bonnie Oakberg, John Cranford, Bernice Mennis, Peaco Todd, and the late Dick Hathaway.

Thanks to the Sewanee Writers' Group, the Lakeway Area Writers' Group, and all those who have given feedback and advice, especially Ashlee Adams Crews, Jennifer Dickinson, Marsha McSpadden, Chad Simpson, Hank Grezlak, Leslie Gathings, Cathy Wilson, Brenda Key, Regina King, Gary Hamrick, Sue Regier, and Suzanne Kingsbury.

Thanks to Beth Miller and Sara Sparkes

Hill for being best friends and brilliant readers.

Thanks to Leigh Feldman, Robin Desser, and Jill McCorkle for making this book happen.

ABOUT THE AUTHOR

Amy Greene was born and raised in the foothills of East Tennessee's Smoky Mountains, where she lives with her husband and two children.